SHADOWS OF THE FALL

BOOK EIGHT
OF THE DUCHY OF TERRA

SHADOWS OF
THE FALL

BOOK EIGHT
OF THE DUCHY OF TERRA

GLYNN STEWART

**FAOLAN'S PEN
PUBLISHING**
faolanspen.com

This edition published in 2020 by:

Faolan's Pen Publishing Inc.

22 King St. S, Suite 300

Waterloo, Ontario

N2J 1N8 Canada

ISBN-13: 978-1-989674-22-2 (print)

A record of this book is available from Library and Archives Canada.

Printed in the United States of America

1 2 3 4 5 6 7 8 9 10

Second edition

First printing: December 2020

Illustration © 2020 Tom Edwards

TomEdwardsDesign.com

Faolan's Pen Publishing logo is a trademark of Faolan's Pen Publishing Inc.

Read more books from Glynn Stewart at faolanspen.com

CHAPTER ONE

CAPTAIN MORGAN CASIMIR COULD ONLY DESCRIBE HER feelings as *awe*. She'd been born on Earth before the A!Tol Imperium —the *!* was a glottal stop, the closest humanity could come to their overlord's beak snap—had annexed humanity's homeworld, and she'd grown up with humanity's membership in that nation.

The Solar System and humanity had benefited immensely from their membership in the Imperium, and Sol buzzed with activity these days, with hundreds of ships plying the spaceways between Earth and Mars and a hundred stations and asteroid colonies.

And compared to the A!To System, mistress of two hundred–plus inhabited worlds and twice as many star systems, Earth was a provincial capital. A wealthy provincial system, but still a recently uplifted star system and species on the edge of the Imperium's territory.

Only a single world in the system was habitable, with the rest of the planets falling outside the liquid-water zone, but that hadn't slowed the amphibious squid-like aliens much. San!Dak, the uninhabitably cold large rocky world orbiting outside A!To itself, had more space stations in orbit than Earth did.

Over a thousand sublight spaceships and hypercapable starships buzzed around the star system, a swarm of gravitational interfaces easily visible to the sensors of Morgan's starship *Defiance*. There were hundreds, possibly thousands, of space stations and asteroid settlements spread through the star system, though concentrated near San!Dak and the single super-Jovian gas giant.

Watching over all of that industry and activity were the looming behemoths of five full squadrons of the Imperial Navy's superbattle-ships, eighty starships individually capable of shattering a planet.

Another hundred lesser capital ships and several hundred escorts made up the rest of Home Fleet. Among those escorts were dozens of ships of equal mass to Morgan's own vessel. *Defiance* was more advanced than the vast majority of Home Fleet, but she remained a single vessel compared to the numbers the Imperium mustered to defend their capital.

"Sir, we are cleared in to A!To orbit," Lesser Commander Hadi El-Amin told her. Morgan's navigator was a dark-skinned man. Today he wore a dark blue headscarf with his black and gold Imperial Navy uniform.

"Docking instructions are for what looks like a refit-and-repair platform," he continued.

"Thank you," the slight blonde Captain replied. "Nystrom, any update to our orders?"

Lesser Commander Passang Nystrom, Morgan's communications officer, shook her head.

"We received confirmation that our orders were to report to A!To on arrival, but no update since," she said. "Is that odd to anyone else?"

Morgan shook her head warningly at Nystrom. That *was* odd, but there was a limit to how much questioning of higher authority they could get away with.

Like most Imperial ships, *Defiance* had a single-species crew—human, in her case. That was a sign of trust in itself, trust that humanity had earned with blood and fire. That Morgan's command was one of the most powerful cruisers in the fleet was another sign of trust.

So was the fact that *Defiance* was normally equipped with a full arsenal of miniaturized starkillers, strategic weapons that the Imperium didn't even officially admit *existed* in the scale Morgan's ship carried.

Her magazines for those weapons were empty right now... because Morgan had used them all against an immense star-eating bioship that had threatened an Imperial colony. Someone had wanted to study that creature, and despite her superior's attempts to protect her, she'd been recalled to A!To.

"Let me know if we hear anything more," she told Nystrom. "Let Liepins know that we're headed into a refit yard. I know we didn't get all the work he wanted done before we were recalled. If we're here, we may as well get *Defiance* fixed up."

Gary Liepins was the cruiser's chief engineer. Morgan trusted him to get the ship back to fighting form as quickly as anyone, but *Defiance* had been badly battered by the sun eater before finishing it off with her starkillers.

"Take us in, Commander El-Amin," she ordered, her eyes on the hundreds of icons marking the wealth and industry of the capital system of the Imperium she served. "It's been long enough getting here. I see no reason to delay."

There was only a small perceivable sensation as *Defiance* moved forward. Her drive operated along the interface line between reality and hyperspace, creating a forward velocity of sixty percent of light-speed in the blink of an eye.

"ETA is twenty minutes, sir," El-Amin reported. "We'll need to slow to maneuvering speeds once we're in orbit."

Morgan nodded silently. Hopefully, there'd be some answers by then of just what her superiors wanted. *Defiance* wasn't really needed out on the edge of the frontier, not when they were reason-ably sure they'd blown the only real threat to stardust, but it was still strange to be abruptly called away and given no clue what to expect at the end of the forty-cycle—thirty-nine-day—voyage to the Imperial capital.

Somehow, Morgan was grimly certain it wasn't going to be *good* news.

———

"SIR, we have a direct com request for you over the hyperfold," Nystrom finally told Morgan ten minutes later. "It's from Echelon Lord Iros."

Defiance was still several light-minutes out from A!To orbit, which meant that the hyperfold coms were the only way to talk to anyone real-time.

"Iros?" Morgan murmured. Iros was a senior intelligence officer, not someone she'd interacted with before. They were a Pibo neuter, one of the gray hairless humanoid aliens that looked like old Earth myths of the Grays. She wasn't sure why they'd be comming her, but at least *someone* was.

"I'll take it in my office," she told Nystrom as she rose from her chair. She glanced around the bridge and smiled. Most of her officers were either off-duty or running their departments from their offices. It was a toss-up between Nystrom and El-Amin who should be in charge, which meant it was her call.

"You have the watch, Nystrom," she decided. The coms officer had fewer regular watches than El-Amin did, so it would be good practice.

She was off the bridge in a few steps and into her office in a few more. The Imperium agreed with most human designers on that point: the captain's quarters and working spaces needed to be close to the bridge.

Morgan slid in behind her desk, taking a moment to breathe and center herself. She was a long way from home here, and she touched a new addition to her desk: a plain gray chunk of rock about the size of her forearm.

There was absolutely nothing special about the piece of granite. It didn't have any historical significance, it held no fossils, nothing. Its only value was that it was from Earth and that her boyfriend had given it to her.

Dr. Rin Dunst, PhD., the boyfriend in question, had carried the rock from Earth himself when he'd traveled to A!To a long time before they'd met. The xenoarcheologist was one of the Imperium's top experts on the ancient Precursor race known as the Alava—and he'd known that becoming that expert would keep him away from Earth.

The reason he'd given *Morgan* the rock was that Morgan's girl-friend back on Earth had promised to replace his. That her significant others had conspired to give her the tiny but thoughtful gift meant a lot to Morgan, and the stone helped her calm her fears before she activated the computer built into the desk.

The sword-and-stylized-rocket symbol of the Imperial Navy flickered above her desk for a moment, and then was replaced by the flat gray-skinned face and large dark eyes of Echelon Lord Iros.

"Captain Casimir," they greeted her. "Welcome to the A!To System. My files say you haven't been here before?"

"I have not," Morgan confirmed. She'd risen to the rank of Commander in the militia of the Duchy of Terra, the semi-autonomous government of the Sol System run by her stepmother. She'd only joined the Imperial Navy after a major attack on Sol by a genocidal faction of the Imperium's old enemies, the Kanzi.

"The capital is impressive, isn't it?" Iros asked.

"It is," Morgan agreed. "Of course, given some of what I've seen..."

Iros bowed their head. They were one of the few beings cleared for everything Morgan knew about the Precursors—and they knew that she'd been present when the Imperium had found the Alavan megastructures that had fueled the threat of the Taljzi, the Kanzi faction that had attacked Sol.

"We pale, of course, in comparison to the achievements of Those

Who Came Before," they agreed. "But we have hundreds of long-cycles yet to rise to their achievements."

"Yes, sir," Morgan agreed. She wasn't sure what the intelligence flag officer wanted yet, but disagreeing with them was never a good plan.

"Your ship has been directed to a repair slip, yes?" Iros asked.

"We have, yes, sir," she confirmed. "I'm not sure what we're doing after that, though."

"Of course not," they said. "You have not yet received your orders. Your crew will go on furlough once you have arrived. A minimum of five cycles; you may tell them that as soon as we finish this conversation."

"Yes, sir. Thank you, sir," Morgan said. "After our encounters out by Kosha, my crew are still under pressure. It's been a quiet flight here, but they can still use the break."

Neither of the two sentients were speaking the same language as each other. Morgan wore earbuds that were loaded with translation software for every major language spoken in the Imperium.

She also spoke French, German and Japanese on her own, and could understand the spoken A!Tol language most of the time. The earbuds were sophisticated enough to remove almost any chance of misunderstanding, though, and held up to thirty languages on their own—and effectively infinite languages if they were networked to a starship's main computers.

"You and your senior officers will not get the break," Iros warned her. "The deployment of a starkiller, especially the Final Dragon starkillers, always requires investigation, Captain.

"Once *Defiance* has arrived, your officers will be given locations to report to. *You*, Captain Casimir, will report to my office in First Home. A shuttle will be standing by to pick you up."

Morgan bowed her head.

"Yes, sir," she said quietly. "Will...I be returning to *Defiance*?"

"Almost certainly, Captain," Iros told her instantly. "There is no plan in place to reassign you or your officers. You may safely leave your possessions aboard your ship, Captain Casimir."

That was the first good sign Morgan had seen so far. She'd been expecting to be told to bring everything with her. That she was expected to resume her command suggested that this review, at least, was mostly formality.

"I understand, sir. I will report to your office as soon as possible."

"I look forward to our conversation, Captain Casimir," Iros told her with a small bow of their head. "What I have already seen in the reports tells me you have encountered spectacular things."

Morgan smiled thinly. The Pibo had *no* idea how badly they were understating things.

Sensor images after the fact could not begin to convey the sheer horror and scale of the sun eater.

CHAPTER TWO

A SMALL CONTINGENT OF HUMAN IMPERIAL MARINES IN DRESS uniforms accompanied Morgan as she exited the shuttle. Without armor or heavy plasma rifles, they were mostly ceremonial. They were, however, required by regulation when the commander of an Imperial starship went planetside while on duty.

On any planet, even A!Tol itself.

First Home was a sprawling city woven into and across an artificial lagoon. Many houses were partially submerged, and canals ran through just as much of the city as the surface roadways. This was not a city built for humans or any of the A!Tol's subject races. This was a city built for the amphibious squids themselves, and Morgan could see hundreds of them traveling around as far as the eye could see.

The lagoon, however, was next to a set of steep foothills leading into a small mountain range. The tallest nearby hills, clearly visible from Morgan's landing pad, held delicately interwoven spires that reminded her of the designs of Imperial warships.

Those spires were deceptively small with the distance, she suspected. They held the Three Houses, the tricameral legislature of the Imperium. There were over a dozen human representatives in those spires, speaking for the interest of the human-settled worlds, the Duchy of Terra, and humanity itself.

Closer to hand, the military headquarters of the Imperium was a set of sharp-edged buildings of middling height for the city. They looked squat to Morgan's eyes, but she'd grown up in a penthouse apartment in Hong Kong.

"Captain Casimir?" an A!Tol waiting nearby asked. They were one of the smaller adult versions of the species Morgan had ever seen —which made them almost certainly male—and they fluttered on their four thicker locomotive tentacles.

"That's me, Lesser Speaker," Morgan acknowledged, reading the alien youth's rank off his harness. He was very young and very junior, which made him a sixteen-tentacled messenger boy.

"I am Lesser Speaker Olot," the A!Tol introduced himself. "Echelon Lord Iros sent me to collect you. Is there anything you need or are your waters clear for the journey?"

"My waters are clear, yes," Morgan said with a small smile at A!Tol idiom. "Lead on, Speaker."

There was only one grade of officer junior to Olot in the Imperial Navy, and given that they were in the *headquarters* of the Imperial Navy, Morgan suspected Olot was related to someone.

Nepotism, in her experience, crossed all species boundaries.

"This way, this way," Olot told her, gesturing for her and her guard to follow him with a flurry of tentacles as his skin flushed with pale streaks of green, red and purple.

A!Tol could never hide their feelings. Olot was determined to get this right, happy to help, and stressed that he was going to get this wrong.

It was a combination of feelings that Morgan could only sympathize with!

IROS ROSE from behind their desk as Morgan entered the office. They were on the top floor of one of the corner buildings of the Naval complex, with windows that gave them an amazing view of the delicate spires of the Imperial Houses.

Another sentient, an older A!Tol female Squadron Lord that Morgan didn't recognize, was standing at those windows and studying the legislative buildings.

"Come in, be seated," Iros ordered.

The guards had remained outside, leaving only the three of them in the corner office. Somehow, Morgan suspected that the office was as much a sign of Iros's rank and authority as it would have been in an Earth organization.

"Echelon Lord Iros," she greeted her host with a salute before taking a seat. "Squadron Lord."

She waited until the A!Tol had turned away from the window and returned her salute before she took her seat, following Iros's invitation and lead.

"Captain, this is Squadron Lord Tan!Cova," Iros introduced the A!Tol. "She is the head of military intelligence for the A!Tol Imperial Navy."

Morgan nodded her understanding—of more than merely the rank. The *Tan!* in the A!Tol's name meant that Tan!Cova was a relative of the Empress. While the Navy tried to keep that from accelerating advancement, it *did* mean that the A!Tol had the ear of the Imperium's ruler.

"We are here to discuss the events near the Kosha System," Tan!Cova told Morgan, her skin dark green with determination. "The events leading up to and necessitating the deployment not merely of a starkiller but of multiple Final Dragon starkillers.

"You understand, Captain Casimir, that we are continuing to attempt to keep the existence of the Mesharom Archive secret, yes? Even without that factor, that we are in possession of miniaturized starkillers is a strategic destabilizer we do not wish to become public."

The Mesharom were the universally acknowledged first race of the Core Powers, the older and more powerful races that dwelled closer to the center of the galaxy. They were the oldest known race and their technology was the best in the galaxy. They had also existed during the times of the Precursors and had a great deal of information on the ancient aliens.

And an archive of *all* of their technological and historical information was in the hands of the A!Tol Imperium thanks to the actions of a much-younger Morgan Casimir.

"I understand all of that, sir," Morgan said levelly. "It was factored into my decision at the time. We had very few options available to us."

"So I understand," Tan!Cova allowed. "I also must note that a Final Dragon starkiller costs almost as much as a standard modern destroyer. You fired *three* of them. Your take on that price tag, Captain?"

"I have to note, sir, that I also used every shuttle, drone, sensor probe and other deployable system on board *Defiance* as decoys for the starkiller strike," Morgan said slowly. "While individually less expensive, the total cost of those nearly rivals the cost of one of the starkillers.

"And we only successfully delivered *one* starkiller to the actual target."

The red flicker of an A!Tol chuckle crossed Tan!Cova's skin.

"This is fair," she allowed. "Did you expect to achieve even that, Captain?"

"I wasn't certain," Morgan admitted. "While all evidence suggested that the sun eater itself couldn't stop the missiles, there were still dozens to hundreds of its progeny between us and the sun it was hauling with it."

She shivered at the memory of those sperm-like starships. Each of them had a natural fusion engine and a natural plasma cannon more powerful than anything mounted by an Imperial warship—and some of them had possessed an organic interface drive, too.

"As it turned out, the one missile that was destroyed was taken out by one of our own ships in the hands of the cultists," she continued. "The Children of the Stars were the more immediate threat in many ways, but the presence of organic interface drives on the bioships..."

She shook her head.

"We have every reason to believe that the sun eater would be able to duplicate the hyperspace drives on the Children's starships, sooner rather than later," Morgan said. "That would have taken the journey to Kosha down from years to days. I judged that we couldn't afford the risk."

"Despite having specific and explicit orders both to leave the Great Mother intact and not to deploy the starkillers?" Iros asked from their desk. The Pibo's tone was deceptively mild.

"When I was given command of *Defiance* and provided the codes to activate the starkillers, it was made clear to me that the responsibility of deploying them was mine," Morgan said slowly. "I was authorized to both refuse orders to deploy them and to use my discretion if it became necessary to deploy them.

"My orders were based on our previous assumptions, that we were looking at an immobile construct built by the Alava that was having its bioships harvested by the Children for their purposes," she continued. "That the sun eater was mobile under its own power and was adapting the technology the Children had in their possession suggested a very different threat level.

"It also communicated with us, demanding that we surrender the matter-conversion core that powers *Defiance*." Morgan shook her head. "I believed then and believe now that allowing it to continue toward Kosha represented a clear and immediate threat to a colony with a population of almost three million, sirs."

"This is not a trial, Captain Casimir," Tan!Cova told her. "Echelon Lord Davor approved your actions to such a level that we would need to put her on trial next to you, and I think the Empress would be highly displeased if we charged either of you."

The office was silent for a moment.

"This is an interview, Captain, the first of what will be many," the A!Tol continued. "We need to understand exactly what you were thinking and what you saw. The Womb, the Great Mother, the sun eater—whatever we call it, the creature you destroyed was an Alavan construction unlike anything we'd seen before."

"It had similar construction and biology to the cloner on Arjtal," Morgan pointed out. "We have seen Alavan biotech before."

It was the only technology from that Precursor empire that still functioned.

"Yes, that was in the report, wasn't it?" Tan!Cova conceded. "And that is my point, I think, Captain Casimir. You were there; you saw all of this yourself. There are elements in the reports that we glance past that you understand the critical importance of.

"We need to make certain nothing of importance is missed," the Squadron Lord insisted. "So far, the Final Dragon Protocol appears to be unbreached despite the deployment of the weapons. That may not last.

"The Empress herself has made it clear that she regards your use of them as justified, Captain, but we need to make certain that we get as much of value out of this situation as we can."

"Not least because of the scans suggesting that the thing reproduced," Iros said grimly. "Echelon Lord Davor's efforts to locate the child have so far failed. We need to know what we might see next."

"These interviews will wear on you, Captain, and it will feel like we are questioning the waters of every flow you swam," Tan!Cova told Morgan. "Your officers as well. We will wring every drop of knowledge from you, but understand that you are *not* on trial.

"We need to know everything you know about this, even the parts you thought irrelevant to your report."

The A!Tol shivered, her tentacles flickering all around her.

"If there are things out there that eat suns, we need to know everything about them."

CHAPTER THREE

Dr. Rin Dunst, PhD in xenoarcheology along with a long list of other qualifications, was trying to meditate. He was generally pretty good at it. Accessing the data library stored at the base of his spine required a very specific type of self-hypnosis, after all.

Today, though, calm and serenity wouldn't come. There was nothing wrong with the space he was trying to work in. He'd spent months of his life in Imperial courier ships, the heavily over-engined messenger ships that ran the ragged edge of "safe velocity" with an interface drive to carry people and cargo across the Imperium.

He'd left Kosha eleven days after Morgan Casimir, when this courier had arrived with orders from the Imperial Archeology Institute calling him home. If someone had bothered to send those orders by starcom or hyperfold com, he could have ridden on *Defiance*, but secrecy was critical to his tasks.

The sandy-haired scientist sighed and opened his eyes. There were tricks he could use to kick himself into the right space to access the data archive, but he wasn't even trying to do that. He was just trying to relax.

The archive implanted in his lower back contained everything the Imperium knew about the Precursor race called the Alava, including how they'd died. Rin was not unaware of the irony that he knew how the Alava's neural implants had wiped out their species... and he was one of the few people in the Imperium with neural implants of his own.

He stretched gently and stepped over to the tiny desk in the courier ship's guest quarters. A small rock lay on the surface and he touched it with a smile. He'd almost missed its arrival, but apparently, Victoria Antonova, Morgan Casimir's girlfriend, had leaned on her authority as an officer in the Ducal Militia to include the package in formal Imperial cargo. It had arrived in Kosha on a similar courier to this one, though that had been a Naval ship.

The rock represented more than the old one had. The old rock, the one he'd given Morgan, had been a reminder of a homeworld he didn't expect to see again for years, if ever. This one was still that, but it was also a reminder that Morgan's other partner approved of their relationship.

Polyamory was outside his prior experience, which meant Antonova's support and approval were critical to him. He had no idea what he was doing, but he figured if Antonova approved and Morgan still wanted him around, he was doing about as well as he could.

"Doctor?"

Rin rose and turned to the intercom.

"Yes, what is it?" he asked.

"This is Lesser Commander Ochas," the courier's second-in-command told him. She, like the rest of the crew, was Tosumi, one of the four-armed avians that had been the A!Tol's third set of subjects.

"The waters of A!To warm to our presence," the officer continued. Like several other species, the Tosumi were an Imperial Race —but that wasn't an entirely positive label. It meant that the A!Tol had uplifted them wrong and wiped out most of their preexisting culture. The Tosumi were by no means an aquatic species, but they had absorbed most of the idioms of the A!Tol culture along the way.

"What's our ETA to the planet?" Rin asked, translating the phrase to *we're almost there.*

"Hyper portal in four hundredth-cycles, orbit one hundredth-cycle after that," Ochas told him. "We should have you on the surface in less than a tenth-cycle. Do you know your final destination, Dr. Dunst?"

"The Imperial Institute, so far as I know," he told the officer. "That may change, but you'll know as soon as I do."

The Tosumi clacked her beak in a chuckle.

"The Courier Service may not be military, but we're close enough to be familiar with *those* waters," Ochas agreed. "We will have a shuttle ready whenever you are, Dr. Dunst. You are not our *only* cargo, but..."

"I'm familiar with being cargo, Commander. I appreciate the ride."

RIN TOOK a few moments once the courier entered the A!To System to confirm that *Defiance* was in-system. It took him a bit longer than he expected, but he eventually located the cruiser in a refit dock.

Defiance had been shredded in her encounter with the sun eater. She'd needed another ship to bring her back into regular space. Her hyperdrive and engines had been fixed when the recall order had arrived, but not much else.

Hopefully, the yards at the heart of the Imperium would finish the work Kosha Station's facilities had begun. He quite liked the ship and her crew, even beyond her captain.

Then he checked in on his mail. A quick notice to the Institute via the courier's hyperfold communicator let them know he had arrived in A!To. A number of e-mails and messages downloaded to his tablet and he glanced through the headers for a moment.

He didn't get more than that before his tablet—a thumb-sized device with a holographic screen and keyboard—chimed to advise of an incoming call. It was a real-time call on the hyperfold com, relayed through the courier's encrypted systems.

"Rin Dunst. Welcome home," the being that appeared on his screen greeted him.

"Director Doad," Rin replied, nodding to his superior.

Doad was Ivida, the second Imperial Race. He was a tall double-jointed biped with a motionless face and red skin. He returned the nod calmly.

"The waters of our work storm in your absence, Rin," Doad told him. "Your own work has brought chaos of its own."

"That is the nature of discovery and science, Director," Rin said. "My recall order was very vague. What's going on?"

"We need to update your copy of the archive with everything we've learned," the Ivida said. "There is no point in storing backup copies in our key scientists if those copies are not up to date."

"There is a cycle for that," Rin said slowly. "I'm not due back at the Institute for another long-cycle."

Six months, give or take. He mostly thought in Imperial cycles now, based on the year of A!To itself.

"We also want to update everyone else's archives with everything you've learned," Doad pointed out. "I hope that you have not trusted *everything* to the vagaries of naval encryption."

"I'm told that is completely secure," Rin said. He'd sent a lot of information on an earlier courier, though. Much of what they knew about the Alava had been stolen, after all, and they didn't want the people they'd robbed to realize that.

"That is true, but some things need even more security," the Ivida told him. "We will need to interview you as well. Strange things were found and learned, and we must know more."

"As you wish, Director," he agreed. "I still have work out by Kosha."

"You left capable subordinates behind, Rin; the expeditions will be fine," Doad insisted. "We will see what is the best course for you once we have combined all the relevant waters."

"Of course. I will be on the surface in a few hundredth-cycles. We can meet in person then."

"I look forward to it. You have been too long in the field, I think. Some rest will be good for you, and we all need to learn what you have learned."

CHAPTER FOUR

THE IMPERIAL ARCHEOLOGY INSTITUTE WAS THE SIZE OF SOME entire universities that Rin Dunst had seen. It was a sprawling complex of buildings, most of them only a few stories high, tucked into a river delta a hundred kilometers south of the capital of First Home.

Doad himself was waiting as Rin Dunst exited the shuttle, the Ivida's eyes focused on Rin in a way that made him uncomfortable. Humid summer heat washed around the two sentients as they greeted each other, and Doad gestured for a robot to take Rin's bag.

"Walk with me, Rin," Doad ordered.

"Of course. Is there more to say that we couldn't talk about on the hyperfold?" Rin asked.

"There are always strange waters that should not be sent over channels that can be intercepted," Doad said. "A meeting of the Directors and the principal researchers has been summoned; they are waiting on us."

Rin swallowed. That was something he would prefer to have been warned about. The "principal researchers" were the archeologists like him, the scientists who knew *everything* the Imperium knew about a particular subject via both intense education and cybernetic implants. The Directors, on the other hand, *merely* ran the Institute.

"What is that important, Doad?" he asked.

"The Empress's orders, Rin," his companion told him. "There are other matters as well, but the Empress wants us to examine everything you learned about the Children and the Great Mother in the context of all we already know of the Alava."

"I was hoping to sit down with the archives and the Institute's data and analysis resources to do some of that on my own," Rin admitted. "But a full meeting of the Directors..."

"The decision was not mine alone," Doad said. "You will be fine, Rin. You did everything entirely correctly."

Rin wasn't so sure of that, but that was at least partially because he knew things he couldn't share with the Institute. He now knew how the archive of Alavan data the Institute worked from had come into their hands—Morgan Casimir had stolen it from a disabled Mesharom war-sphere while she'd rescued its crew.

He suspected the Directors knew that but the other principal researchers didn't. That piece of information had left some of his decisions in doubt.

He still felt he'd done the right things, but it wasn't as certain as Doad implied.

"I work for the Institute and the Imperium," he conceded as they walked through the Institute campus. "If the Directorate wants me to answer questions, I answer questions."

"I know," Doad told him. "I wanted to give you some warning of the waters you were landing in. Once this meeting is done, you should rest. Tomorrow I have a different task for you."

"I am at the Institute's disposal," Rin said.

"We need you to meet with one of our key sponsors," the Ivida said. "You will have to go to her; she can't come to us, but she wants to speak to you."

"Is that as odd as it sounds?" he asked.

Doad made the strange clicking noise of Ivida laughter.

"Yes," he confirmed. "And I can't tell you much more in advance. The sponsor is very secretive and for good reason, but her money and influence help keep the Institute alive and operating."

Rin wracked his brain for a moment, trying to think of a sponsor that fit Doad's description. He thought he'd met all of the Institute's key sponsors, but none of them were that secretive. Though if the sponsor wasn't able to come to the Institute itself for whatever reason, he guessed she couldn't attend the galas where the top researchers made nice with politicians and donors.

"Come on," Doad ordered. "The Directorate is still waiting."

RIN WAS familiar with the conference room that he was led into. There was normally a circular table, where the four principal researchers for a given topic and the six Directors of the Institute sat as theoretical equals.

Today, one of the four segments of the table had been removed, squishing his three colleagues and six bosses together into less space while he was seated alone, facing them all.

The resemblance to a military court-martial was *probably* coincidental.

"Dr. Dunst, please take a seat," the A!Tol at the center of the table ordered. While Doad was the senior Director of the Institute, everyone accepted that L!Ko was the "first among equals" of the rest of the Directors.

Doad slipped into his seat at L!Ko's side as Rin sat down, facing the Directorate. He was the only human in the room, each of the ten scientists representing a different one of the Imperium's twenty-nine species.

"I am at the Directorate's disposal," Rin told them. "My understanding is that you want to ask about the events in the Kosha region and around the Great Mother."

"Eventually," L!Ko told him, her tentacles flickering in a dismissive gesture while the purplish-blue of concern flashed across her skin. "Our understanding is that your expedition was captured by these cultists and that you and your team were held prisoner for some time.

"Are your people well?"

"*Well* would be overstating things," Rin admitted. "Eleven of my people were killed. Their bodies should be home to their families by now. Others suffered from malnutrition or physical injury.

"Most of that was handled by *Defiance*'s sickbay staff before Captain Casimir returned us to Kosha Station. I believe every member of the expedition is undergoing continuing counseling and mental-health observation."

Rin's plans for future expeditions in the region had called for hiring additional medical personnel, including counselors to make sure those programs continued. He'd left those plans with the senior members of the Institute team on site.

"And you, Dr. Dunst?" another Director, an Indiri named Sokan Mal, asked. She was a squat amphibian with a frog-like head and a broad torso covered in russet fur, currently damp from a personal humidifier.

"I spoke to the counselors myself, several times," Rin confirmed. "I was not injured in any of my activities and spent some time working with the counselor aboard *Defiance* as I aided Captain Casimir."

"We will make certain that the resources are available for your people," L!Ko told him. "There will be no shortages or unnecessary stressors. This was a hard time for your people."

"It was, but they rose to the occasion beyond any reasonable expectation," Rin said. "They did well out there."

"Our people are critically important, Dr. Dunst; we appreciate the update," Doad said. "Do you have any concerns about them continuing to operate in your absence?"

Doad himself had noted that Rin had competent subordinates,

but he clearly wanted Rin to commit to that on the record in front of the Directorate.

"None," he assured them. "I left Kelly Lawrence in charge. She's a cyber-archeologist with strong credentials from several Terra-based universities. I have full faith in her abilities as a scientist and an administrator."

He smiled thinly.

"It's not like I was officially in charge of the mission, in any case."

"This is true," L!Ko acknowledged. "Is !Lat prepared to take back over at any point?"

"Like several others, he remains under observation at Kosha, though my understanding is that his prognosis is good," Rin said quietly. !Lat had been the administrator of the expedition, with Rin as his advisor and subject-matter expert. Both he and the A!Tol had been aware of Rin's true role, but !Lat's role had allowed Rin to focus on the archeology instead of the administration.

"We will be in touch with his doctors," Doad assured Rin. "And the others, as well. Our people will be taken care of; you need have no concerns there."

"I have none," Rin confirmed. "If I have concerns, it's over the evidence that the Children of the Stars were originally an Institute expedition from ten years ago."

That was one of the few things that hadn't even been in his physical messages. The Children of the Stars had been a cult, one that had worshipped the sun-eating "Great Mother" and had directly attacked his expedition as well as Captain Casimir's ship.

He'd managed to shock most of the room to silence...but L!Ko waved a tentacle.

"I drew the same conclusions from the information you sent us," she said, her skin flashing green with grim determination. "Their main starship was a long-duration survey vessel, and the classified files from the Navy showed several escort ships present when the sun eater was destroyed.

"I have made inquiries to identify the ships, and the survey vessel,

Child of the Great Mother as the Children renamed her, was ours," she confirmed. "She was *Child of the Rising Storm*, launched twenty-two long-cycles ago. She served on two expeditions and then was assigned to a joint operation with the Imperial Navy for a long-range survey expedition from which she did not return."

"What do we know about this joint operation?" Doad asked.

"We had some early extrapolations from the Archive of what we might find out near Kosha. The colony was just being founded and we wanted to see what we could find," L!Ko said calmly. "The Directorate of the time authorized the project, but it was classified at the highest levels, even here."

Twenty-two long-cycles was ten years, give or take. If Rin remembered right, L!Ko was the only member of that Directorate who was still serving.

She might well know more than she was saying, but this wasn't the place for Rin to push.

"All evidence, unfortunately, suggests that every member of that expedition was somehow coopted by the sun eater," Rin told them. "Or killed. While some of the ones who joined the Children of the Stars may still be alive, the Navy believes most or all of the Children to be dead at this point."

A shiver ran through the room.

"We may believe ourselves immune to delusions of grandeur as scientists, but it is very clear that the sheer scale and power of the Mother, plus her ability to talk to them, overwhelmed anything resembling sense," he continued. "We must be cautious when dealing with future Alavan megastructures and projects. While we know their hard technology has failed, most of their biotech appears to still be operational."

"What little of it we've seen," Sokan Mal said. "It seems odd that we've only encountered a few intact pieces of it, out at the edge of their territory. Why is that, do you think, Dr. Dunst?"

"I believe that we are dealing with a rogue faction, partially or completely detached from the Alava Hegemony," Rin replied. "We have what we believe was a relatively complete census of Hegemony territory in the archive, but it only scrapes the surface of the regions around Arjtal and Kosha. I suspect that the fringe regions of their territory were only loosely in touch with the central government, but that was not how the central government liked to present it.

"Especially not to their slaves, like the Mesharom."

"That leaves much of the data in the Archive suspect," Doad warned. "The vast majority of our data is sourced from the Mesharom and their records of what was going on at the fall of the Alava. They recorded much of what they knew in stone."

"And what they knew was incomplete," Rin concluded. "We should have realized that all along. They were slaves, whatever labels and propaganda the Alava created around them. Why would they have been told all the truth?"

"And in the gaps we find monsters that eat stars and spawn battle fleets," L!Ko said. "These are dangerous waters we swim, especially with a war starting to draw away attention. We nearly missed the sun eater. A world might have died for our mistakes. *Our* mistakes, siblings.

"The Institute studies the Alava, and if there are these kinds of dangers in the Alava's ruins, it is our responsibility to locate them in time to protect the Imperium."

"If we hadn't sent the expedition we sent, the sun eater would never have known to target Kosha," Rin pointed out. "These creations, these dangers, have slept for a hundred thousand long-cycles. If we prod them, we create risks. If we leave them..."

"We allow the risks to grow hidden from us," Doad said grimly. "Protecting the Imperium falls on the Empress's military, but if the Alava's artifacts are a threat...that is *our* responsibility."

"And, thankfully, no one expects us to stop the Wendira and Laians going to war," L!Ko said. "It's going to draw away resources and time that we could use."

"If the Imperium goes to war, that has to be the focus," Rin pointed out.

"But if we miss a creature like the sun eater again, the war might become very irrelevant very fast," L!ko warned. "We must understand as much of the waters of the beast you faced as we can, Dr. Dunst. Please, let us focus on the matter at hand."

"All right." Rin bowed his head, resting his hands on his stomach as he marshaled his thoughts. "I am at the Directorate's disposal," he reiterated. "I think there are some signs we can look for now that would allow us to locate a sun eater, at least.

"I *believe*, from what records we retrieved, that the Great Mother was unique. There may be other biotech constructs in that region. Whoever that faction of Alava was, they were actively trying to keep what they were doing secret from the Hegemony."

"So, the Archive is useless in tracking them," Doad concluded.

"But fifty thousand years of star data might not be," Rin replied. "The star the sun eater was attached to moved, after all. If we study the stars, we might find some answers."

"This is true." L!Ko flickered her tentacles again. "But, again, we had some questions prepared. We have distracted ourselves enough, and the work remains. Are you ready, Dr, Dunst?"

"Of course."

CHAPTER FIVE

AFTER SEVEN DAYS OF EXCRUCIATINGLY DETAILED INTERVIEWS with assorted different people, Morgan almost wished she *were* on trial. At least if she had been on trial, it would have been mostly the same people and she wouldn't have faced the same questions over and over again.

Each interviewer had a different focus, at least, but they all tended to start with similar questions.

But she *had* blown up a star, she supposed, even if that star had been in the grasp of an organic monstrosity that had been using it as a fuel source. So, on the eighth day, she got out of the bed in the guest quarters she'd been given and prepared for another round of questioning.

Her tablet told her she only had one appointment, lasting the entire day.

Morgan sighed as she pulled on her uniform. Hopefully, whoever she was meeting today at least understood the concept of a lunch break. Eight hours in a single round of questioning might be a bit much for her.

"Captain!" her guard slash driver greeted her as she stepped out of the suite.

"Spear Vaquero," she greeted the Marine. Spear Sultan Vaquero—a Petty Officer First Class in Terran parlance—was the noncommissioned Marine in charge of the squad running body-guard for her on the surface. "Do you have the location for today's appointment?"

"Just downloaded to the squad net a hundredth-cycle ago," they confirmed. "Cutting it a little close there, aren't they?"

"We're in the headquarters of an interstellar military. They run the way they want, Spear," Morgan told them. She pulled out her tablet to check something and shook her head. "I don't even have any information on who I'm meeting. Classified, I guess."

"Well, no reason to keep anyone waiting," Vaquero replied. "Fire team bravo has checked over the aircar. We're good to go whenever you are."

"Lead the way, Spear," Morgan ordered.

THE BUILDING they arrived at wasn't quite what Morgan had expected. She'd expected another one of the Navy Headquarters' squat office buildings. Instead, she'd arrived at a miniaturized space-port, one of two multilevel facilities that handled orbital and subor-bital spacecraft for the headquarters campus.

"Our information on the meeting has you on the fifth floor," Vaquero answered her unspoken question, the androgynously pale Marine studying the spaceport themselves. "Permission to bring the fire team, sir?"

The aircar they'd been lent had enough space for a four-person Marine fire team as well as Morgan and her driver. It was clearly designed for VIP transport, and Vaquero had made full use of the space. Including the Spear, who was driving the vehicle, Morgan had five Marines with her—and while they were only carrying plasma pistols on a regular basis, she was well aware there were portable plasma rifles tucked into the aircar as well.

"Granted," she told Vaquero. "Something doesn't feel right."

"Bravo, up and at 'em," the Spear barked. "Fall in on the Captain."

"Oorah!" the Marines chorused.

Morgan concealed a smile. Of the four members of the fire team responding to Vaquero, not one was American. All were at least human, but the old chorus of the United States Marines had long ago infected the A!Tol Imperium's landing forces.

Her nerves had apparently *also* infected her guardians, though. The squad had spent most of the time on the headquarters campus letting her wander around with a single Marine, often Spear Vaquero themselves. Today, the team of five fell in around her in perfect order.

Two of them even paused in the vehicle to acquire those plasma rifles she'd been judiciously ignoring. They were still in dress uniforms instead of power armor, but her escort was loaded for bear.

The spaceport was busy enough that the escort was almost certainly overkill—but that only added to her confusion. Why would she have a meeting in a room in one of the shuttle ports?

Part of the answer revealed itself when she knocked on the door listed for her appointment. It immediately slid open to reveal itself as a three-story bay for a suborbital shuttle, about as small as one of the narrow-bodied aircraft could be.

"Captain Casimir?" someone greeted her in a sharp tone. "Please confirm your ID."

Morgan turned sharply to face the speaker, who turned out to be another Imperial Marine. This one was Pibo, small enough to make the plasma rifle in their hands look strangely out of scale—but the two Pibo *behind* them were in full power armor with full-size plasma rifles.

"I am Captain Morgan Casimir," she confirmed, then reeled off an ID code. "What the hell is going on?"

"Your flight is cleared to leave in one hundredth-cycle," the Pibo told her instead of answering the question. "You are authorized to bring two Marines." They—Pibo genders were unclear at first glance, but the vocal pitch *suggested* this was a neuter—gestured to her escort.

"The rifles can stay here; there is limited space on the shuttle and weapons of that weight aren't permitted at your destination."

"I am not getting on that plane until someone tells me what is going on," Morgan replied, gesturing for her Marines to hold in place. "I have orders to report to this room for an interview, but this is hardly a conference room."

"You are being interviewed, sir," the Marine said firmly. "The individual interviewing you cannot be present on the Navy base due to medical requirements, so you are being transported to them. Their identity and involvement in this process are classified, but you will be briefed prior to meeting them."

"This is all against protocol," Morgan replied. "I need to confirm these orders."

She was reasonably sure someone should have told her if she was being strapped into a suborbital transport and flung god-alone-knew how far around the planet.

"Of course," the Marine replied. "Echelon Lord Iros should be available to take your call, Captain. They are busy, of course, so I suggest you make it quickly."

That the Marine was perfectly willing to let her contact her superiors suggested she was *probably* fine...but she made the call anyway.

"Iros speaking," the Pibo replied instantly. "Captain Casimir, what's going on?"

"I'm hoping you can answer that question for me, sir," she said. "My orders for today have brought me to a suborbital shuttle hangar at Shuttleport A, sir, and I was not expecting to travel today."

"Your destination and this meeting itself are both classified, Captain Casimir," Iros told her. "But yes, you are heading off-site for your interview today. Is that sufficient for your concerns?"

Morgan *really* wanted to ask more questions, but when an Echelon Lord says things are okay, well...

"Yes, sir," she confirmed. "Thank you, sir."

"Be on your way, Captain," they ordered. "The tides wait for no one."

That particular phrase, it seemed, was almost universal among any species whose planet had both oceans and a moon.

THEY WERE in the air for a full tenth-cycle, a quarter of the time Morgan was supposed to be in the interview at all. That was enough for them to cross a significant chunk of A!To's circumference and to bring them to a mountain range full of giants.

Each mountain in the range dwarfed Everest on Earth. Their foothills swept away beneath Morgan's aircraft, twisting roads leading down to cities on the shore.

"That's Adorned Lands," the pilot told them. "It was once the second-largest and -richest nation on the planet. Most histories mark Adorned Lands' acceptance of the Imperial line as the true beginning of the A!Tol Imperium...some four thousand long-cycles ago."

Around when Rome was being sacked by Gauls, Morgan mentally calculated. The Imperium had already been an industrial power then, with limited space travel.

Humanity still had a lot of catching up to do.

"I didn't think the A!Tol had much in the mountains," she said aloud as she realized their course continued toward the immense peaks. "Especially not in mountains *this* big."

"Mines, mostly," the pilot replied. "And religious institutions and similar. We're headed to an old fortress-monastery. You won't see it until we're on top of it. It has more than one layer of defenses."

The Pibo wasn't exaggerating. For several minutes, Morgan thought they were flying directly toward a solid wall of stone, even as the aircraft slowed down.

Then the pilot twisted them through a passageway that was nearly invisible from more than a kilometer away and into a narrow gorge that ran down the side of the mountain. From there, they actually rose up the valley while continuing to shed airspeed toward the sharp walls of the fortress.

The structure wasn't immense, but it was larger than she'd expected. Multiple tiers of walls carved from the living stone surrounded and protected a central structure that could easily house several thousand people.

The A!Tol would find coming up this high difficult enough. To reach these altitudes, overcome multiple layers of defenses, and even then face the solid stone walls of the core structure...it would have been impossible before gunpowder and hard enough even with more modern weapons.

"What is this place?" she asked as they slowed toward the courtyard. They weren't the first ones there, she noted absently. A second suborbital shuttle was on the cleared runway, probably freshly landed. Despite the age of the structure, a modern-looking hangar had been dug into the mountain next to the runway.

The pilot checked something on their console.

"We're far enough in that we're covered by the security fields," they said aloud. "This is a Ki! stronghold. These are where the females who were determined to survive the birthing madness retreated away from their males in the hopes of finding something on the other side of the insanity."

Morgan inhaled sharply. She'd met one Ki!Tol in her life. A!Tol females were among the hardiest sentients in the Imperium, difficult to injure and capable of rapidly healing from almost any injury.

They'd evolved those strengths for one reason: A!Tol reproduction was literally parasitic. They had no wombs and their young literally ate their mothers alive from the inside out. They'd invented birth control and artificial wombs well ahead of any other race, only to find that their bodies had one last brutal trick to play.

Over the course of their lifetime, an A!Tol female's body would build up massive amounts of hormonal imbalances, pushing them ever more fiercely to breed. Even removing the eggs and glands involved only slowed the situation, eventually driving her insane.

Most A!Tol females quietly suicided as they reached that point. Some, more traditional, kept some of their eggs until the end and had them fertilized and reimplanted, dying as their foremothers had.

A small portion tried to push through. Morgan had never really thought about what that would require, but an isolated mountain monastery would probably do the trick. The ones who survived, who found that balance on the far side of insanity, were the Ki!Tol— nearly immortal, indestructible avatars of the A!Tol racial memory.

Their reputation as trickster demons probably had something to do with the walls.

"I'm meeting a Ki!Tol?" Morgan asked.

"I'm not the one to brief you," the pilot told her. "You'll be met when we land."

———

THE FIRST SURPRISE was the passenger of the other suborbital. Rin Dunst looked as surprised to see Morgan as she was to see him, though surprise rapidly turned to a wide grin and a fierce embrace.

"When did you get to A!To?" she demanded.

"Two days ago," he admitted. "Piles of questions since. The Institute has a lot of questions about what we ran into."

"The Navy as well, but I was expecting that," she admitted. "I think everyone thinks we did the right thing, but there's a lot of questions."

"I know." He squeezed her and then stepped back to nod to the Marines. "Spear Vaquero, Lance Hiddleston."

Morgan looked around the runway they'd landed on. It had clearly been blasted out more recently than most of the fortress, attached to the main courtyard that linked smaller structures to the main building.

There was no one there. She expected to see A!Tol moving between the structures, but there was *no one*.

"My pilot said someone would meet us," she said.

"Mine too," Rin replied. "I guess we go to the main doors?"

"Makes sense to me."

The professor fell in beside Morgan as she set off, the Marines following behind them. They made it about halfway across the courtyard before the door to the monastery swung open.

Two Tosumi walked out the door in unpowered body armor, black clamshells locked around their feathered forms. They carried ceremonial spears in one set of hands—and deadly functional plasma rifles in the other.

The two guardians flanked the door silently as a third individual, a Pibo in a plain white robe, walked out.

"Notice something strange?" Rin murmured.

"Beyond everything?" Morgan asked.

"No A!Tol," he replied. "Not since we got on the shuttles, right? All Imperial Races, none of the newer annexations, but not a single A!Tol."

The Pibo met them half a dozen meters in front of the doorway and bowed.

"Welcome to the Fortress Ki!Ron," they greeted the two humans. "You are welcome here, but I ask you to be respectful and as quiet as you can. We have only a handful of Initiates in the fortress at the moment, but they are all at a difficult time."

The Pibo looked down at the ground.

"All Initiates are always at a difficult time," they admitted. "Please, Dr. Dunst, Captain Casimir, walk with me."

"My guards?" Morgan asked.

"They may accompany us if you wish. Our mistress is well protected and you are safe here, but if you desire their company, it will not be blocked." They paused. "The Marines may not enter the final sanctum, however, so they may be better served waiting here."

Morgan considered for a moment, glancing around the fortress.

She suspected that whoever ran the fortress probably had more authority over the pilots who'd delivered them than she did. The Marines couldn't save them if the mistress of the fortress decided to destroy them.

"Spear, stay here and rest," she ordered. "See if they'll get you food or something."

"Sustenance can be arranged," the robed Pibo agreed, gesturing to one of the Tosumi guards. "We don't have human-native food, but we do have supplies of UP."

Universal Protein was a tofu-like substance that had been rendered down to the most basic forms of protein. It could provide most of the critical needs of every species in the Imperium. Combined with easier-to-store vitamin powders, it would feed any species known.

That it was blandly tasteless was inevitable.

"But come. We have plenty of time, but you must have questions that I will answer before you meet your hostess."

THE STILL-UNNAMED PIBO led the two humans deeper into the mountain fortress. None of the people associated with this place and this trip had given Morgan a name yet, and it was starting to make her nervous.

"You are to meet with Ki!Ron herself," the Pibo finally told them. "The fortress was not initially for her, but she was one of its first generations of Initiates. She has been here for so long that it was inevitable the name changed."

"That's impossible," Rin said.

Morgan glanced at him, wondering how he could be so sure.

"The walls, the cuts...I can't be certain without isotope-dating, but this fortress is at least four thousand long-cycles old."

"Six thousand, four hundred and eighty-six," their Pibo guide told them. "Ki!Ron is the oldest known Ki!Tol to still be living. She emerged from the meditation cells in this fortress six thousand one hundred and fifty-two long-cycles ago."

Over thirty-three *centuries* earlier. Morgan shivered. They were being brought to a being who not only predated A!Tol space travel but had been alive while humans had been figuring out how to smelt iron.

"She likely does not have much time left," the guide continued. "She is not, after all, the first Ki!Tol to exist. Merely the oldest left. Her mind is still sharp, but her body betrays her in many ways. If we could move even our remaining Initiates from this fortress, we would. The presence of A!Tol of any kind around her is a stressor she cannot handle.

"As much as possible, she tries to avoid in-person contact with males of any species. That she wishes to interview Dr. Dunst is unusual, but the situation is unusual." The guide shook their head. "I hope it does not prove an error, but I must ask you to keep yourself calm during your meeting."

"Of course," Rin replied before Morgan even finished processing what was being asked.

In theory, a non-A!Tol male should have no impact on a Ki!Tol, but...who knew what could set off the traumas and triggers of a three-thousand-year-old semi-immortal?

"We could have had this meeting remotely," Morgan suggested.

"The security systems of the Imperial Navy headquarters and of this fortress are among the best we can create, but there are matters that cannot be trusted to electronic communication. Anything can be intercepted, Captain Casimir—and, given enough time, anything can be decoded."

The guide made a shrugging gesture.

"And she wished to meet you both."

"What is so secret?" Rin asked. "I'm not aware of much that would require this security, and I am cleared for matters almost no one else is."

"That is not my place to say," the guide told him. "What I can tell you is that even by being in this fortress, you have stepped into matters classified at levels above even the Dragon Protocols. You walk in the most shadowed secrets of our Imperium, Dr. Dunst, and you walk on sacred ground.

"Show Ki!Ron the respect she needs and deserves. Today will be enlightening for you both, I hope, but she has her reasons for summoning you."

And there were reasons, Morgan had to assume, that the word of this aged semi-immortal was enough to summon Imperial military officers and archeologists from across the Imperium.

CHAPTER SIX

THEIR GUIDE LED THEM THROUGH A SET OF OVERSIZED DOORS
into a darkened stone chamber deep inside the fortress. The Pibo
bowed themselves out after Morgan and Rin were in the room and a
shiver ran down Morgan's spine as the door closed.

"Lights," a voice declared in the darkness. "Thirty percent."

Her earbuds were translating perfectly, but Morgan's understanding of the A!Tol primary language told her that the speaker
wasn't using quite the version of the language she was used to. Not
quite to a level of Old English versus modern English, but still an
antiquated dialect and phrasing.

The lights responded to it anyway, the darkness fading into a dim
twilight that allowed Morgan to see her hostess.

Ki!Ron was immense. Morgan had known another Ki!Tol, her
mother's friend and long-standing partner-in-crime Ki!Tana, and
Ki!Tana had towered over other A!Tol at a full three meters in height
on her locomotive tentacles.

Ki!Ron rested in a shallow pool, her tentacles splayed around her,
but her bullet-shaped torso alone was over three meters thick.

Morgan wasn't sure the immense Ki!Tol *could* stand, but she could clearly speak.

"Captain Casimir, Professor Dunst," Ki!Ron greeted them, her tentacles carefully lifting her and shifting around. "Welcome to my home. I understand it might not have been what you expected when you were summoned here, but it is traditional."

"And safe, I hope," Morgan said. Three millennia of experience alone made Ki!Ron a critical asset to the Imperium, a living memory archive of the entire rise of the Imperium from one largish state on a divided planet to the ruling power of hundreds of star systems and nearly thirty species.

"I fear, some days, that the Empress puts more weight on my safety than on her own," Ki!Ron told her. "I am safe, Captain Casimir. And I am more...busy, shall we say, than some might assume. I have a full set of modern communications gear, including a hyperfold communicator."

The Ki!Tol's skin was faded to gray, Morgan noted. There was no emotion showing on the aged sentient's skin. Time had robbed it of that property.

"Hence acting as a patron and influencer in support of the Imperial Institute," Rin said. "How may we assist you, Ki!Ron?"

"There are many things you could do to help me," she replied. "I could interrogate you both for hours on what you found out in the Kosha Sector, but the truth is that I have copies of all of the interviews you both have done. Keeping up with the investigation and study of the sun eater has occupied much of my days of late."

Morgan couldn't help but suspect that wasn't a good thing.

"And what have you learned from that investigation?" she asked.

"That the sentient I chose for that mission was a darkwaters-infested fool," Ki!Ron hissed. "It was *my* tentacle that sent those waters into motion, Captain Casimir. It was *my* influence that assembled a secret scouting mission to seek out the truth behind the hints we had found in the Mesharom Archive."

Morgan froze and Ki!Ron's beak clattered in laughter.

"I am cleared under your Elder Dragon Protocol, Captain Casimir," the ancient Ki!Tol told her. "In fact, you two will now join me in a clearance we admit to even less than the Dragon Protocols. One that predates your species' annexation and one that has never been committed to any electronic record anywhere.

"You will admit nothing I tell you to anyone I do not tell you is cleared to know," Ki!Ron continued. "Right now, the *only* person I will admit knows of this is Empress A!Shall herself. Can you keep a secret that closely, children?"

Morgan swallowed and exchanged a look with Rin. Her boyfriend looked curious and eager, but...

"I have oaths and responsibilities to the Imperial Navy," she told Ki!Ron.

"And this clearance is known to certain members of the Navy," the old sentient told her. "Nothing involved, nothing I ask you to do, will ever be in opposition to the needs of our Imperium. I promise you that.

"But if you accept this burden, Captain Casimir, you may be able to help our Imperium and your humans far more than you possibly imagine."

"I want to know," Rin said beside her. "And yes, I can keep secrets."

"I need to understand," Morgan finally admitted. "And if you can get me confirmation of a *military* order on these secrets..."

Ki!Ron chuckled again, the beak snaps echoing around the chamber she rested in.

"Here, child."

What the Ki!Tol slid across the floor to Morgan was an anachronism for the Imperial Navy, a sheet of physical plastic reinforced to stand up to the ages. It was a written acknowledgement of the existence of a "Last Tsunami" clearance and a requirement for any Imperial officer read into the clearance to observe it.

And it was signed with the mark of the Empress.

"All right," she conceded. "I can live with this, I suppose."

"You are loyal, Captain Casimir, and that is valued beyond treasure when you have lived as long as I have," Ki!Ron told her.

"Now, before all else, we must discuss *why* a covert expedition was sent into the darkness twenty long-cycles ago."

Morgan nodded slowly, looking around to see if there was anywhere she and Rin could sit. There was no furniture in the room around the pool Ki!Ron was resting in. It appeared they were going to have to stand.

"I don't understand why the expedition was so secret," Rin said behind her, the professor's curiosity clearly overcoming any discomfort he had from standing. "The Institute launches a lot of similar projects."

"Not heading out so far or so specifically," Ki!Ron told them. "From the Mesharom Archive, we knew exactly where we were sending the ships. Information from other sources gave us the details to fill in the gaps."

The big A!Tol shivered her tentacles.

"It was a return of a favor, as well," she concluded. "Left to our own currents, the Institute would have sent an expedition before yours, but long after *Child of Rising Storm*'s expedition. But..."

She was silent for several seconds.

"I am part of an association of like-minded individuals across the Core and Arm Powers," she finally told them. "It was these individuals who saw a matter-conversion core delivered to us in exchange for favors rendered in the past, but we owed debts still. Those were called upon to have us investigate certain fragments of the Archive that suggested a threat before any major colonization took place in the region."

"An association," Morgan echoed. That did not sound good.

"Yes," Ki!Ron agreed. "Not a formal body or organization, but individuals across the galaxy, including even some Mesharom, working to see that the technology of the Alava was handled safely. Not necessarily destroyed or hidden, as was the preference of the main Mesharom government, but handled safely."

The Mesharom had made tracking down and removing Alavan tech a major focus of their foreign policy. They'd had ships and hidden bases scattered through the galaxy—but only a small portion of their race could deal with aliens or long-distance travel, and they'd lost a massive fleet to a Taljzi trap.

The loss of resources had forced them to retreat from galactic affairs, but an informal association of supporters...that would help fulfill their mission.

"The Mesharom government doesn't like us much, since we feel that Alavan technology can be studied and replicated, so long as we aren't copying it directly or trying to turn it on," Ki!Ron said with a beak-snap chuckle.

"An interstellar conspiracy," Morgan said quietly. A conspiracy inside an officer's own nation was nightmare enough. One spread across multiple interstellar empires was a horrifying concept. "One that can send Imperial ships and researchers into motion."

"Yes," Ki!Ron agreed bluntly. "But I think we are more fluid than your phrasing suggests. I pay no fealty to anyone but my Empress, but I have contacts and discussions with people across the Core. We try to see the Alavan technology safely contained and studied. Much of the research and study now taking place around Arjtal and Kosha is supported by resources those contacts have made available."

That...made a lot of sense but still made Morgan uncomfortable.

"So, your conspiracy arranged for this mission," Rin said. "What happened?"

"You know what happened," Ki!Ron replied. "Better than I do, I suspect. Sentients I trusted to handle anything spoke with a being beyond our comprehension, and enough of them chose to worship it as a god that they turned on us all."

Morgan grimaced.

"With warships and a transport provided by you," she said.

"Yes," Ki!Ron conceded. "And so, now A!Tol tentacles sweep the region and learn what they can. Most of what we learn will filter back to my associates eventually. You have served our purposes well without knowing them, so I feel you can be of value to both us and the Imperium once more."

"You're why we were both recalled," Morgan realized.

"It didn't take much pushing for those waters to flow," the ancient Ki!Tol told her. "Both of your superiors were already considering bringing you back for debriefing. The interviews you have had over the last few days are of value to the Imperium...but yes, I arranged for you to be recalled."

"Why?" Rin asked.

"Because I want to use you," Ki!Ron said bluntly. "By standing in this room, you have already become part of the conspiracy, as Captain Casimir labels it. You are bound by your existing oaths to keep all I have said secret."

"And if we refuse to cooperate with a shadowy organization spread across half the galaxy?" Morgan demanded.

"Then I ask that you cooperate with the Imperium," their host told them. "I trade favors with my associates, but we all understand that none of us will act against our own nations' best interests. That is why the matter-conversion core that your father's people reverse-engineered came from so far away, Captain Casimir. The associate who provided it saw no threat to *their* people in upgrading our technology."

Morgan wasn't necessarily supposed to know that the Imperium had based their matter-conversion power systems on a stolen generator supplied from a Core Power on the opposite side of the galaxy. Her father, however, was the Ducal Consort of Terra...and the engineer and executive who had organized the labs that had done the work.

And given that Elon Casimir's wife, Morgan's stepmother, was Duchess Annette Bond of Terra, well, a lot of classified things were discussed around their highly secure dinner table.

"Even with these orders"—Morgan waved the plastic paper of the classification writ in the air—"there are still superiors I can report to. What happens if I do?"

"Nothing," Ki!Ron told her. "The Empress is well aware of my activities, Captain Casimir. Your loyalty and courage do you credit, but I am no threat to the Imperium. My associates may be, at times, but not through *my* tentacles."

Rin touched her shoulder and she calmed a bit at his touch, at the reminder that she wasn't alone in there.

"Will it hurt to hear her out?" he asked. "I'm curious, if nothing else."

She sighed.

"All right, Ki!Ron," she told the ancient alien. "*If* we were prepared to help your 'association,' what would you have us do?"

"Your duty," the Ki!Tol replied. "Everything I ask you to do will be covered by proper orders from your superiors, including special authorizations. I need you to go to the border between the Wendira and the Laians, the Dead Zone, and investigate matters there."

Three hundred long-cycles earlier—a hundred and fifty years, by Terran measurements—the Wendira Grand Hive and the Laian Republic had fought a brutal war. Both races were Core Powers, insectoid sentients with massive fleets...and starkillers.

The Dead Zone was the site of the largest-ever use of those weapons. Over the course of a Terran year, the two races had killed over seventy stars and roughly one *trillion* sentient beings. The only stars that remained in the Dead Zone couldn't support life, and the area had been declared a neutral territory in the peace treaty the two shocked and terrified races had signed.

And now those two powers loomed at each other again—and the Imperium was allied with the Laians. Imperial superbattleship squadrons had taken up positions along the Laian side of the front. Ton for ton, the A!Tol warships were just as deadly as the Core Powers they stood alongside, but Wendira and Laian alike were building starships far larger than the Imperium's battleships.

"What kind of *matters*?" Morgan asked. "There's a war going on out there."

"Not quite. Not yet," Ki!Ron told her. "And that, Captain

Casimir, is what I need you to investigate. Official and unofficial channels from the Republic to the Imperium are clear: they are not pushing this war. It is the Wendira who are launching surprise raids."

"I've read the briefings," Morgan said grimly. "The Laians are losing a war-dreadnought every ten to twenty cycles. They have to act sooner or later."

"But my contacts among the Wendira are just as clear as my contacts among the Laians," the Ki!Tol told her. "*They* don't want this war and are trying to deescalate. According to them, Laian warships are raiding their territory and provoking this conflict."

"I trust both," she said with a raised tentacle before Morgan could say anything. "Which means the situation is...complicated. I had reason to suspect a third party was involved, but it was only when the data you recovered from *Child of the Rising Storm* made its way back to me that the answer became clear."

"What answer?" Rin asked.

Of course, the archeologist, professor and teacher was the one asking the questions. Morgan decided that he was probably the best one to do so, too. She tried to subtly stretch to ease aching muscles as Ki!Ron considered the man's question.

"We are not...the only association of like-minded individuals dealing with the Alava," the old being told them slowly. "We have long been aware of others, a mix of corporations and private individuals and military commanders—mostly in the Core—that are attempting to acquire and activate Alavan technology.

"We see, in the starkillers, evidence of the danger of activating Alavan tech," she noted. "*They* see evidence of the power available to those who make it work."

Morgan shivered, and not entirely from the cold. The first starkillers had been developed after an early Mesharom colony had attempted to activate one of their old masters' starships. Whatever the Alava had used as an FTL drive no longer worked as an FTL drive...but it did *wonders* at destabilizing nearby stars into early supernovas.

She'd encountered very little functioning Alavan tech, and outside the biotech, none of it had functioned as intended. That didn't mean it had done *nothing*. In one case, a specialty system design for rapid refueling had become a monstrous death cannon, one that teleported bits of starstuff directly onto any ship using an interface drive.

"I suppose I can see their point, if I didn't think it was more likely to get people killed than help them," she murmured.

"They see the deaths as acceptable losses," Ki!Ron told her. "We have been aware of them for many long-cycles now, occasionally clashing. We have not always succeeded in stopping them from acquiring Alavan tech.

"In general, I feel we have more true influence and say in governments and official actions...but they command more private resources. Almost certainly including, I am afraid, both Laian and Wendira warships and enough wealth to bribe commanders of other warships."

"You think they're starting this war? But why?" Rin asked.

"That was why I didn't think they were involved until I had the information from your mission," Ki!Ron told them. "In the files of *Child of the Rising Storm* and your own examination of the records of the Alava out there, we found evidence of an entire rogue faction that the core Hegemony did not control.

"We had often assumed that the Hegemony's presentation of itself as immutable and all-encompassing was the truth," she continued. "Now we know it was a lie, and a dozen fragments of the Archive fall together in a neat pattern that I did not recognize before.

"At the time of its fall, the Hegemony was at war."

"That would explain what happened, then," Morgan murmured. The Alava had died because they'd built a megastructure at the galactic core that had created an unprecedented and unrepeated effect: it had changed the laws of physics. They had carefully mapped their design to avoid biological processes, so most life—as they understood it, at least—had survived...but their attempt to improve their jump drives had instead broken all of their technology.

And the Alava and their subjects had all been implanted with neural augmentation. Only the Mesharom had a large-enough minority *without* the implants to survive the activation of the device and endure into the modern age.

Morgan had always wondered *why* the Alava had done something so risky...and now she saw at least one reason.

"That is my conclusion as well," Ki!Ron agreed. "More immediately important, however, is that some of those fragments, pieces even the Mesharom were not certain of the meaning of, now suggest details around the deployment of a major Alavan battle fleet to the region that is now the border between the Laians and the Wendira."

"How major is *major*?" Morgan asked at the same time as Rin. The two of them shared a glance and he gestured for her to continue.

"Out by Arjtal, their local military carved up three star systems to build and supply a shipyard," she said. "What does a 'major' fleet look like to a people like that?"

"The standard Alavan mothership was a spherical combatant between a thousand and twelve hundred kilometers in diameter," Ki!Ron told them. "A major fleet would have possessed at least a hundred of them, supported by at least ten times that in smaller units."

"*Smaller* being relative," Rin murmured next to Morgan.

"Exactly."

The underground space was silent for at least a minute.

"So, you think this other conspiracy is hunting that fleet?" Morgan finally asked.

"It fits the data available," Ki!Ron told her. "If I'm wrong, there is still a third party trying to bring two Core Powers to war. Either way, that needs to be stopped."

Morgan nodded, and bowed her head. That wasn't a mission she could turn down, however much she questioned the source.

"What do you want from us?" she asked.

"I have arranged for repairs to *Defiance* to be fast-tracked," the A!Tol told her. "Your ship will be ready inside of three cycles, fully repaired and ready for her mission. Dr. Dunst will be assigned to your vessel as a civilian advisor.

"Officially, your task is to perform an inspection tour of Laian positions along the front to validate what our allies have told us," Ki!Ron said. "You will be operating under direct orders from high command and will *not* be part of Tan!Shallegh's fleet."

"He is the First Fleet Lord," Morgan pointed out. "I'm not exactly going to defy his orders."

"He will recognize the value of your official mission," Ki!Ron replied. "And if he suspects that there is more behind it, he will recognize the value of that as well.

"Once you're on the front, you will also meet with one of our associates who is already in the area. Hopefully, she will have had time to narrow down our probable sources of contact on the Laian side.

"Your mission will have four components, Captain Casimir, Dr. Dunst. First, of course, is the official mission you will receive from your superiors: to survey the Laian defensive positions and confirm to the high command and Fleet Lord Tan!Shallegh that they are in the state and numbers we have been advised.

"Second, you are to locate and confirm the presence of a third party provoking incidents along the Dead Zone.

"Third, if possible, you are to locate the Alavan battle fleet," Ki!Ron instructed. "Once we have located it, other options become available—ranging from its destruction to its study."

The A!Tol's tentacles shivered again.

"Lastly, you are to make certain that the battle fleet does not fall into the hands of those who would attempt to *use* its technology. Even with their nonfunctional systems, those motherships are a critical danger to everyone around them.

"If necessary, you are to use all means at your disposal to destroy the Alavan fleet."

Morgan exhaled a long sigh.

"Starkillers," she said quietly.

"Yes, Captain Casimir. If it comes to that." The Ki!Tol shrugged, a disturbing flutter of tentacles. "We can at least be certain that there is no one living wherever they have ended up. There is no way an Alavan fleet has gone unnoticed in an inhabited system."

"I am not agreeing to join your 'association,'" Morgan warned. "But this mission is in the best interests of the Imperium...of everyone, really. I will await official orders."

"You will find, Captain Casimir, that nothing I will ask you to do will be against the interests of the Imperium," Ki!Ron assured her again. "The three of us share a view of the galaxy, I believe. We swim in the same currents.

"You will see."

"Maybe," Morgan allowed. "Rin? Are you in?"

"I'm not sure how the Institute is going to cover me being assigned to your ship for this one," her boyfriend admitted. "It's in the opposite direction of anything we would be studying."

"Leave that to us," Ki!Ron told him. "If you are prepared to accompany Captain Casimir, there are reasons to explain it. We need you for when she finds the Alavan fleet."

"You have a lot of faith in us," Morgan muttered.

"Yes," Ki!Ron said calmly. "Your actions to date have earned it. Prove me right, Captain Casimir. Complete your mission. Stop a war. We don't want to lose another trillion lives around the Dead Zone."

"Right," Morgan said. "No pressure."

CHAPTER SEVEN

RIN WATCHED THE SHUTTLE CARRYING MORGAN SPLIT AWAY AS the two aircraft descended toward First Home. She'd promised to call him later, but they were both exhausted after standing for the entire conversation with Ki!Ron.

His mind was still whirling with everything the big Ki!Tol had revealed. Not just one conspiracy woven throughout dozens of races and star nations, but two! A shadow conflict over how to handle Alavan artifacts...that one wasn't as much of a surprise to him as he suspected it had been to Morgan.

There were a *lot* of strange events recorded around Alavan sites and artifacts. Many could be explained away by Mesharom operations to destroy or retrieve those artifacts, but other events made a lot more sense now, realizing there could have been as many as *three* different players trying to get their hands on the Precursor ruins.

The suborbital shuttle landed with an almost-imperceptible bump.

"We're here, Professor," the Pibo pilot told him. "My understanding is that the Institute should have sent a car for you."

"Thank you," Rin replied. "What is your name?" he asked, frustrated by the lack of names given on this strange trip.

The Pibo paused.

"Iro," he finally replied. "It's a pleasure to have been of service, Dr. Dunst. Have a good night."

Rin took the name as all he was going to get and left the shuttle. Hopefully, he could get a good night's rest in before he collided with whatever reason Ki!Ron's *associates* came up with for sending him to a war zone.

RIN WAS UTTERLY unsurprised by the messages waiting for him when he woke up. There were several requests for more debriefing meetings, similar to the day before his visit with the Ki!Tol, but also a request from Director Doad for an immediate meeting over breakfast.

Two cups of coffee later found him entering the Director's office, where two covered trays waited on the Ivida's desk. They were, thankfully, on top of fabric mats protecting the desk.

Like most things in Doad's office, the desk was an antique. Made on A!To by some of the first Ivida artisans to permanently move to the capital, it was a hardy wooden structure with delicate inlays celebrating the unity of the two races.

Its age meant that there were hints and symbolism of the Ivida's own culture, lost to historical curiosity now. Desert suns and sand-shrouded plants featured heavily.

Shelves around the room contained more artifacts of a similar theme. Doad's focus of study was on that exact transition, the almost-eight-hundred-long-cycle-past annexation of his people by the A!Tol and the loss of their culture in the uplift.

It was an obsession for some Ivida, Rin knew, though Doad's attention mostly seemed to be purely academic. No one, though, could be entirely dispassionate about that kind of accidental cultural genocide.

Not even the A!Tol themselves. There were reasons the Imperial Races stood high in the favor of the Imperium...and most of them were guilt.

"Director," Rin greeted his host. "Good morning."

"Long morning already, for some of us," the Ivida replied. "I have my own stimulants; I suggest you try the coffee."

Both of them drank from their own cups. The Institute had good coffee, exported all the way from some of the better farms on Terra itself. Some of the Imperium's species were adopting coffee as a morning stimulant of choice—but caffeine was actually toxic to Ivida, so Rin was careful not to spill his cup.

The breakfasts were equally tailored and excellent, and Doad gestured for Rin to dig in while the Director mustered his thoughts. Rin was never one to turn down a good meal—his midsection was quite clear on that topic—and dug into the omelette and toast with good cheer.

"You drew a lot of attention out at Kosha," Doad finally told him. "We don't like to draw that much attention to our principal researchers, so you understand that we want you to keep your head down until it passes, yes?"

"That makes sense to me," Rin admitted. "I'd rather be in the field, though."

He was a good teacher but a terrible academic bureaucrat. Give him a classroom or a dig site, he was fine. Give him an office? He had a bad habit of making enemies—or at least losing friends.

"Wouldn't we all rather be in the field?" Doad agreed. "Duty drives, though. Another option was just dropped into my lap, though, where I think you can both provide value to the Institute and be in the field."

"I'm listening," Rin said, refilling his coffee from a provided carafe.

"Our relationship with the Laian Republic was either nonexistent or strained until recent waters," Doad told him. "Strangely, punching them in the mandibles at Alpha Centauri appeared to make us friends. Our relations have improved since then, and we have slowly opened academic channels of communication.

"One of those channels has finally borne fruit and they have asked that we send several senior researchers to a number of sites they're working on in the Republic, to provide an external set of eyes and experiences. We are, of course, making the same request in turn."

"You want to send me to the Laians, Director? My expertise is the Alava," Rin pointed out. He knew what this was, but he still felt obliged to point out the problem.

"You are also an extremely experienced and well-informed xenoarcheologist in all waters, Dr. Dunst," Doad replied. "Part of the value the Laians are looking for is someone who doesn't have a full immersion in Laian history. An outside perspective on these worlds.

"The ones I'm thinking to send you to are on the far side of the Republic, near the Wendira border."

"Near the war zone," Rin asked.

"Yes," Doad confirmed. "And that is why I want to send you. Anyone we send to the Dead Zone will have to travel on military transport, likely a warship. My understanding is that you handled yourself well aboard *Defiance*."

"I got along well with Captain Casimir and her crew, yes," Rin agreed. "I can do that, Director. Keeps me out of sight, huh?"

"And provides useful value in several ways," the Director agreed. "My understanding, in fact, is that *Defiance* may be sent to the Dead Zone shortly. We will attempt to get you passage aboard her, allowing you to renew your acquaintance with Captain Casimir."

Rin had to grin. Something in the perfectly dry tones Doad's translator was using made it quite clear the Ivida was *very* aware of the nature of Rin's acquaintance with Morgan Casimir!

CHAPTER EIGHT

"WELCOME BACK ABOARD YOUR SHIP, CAPTAIN CASIMIR," the tentacled yardmaster told Morgan. The A!Tol's skin was flushing various shades of red, green and blue—pleasure, determination and curiosity. She was clearly looking forward to showing Morgan what they'd achieved in the last ten cycles.

"It's good to be home," Morgan replied with a smile. There wasn't much visibly different so far. From the outside, the remaining holes had been patched up and the missing chunks of the cruiser's arched wings had been replaced, but that only restored her to her original condition.

"We've been busy since you arrived," the yardmaster, Captain I!Ler, told her. "The Kosha Yards did good work, but they're a repair-and-maintenance facility. *We* are the Imperial Central Yards, Captain, and we pride ourselves on our work."

"So I'm told," Morgan agreed, following the A!Tol onto her own ship. "There's some fascinating work being done in this system."

"There is indeed," I!Ler said. "We received four of the leviathan contracts. Even the slips for those are an entirely new level of technology and sophistication over our prior work. But you would know that, yes? Your father..."

"My father hasn't spoken about anything else beyond basic pleasantries in a long-cycle," Morgan agreed with a chuckle. "Four more of those yards are going in at Sol. I think it was Indir and !Nala that got the other eight, right?"

"Yes, yes," I!Ler confirmed. "Watch your step, Captain; we're still retrieving teams and equipment."

The leviathans were the Imperium's newest ship type. Not a new class of warships but an entirely new *type*, targeted at sixty million tons, compared to the superbattleships that had crept up to twenty-five megatons.

They were intended to be the answer to the Core Powers' super-warships, capital ships able to fight on the same scale as a Wendira star hive or a Laian war-dreadnought.

Once they were built—and as I!Ler noted, Morgan's father had spent the last year consumed by the process of designing the *construction slips* for the massive starships. A full squadron of sixteen would shortly start construction, but it would be at least two years—four long-cycles—before anyone expected them to enter service.

Stepping over a set of cables that stretched across *Defiance*'s boat bay, Morgan reflected that there were a *lot* of reasons the A!Tol Imperium didn't want to go to war with the Wendira right now.

"You won't see much visible change around the ship herself, of course," I!Ler said, gesturing around the boat bay. The metal walls and composite floors gleamed like the day Morgan had boarded the still-under-construction warship two long-cycles earlier. "We were working to the original designs and drawings, so everything inside and out should look the same as before. It is all back in place and checked out."

"That's all we need, isn't it?" Morgan asked. "*Defiance* was one of our most advanced warships already. *Back in place* still puts her above most of the galaxy."

"It would have, yes," I!Ler said with a beak-clack of laughter and a deeper flush of pleased red to her skin. "We did have a few aspects we could upgrade, though, even in our limited time currents."

Morgan arched an eyebrow as they entered the elevator that would take them to the bridge. Most of her crew would return aboard ship over the next cycle, with *Defiance* scheduled to ship out toward the Wendira front in three cycles.

"Upgrades already?" she asked.

"There are always changes," I!Ler replied. "Especially to a new design we've only just begun to field. Reports from you as well as the other *Armored Dream* captains are being incorporated into the new vessels under construction, and some new technology has become available."

"All right," Morgan conceded as the elevator came to a halt. The corridor between the elevator and the bridge was short and familiar, and she concealed a sigh of relief as she walked past her office and nodded to the two Marines standing at parade rest on either side of the security hatch.

With most of the cruiser's crew on furlough and at the heart of the Imperium, the guards were A!Tol soldiers on loan from the system's Marine command. They responded to her nod with a respectful tentacle flutter.

The bridge slid open at the touch of her hand to the DNA reader next to the hatch, and she stepped into her command center and inhaled deeply. It wasn't a new-ship smell, that could never truly be duplicated, but the scent of a ship that had undergone a full air purge-and-replacement was distinct in its own way.

"If we've made changes, brief me," she told I!Ler. She couldn't technically *order* the yardmaster, they were of the same rank, but *Defiance* was *her* ship.

"You'd lost your starboard wingtip plasma lance and your port lance was moderately damaged," I!Ler told her. "We could have repaired the port lance easily enough, but we had new-version plasma lances in the stockpile and we didn't want to leave you with an unbalanced set of batteries.

"So, your Bravo Battery is fully upgraded with the next-generation plasma lances," the A!Tol concluded. "Impact power is basically the same but the magnetic tube has been extended by another five hundred thousand kilometers, bringing you to an effective range of just over seventeen light-seconds."

Five million kilometers. For a lightspeed weapon, that was incredible—and it was only made possible by the magnetic tube that would attach itself to a target's metal hull. Against the bioships the Great Mother had spawned, *Defiance*'s plasma lances had proven far more difficult to deploy.

"We also had to replace two of your four secondary fusion-power cores," I!Ler said. "Kosha repaired all four in place, but our assessment was that your Secondary-Two and Secondary-Three power plants would have a working life of under one long-cycle.

"The new cores are slightly smaller and more powerful. We used the extra space to increase your general fuel capacity by three percent."

"Not as insignificant as it sounds," Morgan murmured. *Defiance* was rated for a full long-cycle of operation without major replenishment. Three percent was several days' worth of full power from the matter converter and fusion cores.

"The updates to your antimatter systems were mostly software," I!Ler said. "They're pure safety concerns, reducing the likelihood of failure by seventy-six percent." Tentacles fluttered. "That's from point zero zero zero zero six percent per cycle of operation to point zero zero zero zero one four percent."

The two antimatter cores that backed up *Defiance*'s matter-conversion power plant were the most temperamental of the three power sources the ship carried. Fusion plants were controlled thermonuclear reactions, but an antimatter plant was a controlled *annihilation* reaction.

The order of failure was low enough that Morgan wasn't particularly worried about it—but she was pleased to hear it had been reduced even lower.

"In general, that is the theme of most of the upgrades," I!Ler explained. "Minor new software and hardware upgrades throughout the ship, small efficiency boosts and better safety margins. With some small modifications, we squeezed an extra two percent power transmission into your hyperfold cannons."

"I don't suppose we found any extra velocity for the sublight missiles?" Morgan asked.

She knew the answer. So far as even the Core Powers had found, point eight five c was a hard max for the interface drive. Even the hardware couldn't survive the gravity tides and radiation that leaked through at any higher velocity—and most organics couldn't survive anything above the point seven c of *Defiance*'s sprint mode.

"No, but we did swap out your magazines for upgraded missiles," the A!Tol told her. "Velocity is the same, but there's more electronic warfare capabilities built into them. Not, as I understand, up to the level of Laian or Wendira missiles, but closer."

"That'll help on the front," Morgan murmured. "I hope Fleet Lord Tan!Shallegh's forces are receiving them?"

"First shipment of one point six million missiles left for the Fleet Lord's central position fifteen cycles ago," I!Ler confirmed. "We all hope there won't be a war, but...we must prepare as if there's going to be."

Morgan grimaced, glancing around the bridge and taking a seat on the Captain's chair. The screens woke up at her touch, confirming the security fields were active and that the two of them were alone on the bridge.

"Final Dragon systems?" she asked quietly. There was no way the sentient in charge of *Defiance*'s refit *wasn't* cleared to know about her strategic weapons.

"No upgrades there," I!Ler told her. "Her Majesty countersigned replenishing your stock, so you are back to three Final Dragon weapons." There was a long pause. "No one has told me quite what you fired the last three at."

"And no one is going to," Morgan confirmed. "That's classified, Captain I!Ler."

"I expected those currents," the A!Tol agreed. "Curiosity is always a hungry fish, though."

"That it is," Morgan said. "How long until all of your people are done and off-ship? I have orders to ship out in three cycles."

She was waiting on most of her crew and her two civilian delegations, plus more detail on her orders. So far, she'd received the official mission Ki!Ron had told her she'd get. She had not received any orders from her naval superiors about the *other* mission.

Hopefully, she'd get some. She expected she *would*, but she was curious how'd she'd get them.

"We'll be done within a cycle," I!Ler told her. "After that, *Defiance* is once again wholly yours, Captain Casimir." She paused. "Please try to break her less next time?"

Morgan laughed.

"I wasn't trying to break her *last* time, so I can't make many promises," she admitted. "But we do what we can."

And if she was very lucky, she might eventually sleep without nightmares about the crew who hadn't made it. She'd made a point of learning as many faces as she could...and part of her regretted that now.

She was still going to memorize faces again, though. Carrying that weight was part of the job. It wasn't *supposed* to be easy.

CHAPTER NINE

MORGAN'S EXECUTIVE OFFICER WAS THE FIRST PERSON TO JOIN her on the bridge, arriving less than half an hour after I!Ler had left.

Commander Bethany Rogers was a younger redheaded woman and one of the first humans born outside the Solar System. She'd signed on for the Imperial military, while Morgan had initially served in the Duchy of Terra Militia, but her service had been exemplary enough to make her a Commander while still quite young.

"Nice to have the girl back together," Rogers told Morgan as she crossed the horseshoe-shaped bridge. "Feels weird to have so few of our people aboard her, though."

"That'll change quickly enough," Morgan replied. "How was your furlough?"

"Eight hours a day of meetings and interviews; how was yours?" the XO asked.

"Much the same," Morgan confirmed. "Apparently, blowing up a star earns a lot of questions."

"Even for me, who was entirely locked out of that decision," Rogers pointed out. "I appreciate what you were trying to do, but I had full sensor access. There wasn't much to hide once the star the Great Mother was chewing on went boom."

"It still protected you from sharing responsibility for my decisions," Morgan said calmly. "There were definitely a lot of people who wanted to properly analyze that thing. In a perfect world, we'd have removed the bioships and the Children and then basically dissected it piece by piece for a few centuries."

"And how long do you think it would have taken it to build a hyperdrive if we hadn't blown it up?"

"A year. Maybe two," Morgan said instantly. "Its biggest problem was powering it. It could only extract so much energy from the star, and it needed a hyper portal on a scale we've never seen."

She shivered.

"Davor thinks it might have been able to duplicate our matter-conversion core from the scans," she told her XO. "Given that...I don't think there was another choice."

"Everyone seems to agree with you, though some of my interviewers wanted to see whether I was out of the loop because I didn't."

"I didn't give you a chance to," Morgan said with a chuckle.

"And I'd have backed you all the way if you had," Rogers replied. "Part of my job as XO, sir."

"Part of the job is to tell me when I'm wrong, too," Morgan pointed out. "But it's also part of *my* job, sometimes, to take full responsibility for my decisions to protect valuable officers under my command."

Her XO snorted.

"It's appreciated," Rogers repeated. "Any concerns about the yard work?"

"Shouldn't you be the one with those?" Morgan asked.

"I was busy with interviews, couldn't ride herd on the yard workers the way I'd like," the XO said. "I kept an eye on it, but you just met with the being in charge."

"I did, and I don't have any concerns," Morgan admitted. "I'll wait until Liepins is back aboard and get his opinion before I confirm that we're happy with the work. Do *you* have concerns?"

"Nothing I've noticed," Rogers said. "Stunned by how fast they did it all. Even our yards back home would have taken half again this long to get the work done."

"I think you underestimate the Raging Waters of Friendship," Morgan said. The fancifully named shipyards at Sol were a joint project between the Terran and Indiri Duchies, which had allowed the Imperium's second-largest shipbuilder to profit from Sol's growth from nothing to the Imperium's *third*-largest shipbuilder.

Part-ownership always helped assuage a competitor's fears.

"Maybe, but I still don't think they could have done all this in ten cycles."

"Perhaps not, but they'd have done well by us," Morgan said. She was still a bit in awe of the sheer scale of A!To's orbital industry. It didn't match the scale of the Alavan megastructures she'd seen, but this hadn't been built by an ancient race that may as well have been gods.

"True enough."

The two women looked at the screens showing the yards around them. Space stations and starships added dozens of tiny moving constellations to the stars they could see—there, in orbit of A!To, it was more likely a given "star" was a spaceship than anything else!

"I have something for you," Rogers finally said. "Weirdest thing I've seen since signing up for Imperial service."

"Oh?" Morgan asked carefully.

"I was ordered to report to Echelon Lord Iros's office before I reported aboard *Defiance*," the XO told her. "That's the only reason I wasn't available for I!Ler's show. They then gave me a physical package of orders to deliver to you. DNA-secured, your eyes only."

Rogers removed a folder-sized envelope from inside her jacket. It had been invisible there, the redhead clearly guessing that the orders needed to be secret.

"Since when do we do physical orders, Captain?" Rogers asked.

"The last time I got them, it was with regards to Dragon Protocol affairs," Morgan told Rogers. "So, I would guess the answer to that question, Commander Rogers, is classified."

Her XO chuckled and handed her the envelope.

"That was my guess, too. I don't know what's in there, sir, but I suspect it's going to bite me in the ass later. Fill me in on what you can once you've read it, hey?"

"Everything I can," Morgan promised absently, her attention focused on the plain logo inked onto the plastic envelope above the DNA seal: the symbol of a stylized tidal wave.

A tsunami was an even more devastating event to a species that was still mostly amphibious and never settled far inland. While the A!Tol word translated correctly as *tsunami*, the connotations were closer to *Armageddon*.

WITH THE SECURITY SYSTEMS ENGAGED, Morgan's office was as private a sanctum as any known to the Imperium. It was only in the last ten long-cycles that some of the systems built into her office had become available, finally shielding at least offline storage from Core Power scanners.

They couldn't maintain that security and run a starship, however, which meant that some things were never committed to electronic storage. The documents in the Tsunami envelope were the classic kind: orders that didn't officially exist.

It was a single sheet of plastic and it didn't tell her anything she wasn't expecting. She was officially tasked with carrying the Ivida envoy Awav on a tour of the Laian side of the Dead Zone. Which stations she visited was left to her discretion on discussions with Awav.

She was also to make contact with a "freelance agent" at a specific set of coordinates. Plugging them into her computer gave her a position in deep space, roughly two light-years away from the star system currently playing host to an Imperial Grand Fleet.

Once she had the agent aboard, she was to carry on with the inspections while investigating any and all evidence around third parties intervening in the conflict. She was to gather intelligence on the third parties and neutralize their operations where possible.

These orders confirmed the belief in the existence of an Alavan fleet somewhere in the Dead Zone and authorized her to follow up on any leads she found on the subject. In the pursuit of this, she was being assigned Rin Dunst and would assist in his official mission of meeting with Laian archeologists in the area.

Lastly, she was authorized to secure the Alavan fleet by any means necessary, whether that was bringing Tan!Shallegh into the loop to deploy Imperial ships...or using her own starkillers to deny the fleet to any non-Imperial power.

"No pressure," she murmured aloud, going through the text on the plastic again.

She just had to sneak her way along the edge of a near-war zone, delivering an archeologist and an envoy to their destinations, while asking all sorts of awkward questions and poking at the people who were probably trying to start a war.

Morgan could see a lot of ways this operation could go wrong... but she also recognized the potential threat if she failed. Anything more obvious would cause as many problems as it fixed, so a single ship was all they could send.

And since she'd already fallen into the deep end and walked out, well...it made as much sense to send her as anyone else.

CHAPTER TEN

"Welcome back aboard *Defiance*, Professor."

Rin returned Commander Rogers's greeting with a firm nod as he glanced around the shuttle bay. It looked oddly pristine to him, a cleanliness and freshness the warship hadn't even had when he'd first reported aboard.

It was missing one key factor he was looking for, though.

"Captain Casimir was called back to the surface to meet the Imperial envoy," Rogers told him apologetically. "She told me to pass on her apologies, but the plan changed very suddenly."

"Is that why I got the formal welcome?" Rin replied, gesturing at the files of Marines who'd escorted him aboard.

"You do rate that welcome, Professor," the executive officer pointed out. "Captain Casimir might not have done it, but..." She shrugged.

"Fair enough." Rin waved delicately at the Marines, any of whom could have broken him with one hand. "I'm not going to pretend I can salute, people," he continued somewhat more loudly, "but you're appreciated and recognized, I promise!"

He had a decent idea of how much protocol he'd violated in one extended sentence, but the smothered chuckles from the troopers were worth it.

"Company, at ease!" the Spear in charge of the formation snapped. "Welcome aboard, Dr. Dunst."

"Are you bringing any staff?" Rogers asked.

"No, this is a far smaller-scale endeavor than our tour around Kosha," Rin said. "I'm just meeting with some Laian archeologists to provide a different perspective on what they've found. I'm only aboard *Defiance* because we're going the same way."

"Walk with me," the XO instructed as she turned precisely on her heel. The Marines dissipated in answer to an unspoken but clear dismissal, and Rin obeyed, falling in beside Rogers as he hauled his carrying case behind him.

"Let me take that, Doctor," one of the Marines said, intercepting him well short of the bay. "Sir, what quarters is he in?"

"Deck eleven, B66," Rogers said instantly.

"Yes, sir."

The Marine took off at a brisk pace that rapidly left Rin and Rogers behind—before he could even say one word about being capable of carrying his own luggage.

"You have no idea how hard it is to find a free set of quarters on the same deck as the bridge," Rogers murmured as the crew shifted away from them, a practiced Brownian motion that gave them some privacy. "The Navy likes to keep those rooms for the bridge crew to make battle stations easier.

"Guests are supposed to go in a specific set of quarters, but it's harder to sneak into the Captain's quarters from there."

Rin felt his cheeks heat as he blushed. He knew that Rogers was aware of his relationship with Morgan, but he hadn't considered that she'd incorporate that into picking his room.

"I appreciate the thought, Commander," he said as levelly as he could.

"Please, Doctor, you've done this ship more favors than I can count *and* you're sleeping with my Captain," Rogers noted. "You can call me Beth."

"Then please, Beth, call me Rin," he instructed. "And I'll admit I'm less than concerned about my quarters, though their sneaky access to Morgan's *is* relevant. What do I have for lab space?"

"I thought you were just with us as a passenger, Rin?" Rogers asked with an arched eyebrow.

"You never know what you'll find," he replied with an innocent smile. "And since you've *got* me, I may as well plan to be of use. I also have no idea just what the Laians are going to give me for data and analyses, but I'm likely better off going through their discoveries on my own machines."

"I had a workshop put aside for you," the XO said with an innocent smile of her own. "It should have enough space for you to set up, though I'm not sure what you'll need for tools. Let Lesser Commander Trifonov know and he'll make sure we'll either get it here or fabricate it en route."

"Appreciated again, Commander," Rin said. "If you can guide me to the workshop, I'll take a look."

ROGERS HAD, to Rin's complete lack of surprise, understated the space she'd arranged for him to use. The workshop was far more space than he was going to need, and she'd had a proper console setup installed—with access to the cruiser's sensors.

She left him to putter around the space and put together a wish list of items he'd need, but he had to admit that he really didn't need much more than space, some tables, and a really good computer. He'd set up his stand-alone secured console as well, for the Dragon Protocol items he couldn't even let a military computer see, and he'd be good.

He settled down into the chair and pulled up the sensor displays.

He was aware of the level of activity in A!To orbit, but he saw it rarely enough that it was stunning. Hundreds of stations and ships.

He couldn't help but compare it to some of the systems he'd seen out at the edge of the Imperium, the ruins and wreckage left over from colonies that had died fifty thousand years earlier. He could run the analysis backward, after all, and assess what would still be there fifty thousand years after the A!Tol fell.

Less than many would guess. Even orbits regarded as stable by space station standards still required some adjustment—and the satellites in unstable orbits wouldn't help the stable ones stay up.

Sighing, he shut down the screen and closed his eyes, settling into the state of altered consciousness that let him access the computer at the base of his spine.

The file he'd been working on appeared against the inside of his eyelids, and he skimmed through the data again.

He agreed with Ki!Ron's assessment that there was *something* in the Dead Zone. There had been a major Alavan fleet base near there, one that the Mesharom had "cleaned up" a long time before the Laians and Wendira had fought their war.

They didn't have detailed reports of that operation—even Mesharom data-storage technology didn't let one of their ships carry *all* of their data, after all—but the summaries in the data Rin had access to suggested that there had been fewer ships than expected.

The Mesharom had marked that off as bad data, a common problem when your data source was stone tablets where your ancestors had written down everything they knew of the Hegemony. Those age-old Mesharom had done the galaxy more of a service than they could have realized, but they'd only known so much and they probably hadn't managed to write it all down in the first place!

The other fragment was several places where the Mesharom tablets had said there should be Alavan bases or colonies and the Mesharom scout fleets had found nothing. Colonies of a billion or more souls, Alava and subject races combined, just...gone.

The Mesharom had assumed bad data again, but Rin and Ki!Ron

had drawn the pattern. A broad but clear line, the course of some kind of invasion fleet coming in from the outer regions. Drawing the line back didn't head directly to the faction near Kosha, but it wasn't an entirely straight line.

It *could* have been a fleet from the rogue faction working in biotech against the Hegemony's strictures. It could have been a lot of things—but it had wiped out several worlds, and the fleet base near the Dead Zone would have been the right place to send a fleet from.

What Rin couldn't calculate from the data he had was where the fleet would have gone. Quite possibly, they'd met their enemy somewhere in the stars the Laians and Wendira had destroyed.

The Alavan jump drive had had a limited range and used a lot of fuel. That was why the Alava had their small refueling stations scattered across their empire. The fleet could have been anywhere, really, but it seemed likely that they were within two or three jumps of the old fleet base.

That only narrowed it down to a ninety-light-year sphere that contained six or seven hundred star systems, several nebulas and the entirety of the Dead Zone.

Rin had no idea how they were going to find that fleet...or how the people starting a war to hide their search were planning on finding it, either.

CHAPTER ELEVEN

A!Tol Marines snapped to attention as Morgan walked through the halls of the Imperial Palace. Four Ivida Marines had reinforced her detail of four human Marines from *Defiance*, doubling her escort for hopefully ceremonial purposes.

One of the Ivida soldiers was guiding her, and she was starting to have a sinking feeling that she wasn't *just* meeting an envoy as their route headed deeper and deeper into the Palace.

Finally, they emerged from the structure into an interior courtyard. The soothing sound of gently running water washed over Morgan's hearing, and she found herself looking at a water feature slash garden at least a hundred meters on a side.

"We wait here," the Marine told her. "You are to approach the Empress."

Morgan swallowed as she finally registered the A!Tol reclining on a couch at the center of the garden. There was an Ivida standing stiffly next to her, but those two were the only people on the artificial island.

"Thank you," she told her escort, then swallowed her moment of anxiety and strode forward.

It was hard to be nervous in the space. It had been designed to soothe the nerves of an A!Tol, but many of the same features could soothe the mind of a human. Soft natural light. Murmuring waters. Delicate scents and colors from plants and flowers brought from a hundred worlds.

Morgan didn't need to ask to realize she was in the private garden of the Empress, and she bowed deeply as she reached the central island.

"Your Majesty, Captain Morgan Casimir," she said softly.

"I know who you are, Captain Casimir. Please, sit," A!Shall instructed. A human-style chair was already in position in front of the couch A!Shall occupied. "And you, Envoy Awav, please."

From the Ivida's body language, he'd already refused once. Now that Morgan was there, though, Awav finally obeyed and carefully took a seat in a chair designed for his double-jointed limbs.

Morgan studied the Empress for a moment. She'd seen images of A!Shall, of course, and heard her stepmother speak of the being, but it was the first time she'd been in the Imperial presence herself.

A!Shall's skin was an even pale gray tone, a shade Morgan had rarely seen on an A!Tol. There were no swirls of color on the Empress's skin. Whatever emotions the leader of the Imperium felt, she did not show them to the world.

She had, Morgan supposed, been trained from birth to lead the Imperium.

"You will both shortly set out for the edge of the Dead Zone," A!Shall reminded them. "Awav, it falls to you to make certain that our allies are telling us the truth. They have assured us that the fortifications and bases along the frontier are secure, that the Wendira won't dare a war because they cannot overcome those barriers.

"I do not believe them," the Empress noted. "Too many times in the history of the races of the Imperium alone has a belief in impenetrable defenses led to failure and disaster. My oaths and the agreements of the Houses of the Imperium commit us to this conflict.

"I would not see my allies fall because they misread their own currents."

"I understand my mission, Empress," Awav said firmly.

"I know you do, Awav," A!Shall told him. "But its importance cannot be understated...and it is only the *second* most important task laid upon the ship that carries you."

Ivida faces were armored plates, unmoving and unmoved by emotion. The race showed their emotions in their eyes and the posture of their shoulders. Morgan wasn't *good* at reading Ivida, but she'd served with a few.

She recognized Awav's surprise.

"Secrets and shadows swirl in these waters, my envoy," A!Shall continued. "I do not feel that it is the time to unveil them all, but I want to be clear on one thing before you leave: Captain Morgan Casimir commands your mission. She has my full faith and orders and tasks you know nothing of.

"There may—there *will*—come a time when currents she is aware of require you to abandon your tasks in favor of hers. You will do so without question or hesitation. Are the waters clear, Awav?"

"They are," the envoy said slowly. "I question, my Empress, why I am not trusted to know this mission."

"Because the nature of Captain Casimir's task is of the utmost secrecy and I will drag no one into those dark waters that is not already aware of them," A!Shall told him. "Fate has dragged Captain Casimir into these depths already. Her actions and her nest-mother's actions assure me that she can handle this task, but it must remain as secret as possible."

"I believe I understand," Awav said. "I am your servant in this, as in all things."

"I know," the Empress confirmed, then turned to Morgan. "Captain Casimir, do not fail my trust."

"I understand the weight of this mission," Morgan replied. She had only the vaguest idea of what an Alavan battle fleet would even look like, but she knew they didn't want it in the hands of someone who would try and *use* it.

"This trust is placed in you for your own efforts, Captain Casimir," A!Shall told her. "Your nest-mother's prior acts *encourage* me to place my faith in you, but the decision is based on your own actions, not Duchess Bond's. Are those waters clear?"

"They are, my Empress."

"Good."

A!Shall rose from the couch. She was still small for a female A!Tol, scarcely larger than a full-grown male—a sign of her relative youth.

"I have faith in you both," she told them. "You will travel to *Defiance* together and then to the front lines of this ice-cursed war. Bring my regards to Tan!Shallegh. My sibling's child continues to serve the Imperium well."

CHAPTER TWELVE

"I WILL NOT ASK YOU TO REVEAL ANY SECRETS," AWAV SAID later, as their shuttle lifted into space toward *Defiance*. "You understand that this situation is strange to me."

"For all of us, Envoy," Morgan told him. They had a separate compartment from their security detachments, giving them some amount of privacy for this conversation. "In a perfect world, none of this would be necessary."

Awav paused, clearly interpreting the concept.

"This is not a perfect world," he finally concluded. "The Dead Zone alone is proof of that."

"I know." Morgan studied the world behind them. "I know Laians relatively well, Envoy. I grew up with some of the Exiles. I presume, though, that the Republic and the Exiles are not fully aligned in terms of culture."

The Ivida chuckled.

"They are quite different, yes," he agreed. "Not so much that you are likely to cause offense with your knowledge of their culture, though. The Republic is determined to value our alliance, at least publicly."

"And in private?" she asked.

"In private, it depends on the Laian," Awav admitted. "I have spent much of the last ten long-cycles in the Republic, Captain. Some of them recognize the rapid expansion and enhancement of our military.

"Others consider any Arm Power a waste of water and dismiss any contribution we could bring. It is not, after all, as though your nest-mother succeeded in destroying the war-dreadnought that came to Alpha Centauri."

"That was before we had hyperfold cannons and hyperspace missiles," Morgan noted.

"Exactly," he agreed. "I think the size of our warships helps them underestimate us, which may be useful in future. Even if it's annoying when negotiating."

"Are we likely to have problems with the inspection tour?" she asked.

"No," Awav said. "All of this has been prearranged, including that we will visit them in a random order of our choice. These currents are known to them."

"Good." Morgan shook her head. She suspected some of the questions she was going to be asking would be less welcome, but that was part of the plan. To a certain extent, she was *intending* to provoke people—at least the people involved in the plot she was hunting.

"We are nearly at *Defiance*," she told Awav. "Is there anything else we will need to bring aboard for you?"

"I have a staff of three who should be aboard within the next tenth-cycle," the envoy told her. "Normally, I would have four, but I was instructed not to bring any A!Tol with me. Do you know why, Captain?"

"I'm not aware of that instruction, Envoy," Morgan admitted. "I will have to look into it, but I assume it was given with a good reason."

That was...odd. There were no A!Tol aboard *Defiance*—less than five percent of the Navy's ships were multi-species—but it was strange that the envoy would have been told *not* to bring one with him.

"There is no need and, I suspect, no time," Awav told her. "If my people are aboard as quickly as planned, when will we leave?"

"Tonight," Morgan said. "Within half a cycle. Depending on hyperspace currents, it's between a twenty-five- and a thirty-eight-cycle voyage to Tan!Shallegh's fleet.

"A war could be fought and lost in that time, Envoy. The sooner we are in motion, the more likely we are to arrive in time to complete our missions."

The Ivida made a wordless sound of acknowledgement.

"Then let us be on our way," he concluded. "I will talk to my people and make certain there is no delay."

MORGAN WAS DELIGHTED to see that Rogers had managed to corral Rin up to join the greeting party as she and Awav boarded *Defiance*.

"Welcome aboard, Envoy," she told the Ivida after Awav exchanged greetings with Rogers. "First Sword, do you have quarters prepared for the Envoy and his staff?"

First Sword was the Imperial equivalent to *executive officer*. Most of the time, a human-crewed ship like *Defiance* would use the XO title, but Awav wouldn't be familiar with it.

"I had our guest quarters spruced up and made ready for them, yes," Rogers said with a smile.

The *Armored Dream*–class ships like *Defiance* weren't designed to act as flagships or VIP transports. They had a grand total of four sets of rooms awkwardly tucked away that were marked as guest quarters.

Most ships of *Defiance*'s size would have been intended to act as at least small-squadron flagships, but the *Dream* class had so many weapons crammed into their hulls that there was no space to spare for a flag deck.

"I'll warn you, Awav, that our guest quarters may not be what you're used to," Morgan told the envoy. "Dr. Dunst can share his prior experience in them."

"I am certain they will be more than acceptable, Captain Casimir," Awav told her. "And if my staff disagree, you won't hear about it."

"If you have everything, Envoy Awav, I'll have someone collect your bags and show you to your quarters," Rogers told him. "There's a briefing ready in your office, Captain, though not much happened while you were gone."

Morgan traded a small smile with Rin as the greeting party dissolved into mostly organized chaos. Somehow, the Marines and crew around them managed to allow her and Rin to end up next to each other as Awav was led away.

"Your people have given me more than I need this time," Rin told her. "I'm ready to move whenever everyone else is."

"A few hours; we're just waiting on Awav's staff," Morgan replied. "I need to get to the bridge for the next few hours, but there will be a dinner in the officers' mess with Awav and the senior crew."

"May I hope for your presence, Dr. Dunst?"

His eyes sparkled with amusement, the liveliness that drew her to the soft-fleshed archeologist.

"I think you can hope for that, Captain Casimir," he agreed. "Have your staff talk to my staff?"

She snorted.

"I believe you are your staff on this trip, Rin," she reminded him.

"Drat. Well, let the computers talk to each other, then," he said with a chuckle. "I'll see you at dinner?"

CHAPTER THIRTEEN

"Course is set, but we are receiving hyperspace coordinates from Logistics Command," El-Amin reported. "Do I want to know what those coordinates are?"

"Opening point of a hyperspace current that should take us most of the way to Tan!Shallegh's primary anchorage," Morgan told him. "I received the briefing this morning."

"We're just...that lucky, are we?" the Lesser Commander asked. "A natural current, exactly on our route?"

"Yes, just that lucky," Morgan said dryly. It was a poorly kept secret that the Imperium had a small fleet of couriers with the ability to increase the local density of hyperspace and hence their realspace pseudovelocity.

That was a Mesharom technology they wanted to keep their access to secret, but its sheer usefulness made it hard to keep it under wraps. The Grand Fleet Current, on the other hand, was even more blatant in many ways.

Most of the Core Powers had tech to increase hyperspace density to one degree or another, but creating an artificial current was beyond most of them due to the sheer scale required. Even the Mesharom weren't up to creating a current that lasted more than a few days.

The Imperium's best system created a current that lasted twelve tenth-cycles. The Grand Fleet Current had a series of ships flying six tenth-cycles one way, creating the current, and then six tenth-cycles back.

The briefing said there were thirty ships in place, creating a current that would take fifteen cycles to traverse...and that would cut seven cycles off the time to travel to Tan!Shallegh's Grand Fleet.

Seventeen to twenty cycles sounded a lot better to Morgan than twenty-five to thirty-eight. She understood why she'd only received the briefing at the last minute, but it was still frustrating.

"We're clear to leave the station," the navigator said with a shake of his head. "Once we're clear, hyper portal in one hundredth-cycle. One twentieth-cycle after that, we'll hit the coordinates from Logistics."

Eighty-four minutes, give or take. Morgan leaned back in her chair and smiled.

"Get us under way, Lesser Commander," she ordered. "Logistics has found us a shortcut, but I see no reason to delay any longer than we have to."

"All umbilicals detached...now," he reported. "Interface drive online at minimum power. Separation one kilometer...ten kilometers...one hundred kilometers. Increasing drive power."

The numbers were on Morgan's screen, watching as the ship's exotic-matter arrays dug deep into the barrier between reality and hyperspace. A few kilometers a second became dozens of kilometers a second, and then El-Amin gave the interface drive full power.

Six seconds later, *Defiance* lunged toward the outer limits of the A!To System at sixty percent of lightspeed.

Morgan doubted she'd fully escaped the reality of shadows and conspiracies, but at least out in deep space, she could *do* something about them. In A!To, all she seemed to get were shadowy orders and terrifying revelations.

And now she was under way, she could have guests in her mess for dinner—and make sure a certain archeologist didn't make it back to his quarters afterward!

CHAPTER FOURTEEN

If the A!To System was a monument to the economic strength of a rising Arm Power, the Tohrohsail System was a monument to the military might of a Core Power. The current anchorage of the A!Tol Imperial Grand Fleet was a massive fleet base whose refueling facilities and storage depots filled the skies of a super-Jovian gas giant orbiting a red giant.

As *Defiance* crossed the empty space toward the gathered warships, Morgan tried to match up her information on the system with the icons on her tactical displays and the bright stars on her camera feeds.

Twenty squadrons of Imperial capital ships—three hundred and twenty battleships and superbattleships—had joined the Laian Republic's First Defense Fleet. Another seven hundred cruisers and destroyers orbited those capital ships. All told, the Grand Fleet represented a third of the Imperial Navy's hulls and, given the concentration of hyperspace missile–equipped ships in the Grand Fleet, slightly over half its firepower.

Those billions of tons of warships, however, were still the *smaller* of the two fleets present in the Tohrohsail System. The name translated as something like "Citadel of Hope," and while the system had no habitable planets, it was still home to tens of millions of Laians.

Many of those Laians served aboard the exactly one hundred war-dreadnoughts that formed the striking fist of the First Defense Fleet. Each dreadnought had ten cruisers for escorts, but while the Defense Fleet only barely outnumbered the Imperial Grand Fleet, those dreadnoughts outmassed their Imperial superbattleship counterparts by ten to one.

"We have clearance from Tohrohsail Base Control to approach *Storm Sentinel*," Lesser Commander Passang Nystrom announced. The green-eyed communications officer looked back at Morgan. "Fleet Lord Tan!Shallegh sends his regards and requests that you report aboard *Sentinel* at your earliest convenience, Captain."

Morgan nodded.

"Thank you, Commander," she told Nystrom. "Do we have coordinates for El-Amin?"

"Received and forwarding," Nystrom confirmed.

All of Morgan's senior officers were on the bridge right now. She put it up to curiosity—like her, they'd seen the reports and numbers, but it was something else to look at live camera feeds and sensor data of one of the key fleets of a Core Power.

The allied fleet there mustered over twenty-five *billion* tons of firepower. Both the A!Tol and Laian fleets had starkillers concealed among their escorts as well, Morgan knew. The only Final Dragon weapons in the area, though, were aboard *Defiance*.

The A!Tol Imperium and the Laian Republic were allies...but that didn't mean the Imperium was revealing *all* of their secrets.

"Who's in command of the Defense Fleet?" Morgan asked.

"Eleventh Voice of the Republic Tidirok," Speaker Toma Murtas answered from his console. The gaunt man in the cyberwarfare section of *Defiance*'s bridge was Morgan's intelligence officer.

"Any relation to Admiral Tidikat?" Morgan asked. Vice Admiral Tidikat was the senior Laian officer of the Duchy of Terra Militia, representing the Laian Exile Enclaves on Mars and in the Australian Outback.

"Distantly, yes," Murtas confirmed. "Laian family structures are...complicated, but it looks like they're descended from the same pre-Republic noble family. One branch went into exile, one branch collaborated."

"So, not inviting each other to reunions," Morgan murmured. "Anyone else I should be watching for?"

"Seventh Pincer of the Republic Kanmorad commands the escorts," the intelligence officer told her. "Did you deal much with him during the Arjtal Campaigns?"

Kanmorad had commanded the Laian contingent that had helped the Imperium and the Kanzi deal with the Kanzi's genocidal offshoot. Morgan had been a battleship XO at the time, though, so...

"Not really," she murmured. "I think I met the Kanzi High Warlord more."

Shairon Cawl, now generally considered co-ruler of the Kanzi Theocracy, had been a *mere* Fleet Master then. When the Theocracy had descended into civil war after the Arjtal Campaigns, he'd chosen the side of the High Priestess and proceeded to shatter every force that had opposed her.

That civil war wasn't *quite* over—but the end was sufficiently certain that the Imperium had drawn down some of its forces facing the Theocracy to reinforce the Grand Fleet. The Kanzi might be the Imperium's age-old enemies, but the Imperium's leadership trusted Shairon Cawl.

Not enough to have *no* defenses on that border, but enough to spare ships for the war Morgan was supposed to prevent. Somehow.

"Let Vichy know I'll need a shuttle and an escort," Morgan said aloud after a moment's thought. "I'm pretty sure I know what a Fleet Lord means by *at your earliest convenience*. I'll be on my way as soon as we're in position."

BATTALION COMMANDER PIERRE VICHY was the senior officer of *Defiance's* Marine attachment, a darkly handsome French officer with an astonishing ability to irritate his superiors while holding his men's undying respect and loyalty.

He'd grown on Morgan, she supposed, but she wasn't expecting to find him waiting for her with a squad of Marines when she reached the shuttle bay.

"Aren't you a little senior for squad command, Commander Vichy?" she asked drily.

"Oui, oui," he confirmed brightly. "But to command the escort of our dearest Captain, well, nothing is too much."

"Right," she said. "You're in command of the Marines, I suppose. Do we have a shuttle?"

"Of course," he agreed, his accent noticeably stronger than usual. "Even a pilot. Shall we, mon Capitaine?"

"Fall in," Morgan ordered the Marines. "We're not going to impress a Fleet Lord, so let's settle for not embarrassing ourselves, shall we?"

The Marines smothered any chuckles they might have been considering at the interplay between their CO and the ship's Captain, smoothing their faces into proper deportment as they trooped onto the shuttle in their picture-perfect dress uniforms.

There were *some* advantages to having a French dandy as her senior Marine, Morgan supposed. Her escort's dress uniforms were less decorated than her own black-and-gold suit, but they were noticeably more perfectly pressed and arranged.

And she'd thought her steward had done a good job!

"WELCOME ABOARD *STORM SENTINEL*," Tan!Shallegh told Morgan as she saluted crisply. Lines of human and A!Tol Marines flanked her and Vichy as they approached the Fleet Lord—and only a fraction of the Marines came from *Defiance*.

For as long as Morgan had been a member of the Imperial military, Tan!Shallegh had commanded his forces from multi-species warships. One of the few male A!Tol to rise to the rank of Fleet Lord *ever*, he'd also earned himself a surprising groundswell of respect from the rest of the Imperium.

Including, strangely enough, Earth. He'd been the fleet commander who'd conquered humanity—and then the one who'd saved them. Twice. There was a *reason* the Fleet Lord's personal bodyguard was half-A!Tol...and half-human.

"It is a rare Captain who does not hurry when a Fleet Lord calls, sir," Morgan told the A!Tol. He was a friend of her parents, which gave her some leeway another Captain might not have, though his reputation suggested she could have got away with that much regardless.

"That is true, Captain Casimir, even when they are not under said Fleet Lord's command."

That was said quietly, the translator edging down to make sure only the two of them heard him.

"That was not my choice, sir," Morgan said.

"So I suspected. But it does draw some attention, I must admit. Commander Vichy," Tan!Shallegh inclined his bullet-shaped torso to the Marine. "May I borrow your Captain for a private meeting?

"I believe she and I have matters to discuss in private."

CHAPTER FIFTEEN

Tan!Shallegh's office aboard *Storm Sentinel* was immense. His flagship was one of the new *Galileo*-class superbattleships, a twenty-two-megaton behemoth two and a half kilometers long with a hundred hyperspace missile launchers amidst her hundreds of weapons.

Dwarfed ten to one by the Laian warships around her, she was still, ton for ton, the most powerful warship in the Tohrohsail System. Tan!Shallegh commanded three full squadrons of her sisters.

The size of the ships enabled an office for the fleet commander that was at least five meters on a side. The walls were lined with display cases holding sculptures of various kinds, most unrecognizable to Morgan—but several were pieces by Terran artists she recognized.

Living artists.

Tan!Shallegh had sponsored current artists on worlds across the Imperium, filling his office with the culture of the Imperium's species without taking away from their history.

"I am at your disposal, Fleet Lord," Morgan told him as the Fleet

Lord settled into the couch behind his desk. She remained standing at attention, facing the A!Tol. "What do you need from me?"

"Honesty, Captain Casimir," the A!Tol replied. "Though first... the artificial current. Your thoughts?"

"We made it here in nineteen cycles instead of a minimum of twenty-five," she admitted. "I question whether it will avoid notice for long, but I can't argue its value."

"Thirty ships, each the size of a destroyer and the cost of a cruiser," Tan!Shallegh noted. "Once our enemies realize what we're doing, they will require escorts. *Specialty* escorts, at that, since our ships become less-effective hyperspace combatants as time goes on."

Morgan nodded grimly. Both the hyperfold cannons and the hyperspace missiles that formed *Defiance*'s main battery were useless in hyperspace. Her warship carried weapons that did work in hyperspace, but she had the sublight missiles of an older warship two-thirds her size.

"But as you say, the value of swift currents cannot be understated," the Fleet Lord agreed. His skin flushed with blue curiosity as his tentacles shivered. "Against the Wendira, we will lean on many options we would otherwise still conceal."

"It will be war, then?" Morgan asked softly.

"I hope not," he told her. "We are not entirely neutral in this affair, but we have made very clear that our alliance with the Republic is *defensive* in nature. That has been...enough, I think."

"They're going to talk?"

"The Voice of the Republic and I will be traveling to a system in the Dead Zone soon," the Fleet Lord confirmed. "That does not leave this room yet, Captain. I share it because I suspect it may have some bearing on your mission."

"I'm carrying an inspector to the Laian fortifications," Morgan reminded him.

"No, you're not." Tan!Shallegh's skin flickered the dark green of determination. "I will not force you to reveal my Empress's confidences, Captain, but please recognize the waters I swim in. I am not blind and I asked for honesty."

Morgan swallowed and nodded.

"My apologies, Fleet Lord," she told him. "My orders, as you say, come directly from Empress A!Shall and included the pressure for absolute secrecy."

"So I expect."

The room was silent for several seconds as Morgan considered the situation. If Ki!Ron's third party was in play, a peace summit could be in great danger.

"You realize that a summit is a target if there are other players?" she finally asked.

"And that, Captain, is why very few people know what is going on, on either side of the Dead Zone," Tan!Shallegh told her. "In twenty-six cycles, Voice Tidirok and I will be at the Exelkhan System to meet with Princess Oxtashah.

"She is a Wendira Royal of the highest castes and bloodlines, not a Fleet Commandant. She speaks for the Grand Hive, as the Voice of the Republic speaks for the Grand Parliament. We *hope* that this can be resolved—especially since both sides are saying they aren't authorizing the raids and battles that have occurred."

"That is hopeful, at least," Morgan murmured.

"But if they are telling the truth, something else is in the dark waters here, and I can't help but feel your mission is related to that," he told her. "Am I wrong?"

"I cannot say that you are right," she replied slowly. "My orders are clear."

"I see the waters," Tan!Shallegh said. "And your honesty is appreciated. The official support I can give is limited, but I will give it. I will *also* provide you with full details of the peace summit."

"Fleet Lord, I'm not sure what use that will be to me," Morgan admitted. Even if she found the conspiracy, she might not find enough evidence to change the discussions.

"If nothing else, you will know where to find me," the Fleet Lord told her. "Any evidence you find of what is going on in the dark waters among these dead stars may be worth more than you can imagine.

"I will fight the Wendira if I must, but I would rather make peace if I can."

"I can't promise I'll find that proof," Morgan said. "There are multiple parts to my mission."

"So I presume," he conceded. "And the orders you carry place you outside my command without dire need. But if you find any proof, that need exists, Captain Casimir."

"I know," she agreed. "How long do you expect to remain at Exelkhan?"

"Some cycles; I do not know for certain," Tan!Shallegh said. "The waters are far from clear enough for easy swimming."

"We'll see what we find," Morgan promised. "If we find it, we'll bring it to Exelkhan."

She'd probably have to find the Alavan fleet first, but she *would* bring the Fleet Lord the evidence he needed if she found it.

Morgan wasn't going to watch another hundred stars wiped from the galaxy because she didn't hand over the information she found, after all.

CHAPTER SIXTEEN

"Professor Dunst, welcome."

The Laian on the screen resembled an old Egyptian scarab beetle to Rin, a glittering six-limbed insectoid with a carapace of gold and turquoise. Her size told him the researcher was female, but he didn't know much about their dimorphism beyond that.

"Greetings, Past-Seeker," Rin said, bowing his head to the Laian. He at least knew the right *title* for a xenoarcheologist in Laian space. "I must admit, I was surprised to realize one of the sites I'd been asked to check in at was here in Tohrohsail."

"It is an unusual excavation," she replied. "I am Lodotan, senior Past-Seeker of the Republic's Hive of Inquiries in Ancient Pasts. This is a...frustrating site, in fact."

"I'd be delighted to tour the site if you wish, though I know my time in the system is limited," Rin told her. "I am dependent on the Imperial Navy for transport, and the ship I am traveling aboard is touring the edge of the Dead Zone."

"Of course, of course," Lodotan said. "I can give you the shell-shine to begin with and then we can see where you might provide new light."

Shellshine presumably meant *highlights*. Rin gestured for the Laian to continue and adjusted his seat. He was in the workshop aboard *Defiance*, linked to the Laian research station—apparently orbiting one of the unnamed gas giant's moons—by hyperfold coms.

"Tohrohsail was not a system of import before the Great War with the Wendira," Lodotan told him. "When the Dead Zone...came into existence, the star drew attention, as the large gas giant made for an excellent fueling depot in a central position along the new frontier.

"Over the time since, our Navy has built and expanded on their stations here, but it was only twenty orbits ago that a mining expedition on the seventh moon uncovered this site."

Rin brought up the information on the seventh moon as Lodotan mentioned it. A rival for Io in Sol, the planetoid was roughly half the size of Earth and had a thin, unbreathable atmosphere.

"How did they find it?" he asked. "It doesn't look like the moon has much."

"It has some veins of heavy metals, but that's part of what led to identifying the site," she told him. "An extraction team was following one of those veins when it simply ended. Something else had dug out the rest of the vein from the other end."

Images appeared on the screen with Lodotan.

"Initially, they thought the planet might have some native life that had been missed, but the scale of the tunnels was far larger than any likely life form. The moon only has bacteria, after all."

"But those tunnels look like they were dug by worms," Rin agreed. "I don't have a scale, Past-Seeker. How large are these?"

"We've excavated and found several large networks of these tunnels on the moon," Lodotan told him. "Each has tunnels varying from one to four meters in diameter. If the soldiers and miners had found *anything* that could have dug those tunnels, we might have dismissed it.

"Instead, they found that each network of tunnels connects to a central point that initially we assumed was a meteorite impact."

"And, on later examination, you believe to be a ship landing?" Rin asked.

"At a higher velocity than any ship we would land, but yes," the Laian Past-Seeker agreed. "Six sites, in fact, Dr. Dunst. Six high-speed objects made of clearly artificial materials impacted this moon and began the extraction of any minerals of value near the sites.

"We have only closely investigated one of the landing sites, but... it was definitely an advanced sentient settlement for at least some time."

More images appeared on the screen and Rin nodded slowly. A map of the settlement was the first one, showing the lines circling around the initial impact slash landing zone. It was clear the first tunnels had been dug at fixed intervals and then the circles dug linking them together.

Once the initial space had been created, the tunnels appeared to head directly for targeted veins of metal. The diggers had known exactly where they were heading.

"If there was furniture or equipment here, it's long gone," Lodotan noted. "But, like the surface craters, there are fragments of artificial material remaining. We're cataloging and trying to identify, but most of the fragments are very small."

"Can you send me your spectrographic data on the fragments?" Rin asked. "Imagery of the larger ones would be helpful as well."

The images of the tunnels themselves weren't particularly telling. Whatever had been in them when they'd been occupied was long gone, along with the ships that had landed.

"Do you know time frames?" he continued.

"Not with certainty," Lodotan admitted. "Forty-nine thousand years ago, we think, but variance is at least five percent."

That put it in a concerning range for Rin. That would easily be over fifty thousand years ago...and in the time frame of the Alava. But this didn't *look* like an Alavan structure.

"I see what you mean by a *strange site*," he admitted. "If it wasn't for the artificial materials, I might even write off the pattern of the settlement site as a home den for some kind of digging worm, but..."

"No remains, clear use of sensors to locate valuable minerals, targeting solely heavy metals and fissionables for digging..." Lodotan listed off the oddities. "There's no sign of anything except the digging other than the fact that someone clearly landed a starship on the center site and left with whatever did the digging."

"And a lot of heavy metals and fissionables," Rin said. "What kind of scale are we looking at for the overall tunnels?"

A new map of the moon appeared on the data and he inhaled sharply. Each of the six landing sites was surrounded by a thousand-kilometer radius warren of tunnels.

"According to our scans, every heavy metal and fissionable of extractable value inside eleven to twelve hundred kilometers of a landing site is gone," the Past-Seeker told him. "It appears to have been a highly efficient mining operation, but there was definitely some short-term settlement here as well, just from the nature of the tunnels."

"Short-term?" Rin asked. "Why *short-term*?"

"Our best guess is that all of this was done in about two years," she told him. "Twenty-five percent variance, but..."

"'But' indeed," he agreed. Efficient indeed, though it paled against some Alavan methods. If you weren't going to crack planets to get at the cores, though...this was effective enough.

"I'll send you all that we have, Dr. Dunst, and I can arrange a tour in about seventeen and a half hours, if you'd like?"

All of the measurements the Laian was giving him were being translated into Terran numbers. Seventeen and a half hours was a Laian day.

"Hopefully, I'll have time for that," he agreed. "I don't know if I'll have a point of view you don't already, but I'll see what it all looks like when I put it together."

The timing meant his expertise might be more valuable than he'd thought. This didn't *look* like an Alavan project...but there shouldn't have been anyone *else* around in the time period of the site.

Rin was here to support Morgan's mission, but this site...this site intrigued his curiosity.

IT WAS NO LESS intriguing in person, he discovered, though he suspected most non-archeologists would have questioned just what he was seeing. Dirt had slowly collapsed into the chambers that had been excavated thousands of years earlier, but the Laian excavators had made good progress in clearing them out.

"I see what you mean by *clearly sentient settlement*," he told Lodotan as he and the Laian paced their way through the caves. "Storage chambers, clear organization..." He shook his head. "I'd expect to see more debris, but the layout looks like people lived here."

"But not many, and that was part of our initial confusion," his counterpart told him, her mandibles clicking behind her oxygen mask as she looked around the cave. The Laians had pressurized the space, but the air was still only mostly breathable and the masks were a logical precaution.

"From the scale of the mining operations, we were expecting more people in the settlement portion," she continued. "But it seems like the mining was mostly automated and there were only a dozen people at most living in the settlement."

Rin considered the size of the space. The settlement looked like it had mostly been a storage depot, with limited working or living spaces—except that hundreds of kilometers of excavation tunnels spread out from this point. That kind of work should have taken dozens of workers, even with the best equipment.

He ran his fingers over the wall. What looked mostly smooth at a distance was actually ridged, a distinctive pattern.

"What dug these?" he asked.

"That's the other odd part," she told him. "Originally, this was a xenobiology project, as the tunnels have every sign of being dug by a lifeform, a giant worm of some kind. But the planet doesn't have any life of that size."

"Or any macro-organisms at all," Rin agreed. "Precursor biotech?"

The cave was silent.

"We've heard of such but never encountered examples in our space," Lodotan admitted. "It's possible, but...it seems almost too small-scale for a project of Those Who Came Before."

"A test, perhaps," he murmured. Or a small-scale endeavor by the rogues who'd challenged the Alava Hegemony. He wasn't going to talk to Lodotan about that, though...extracting supplies from a useless planet to fuel a forward scouting operation or a fleet would fit the bill.

"There isn't much else to see," Lodotan told him. "It's all much the same, but I felt that you should touch it with your own claws before you judged."

"There's no real judging here," Rin said. "I was asked to provide a different point of view; that's all." He shook his head. "I think I have another day in Tohrohsail before Captain Casimir and Envoy Awav need to move on. I'll go through your data and send you any conclusions I can come to, but..."

"But?"

"I think your biologists had a point," he told her. "I think you're looking at a test site, potentially, for mid-scale mining biotech. A stage between whatever the Precursors did on their own planets and their tendency to carve up planets they didn't have a use for.

"If six sets of miners extracted every valuable resource within a thousand kilometers of their landing site in two years, I could very easily see that being a tool that could strip a world of its resources in a decade or two," Rin pointed out. "That...that seems very much in the Alava's style."

"Those Who Came Before do seem to always have thought on a large scale," Lodotan agreed. "I would be curious to see your more-detailed thoughts once you've reviewed the work of our claws, Dr. Dunst.

"I will take away your concept, though, and compare it to what we have learned so far," she concluded. "Your 'different point of view' may be nearly as valuable as some of my superiors hoped it would be."

Rin concealed a grin. Lodotan had been as cooperative as he could have wished, but from the sounds of that statement, she hadn't actually expected his contribution to be significant.

To be fair, neither had Rin!

CHAPTER SEVENTEEN

"ALL RIGHT, EVERYONE, WE HAVE PLACES TO BE AND PEOPLE TO see," Morgan told her senior staff. "Any reasons left to stick around in Tohrohsail?"

Her team looked around at each other and shrugged almost as one.

"We're fully restocked and refueled," Trifonov reported, the logistics officer leaning back in his chair and steepling his dark-skinned fingers. "The Grand Fleet has a full logistics train with them, which definitely bodes well for any needs we have in the near future."

"On the other hand, they don't have much in terms of repair facilities," Liepins pointed out, the Latvian engineer sounding grumpy. "If we get ourselves shot up again, we'll either need to fall back to Imperial space or beg help from the Laians."

"While the Laians could probably help, we are under no circumstances letting Laian engineers poke around inside this ship," Morgan pointed out. The Laian fleet had multiple mobile shipyards with them, each designed to hold a war-dreadnought or dozens of cruisers, as well as the repair slips of the Tohrohsail base itself.

The problem was that *Defiance* was back up to three Final Dragon starkillers *and* was a hyperspace-missile platform, two technologies the Imperium knew the Laians didn't share. They'd fight with and for the Laians if necessary, but they weren't giving up their handful of surprises.

"Then I suggest we try not to get shot," the engineer told her.

"This is just a tour of the front, Commander," Morgan replied. "I don't expect to get shot at much."

"Our last mission was supposed to be survey and exploration," Rogers noted. "We all know how *that* ended."

"Messily," Morgan conceded. "We'll try to keep this one calmer, even if we do go beyond the mission brief."

She wasn't allowed to brief her staff on the Tsunami part of her mission just yet. That decision was at her sole discretion, but she wanted to be well clear of the rest of the Imperial fleet before she started sharing that information.

"Dr. Dunst, Awav?" She turned to their two civilians. "Anything you need here in Tohrohsail?"

"I think I've provided as much value to the archeology work as I can," Rin replied. "I have a few pieces of their data I'm chewing on, but I don't need to be here to give them their answers."

"For myself, remaining in Tohrohsail is actively against the currents of my mission," Awav told her. "The Laian fortifications and ships in the system are well known to the Imperium. The other sites on our journey are far darker waters and it is there that I can serve my purpose."

"All right," Morgan said. "In the absence of counter-orders from home, we'll move out in three tenth-cycles. I expect all departments to check in three hundredth-cycles before we depart, to confirm we're ready to go."

That was, roughly, seven hours and forty-two minutes, respectively.

"I DIDN'T GET a chance to ask how your visit to the dig site was," Morgan said after she and Rin retreated to her quarters. She'd been swamped with one task or another since arriving in the Laian base system.

"Fascinating," he told her. "In both good and bad ways, I think."

She arched an eyebrow at her lover, waving him to the couch as she started a pot of coffee.

"That's an interesting combination. Dangerous?"

"Fifty thousand years dead, so no more dangerous than anything we're poking at," he admitted. "Unlikely to eat stars or start tele- porting starstuff at ships, in any case."

"All right, so I guess the other question is whether it's relevant to our mission here," Morgan told him as she laid out the cups and the sugar for Rin's coffee. Her own was black, but she wasn't going to argue with someone over their coffee choices.

"I don't think so," he admitted. "It looks like Alavan biotech, but... not quite."

"*Not quite?*"

She handed Rin a coffee and dropped herself onto the couch next to him, leaning her leg against his.

"The scale is smaller than I'd expect from the Alava, though it could be an experiment," he said. "Or just a smaller operation being run by the rogues from the outside, potentially laying groundwork for the invasion."

He didn't sound certain, and Morgan eyed him over her coffee cup.

"But?"

"I have samples of the materials the Laians found in the tunnels," he told her. "Well, full data workups on them, anyway. The protein structures, the materials—it's definitely close to what we've seen of Alavan biotech, but it's not quite the same. Cruder in some ways."

"But the bioships from the Great Mother and the cloner on Arjtal were identical at that level," Morgan pointed out.

"I know," Rin agreed. "Hence, fascinating. I'm pretty certain we're looking at Alavan work, but it's possible we're looking at something post-Fall. So, maybe we're looking at somebody with left-over or evolved biotech after everything came apart?"

"But the only people we know of are the Mesharom," Morgan said.

"Which would tie with large tunnels and small numbers of individuals, if we're looking at a biotech operation by a small Mesharom group after the Fall," he said. "Or...it could be something entirely new."

"This is pretty deep in space the Mesharom are certain was Alavan," she noted.

"I know. So, *something new* seems unlikely," he admitted. "So, I'm back to what I suggested to the Laians: an experiment by the Alava, potentially some of their earliest biotech. But unless they've got the time frame way off, we may have misestimated when the Alava started working with biotech.

"The oldest time frame for this site is only about fifty-two thousand years ago."

"Two thousand years sounds like enough time for the rogue and semi-rogue factions experimenting with biotech to take shape on the frontier to me," Morgan said. "That fits."

"Yeah," he conceded. "But...it's an awkward fit, Morgan. I feel like I'm missing something."

"Well, it doesn't sound like our problem today," she told him. "Not unless it's going to lead us to the Alavan fleet or the conspirators."

"I don't think so," he said. "It's just a curious itch, I think. But, well...I didn't become a premier xenoarcheologist by not trying to satisfy my curiosity!"

"I'll keep an eye out for hints to give you," Morgan replied. "We'll see what we find out here."

Hopefully, everything they found was either useful or harmless.

"Speaking of, does your crew know where we're going from here?" Rin asked.

"El-Amin has the coordinates for our rendezvous," she confirmed. The navigator hadn't even blinked at being given deep-space coordinates to navigate to. She wasn't sure if he'd guessed there was more going on than anyone had admitted to or if he was just taking everything in stride.

Bit of both, she thought.

"And from there?"

"We'll see what the contact says," Morgan said. "The plan is to visit all of the Laian bases and your archeology sites over the next thirty cycles, but I have full discretion over the order we visit them in, and I plan to use it.

"Even for Awav, showing up when they don't expect us is handy. Hopefully, the contact has some useful information to help guide our way."

CHAPTER EIGHTEEN

"Hyper portal opening," El-Amin announced, his voice clearly showing his curiosity as *Defiance* tore her way back into regular space well over two light-years from any star system on her charts or scanners.

"Commander Nguyen, let me know the moment you spot anything," Morgan ordered as the ever-shifting gray void of hyper-space faded away behind them. "Are we alone?"

Lesser Commander Thu Nguyen was the woman in charge of *Defiance*'s arsenal and sensors. As yet, she hadn't been briefed on the Tsunami part of their mission, but she was focused on the right things as they emerged into darkness.

"We are," Nguyen confirmed. "I'm not sure why we're here, but there's nobody else here."

Morgan nodded.

"That's what I was expecting. El-Amin, secure the ship to station-keeping. Nguyen, keep a full active sensor sweep and begin post-processing our scanner data for stealth ships."

The Imperium's scanners were theoretically capable of picking up the small disturbances in gravity and radiation that revealed the presence of a ship hidden in a stealth field. In practice, finding those disturbances required dedicating a significant portion of a ship's computing power to reprocessing the sensor data multiple different ways to find those anomalies.

They were down to taking fifteen minutes to identify where a stealth ship had been. It wasn't a perfect science or an entirely useful trick, but it at least told the Imperium when they had been ghosted.

"We're expecting company?" Nguyen asked.

"There will be a briefing for all senior officers at the sixth tenth-cycle," Morgan told her—and made a mental note to schedule said briefing—"but what you need to know right now is that we are meeting someone here, a contact who has been carrying out her own investigations along the Dead Zone."

Several of her officers shivered and she shook her head slightly in sympathy. This close to the Dead Zone, it was a visible blotch of missing stars in the sky and on their scanners. Even without knowing the history, looking at that bit of sky just felt *wrong*.

"Permission to deploy Buckler platforms?" Nguyen said after a few moments. "My skin is crawling, and while that *might* just be a stealthed friend..."

Sword and Buckler was the code name for the two-tiered missile-defense system installed on every Imperial warship. Designed by a team of engineers led by Morgan's father, it had started as a high-efficiency laser antimissile system based around shipboard turrets—the Sword system—and parasite drones—the Bucklers.

These days, the drones and turrets used a mix of lasers, plasma beams and light hyperfold cannons to maximize their efficiency and range. It wasn't perfect—the standard sublight combat missile of both the Imperium and the Core Powers traveled at eighty-five percent of lightspeed, after all—but deploying the Bucklers dramatically increased *Defiance*'s survivability.

"Shouldn't be necessary," Morgan replied, "but let's not start distrusting our intuition today, shall we? Go to stage two Buckler deployment."

That would put one of the parasite platforms at each of the ship's six cardinal points, roughly a quarter of the number they'd have out for a full deployment...but running the platforms wasn't free, either.

"Understood; deploying platforms."

New icons appeared on the displays around Morgan as six of the robotic spacecraft dropped away from *Defiance* and took up their positions. She was about to ask for an update on the processing when a seventh icon appeared on the screen.

"New contact, danger close!" Nguyen snapped. "Contact at five light-seconds, unknown class. Energy levels...suggest no heavy weaponry."

Morgan could hear the move from concern to calm in her tactical officer's voice over the few seconds of her report, and brought up the data on the ship.

"Looks like one of ours," she noted. "A!Tol-manufacture interface drive, anyway, though I don't think our stealth fields could have got her that close."

They were getting there, but the stealth fields were one of the technologies in the Mesharom Archives that the Imperium's scientists and engineers were having difficulty with.

"Incoming laser com," one of Nystrom's deputies reported, the young man sounding worried. "Imperial codes, captain's eyes only."

"Understood," Morgan replied. She considered for a moment. She *had* a privacy shield that could drop around her in the middle of the bridge, but it wasn't always entirely reliable—and it was mildly claustrophobic, too.

"I'll take it in my office," she told the deputy. "Commander Nguyen, you have the bridge."

———

BY THE TIME Morgan reached her office—all of forty seconds after leaving the bridge—Nguyen's teams had the beginning of a detailed workup on the stranger. It was a small ship, smaller than most hypercapable starships Morgan had seen. It was barely two-thirds the size of an Imperial courier ship.

At its core, it was definitely A!Tol in construction, but its energy signature was something else. Morgan recognized some of the variation, though, and wondered just where the ship had come from—it had been built by the A!Tol, but it had definitely been upgraded by the *Mesharom*...and no one had seen a Mesharom ship outside their borders in years.

A tapped command accepted the encrypted link from the other ship, still hovering five light-seconds clear of *Defiance*. It promptly asked for more codes and a Tsunami authorization, all of which Morgan typed in.

Finally, the link opened, resolving into a video transmission of a large A!Tol. The being on the screen didn't rival Ki!Ron for size, but she was still an immense creature...and a familiar one to Morgan Casimir.

"Captain Casimir of *Defiance* speaking," she reeled off before the image of her stepmother's first A!Tol friend fully registered.

"Ki!Tana?" she demanded a moment later.

"Morgan," the Ki!Tol greeted her with a flush of red contentment and a beak snap of amusement. "No one actually told me which Captain Ki!Ron had recruited and sent out, but I was still half-expecting it to be you. Your family always finds the deepest waters, don't they?"

"So it seems," Morgan conceded. "Does Mom know about any of this?"

"Annette suspects that my connections outside the Imperium are far more complicated than I have admitted, and knew that I acted as an agent of the Mesharom," Ki!Tana told her. "I do not believe she knows of Ki!Ron's...association, as my old friend calls it."

"But you're part of it?" Morgan asked.

"Less so than Ki!Ron," Ki!Tana said. "I came into these waters from being a Mesharom agent out here, but I agree with their goals and have helped their purposes. And this current mess..."

"Is ugly," Morgan finished. "Ki!Ron wants me to stop a war. Not quite sure how I'm going to do that."

"An ancient and honorable task, if also usually an impossible one," the Ki!Tol admitted. "I've been retrieving data from sensor stations we'd seeded along this frontier for a bit now, and I think I might have *some* clues."

"Good. That's more than I have beyond 'There's an Alavan fleet out here somewhere,'" Morgan said. "I need to brief my officers. Can you come aboard?"

"Unless I miss my guess, I should be able to bring *Dark Eyes* into one of your small craft bays," Ki!Tana told her. "She's hyper-capable on her own, but I suspect a surprise stealth ship might be useful in these waters."

———

"DOES anyone else find it suspicious that the ship *exactly* fits our boat bay if we transfer all the shuttles to the other one?" Pierre Vichy asked dryly as he watched his people assemble a proper honor guard for one of the people regarded as founders of the Duchy of Terra.

"A cruiser boat bay for the Imperial Navy is a pretty standard size," Morgan pointed out to her Marine CO. The Marines were now in a neat line on this side of the blast doors, waiting for *Dark Eyes* to finish her very careful approach into the bay. "I suspect *Dark Eyes* was specifically designed to fit in one rather than the other way around."

"C'est vrai, but still." The Marine shook his head. "Makes me paranoid."

"Paranoia is in your job description, Commander Vichy," she reminded him. "Are we ready?"

"To greet an ancient trickster-demon who is directly responsible for your stepmother's rule of humanity, has probably saved Earth three or four times over, and almost certainly knows more about what we're doing out here than I do? Sure! If, on the other hand, this is some dark conspiracy and we are swarmed by Mesharom combat robots, we're probably a little under-gunned."

"I'm not expecting *Dark Eyes* to be a trojan horse, Commander."

"No one ever expects anything to be a trojan horse. That's why the tactic works, mon capitaine," Vichy said.

"And do you have a fallback plan if the Captain's old family friend is actually an AI simulacrum being used to trap us?" Commander Rogers asked, the XO grinning at the Marine.

"Two squads behind those bulkheads in full armor," the Marine CO said instantly, gesturing. "The boat bay itself has remote-controlled weapons, the control center for those is manned, and we are maintaining surveillance of the exterior of Ki!Tana's ship. We might be overrun if it is a trap, sir, but ils sauront qu'ils nous ont rencontrés."

They will know they met us.

"Let's hope it doesn't come to that," Morgan replied.

"Docking complete," the boat bay officer's voice reported calmly. "Interface drive offline. *Dark Eyes* is in place and we are locked down. Opening the blast doors."

"You're on, Commander Vichy. Time to look pretty."

"Now, that, Captain Casimir, there is no question of our ability to achieve."

THE DRESS-UNIFORMED MARINES trooped out in front of Morgan and her companions, and the officers followed behind. The access hatch to *Dark Eyes* flowed down, the hull's active matrix of microbots turning into a ramp.

That ramp sat empty for at least twenty seconds as the Marines smoothly flanked it, their weapons at a respectful-but-ready angle.

Morgan didn't doubt the truth of Vichy's statements, either. Her Marine CO faked being an egotistical dandy extremely well, but he took the security of his charges deadly seriously as well.

After those twenty-odd seconds had passed, the three-meter-tall squid-like form of Ki!Tana emerged from the ship. A flush of surprise flickered across her skin at the sight of the Marine honor guard, but she gamely moved down the ramp toward Morgan and her senior officers.

"Captain Casimir, I was not expecting...this," Ki!Tana admitted.

"You are one of the founders of the Duchy of Terra and respected by humanity, above and beyond the respect due to a Ki!Tol of the Imperium," Morgan told her. "Welcome aboard *Defiance*, Ki!Tana. This is Commander Bethany Rogers, my First Sword, and Battalion Commander Pierre Vichy, my Marine commander."

"Thank you for the warm waters," Ki!Tana told them. "These are dark tides we swim in. I worry we may not have much time."

"I know exactly how much time we have," Morgan said grimly. "I have scheduled a briefing for my officers in just over a twentieth-cycle, where I will update them on our mission out here. Can you share your own discoveries then, or should you and I speak in private?"

"Most of what I have learned I can share with your officers if you're briefing them," Ki!Tana told her. "Some we will discuss afterward."

A flush of red pleasure suffused the old A!Tol's skin.

"It's good to see you, Morgan Casimir," she told Morgan. "I truly should have spent more time on Earth."

Morgan coughed awkwardly.

"That might not help you see me much," she admitted. "Duty keeps me away from home these days."

And if that was a choice Morgan had made herself, to let her girl-friend's marriage to the partner who was physically present on Earth bother her less, well, that was a private affair.

CHAPTER NINETEEN

"So, as most of you have guessed by now, our formal missions out here are a cover," Morgan told her senior officers, looking around the briefing room with level eyes. "This room is currently sealed under Dragon Protocols because that's as high as we get for clearance.

"I'm not even going to tell you what codes this is secured under, as you are only learning about our mission because you need to know."

She had everyone's attention now, even if several of the officers in the room were clearly eyeing Rin Dunst and Ki!Tana and questioning their presence.

Rogers and Vichy, as the next-most-senior officers after Morgan herself, were seated at the far end of the table. Nguyen, El-Amin and Nystrom sat on the left side, the three bridge officers probably the least surprised by the briefing. They might not know what was going on, but they knew *something* was going on.

Facing them were Liepins and Trifonov, engineering and administration respectively, and the sole Speaker-ranked officer in the room: Speaker Murtas, the cruiser's intelligence officer.

Rin and Ki!Tana sat next to Morgan, bringing the number of people in the room to eleven. Morgan had debated inviting Awav but had eventually decided that keeping the diplomat out of the loop worked best for everyone.

"The Imperium has reason to believe that a third party is attempting to trigger a conflict between the Wendira and Laians as cover for their own activities near the Dead Zone," Morgan told them all, her tone flat. "At this point, any unidentified movement detected by hyperspace anomaly scanners would be assumed to be a fleet movement by the other side.

"Given the difficulty of hyperspace interception, the conflict removes any likely questions as to who is moving significant numbers of ships or why," Morgan continued. "Tens of thousands are already dead in the *incidents* that have brought us to the edge of this war, but against the prize our target is seeking, those deaths have been judged necessary."

She shook her head.

"I disagree with the people making that assessment," she told her people, "but I can almost see where they are coming from. They believe, officers, that they have located an Alavan battle fleet that the Mesharom haven't cleaned up."

The room was silent. Only Rin and Ki!Tana had known the prize on the board, and everyone else was stunned.

"How is that possible?" Rogers finally asked. "We're *in* the Core; the Mesharom have swept these regions a dozen times."

"Because thanks to various fragments and what we learned out in the Kosha Sector, we now believe that a major Alavan deployment was underway when the Fall happened," Morgan explained. "The Mesharom targeted bases and colonies. They couldn't find a fleet in motion, lost either in deep space or in an uninhabited system."

"Deep space is unlikely," Rin interjected. "The nature of the Alavan jump drive means it's unlikely they'd end up far away from a gravity well."

"We believe they were deployed against a force from one of the rogue Alavan factions we have identified," Morgan continued with a nod to the archeologist. "Obviously, the Imperium wants to take possession of these ships if possible.

"On the other hand, given the known dangers of Alavan technology, we are ordered to destroy the fleet before allowing it to fall into unknown hands."

Morgan waited while that sank in and smiled grimly.

"Our orders are fundamentally threefold," she concluded. "First, the mission we are officially performing is not without value. Envoy Awav and Dr. Dunst do need to visit the various locations we are scheduled to visit. Conveniently, that allows us to access Dr. Dunst's knowledge of the Alava for our primary mission.

"Secondly, we need to learn more about who is trying to start this conflict. If at all possible, we are to find sufficient evidence of their actions to provide Fleet Lord Tan!Shallegh with the leverage he needs to deescalate the situation at the peace conference he has organized in twenty-five cycles." She looked at her officers grimly.

"That's our first time limit, people," she told them. "If at all possible, I want enough data to end this fucking war in Fleet Lord Tan!Shallegh's tentacles by the time he meets with the Laian and Wendira representatives.

"Our third mission is parallel to that. We need to find the Alavan fleet before the conspirators do. That may require us to steal information from them, stalk them, or potentially even engage them in battle to get to the graveyard first.

"We will do whatever is required to complete our missions," Morgan finished. "Questions? Suggestions?"

"What do we even know about this 'third party'?" Rogers asked.

"Not much," Morgan admitted. "Our best guess is a group of politicians, military officers, and industrialists from at least the Wendira and Laian star nations. They want to get their hands on intact Alavan technology—but I have to remind everyone that experimenting with intact Alavan technology is how the Mesharom discovered how to build starkillers."

"Yeah, so we don't let them do that," Rogers agreed. "But we're hunting ghosts and shadows without more data."

"I can help a bit there," Ki!Tana told them, "though I would wait for the Captain to finish?"

Morgan nodded to the A!Tol and glanced around the room again. "Anyone?"

"Any idea how much force these 'shadows' might have?" Nguyen asked.

"Most likely, they either have or can borrow a medium-sized raiding force from both the Wendira and the Laians," Morgan admitted. "A direct conflict with their search fleet is almost certainly unwinnable, so we'll need to be very careful."

She waited for a few more moments, then gestured to Ki!Tana.

"Ki!Tana has been scouting this area for evidence of the situation for some time. If you would brief us on everything you can share?"

The Ki!Tol lifted herself to her locomotive tentacles, looming over the room as she rose to her full three-meter height.

"For reasons I won't go into, there are a number of covert sensor platforms seeded along this frontier," she told them. "I have spent the last few ten-cycles downloading their data and making my own sensor sweeps.

"I can confirm one of our worst fears right away: there is definitely an independent force moving around, carrying out at least a portion of the provocative incidents while also searching for something, presumably our target.

"However, a review of the actions and tentacles in play tells me that that force is *not* the only factor in motion. At least a third of the raids are being carried out by forces from the fleet bases along the frontier, Laian and Wendira alike.

"Either these are officers operating on their own or orders are coming down from higher up. The main nodal forces on both sides have remained watchful but inactive as this continues, but secondary fleets have carried out raids and counter-raids."

"It almost looks like a real war," Rogers said grimly.

"That, I imagine, is the intent," Ki!Tana agreed. "It is those fleets, those small actions and the officers and ships that carried them out, that I believe may be the vulnerability for our enemy."

A holographic map of the Dead Zone and the stars around it filled the air. One side was lit up in green to mark the Laian Republic, the other side in orange to mark the Wendira Grand Hive.

"Despite the name, the Dead Zone is hardly empty," Ki!Tana reminded everyone. "Over a hundred stars died, but only one star in three was inhabited. While mostly only smaller and dimmer stars remain, so does the Astoroko Nebula, a stellar nursery in the process of birthing at least half a dozen stars.

"While every star system around Astoroko that had a living world is now dead, there are still two hundred star systems in the Dead Zone. Not all of these are empty."

Nine stars in the Laian section were highlighted in a darker green, as were six stars in the Dead Zone itself.

"These are the active Laian defense bases in the region," the A!Tol said. "Outside of Tohrohsail, none have more than three dreadnoughts, but there are forty capital ships and roughly five hundred warships spread across the other fourteen bases."

"The Wendira have a similar arrangement on their side," Morgan told her people, "but we have access to the Laian bases. We are authorized, in fact, to visit and inspect all fourteen of those fleet positions."

Ki!Tana flickered her tentacles in acknowledgement and then highlighted three of the systems in flashing crimson.

One was in the Republic proper, but two were in the Dead Zone, both close to the Nebula.

"These three systems appear to have been used as bases for raids into Wendira space," she told them. "I *think* that forces from these two"—a tentacle indicated the two systems close to the Astoroko Nebula—"combined with our mystery fleet to destroy the Wendira base at Ritchit."

"Currently the largest single provocation," Morgan murmured.

Ritchit had been a small forward base with a minimal civilian population, but the entire base had been destroyed by orbital bombardment.

"Exactly. Both sides are trying to work out what happened there, but since the Laians didn't officially order it, they're having trouble identifying the attackers—but the Wendira have clear and distinct sensor data of war-dreadnoughts bombarding a planetary base."

"Wonderful," Rogers said. "I suppose there's also the possibility our allies are seriously screwing us and setting up a conflict they can blame the Wendira for to bring us in?"

"It's possible, but all evidence I've seen suggests the Laians are aboveboard," Morgan replied. "This system"—she tapped the suspect base still in Republic space—"is on our way to the other two. I think it's our first stop. We use Awav's access to ask all kinds of awkward questions and we see how they react—while Ki!Tana and Speaker Murtas tear into their systems, hopefully without getting caught.

"Any answers we can find are a step in the right direction, everyone. If we can prevent a war, I'm pretty sure the Laians will forgive us a few criminal acts of espionage."

CHAPTER TWENTY

AFTER THE MEETING, KI!TANA JOINED MORGAN AND RIN IN the Captain's office, collapsing into an A!Tol couch with an audible beak-snap of relief.

"Solitude comes naturally to me at this point," she admitted, "but I do enjoy the company of others. Just...not my own race."

"And that would be why Awav was told not to bring his A!Tol aide," Morgan guessed. It had seemed suspicious to her when she'd heard, though she hadn't necessarily expected the agent to be Ki!Tana.

"Most likely," Ki!Tana agreed. "Female A!Tol are usually fine, though I'm finding them a little stressful of late. Males..."

The thought sent a disturbing shiver through her tentacles.

"By the time I became Ki!Tol, we knew better than to let males near Ki!Tol," she finally said. "We'd worked that out a *long* time before."

"Ki!Ron had no A!Tol around her at all," Rin said. "It gets that bad, does it?"

Ki!Tana was silent, her skin dark with unspoken grief. Finally, she snapped her beak again.

"However bad you think the chaos of our hormones is, you under-estimate the depths of the water," she told them. "It is bad enough for me, though I can tolerate females of my own kind for a while. Ki!Ron was already ancient among us when I emerged from my initiation cell with fragmented memories and a new lease on life."

"So, she is surrounded by aliens forever," Morgan murmured. "Not sure I'd make that trade."

"Immortality is a tempting current," Ki!Tana replied. "I am not certain I would choose to follow this course a second time, but now that I am on it, I will not give it up."

"From my perspective, having the Ki!Tol around as a living memory..." Rin shook his head. "I can't even imagine the value for historical and archeological studies, even if I had to send my questions in writing."

"We don't remember much from before we became Ki!Tol," Ki!Tana said. "But Ki!Ron, for example, has been watching our species and civilization grow for thousands of long-cycles. She gets more than a few messages like that."

Morgan nodded as she tapped a command and brought the holographic map of the Dead Zone up.

"How much more do you know than what you told my officers?" she asked bluntly.

"Not a lot," Ki!Tana said. "Files are in your people's tentacles of what I learned about the operations out of the three bases I flagged. I know a bit more about the actual scout fleet than I admitted."

"What am I looking at?" Morgan asked.

"It's a mix of Laian and Wendira ships," the old spy told them. "At least one star hive and one war-dreadnought, plus escorts. There may be other Core Power ships present, but all of the capital ships are Laian or Wendira."

"Are they active military ships?" Morgan said, considering that. "If so, can we trace their assignments?"

"So far as I can tell, the ships don't officially exist," Ki!Tana admitted. "I can't speak to the war-dreadnought, but between myself and our associates in the Grand Hive, we managed to ID the star hive.

"Or...fail to, where we should have succeeded," she said with a beak snap of a bitter chuckle. "My associate's guess is that she was built in the same yards as the Grand Hive's ships but was never ordered or paid for by the Wendira's military. An extra unit for the purposes of the people who owned the shipyard."

"I suppose owning the shipyards gives you that kind of option," Morgan agreed. "I can't see my father building warships for himself, but he's in deep with the ducal government at this point."

"Arguably, you could say the entire Terran Militia is basically built on that kind of scheme," Rin said quietly. "Since the Duchy owns a significant portion of the Raging Waters complex."

Morgan had never thought of it that way. The Raging Waters of Friendship Yards had *always* been intended to build the warships for the Duchy, but thinking about it, she realized the Duchy of Terra probably had access to far better technology than they would have if the Raging Waters Yards *hadn't* been a major refit-and-construction yard for the Imperial Navy.

She gave her lover a pained smile and gestured for Ki!Tana to continue.

"A star hive alone is a hundred-million-plus-ton warship with over a thousand starfighters aboard," the spy noted. "I don't think *Defiance* is up to that fight."

"Not in a straight-up brawl, no," Morgan conceded. If the geography was right, she could blow up a star to level the odds—but tactical use of starkillers would *probably* get her in trouble.

"The one other thing I've noted about the fleet is that the movements I have been able to confirm as theirs are heading closer and closer to the Astoroko Nebula," Ki!Tana told them. "I suspect, though I have no solid data to support this current, that they believe the Alavan fleet is somewhere in the stellar nursery."

"That would suggest...what?" Rin asked. "I feel like there'd be some logic to them being in the nebula."

Morgan considered the map. The Astoroko Nebula was fifteen light-years across, an area of dangerously variable density both in regular space and hyperspace. In several key locations, that density was converging in the slow birth of stars.

"It means someone was hiding," she told Rin. "That area is hard to chase someone through. For the Alavan with their jump drives? It might even have been worse than it was for us. I'd guess they'd actually fought the battle the fleet went out for and the Alava were pursuing someone into the nebula."

"If their enemy was hiding in the nursery, they'd be hard for the Alava to find," Ki!Tana agreed. "I'm not as familiar with their tech and systems as others would be, but I understand that the jump drive wouldn't lend itself to easily sweeping a fifteen-light-year sphere."

"Probably not," Morgan agreed. "We have limited visibility from hyperspace into regular space, but they would have had no visibility into the space between their jump points."

"That gives us somewhere to look, doesn't it?" Rin asked. "Should we be heading right there?"

"The Salroduk System is on the way, anyway," Morgan pointed out. "And if we can get some groundwork data before we walk right into the zone where we *know* our shadowy friends are operating, that gives some idea of what we're doing. And what they're doing."

"I can sweep the system in *Dark Eyes* once we're in," Ki!Tana offered. "I have some idea of what to look for in the ships that engaged in the raid."

"And I'll ask awkward questions with Away," Morgan said. "Rin, I don't believe there's one of your sites in Salroduk, is there?"

"No. The two by the nebula both have one, though," he said. "The civilians at those sites might even have data on the military movements we can use."

"An uninvolved party may have seen things our shadows didn't think they did," Morgan agreed. "They could be useful. First, though, Salroduk. Let's see how the commanders there spin sending a dreadnought battle group into Wendira space."

CHAPTER TWENTY-ONE

THE ADVANTAGE OF DROPPING BACK INTO REGULAR SPACE TO pick up Ki!Tana, even in the middle of nowhere, was that *Defiance* linked back into the Laians' network of hyperfold relays. The hyper-fold communicator had a maximum range of about ten light-years, a distance where transmission delays were around twelve hours.

It wasn't enough for instantaneous communications, but in most places in the Core or the A!Tol Imperium, it was enough to get to a starcom, which *was* instantaneous, within thirty-six hours. Inter-stellar mail was faster than it had ever been, but it was still *mail*, not phone calls outside of the systems with starcoms.

That meant that Morgan heard from her girlfriend on Earth roughly two days after Victoria Antonova sent her messages. She was gratified to still be *getting* said messages, since it had been over a year since she'd returned home.

They'd agreed on an open relationship due to Morgan's duties away from Sol years earlier, but Victoria marrying her other girlfriend had been a bit...much. Shelly was a wonderful person, in Morgan's probably unbiased opinion, but going from the primary-who-wasn't-there-much-partner to the definitely-secondary-partner was still hard.

But the mail download they got while picking up *Dark Eyes* included a message from Victoria. Leaving Rin to sleep when she woke up, Morgan slipped into her office to play the message.

Making time to keep in touch with Victoria had been hard enough before she had her second partner on ship with her. She didn't begrudge the time spent on either of them, but the balance was hard.

"Hey, Morgan," the elegantly tall blonde woman greeted her from the video feed. "Notice anything different?"

Victoria leaned into the camera, allowing her collar insignia to glitter in the light of her office. Even if Morgan hadn't been warned, she'd probably have noticed the silver eagle that had replaced her lover's three gold bars.

"I just got the update yesterday," Victoria continued. "Promoted to Captain at last." She grinned. "I'm catching up with you, my love. My CO had apparently told Shelly before anyone let me know, so I got jumped with a surprise party or I'd have messaged you sooner."

The grin widened.

"I'm taking over one of the Terran defense platforms in three weeks," she announced. "I know, I know, there's sixty of them and my new baby doesn't even have a *name*, but she's still a cruiser-sized space station with eight hundred people aboard. A little less glamorous than a heavy cruiser, but still my own command."

Morgan was grinning herself now. Victoria might be talking it down, but there was an extra layer she wasn't mentioning. Her former superiors were *very* careful about who got command of the platforms above Earth itself. Fortress Command was the final line of defense if everything else went wrong.

If Victoria Antonova was taking command of one of those fortresses, even one of the smaller ones, her superiors had complete faith in her.

"You were the first person I wanted to tell," Victoria said. "Especially since Shelly apparently already knew. It's...it's huge, love. I want to show you every inch of my baby when you're back. I know you can't show me all of *your* ship, but you have the clearance for everything on the platform."

The blonde Russian came to a halt, her grin shrinking into a shy smile.

"I miss you," she admitted. "I'm glad you have Rin and I have Shelly, but I still miss *you*. Let me know if you have any idea when you'll be back on Earth. I want to actually *meet* Rin. Trading messages with him isn't the same—and neither is trading messages with you.

"Look forward to hearing from you. I'll send you another message once I'm on the station—I get the feeling the next few weeks are going to be *very* busy. Love you."

Victoria blew a kiss at the camera and the recording ended, leaving Morgan smiling at the screen with mixed feelings. She *wanted* to go home, but she had the niggling feeling that the situation out here at the Dead Zone wasn't going to resolve anytime soon.

Even if they completed her Tsunami orders, she suspected Tan!Shallegh was going to try and hang on to her ship. Even putting aside that *Defiance* was a powerful cruiser in her own right, she was also a covert strategic weapons platform.

No sane fleet commander was going to let *Defiance* slip through their fingers until they were certain of peace.

Exhaling a long sigh, Morgan let that fear go and focused on Victoria's good news. Letting the smile cover her face again, she started the recorder on her desk.

"I just got your message," she told the frozen image of her lover. "That is *amazing* news!"

CHAPTER TWENTY-TWO

SALRODUK WAS OUTSIDE THE DEAD ZONE, ONE OF THE inhabited Laian systems closest to the Wendira Grand Hive. It wasn't a heavily populated system, with one inhabited world that wasn't entirely in line with Laian needs.

To Morgan's amusement, her review of the scan data suggested that Salroduk was a near-paradise for humans. Slightly more surface water than Earth with less axial tilt, it was humid and comfortably warm across most latitudes.

For the Laians, it was cold and damp. The Exile Enclave on Earth, after all, had settled in the Australian Outback. Still, the colony was home to just over a billion people and Salroduk had a moon as large as Earth's Luna.

The moon was the anchor point for half of the fleet base. The other half was positioned in the usual spot, attached to a refueling depot around the gas giant. The refit yards were out at the gas giant, but the main fleet position was above Salroduk.

Three war-dreadnoughts orbited the bases, supported by ten cruisers each and a flotilla of defensive platforms in each location.

While *Defiance* could probably handle any of the forty cruisers in the system one-on-one, she was outmassed some seventy to one by the war-dreadnoughts.

"Let's be very polite," Morgan murmured to her bridge staff as her cruiser slowed toward Salroduk's moon. "I'd rather not test the theory that a war-dreadnought could vaporize us in a single salvo."

Depending on the class, the war-dreadnought had somewhere between thirty and *sixty* times as many hyperfold cannons as *Defiance* did, with an even higher ratio for sublight interface drive missiles. Those missiles no longer had a speed advantage over Imperial weapons, but they *were* smarter and equipped with better electronic warfare systems.

"We've received docking instructions from Salroduk Base Control," El-Amin reported. "ETA is eleven thousandth-cycles."

"Lesser Commander Nystrom, please inform the Envoy that we are nearly at the first base for his inspection," Morgan told her communications officer. "I believe organizing the next stage is on him."

"Passing that on, sir," Nystrom confirmed. She paused, listening to a conversation transmitted to her translator earbuds. "The Envoy is asking if you want to accompany him on his inspection, sir."

Awav, Morgan reflected, had been *told* there was more going on than he was being briefed on. He was doing his best to be cooperative.

"Yes, let the Envoy know that I would appreciate that," she told Nystrom.

"Yes, sir. He says he'll let you know when he is planning on going aboard."

Morgan nodded her thanks to the communications officer.

"Is *Dark Eyes* clear?" she asked her XO. Rogers was keeping an eye on that half of their plan from the backup bridge.

"She is launching...now," Rogers reported. "We're still a good eight light-minutes clear of everything, so that should be more than enough distance to keep her dark. Stealth fields were up before she cleared the boat bay."

The Commander snorted.

"I could barely see her *in our boat bay*, so I think the Laians might have trouble," she concluded.

"Good, good," Morgan replied. *Dark Eyes* would do a scout of the outer system base before Awav officially headed out to inspect it. If there were ships that their allies were trying to hide—damaged ships that hadn't officially seen action, for example—they'd be at the gas-giant half of the base.

The next cycle or two of poking and prodding was going to be *interesting*. Morgan was going to have all kinds of questions to ask... questions that the local officers probably weren't going to like.

Fortunately, she was decent at reading Laian body language. That skill might prove necessary to avoiding an interstellar incident here.

Or, quite possibly, to surviving the next few cycles at all.

AWAV and his team were waiting when Morgan joined them on the crowded floor of *Defiance*'s port shuttle bay. The three analysts the Envoy had brought were a surprisingly diverse mix, even for Imperial officials: one Rekiki, a crocodilian centaur with a sharp-toothed grin; a barrel-bodied four-armed Anbrai; and one Yin, a blue-feathered humanoid.

All were races Morgan was familiar with, though she didn't know these individuals. She inclined her head to the three as she joined them.

"Envoy Awav," she greeted the Ivida. "Are you ready?"

"I am, yes," he confirmed. "We were reviewing the information we had on this base. I can summarize for you if you wish as we fly over?"

"That would be helpful," she agreed. "Thank you."

"I don't recall this bay being quite as crowded when we arrived," the Yin noted, surveying the shuttle bay with his beak slightly open.

"We are merely passengers aboard Captain Casimir's ship, Sorl," Awav said sharply. "Not all aspects of her operations must be explained to us."

"True, true," Sorl conceded. "My apologies for my rudeness, Captain."

"Unnecessary," Morgan told him, though she also didn't make any effort to answer his implied question. "After you, Envoy."

Awav led them onto the shuttle, his unmoving face showing no sign of surprise as four Marines followed them aboard.

Morgan wasn't actually *allowed* to leave *Defiance* without an escort outside of Imperial space, and she had no intention of letting the Envoy and his people wander around without protection, either. She hadn't discussed it with him because, well, she was the Captain.

Some things didn't need to be discussed. From Awav's calm demeanor, he'd expected as much. His staffers seemed more taken aback, but they took their lead from the Envoy.

"So, the base here?" she asked him as she took her seat across from him.

"One of thirteen refueling and security positions placed to support the nodal position at Tohrohsail," he said. "According to the details we were provided, guarded by four war-dreadnoughts, forty escort cruisers, thirty frigates and fifty defensive platforms. Refueling capacity was listed at one hundred million cubic meters per cycle. Sufficient to refuel all of the Grand Fleet from empty tanks in just a few cycles.

"Now, *all* of the secondary bases were listed at the same refueling capacity," Awav pointed out. "That is my single largest doubt with regards to these facilities."

"I'm not familiar with Laian frigates," Morgan noted. "War-dreadnoughts I know and escort cruisers I know."

"Laian frigates are rarely used in their main combat formations, as they are generally equipped with extremely limited fuel capacity," the Envoy told her. "They're usually between ten and twenty megatons but only have twenty to thirty Laian days of operations without refueling.

"They are intended as short-range defensive units and would never be seen outside of a defensive position like this."

Morgan nodded slowly.

"We didn't see any units like that on our initial scans," she said. "Does that suggest they overstated their defenses here?"

"Potentially," Awav agreed. "That is exactly what this tour is supposed to be about, Captain. Most likely, the frigates are at the outer system base, but we are trying to validate the currents of the information the Laians have provided us.

"If we base our operations in support of their fleet on the data they provide, we could find ourselves badly out of position if they have lied to us." The Ivida made a wordless noncommittal sound.

"I do not expect to find any great variance between the information they provided us and their true force positions," he noted. "But verification is necessary. Doing so in a random order helps maintain the integrity of the data and supports your true mission."

Morgan shook her head.

"I don't think we're supposed to admit there's anything else going on, Envoy," she pointed out.

"Of course not. I know nothing," he agreed. "And so, I continue my mission, but I am aware that there are other currents here, Captain. We are at your disposal."

"Today, just do your job," Morgan told him. "And try not to be too surprised by any questions I might ask."

"Captain Casimir, I have been a diplomat in the Empress's service for sixty long-cycles," Awav said gently. "It is unlikely that you can surprise me and very likely they will not realize if you do. Ivida lie far more readily than our color-changing leaders."

THE MAIN STRUCTURE of the Laian fleet base was on the surface of the moon, a sprawling base that covered at least a hundred square kilometers in domes, tunnels, docking platforms and weapons emplacements.

Any attacker that ignored Salroduk's moon would discover that it had the hyperfold cannons and missile arsenal of multiple war-dreadnoughts. That would be an ugly surprise, one Morgan was more than happy to inflict on that theoretical mutual enemy.

Their focus was on the docking platforms, and the pilot tucked the Imperial shuttle neatly onto the platform they were sent to. A dome extended up over the platform and quickly pressurized while they waited.

A dozen power-armored Laian soldiers moved out onto the platform while the pressurization process completed, forming a neat pathway for the Imperial delegation.

"Air pressure is clear; you can leave whenever you want," the pilot told them.

"There should be arrangements made for you, Braddock," Morgan told the pilot. "Lock the shuttle down once you've sorted those out with the locals. Everything *should* be clean and easy."

"I like clean and easy," Lesser Speaker Braddock replied with a chuckle.

"So do we," Awav muttered. "Shall we, Captain?"

"This is your show, Envoy," Morgan replied. "I'm just a spoiler. Lead on."

"Spoiler, Captain?" the Ividia asked.

"Not sure how to explain the metaphor," Morgan admitted as she followed the diplomat. "Mostly, it means I'm here to ask questions that make your life more difficult."

"I see," Awav replied. "That, then, is exactly what I expected when I invited you to join us, Captain Casimir."

Morgan managed *not* to audibly giggle as they approached the airlock and its waiting contingent of Laian officers. They probably didn't know human or Ivida body language well enough to get her amusement, but she also figured that laughing in front of them wouldn't start things off on the right foot—especially when there was no way she could explain the joke!

CHAPTER TWENTY-THREE

THE CENTRAL FIGURE IN THE GREETING PARTY WAS ONE OF THE larger Laians Morgan had ever met. Like A!Tol females, size among Laians was directly correlated to both age and sex. Male Laians were larger and had simpler coloring than their female counterparts, but both kept growing until death.

"Envoy Awav," the large bronze alien greeted the A!Tol Imperium's diplomat. "I am Twenty-Third Sword of the Republic Katavan, the commanding officer of the Salroduk Defense Base. Welcome to our facility."

"Thank you, Twenty-Third Sword," Awav said with a small bow. "May I introduce my escort commander, Captain Morgan Casimir?"

"Welcome to Salroduk, Captain," Katavan told Morgan.

Morgan gave the Laian a crisp salute. While their rank was arguably the same, authority among the thousands of officers with the rank "Sword of the Republic" went entirely by seniority. The Twenty-Third Sword was closer to a senior Militia Commodore or Imperial Division Lord than a Captain, as indicated by his command of a four-dreadnought battle group.

On the other hand, to *only* be a Sword of the Republic at Katavan's clearly advanced age suggested a career that had potentially stalled out. Seniority would eventually make him the most senior Sword, but it wouldn't be enough to promote him to Pincer on its own.

She filed that away in the back of her mind. A bitter officer who felt passed over was one at risk of subversion.

"I will admit, Envoy, that we did not expect your tour to begin here," Katavan continued. "We are quite some distance from Tohrohsail."

"While my government has no real reason to suspect deception on the part of the Republic, we must verify the transparency of even the friendliest waters," Awav told the Sword. "Starting and continuing our tour at random helps that verification."

"As the sands blow," the Laian allowed. "May I escort you to our main command center? You should be able to verify much of what you wish to see there."

"Of course, Sword Katavan. Lead the way."

Morgan tailed along as Katavan turned and walked into an elevator. The sheer size of the base meant the Laians could still play a lot of games with what they showed Awav. They'd had no reason to be *ready* to play those games, though, which meant the Envoy should end up seeing a true image.

Unless, of course, Katavan had been ready to conceal something from his own people...because, say, he'd been carrying out unauthorized adventures into Wendira space.

"AS YOU CAN SEE LOOKING AROUND, this base was at one point planned to act as a secondary command node after the Tohrohsail base," Katavan told them as he led them into the main command center.

They stood on a balcony that jutted out into an open space at least five hundred meters long and half that wide. Row upon row of communications consoles, holoprojections and screens stretched out under them, enough for not only a fleet but *multiple* fleets.

Most of the room was only dimly lit, with cloths draped over the consoles to protect them from the effects of time. A central core was fully lit and the consoles active, with at least fifty Laians operating consoles and checking in with each other.

A massive holographic projection of the Salroduk System hung in front of the balcony, giving the watch officer a clear view of everything going on in the star system.

Morgan's quick check confirmed at least one thing: the Laians couldn't detect Ki!Tana's ship.

"You should be able to see my entire command here," Katavan told them brightly. "I have the war-dreadnoughts *Dreamer of Hope*, *Reaper of Oaths*, *Harvester of Red* and *Driver of Blades*, plus their cruiser escorts and the local frigate squadrons.

"We also have significant fortifications, as you can see," he continued. "I don't know what you seek to verify, Envoy Awav, but the Salroduk Base is fully prepared for the war to come and ready to hold this position against the Wendira."

"Are any of your ships deployed?" Morgan asked.

"Of course," Katavan agreed. "We have four cruisers and ten frigates on local patrols. We are close to the Dead Zone, a favored location for pirates like the Ascendancy Exiles, and are responsible for the security of several less fortified systems."

Morgan left that for Awav to assess as she stepped closer to the hologram. As they'd guessed, it looked like most of the frigates were out at the gas giant. Ten of them orbited with the refueling station, and ten were scattered throughout the star system.

That lined up with Katavan's numbers, at least. Something about the Laian officer's eagerness to provide any and all data made her neck itch, though. She'd expected at least some resistance. The openness felt wrong.

"Will it be possible to tour the war-dreadnoughts?" Awav asked behind her.

"I will need time to prepare for that," Katavan warned, "but I can make it possible. Obviously, the entire ship would not be available. We are allies, but that does not mean we share everything."

"Of course not," the envoy agreed.

Morgan smiled to herself as she realized at least one small deception the Sword was engaging in. All of the *ships* were present and the Laian iconography was unfamiliar to her, but she was reasonably certain that the status indicators marking if the ships were damaged were missing from the display.

"And how far toward the Wendira border do you send your ships, Sword?" she asked.

"My pincers are only authorized to protect my area of responsibility," Katavan replied. "Outside of patrols of the closest portion of the Dead Zone, my ships do not go anywhere near the border."

"So, your dreadnoughts haven't left Salroduk?"

"I didn't say that," Katavan said. Any concern in his tone was lost in the translation, but Morgan knew Laian body language. He was irritated now, but it was forced. He *was* covering something. "I've occasionally sent one of them on patrol. That's part of why I have them. I'm not sure I understand your purpose, Captain."

"I'm just noticing that Salroduk would have made a solid launching point for several of the raids the Wendira are claiming the Republic has launched on their territory," Morgan told him. "But since the Wendira claimed there were war-dreadnoughts in those strikes, I presumed your ships couldn't have been involved."

"I trust every dreadnought captain under my command," Katavan snapped. "None of them have launched the kind of unauthorized expedition you are implying."

"Of course, of course," Morgan agreed. "You know your officers better than we would, of course. But you must understand, Sword, that the Imperium signed a defensive treaty with the Republic. Given the Wendira's accusations, we must be certain your people are not provoking this war."

"Envoy, I believe the good Captain's role in this meeting may be over," the Sword told Awav flatly. "I will not—"

"She is asking very good questions, Sword, around exactly the points I am tasked to investigate," the envoy cut him off. "So, tell me, Sword Katavan, how certain *are* you that none of your dreadnought commanders have left the waters you ordered them into?"

The balcony above the command center was dead silent for several seconds.

"I am more certain that my subordinates have done their duty than I am that you speak for the A!Tol Imperium," the Sword finally told them. "And I do not doubt the authorizations and warrants you bear, Envoy Awav. My officers are loyal servants of the Republic who would never exceed their orders."

"Of course, Sword," Awav agreed. "But you must understand that trust is easily given but verification requires action."

"We trust the Republic and we trust you," Morgan added, understanding the envoy's point instantly, "but we must verify as best as we can. If you would provide us with the schedules and movements of when your dreadnoughts left Salroduk, we would be able to verify that it was impossible for your ships to take part in the raids."

"I begin to understand why some in the Parliament feel this alliance is not worth it," Katavan replied. "But very well. The sands will part for your desires. Give me some time to have my staff assemble the data, but you will have it."

"I appreciate your efforts to meet our needs, Sword of the Republic," Awav told him. "This will be reflected in my reports and will shine fair light and waters upon you."

"So I hope," Katavan said. "Now, Envoy, Captain. Shall we continue the tour?"

MORGAN TOOK a break after several hours of being run through the less-classified portions of the moon base to return to her shuttle.

One of the Marines was standing next to the ramp and nodded to her as she approached.

"No one's caused any trouble, sir," she reported. "Lesser Speaker Braddock is getting lunch. From what the other Marines say, the Laians make the same tasteless mush of UP that we do."

"Thank you, Lance," Morgan replied. "I'll need privacy on the shuttle for a few minutes. Think you can keep the door closed?"

"Five by five, Captain."

Morgan grinned and stepped past the Marine. Once she was in the shuttle, she beelined for the small command module tucked almost out of sight. The module wasn't much more than a virtual reality pod, intended to be used for coordinating Marine squads in a landing action, but it had encrypted communicators.

"*Defiance*, this is Captain Casimir, come in."

The hyperfold communicator was *supposed* to be uninterceptable. *Supposed to be* wasn't good enough, and a series of electronic handshakes took place as the two systems synchronized the highest level of encryption they could manage.

"This is Rogers," Morgan's XO replied. "What's the situation?"

"We're poking Sword Katavan in places he doesn't like," Morgan told the other woman. "His staff is supposedly putting together a set of reports on when his war-dreadnoughts left the system and where they went.

"I want Murtas to verify that report. Do you understand what I mean?"

Even on an encrypted hyperfold channel, Morgan wasn't going to explicitly order her intelligence officer to hack into the databases of an allied power. Katavan's reaction left her grimly certain that the officer *was* involved and it *had* been his ships at the raids Ki!Tana had flagged.

That meant the report they'd get was going to have been massaged at the very least—and potentially completely falsified. The only way they could confirm that was by breaking into Katavan's computer systems.

"I'll let him know," Rogers promised. "Anything else we should be watching for?"

"Envoy Awav is scheduling tours of the war-dreadnoughts," Morgan said. "I won't be accompanying him, but we'll want to provide transport between the ships. Keep in touch with his staff and make sure we provide whatever they need."

"Understood. Do you have a timeline on your return aboard?" the XO asked. "I can First Sword it up as long as you'd like, but it's *my* job to remind *you* that your job is aboard *Defiance*. Diplomacy is part of the parcel, but..."

"My butt belongs in a chair on that bridge, I know," Morgan agreed. "I think we've got a few more hours here, though I don't think the Laians will try to feed us. I'll be back aboard by the ninth tenth-cycle, I think."

"We'll hold the fort until then," Rogers confirmed.

CHAPTER TWENTY-FOUR

"WELL. THE SWORD OF THE REPUBLIC IS LYING THROUGH HIS lovely mandibles," Speaker Toma Murtas told Morgan and the other senior officers the following day. "I mean, seriously, that shell color? *Amazing.*"

"It's relatively rare for Laians, as I understand," Rin agreed. "But I'm not sure whether we think bronze is a good color on him is relevant."

Murtas looked momentarily awkwardly at the civilian, then shrugged.

"We're still waiting for Ki!Tana to come back aboard from her tour of the outer system," the intelligence officer told them. "But I followed the Sword's staff through their work building the report we got on the dreadnought deployments—and borrowed some data from a few local civilian sensor platforms."

"And?" Rogers asked.

"He shifted the dates of deployment for every dreadnought operation," Murtas told them. "By between three and ten cycles each. He cut the time they were out of Salroduk by enough that none of them could have crossed the Dead Zone...except that there were at least five deployments that *definitely* could have."

"You confirmed that?" Morgan demanded.

"The civilian data is clear and his own data agrees with it everywhere else," the junior officer told them. "He's hiding something, and we have five deployments of a war-dreadnought with full escort that could have reached the Wendira bases in the Dead Zone."

"Do they match up with the time stamps we have for raids?" Nguyen asked, the tactical officer looking concerned.

"Three of them could, yes," Murtas confirmed. "The data is on all your tablets. They adjusted the timing on every one of nine dreadnought deployments in the last long-cycle, but only three of the original dates line up with attacks we're watching for.

"Given that we can be reasonably sure those three are lies, I would hesitate to trust any information we have on the other six."

"Because what we need is another mystery," Morgan said. "Beyond confirming that Katavan, at the very least, is covering for officers who are trying to provoke this war, what does this tell us?"

"It's possible those other six deployments were looking for the Alavan fleet," Murtas suggested. "I can plug them into our map and see if I can establish a zone that Katavan's people already swept. Might save us some time as we go hunting ourselves."

"I presume there's nothing in their computers about that?" Rin asked. "They wouldn't be that stupid, would they?"

"I can only dig so deep into a Core Power's computer network," the intelligence officer admitted. "Their computers are still better than ours. I'm using some prototype reconstructed Mesharom hardware and code, but the edge is slim.

"Following one of their people and piggybacking on what they pull? I can do that. Hard-hacking into a database that isn't currently open to pull data they're actively hiding? That's beyond my tools, sirs."

"Damn," Morgan conceded. "That's fair enough, Speaker. Thoughts, people?"

"If Katavan's ships did carry out those raids, the Wendira reported kicking the ever-loving *shit* out of one of the dreadnoughts involved," Nguyen pointed out, the tactical officer looking at the data on her tablet. "So, Ki!Tana's tour and Awav's inspections are probably going to find a damaged ship that should be fine."

"I suspect Katavan has a plan for Awav's inspections," Morgan said. "We'll see how that goes. But Ki!Tana will see; that's for certain."

"The other thing to consider is the threat level to *Defiance*, sir," Nguyen replied. "You poked Katavan pretty openly and he has to suspect that we suspect. Any one of his war-dreadnoughts could obliterate us in a thought."

"So long as we're in Salroduk, where there are civilians with hyperfold coms to the rest of the Republic, I think we're safe," Morgan replied after a moment's thought. "Once we're on our way, though...all bets are off. We need to be careful; you're right."

"What do we do next?" Rogers asked. "Knowing Katavan is involved doesn't actually help us unless we can use him to locate the shadow fleet or the Alavan graveyard."

"It does give us some evidence that we can forward to Fleet Lord Tan!Shallegh," Morgan said. "That's not worthless. Any evidence that the Laians are provoking this can be used as a lever to force people to back down."

"Doesn't help get the Wendira to back down, though," Rin said. "You need proof of a third party to pull that off. Without anything around Katavan's motives..."

"I know," she admitted. "Hopefully, Tan!Shallegh and some quiet Laian friends can investigate more. We've confirmed he's dirty, but we have no authority to act against him. I'm quite sure the Laians have somebody who can clean up this mess."

"I hope whoever it is has war-dreadnoughts of their own," Murtas said. "Because while only about half of his cruisers were involved in the trips we're talking about, all four of his dreadnoughts have gone out."

"And if they'll follow his orders to start a war, they might fight for him when the Parliament orders his arrest," Rogers agreed. "We need a better plan than poking the bear, sir."

"Right now, what I think we actually need is to know where those other six dreadnought missions actually went," Morgan replied. "Because if he messed with the reports for them, those were also something he was trying to conceal.

"And that means I want to know what it was. Sword Katavan is allowed no secrets, people. Too many of his lies are covering for our damned shadows."

"I can't break into the dreadnought computers," Murtas argued. "I might be able to get deeper into the base's systems, but the risk that they'll ID the source is high."

"Don't touch the military systems," Morgan ordered. "Not first, anyway. Somewhere in this system there has to be a civilian hyper-space anomaly scanner. Find it. Then steal their data—or, hell, *buy* it if we can do it quietly enough.

"That will tell us where those dreadnoughts went, and *that*, my friends, will let us come up with that better plan of Commander Rogers's. Poking the bear only takes us so far, but it's a necessary first step."

Her tablet chimed before anyone could respond to that, and Morgan grinned.

"Ki!Tana is back. Rin, I think you and I should meet with her first. Murtas—make that dig for the civilian data. Ki!Tana might have an answer for the military systems."

If anyone had a fully functioning Mesharom holographic data scanner, it would be Ki!Tana, after all.

KI!TANA arrived in Morgan's office moments after she and Rin did, interrupting an embrace they thought they'd have the time for.

Morgan arched an eyebrow at her stepmother's friend as she gave her lover a slightly harder squeeze and stepped away.

"I see you never learned to knock," she noted.

"I was already invited. I didn't intend to interrupt," the Ki!Tol told her. "I can come back, I suppose?"

"It's fine," Rin said, flushing adorably as he realized they weren't alone.

"Everybody grab a seat," Morgan ordered. "Katavan stinks from our side, Ki!Tana. What did you find?"

"One of his war-dreadnoughts got on the wrong side of a Wendira fighter strike," Ki!Tana said. "They've covered up the blatant damage with radar-reflecting cloth, but that doesn't do much against tachyon scanners.

"I'd guess he's being very careful which ships are allowed out at the refueling-and-refit station right now, until the damage is repaired. And I *know* the Wendira have kicked the personal waters out of at least a few dreadnoughts during the raids."

"We've got a solid idea on the timing of when his ships left," Morgan told her ally. "It lines up with three of the raids, including one of the ones where the Wendira say they crippled a dreadnought."

"They overstated it, I think, but *Harvester of Red* is in rough shape for a ship that isn't supposed to have been in a fight in the last fifty long-cycles," Ki!Tana replied. "I guess we pass that information on to the Republic?"

"We'll put together a report for Fleet Lord Tan!Shallegh," Morgan said. "Whether or not we tell our allies that one of their regional commanders has gone rogue is up to him.

"What *we* need is something that points us to our conspirators or the Alavan fleet, and honestly, I'm not sure we've found anything here that does that," she admitted. "My cyberwarfare team are hesitant to try to crack secured Laian databases."

"Would it help if I handed them a copy of *Harvester*'s databanks?" Ki!Tana asked.

Morgan blinked and eyed the A!Tol as a flash of red humor flickered across her skin.

"You copied their database?" she asked.

"It was offline for repairs, which meant the security protocols were inactive," Ki!Tana said. "Copied everything at a distance. It *will* be incomplete, but the alert programs can't tell anyone what we're doing if we're operating in a virtual environment."

"I leave whether or not that's possible to you and Murtas," Morgan finally said. "Rin, can you help?"

Xenoarcheology involved a lot of very strange computer work, after all.

"Probably," he agreed. "I've built virtual environments like that before. Ki!Tana, shall we go check in with Speaker Murtas and see what the three of us can pull together?"

Ki!Tana flushed red again and snapped her beak in agreement.

"We need answers," she told Morgan. "If nothing else, the database should give us some idea of what the Laian conspirators are saying to each other and their subordinates."

"Get to it," Morgan ordered. "We poked a beehive here and I want it to have been worth it; am I clear?"

CHAPTER TWENTY-FIVE

RIN CHECKED THE SOFTWARE ON THE SETUP ONE MORE TIME. As it turned out, he had significantly more practical experience with building virtual environments for copies of alien databases than Speaker Murtas's cyberwarfare team.

"That should do," he told Murtas. "Can you check the hardware?"

The hardware they were using was outside of his experience, but the code wasn't. The molecular computer cores were a step beyond the delicate spikes of crystal often used in A!Tol computers. These were *Mesharom* cores, for all intents and purposes.

Ki!Tana was familiar with those as well, and she leaned past one of the spacers to tap a connection into place with a long manipulator tentacle.

"We're good here," the old alien told them. "What happens if the security protocols try to slag the hardware, Dr. Dunst?"

"The hardware the security protocols can see doesn't exist, Ki!Tana," Rin told her. "That's the point of the virtual environment. There's a secondary set of security protocols to prevent them from affecting the actual hardware as well, just in case they allowed for that possibility, plus a built-in delay where all code is examined for threats before it's activated."

Rin shrugged.

"It's possible they might be smarter than we all are, in which case they might manage to slag this setup."

"Which is why this is a secured room with a Faraday cage and an independent fire-suppression system," Murtas's senior cybertech reminded them. Lesser Speaker Dorji MacBaird was a dark-skinned officer wearing both eyeshadow and faint stubble.

"Even if the Laians are far better than we anticipate," they continued, "the worst case is we lose this setup itself. That would be expensive, but not insurmountable."

"All right." Rin shook his head as he eyed the glowing cubes of the half-Mesharom, half-A!Tol computer setup. "Let's boot it up and see if your people can crack open the Laians' data."

Murtas tapped a command on the console linked to the cores. A soft humming and a slightly brighter glow on the molycirc cubes announced their initial success.

"Intrusion software online," MacBaird said in a distracted voice as they leaned over their own console. "It helps that we have *some* authorization codes for prodding Laian systems."

"You can stick around if you want, Dr. Dunst, Ki!Tana," Murtas told them. "I warn you, this is not the most exciting process to watch if we do it right."

"Stick around?" Rin asked, grinning at the younger man. "Please, Speaker Murtas, I've done almost as much of this as most of your people. I'm not trained for military hacking, but I've decrypted databases written in languages that have been dead for a thousand years.

"I think I can manage to be helpful."

Ki!Tana clacked her beak in amusement.

"I am somewhat out of date with Laian hardware," she admitted, "but I worked aboard an Exile cruiser for a long time. I think I can still be of some use as well."

"WELL, THAT'S INTERESTING BUT EXPECTED," Murtas said a moment after his tablet chimed.

"Speaker?" Rin asked.

"Katavan is couching it in all kinds of flowery language, but he wants to run Awav around in one of his shuttles," the intelligence officer told him. "Gives him control of the inspector."

"And almost certainly means the envoy doesn't actually set foot on *Harvester of Red*," MacBaird added. "Or if he does, that he doesn't see the damaged parts."

"One of our shuttles would see through the covers that Ki!Tana mentioned, wouldn't they?" Rin asked.

"Fifty-fifty," MacBaird replied. "They don't carry tachyon scanners as a rule. Not every pilot would run their sensors at enough detail to pick out the inconsistencies approaching a theoretically friendly ship."

"I suspect Vichy's people would," Murtas said. "But this way, Katavan avoids that risk. He controls what Awav sees, and, well, technically, all Awav is looking for is whether the ships exist that we were told exist."

"Which we already know," Rin agreed. He looked at his console. "We're making progress here. And I think this might be more useful than Awav's tour."

"Almost certainly now," Murtas agreed. "He has to do it, but his mission doesn't quite align with ours. I worry what will happen if we end up in opposition to his."

"Don't," the archeologist told him. "It's been taken care of."

Murtas gave Rin A Look but sighed and shook his head.

"Sometimes, Dr. Dunst, I feel like you know more about what's going on than you should," he admitted. "And I don't think that it's because you're the Captain's boyfriend."

"I'm here for if we find the Alava, Speaker, which means I'm fully informed on the details of that mission," Rin replied. "I'm hoping we find *some* answers here."

"Well, included in the mail I just got was the data we purchased under the table from the local astronomy society," Murtas told him. "We found a convenient broker willing to ask no questions to buy it. I'm not sure *how* Ki!Tana knew to find that broker."

The A!Tol flickered the blue of curious questioning as she fluttered her tentacles in a shrug.

"My second team is running that data against the official destinations of the dreadnoughts when they went out," Murtas concluded. "We'll have some data there shortly. That will help us know where the dreadnoughts that *didn't* raid Wendira space went."

"Hopefully, you'll find a consistent rendezvous point," Rin suggested. "That would help us locate our third party."

"I'm in," MacBaird snapped. "Not all the way, some of the data files are under a second layer of encryption, but I have mid-level access to the entire database."

"Everybody else hold up and see if you can copy those credentials," Murtas ordered. "Let's not risk breaking it when we're already in."

"Then we hunt," MacBaird said, their tone eager. "What are we looking for, sir?"

"Any details on how *Harvester* got her ass kicked, but also everything she's got recorded about where she's been in the last year, people. She left Salroduk four times. I want to know where she went every time—and I want to know who she met."

Rin was already linking his console to the access credentials MacBaird had created. There was a lot of data to go through...but if there was one thing a research academic knew better than anyone else, it was how to find the valuable bits in a lot of data.

"THOSE SEALED files are going to stay sealed," MacBaird admitted later. "I don't want to push harder against their security in a copy of the database we've otherwise opened up. They have some nasty countermeasures, code that I think might well be able to slag the setup despite our security measures."

"We may need to take that risk," Rin told them, looking at the others in the room. "We've gone through the rest of the database. We *know* where *Harvester* went initially, but that's not as useful as we hoped."

"It's not useless," Ki!Tana said. "We can presume she was rendezvousing with our mystery fleet, which means we have more data points to track their course across the Dead Zone and surrounding space. The more places we know they've *been*, the easier it is to guess where they're going."

"That's true," Rin admitted. "And I imagine your team will find all sorts of useful data in here, but I'm not seeing any answers to the job before us today."

"Those rendezvous points are useful," Murtas agreed. "And, yeah, there's a lot of useful data in here. We now have fuller specifications on our allies' dreadnoughts than they ever gave us, for example."

"And these files prove that Katavan was provoking the Wendira," MacBaird said. "We can take another copy of this database and keep working on the sealed files, but we're talking days of work, not hours, to crack those."

"We've got what we're getting for today, sir, Dr. Dunst."

"And it's better than nothing," Rin replied. "More useful in some ways than what Envoy Awav has learned for us today, I'm sure."

"So, what do we do now?" Murtas asked.

"That's Captain Casimir's job," Rin said. "But I'm guessing we head to another one of the systems Ki!Tana flagged and try and steal ourselves another database. The more data points we can build on our shadow fleet, the better off we are—and who knows, maybe the commander at the next system will be less careful with their data!"

CHAPTER TWENTY-SIX

"So, how transparent do you think the Sword was being, Envoy Awav?" Morgan asked as the Ivida poked diffidently at the carefully spiralized UP on his plate. Her steward was *trying*, but there was only so much they could do with the tofu-like food and a collection of vitamin powders for Ivida.

"He was very transparent, I think," Awav noted. "He was very careful what waters he allowed us to see into, though. In the waves he wished us to see, he showed more than I expected. Elsewhere, though..."

"That's my impression as well," Morgan agreed. "I found his responses to some of my questions fascinating."

"And I'm sure your people have happily poked away in a dozen ways I do not want to know anything about," the envoy confirmed.

At Morgan's right hand, Rin was suddenly very fascinated with his spaghetti. She knew the man well at this point, though, and didn't think Awav picked up on it.

Not that it would matter. The only reason Awav didn't know what was going on was because he didn't want to. He and Morgan clearly agreed that he was better off not knowing.

"Are you done here, then?" Morgan asked.

"I am," he confirmed. "If we can wait half a cycle for my team to finish drafting their report and transmit it back to Fleet Lord Tan!Shallegh, that would be optimal, but I have completed my review. The defenses at Salroduk are basically what we were told they were."

Double-jointed arms swung up in a vague shrug.

"Are they sufficient if war comes to the system? I do not know, but that is not my task to judge," he admitted. "I am here to confirm our allies' words. We trust, but we must verify."

"And mostly, they seem to accept that," Morgan said. "We will move on to our next destination once your people have sent their report in."

Hyperfold communicators didn't work in hyperspace. *Defiance* could not transmit or receive interstellar communications while she was in FTL. Larger ships could carry starcom receivers, which could at least receive messages, but *Defiance* was too small and too packed full of other systems to carry one of those.

"And where is our next destination?" Awav asked. "A random one, as per the plan, or one tied to your other mission?"

"Both," Morgan replied with a grin. "If we keep poking at our targets, we get even more suspicious to everybody *and* some questions will start to get asked as to how we know as much as we do.

"That will draw attention we don't want, both to ourselves and to our agents in the region."

No one had told Morgan that Ki!Tana hadn't been working alone, but she was a starship commander. She could see the pattern in the data that Ki!Tana had given her and *knew* there was no way that Ki!Tana had gathered all of the information on her own with one ship, however capable *Dark Eyes* was.

There were other "associates" of Ki!Ron's organization scattered through the region, Laian and Wendira alike. Probably other semi-neutrals from the other Core Powers as well. A thousand eyes, many of them supposedly looking in different directions, had provided the data that was feeding Morgan's operation.

She owed it to those anonymous agents to minimize their risk. Even if she and they didn't know each other directly, responsibility flowed both ways.

"We are heading to the Kasad System," she told Awav. "One of the dig sites Professor Dunst is supposed to visit is there, as is one of the bases you are supposed to review. While it isn't on the direct route to the next location flagged for my main mission, it is closer than Salroduk.

"Our goal is to at least *appear* to be following a random pattern to support your inspections," she concluded. "While working through the intelligence we have."

There was a vague pattern in the data that Rin and Murtas had acquired, too, though not one she was willing to rely on yet. Either way, though, she appeared to be heading for the Astoroko Nebula.

"I do not wish to know more," Awav reminded her. "So long as we continue to visit the systems on my list, I am content to provide a cover for your operations while completing my mission. If we visit systems that are not on my list, I do not know how much assistance I can provide.

"I will, of course, assist as best I can."

"Your cooperation is appreciated, Envoy," Morgan told him. Since Awav was officially the reason for *Defiance* being there, he could cause her a lot of headaches if he decided to be troublesome.

"I look forward to what the Laians want me to look at in Kasad," Rin said. "The dig at Tohrohsail was more fascinating than I expected. I was expecting to see post-Fall ruins, not potential Alavan experiments."

"We know so little of the time period before the Fall," Awav noted. "I envy you your focus, Professor, and your knowledge of that deep past. My own studies have been of far more recent history."

"We each have our own skills and focuses," Rin noted. "I could not negotiate with a Laian fleet commander to inspect his forces or command a starship. But I believe I'd do a far better job organizing an archeological dig than either of you."

"Of course," the Ivida agreed. He eyed the UP on his plate and then scooped a large portion of it into his mouth with a sound that didn't quite mirror a human sigh.

"If you have suggestions for my steward on the food, Envoy, I think they'd be delighted," Morgan told him. "I think they're feeling guilty with how little they can do for you."

"This suffices," Awav said. "I have been fed far worse things by cooks limited to Universal Protein. As have we all, I suspect!"

AFTER DINNER, Rin remained in Morgan's quarters and dropped himself on the couch. He looked even more thoughtful than usual to her as she sat next to him.

"What is it, Rin?" she asked.

"This whole situation is making me...nervous, I guess," he admitted. "The last time we were flailing around in the dark, we found a thing that ate *stars*."

"Well, you tell me," Morgan said. "How many of those do you think the Alava built?"

"A year ago, I'd have said none," he pointed out. "I'm not sure now. I understood the Alava to be utterly hostile to the concept of biotech, especially on that scale, and now I feel like we overestimated just how accurate the Mesharom's impression of their old masters was."

"We always knew we were running off an archive that was the memories of a few well-informed Mesharom on what their masters were up to," Morgan agreed. "We should have questioned its completeness and accuracy before this, but..."

"But it was the *Mesharom*," Rin said. "The Old Wyrms, the First Elders. Nobody questioned them."

"And truthfully, I question their destruction and restriction of

Alavan tech even less now," Morgan admitted. "The more I learn about the Precursors, the more I find myself wishing they'd done a better job of wiping themselves out!"

"I have spent my life studying them and I can't argue with that conclusion," her lover admitted. "And then there's people's reactions to what they left behind. Tens of thousands have already died in these provocations, haven't they?"

"At least that," Morgan agreed. She suspected the official reports from both sides were downplaying their losses. The deaths were probably up into the hundreds of thousands, if not more.

"And all to make it *easier* for someone to find this graveyard of Alavan ships without being caught." Rin shook his head. "It's grotesque to me, Morgan. I'm no soldier."

"I am a soldier," she said flatly, "and it's *still* fucking grotesque."

He paused, silent for several seconds.

"I'm sorry; I didn't mean to imply it would mean less to you," he said. "I don't know what I meant, really. I'm sorry."

"I know." She was still stiff, but as Rin leaned back against her, she relaxed slightly, wrapping an arm around his shoulders. "It's a nightmare, my love, the exact kind of thing I joined the Militia and the Navy to stop. The people who are dying may not be human or Imperials, but they're still *people*. Some of them soldiers, some of them civilians, but none of them should be facing this fucking nightmare."

"So, we stop these bastards?"

"We stop them," Morgan confirmed. "We find this damn Alavan fleet and we make damn sure it never haunts anyone else—and then we make damn sure this group of conspirators gets ripped apart by their own governments.

"The more we know about them, the better the Republic and the Hive can wipe them out once we drag them into the open." She smiled coldly. "Sword Katavan doesn't know it yet, but he's already fucked. I've sent enough to Tan!Shallegh for the Laian Parliament to nail him to a wall for treason."

"Good." Rin shivered in her arms. "Someone has to pay for this."

"A lot of people are going to pay for this," she promised. "And if we can manage it—and I think we can get a good chunk of the way—we're going to get every last one of the bastards who set this in motion to pay for it.

"I *am* a soldier," she echoed, "and that means I will *never* stand by while someone tries to get *other people* into a war for their own profit!"

CHAPTER TWENTY-SEVEN

DEFIANCE WAS BARELY A TENTH-CYCLE, TWO HOURS AND twenty minutes, out of Salroduk before Morgan knew they weren't alone.

"Two new hyperspace anomaly contacts behind us," Nguyen reported. "They either just left Salroduk or were waiting next to the system with their interface drives down." The tactical officer shrugged. "We're too far away to detect portals, but we can see their movement."

Morgan nodded silently as the two contacts, flashing orange for unknown, appeared on her screens. They were one point four light-hours behind *Defiance* in hyperspace, which meant they were several light-weeks behind in realspace.

Plus or minus a significant percentage. Hyperspace and realspace didn't correlate at anything resembling a consistent ratio. It was usually mappable, but even those maps only had estimates at best, and the flight time between any two systems could change by as much as fifty percent depending on the conditions.

Hyperspace was also hard to see through. The anomaly of a moving ship could be detected at a significant distance, but false positives were common and localizing the anomaly was difficult. Morgan's father had used anomaly scanners to realize humanity was far from alone in the galaxy, mapping hundreds of hyperspace flight paths with sensors in Sol, but chasing someone with them was a risky game unless you knew their destination.

"Are they pursuing?" Morgan asked. Katavan didn't know where she was going next, but he could guess what the most *dangerous* course for him was. If she was heading toward the Astoroko Nebula, then those two ships would be able to follow her.

"Yes, sir," Nguyen confirmed. "Estimate velocity at point six two to point six three light speed."

Seventy hours to intercept, then. The realspace intercept location would be hard to predict, but a point oh two *c* velocity advantage would close up the gap in seventy hours if Morgan did nothing.

They'd be in interface-missile range well before then, but targeting would suffer the same issues as pursuit magnified tenfold. It was only in the last light-second or so that hyperspace really became clear to most scanners.

Beyond that, they could detect the anomaly of each other's interface drives and fire missiles at those. *Assuming* these two ships were hostile.

"Any idea on mass?" Morgan asked, even though she knew the answer.

"Nothing, sir," Nguyen admitted. "From the velocity, I'd *guess* we're looking at a pair of Laian cruisers rather than war-dreadnoughts or frigates, but that's the most likely scenario no matter what."

"Understood."

Morgan eyed the flashing orange icons for a few more seconds.

"Maintain course, El-Amin," she ordered the navigator. "Nguyen, let's bring the ship to Status Three. I don't think we need to go higher yet, but let's keep our eyes open."

Status Three didn't change the number of staff on duty at any of *Defiance*'s stations. It did charge the cruiser's weapon capacitors, refresh the ready magazines, and bring targeting sensors online.

Almost as importantly, it was Morgan giving any officer of the watch authorization to *use* those weapons in *Defiance*'s defense without waiting for the Captain's permission. Even if it came to a fight, it wouldn't be one for several days yet.

There was no reason for her to remain on the bridge for the next seventy hours.

THE NEXT TWO days passed much as Morgan had expected. The two probably-Laian cruisers slowly gained on *Defiance*, spreading their courses wide enough to make sure at least one continued to pursue the Imperial cruiser no matter what tricks she pulled.

"Interface missile range in one twentieth-cycle," Nguyen reported. "Thirty thousandth-cycles after that to minimum range."

Morgan nodded her acknowledgement. Seventy minutes to range, then forty-three to point-blank range.

She could outrun the Laian ships for a while if she chose to. *Defiance* had a sprint mode that could bring her up to point seven *c*, but she couldn't sustain it for more than twelve hours. That was all the engines could take of that pace—and more than that was actively dangerous for her crew, too.

Radiation and gravity tides were *not* kind to living beings, even if Imperial technology meant they could survive it.

"Murtas, what does intelligence say about a Laian equivalent to our sprint mode?" she asked her intelligence officer.

"We're not certain," the younger man admitted. "Estimates are sixty-forty in favor of them having the same point seven sprint we have, though. Imperial physicists tell us that anything higher than that is basically suicide for a living crew."

Which didn't stop Wendira starfighters from hitting point eight *c*, almost as fast as the missiles in everyone's magazines. Of course, Wendira starfighters were flown by drones, a rapidly maturing and sterile subcaste with a life expectancy of only about twenty long-cycles to begin with.

"So, if we run, they can probably keep up with us," Morgan muttered.

"I also have to remind you, sir, that we know the Laians have stealth fields that work in hyperspace," her intelligence officer said. "Those are the two ships we can *see*."

Morgan hadn't quite forgotten about that, but she hadn't been considering it, either.

"Thank you, Speaker," she told him. "I'm correct in presuming post-processing won't help us in hyperspace?"

"You are, sir," Murtas admitted. "Not unless they're inside the one-light-second bubble, where…"

"We'd see them anyway," Morgan finished. She studied the icons behind her for a few more seconds, then shook her head and flipped open a covered button on the arm of her command seat.

"Battle stations," she said aloud as the button opened an all-hands channel and started alarms blaring through the hull. "All hands to battle stations; this is not a drill."

Her repeater screens lit up with readiness indicators for every department on the ship as Morgan considered her pursuers. Even in hyperspace, Morgan figured she could take one Laian cruiser. They outmassed her by two-thirds but she had faith in her crew.

In regular space, she was reasonably sure she could take both so long as she could set the range. Her hyperspace missiles vastly outranged anything the Laians had, and her tachyon scanners would give her real-time targeting data over a good chunk of that range.

Even one more stealthed cruiser, though…

"We can't fight them in hyperspace," she concluded. "El-Amin!"

The navigator was still crossing the bridge, tightening his head-scarf as he headed to his duty station.

"Sir!"

"Prepare for hyperspace exit," she ordered. "If these people want a fight, they can have it on *my* terms."

"Yes, sir!" El-Amin confirmed, dropping into his chair. "Translation in ten minutes?"

"Make it five," Morgan replied. "Let's see what they do."

"PORTAL...NOW."

Exotic-matter emitters flared to life with El-Amin's words, carving a hole in reality half a million kilometers ahead of the cruiser. At sixty percent of lightspeed, *Defiance* flashed through that hole seconds later and closed it behind her, dropping back into realspace light-years away from any star system.

"El-Amin, get me a fix on our location and get us moving from our emergence point," Morgan ordered. "Nguyen, see if you can lock in our friends on the anomaly scanner, and get the HSM batteries online. Keep the internal portals off for now, but get the capacitors charged."

"On it," her two officers chorused and Morgan studied her screens.

Her pursuers probably wouldn't be able to detect the miniature portals for her HSM launchers, but leaving them off would hopefully keep them invisible from hyperspace. She could see *into* hyperspace with her anomaly scanners, but they couldn't see out.

That gave her the advantage.

"I have them," Nguyen reported. "Pseudovelocity estimate two thousand *c*. One light-week away."

Anomaly scanners were even *more* inaccurate across the barrier than they were when both sides were in hyperspace, but they could see FTL ships coming.

"ETA five minutes."

"Let's see what you do, shall we?" Morgan murmured. "Stand by all batteries."

Back in realspace, she had her hyperspace missiles and her hyperfold cannons. Her opponents would have hyperfold guns of their own, but she'd make that trade.

"Sword and Buckler deployed and online," Nguyen said. "Shields are up and at full power. We are ready to engage."

Morgan nodded her receipt of Nguyen's report and waited in silence as the minutes counted by.

"New anomaly!" Nguyen suddenly snapped. "I have a third contact on the anomaly scanner, heading for rendezvous with the first two."

"At our zero-distance point?" Morgan guessed.

"Hard to say, sir," the tactical officer confirmed. "Their stealth field is less effective against us here, but their signature is extremely diffuse. I'd say its possible, at least."

Morgan inhaled softly, watching the icons sweep toward her command. El-Amin had them moving away from their emergence point, every second adding hundreds of thousands of kilometers to the zone their enemies would expect them in.

Five minutes. There was no hyper portal.

"Contacts have passed our emergence point," Nguyen reported. "Pseudovelocity is shifting but I think that's hyperspatial density. They are continuing on course."

"Interesting," Morgan murmured. "Maintain battle stations and keep a close eye on them."

She wondered what her counterparts were thinking. The three ships were heading to a rendezvous at about the point where they would have caught up to *Defiance*. She knew they could find her, they'd known exactly where she'd emerged and the light-minutes of space she'd bought weren't enough to escape.

They *were* enough that she could all but guarantee they'd have to close through her hyperspace missile range before they reached their own range. Laian stealth fields were decent in hyperspace, but the Imperium's tachyon scanners could penetrate them well outside sublight missile range.

"Anomalies have rendezvoused...and all of them are now under stealth fields," Nguyen reported grimly. "Contacts are now uncertain but...they appear to be continuing on their way, using the stealth fields to conceal their course from us."

"Someone doesn't want to play with HSMs, I think," Morgan said aloud. "All right. Scaring them off is actually the best result, people," she told her bridge crew. "We'll give them half a cycle to get well out of range, and then we'll continue on our way."

She forced a wide grin.

"We still have work to do, and I don't plan to be scared out of it by a handful of cruisers who appear to be *terrified* of *me*."

CHAPTER TWENTY-EIGHT

THE REST OF THE TRIP TO KASAD PASSED WITHOUT FURTHER incident, though there were enough blips on the anomaly scanners for Morgan to be grimly certain *Defiance* was still being hunted. Her ghosts never came close enough to register as solid contacts, though, which meant all she could do was be paranoid.

A feeling not helped by their arrival in the Kasad System. Unlike Tohrohsail or Salroduk, Kasad was in the Dead Zone. The star itself was a blue giant bright enough that the bridge screens automatically dimmed, even at almost twenty light-minutes' distance.

Around and beyond it, though, the sky was noticeably empty. The Dead Zone had died long enough before that not even ghost light reached this system now. Some dwarfs and giants remained of the nearby stars, but every star that should have supported life on one side of the star system was gone.

Morgan shivered and focused her attention on the star system in front of her. Like Tohrohsail, there were no habitable planets and the Laian base was anchored on a gas giant. Here, there were no super-Jovian planets, though.

Instead, Kasad's two gas giants were trapped in a massive binary planetary system. Both of the planets were about the size of Sol's Neptune, and they orbited a common point halfway between them even as they orbited the blue giant in turn.

Moons and ice comets littered the space around the Kasad Pair, a dozen of them host to extraction facilities that produced fuel for the Laian defensive and scout fleets.

"We have clearance to Kasad Base Prime," Nystrom reported. "They've provided a detailed course, Commander El-Amin, and strongly recommend following it. They have the debris fields mapped and...unless I miss my guess, they also have the debris field mined."

Mines were only so useful in space, but in an environment like this with only a handful of easy paths, laying antimatter bombs made some sense. Morgan might not have included them in the base's defenses herself, but she could see the value.

"Envoy Awav, what are we expecting here?" she asked. The diplomat had joined her on the bridge, taking one of the observer chairs to allow him to study their scan data as they approached.

"Fueling station, two war-dreadnoughts, twenty cruisers," the Ivida reeled off instantly. "Like Salroduk, fueling capacity is listed at one hundred million cubic meters per cycle."

"And you expect..." Morgan asked.

"Salroduk was about ninety million in truth," Awav told her. "I expect Kasad to be closer to one fifty. I'm not sure why they gave us the average—it might have been an oversight; the waters of their data have been transparent enough so far."

"Seems possible, if not likely," she said. "What's the plan for your side?"

"I will make contact with the Seventy-Eighth Sword as we approach the base, and clear the waters for our meeting. Will you wish to attend again?"

"I may as well," Morgan told him. "Let's not do anything different without a reason."

"Of course, Captain," Awav agreed with a bowed head. "Do we know what ruins your partner is scheduled to look at?"

Morgan chuckled.

"Dr. Dunst doesn't know what ruins he's looking at in any given system," she admitted. "They want an unbiased perspective, apparently, so they're not telling him anything in advance."

"I see the waters," the envoy said. "I shall continue to review the scan data for a few more thousandth-cycles and then make contact with the base. I appreciate your assistance as always, Captain Casimir."

Morgan waved him off. They both knew that Awav was providing more help for *her* mission than she was for *his*, after all.

THE SHUTTLE FLIGHT over to the war-dreadnought *Dreamer of Liberty* was awe-inspiring. Morgan had seen dozens of gas giants in her life, but the Kasad Pair was something else entirely. The gas giants were close enough that they were occasionally flaring jets of gas at each other, and any comet that flew between them was torn to pieces by the tidal forces.

The Laian base was carefully positioned to orbit the Pair's center of gravity at the same distance as the Pair themselves, while the cloudscoops extracting hydrogen from the two gas giants were all mobile enough to avoid being pulled into the middle.

Dreamer of Liberty and *Deliverer of Glory* orbited even farther out, between two of the double-centered rings wrapped around the Pair, and a host of icy comets flickered around them as their shuttle made the approach.

"It's pretty," she finally said aloud.

"It's certainly impressive," Awav agreed. "I'm not certain it was wise to put a base here, though."

"The Pair have swept up basically every piece of significant mass in the system," Morgan pointed out. "It makes for easy extraction, even if it also makes them easy to find. I wouldn't want to try and fight my way in here, either. My targeting data would be garbage."

Hyperspace missiles would be useless against a base and a fleet concealed in the Pair's planetary system. Few places in space were *this* densely crowded.

"I'm surprised that the Seventy-Eighth Sword invited us onto his ship, though," she told Awav. "I was expecting to head aboard the base, as we did at Salroduk."

"So was I," Awav admitted. "I am not certain if these are promising waters or not, but it seems that Seventy-Eighth Sword Lodovoch has, perhaps, less to hide than Sword Katavan."

"Though it may also be as simple as the Seventy-Eighth Sword is a ship captain who also has authority over a base, where the Twenty-Third Sword was solely a base commander," Morgan suggested. "She is that much more junior of an officer, after all."

"Perhaps," Awav agreed. "We shall learn soon enough. We are here."

AS WITH THE base in Salroduk, a formal line of power-armored Laian soldiers awaited them as they stepped onto *Dreamer of Liberty*'s decks. The Laian officers waiting for them were dressed almost identically, though Lodovoch was much smaller than Katavan.

Where Katavan had been a solid, if attractive to human eyes, bronze color, Lodovoch was a glittering creature of blues and red that shone in the lights of her ship's shuttle bay. She approached and bowed to the two Imperial representatives.

"Welcome aboard *Dreamer of Liberty*, Envoy Awav, Captain Casimir," she said. "I am Lodovoch, the Seventy-Eighth Sword of the Republic. I have, of course, been advised of your mission."

"Then you have a good idea of my needs," Awav told her. "I will need full data on your fueling, defenses, warships and recent excursions."

"Recent excursions?" Lodovoch asked slowly.

"Yes," Morgan confirmed. "We are parties to a defensive treaty with the Republic, Sword Lodovoch. The Wendira claim that the Republic has been attacking their facilities and ships and is provoking the conflict we all fear. If that is true, then the Imperium may not be bound by the terms of the treaty.

"We are obliged by our duties to our own citizens and soldiers to make absolutely certain that this is not the case."

Morgan knew Laian body language, but she found Lodovoch hard to read. The Laian was very good at concealing her emotions, which was fascinating—not least in that she was very clearly doing so.

"Of course, of course," the Sword finally allowed. "May I give you a tour of my vessel as I have my staff work on preparing that data for you? I also understand that you have a Past-Seeker on board who will be visiting the investigation sites?"

"We do, though I leave that part of our mission to him," Morgan said.

"I will make certain my staff enable Past-Seeker Lodokan to make contact," Lodovoch told her. "The Past-Seeker is my clan-mate. He may...forget if he is not reminded."

Morgan swallowed a chuckle. Certain stereotypes of professors, it seemed, were universal.

CHAPTER TWENTY-NINE

The tour of the vessel was *FASCINATING*. Morgan had skipped the tour of the dreadnoughts in Salroduk, leaving that to Awav, but she'd also received the impression that the tour Awav had received had been abbreviated and highly controlled.

Lodovoch, on the other hand, was delighted to show off her ship. Some aspects were classified and she couldn't, for example, show them the shield generators or hyperfold cannons, but she seemed upfront enough.

That made Morgan mentally pass over the first set of open panels and teams clearly working on repairs. The second time they moved swiftly past a section of the ship where teams of the big insectoids were fixing broken conduits, she started to get suspicious.

It was the smell that finally convinced her, though. They stopped outside a set of secured blast doors, and Morgan could pick up the actinic smell of welders...but under that, she smelled the distinctive scent of vaporized metal.

And, unless she was wrong, the oddly pepperish smell of burnt Laian shell. She'd only smelled that twice in her life before, but it wasn't something she was likely to forget.

"Through here is our primary starboard hyperfold cannon array," Lodovoch told them, gesturing at the door. "Obviously, I won't be showing them to you, so we can continue on to—"

"What happened to this ship?" Morgan interrupted. "Sword Lodovoch, we've passed multiple places where your crew are carrying out repairs, and from here I can smell the signs of a breach in the hull...and death.

"I didn't think this ship had gone anywhere, let alone been in a fight."

The base commander's stiff body language grew stiffer for several seconds, and then her upper arms collapsed inward in distress. It only lasted moments before her formality returned, but Morgan caught it and held her gaze on the Laian's multifaceted eyes.

"I think, Captain Casimir, that this is a conversation we should have in private," she finally told Morgan and Awav. "Your earlier comments..." She chittered, a softly distressed noise.

"I believe I now have an answer to a question that had bothered me," she concluded. "That answer may be relevant to you. Let us speak of these winds and sands in private."

"Of course, Sword of the Republic," Awav said formally. "We are at your disposal."

DESPITE THE DIFFERENCE in species and culture and everything else, Sword Lodovoch's office looked very familiar to Morgan. It was close to the bridge, it had viewscreens that showed the outside of the ship, it had a single large desk and multiple chairs...

Warships tended toward function over form and so tended to congregate toward particular forms. Swap out the artwork for something in human-visible wavelengths and adjust the chairs for four-limbed humanoids instead of six-limbed insectoids, and the room could have dropped into *Defiance* without a ripple.

Lodovoch gestured them to seats in front of her desk as she took a seat behind it. Someone had brought in chairs that worked for humans and Ivida while they were touring the ship, and Morgan was surprised by how comfortable they were.

The Sword was silent for a minute or so as the Imperials waited. Finally, she chittered her mandibles in a soft sigh.

"As Captain Casimir presumed, *Dreamer of Liberty* saw action eleven Laian days ago," she said calmly. "We fought a meeting engagement with a Wendira star hive and six star shields that ended with both primary capital ships being forced to withdraw with material but repairable damage."

That was roughly one hundred eighty-seven hours earlier. Even if a formal report had been filed, Morgan wouldn't have heard about it yet.

"That's not a small battle group to clash with," Morgan noted. A star shield was equivalent to somewhere between an Imperial battleship and a superbattleship, a ten- to fifteen-megaton warship intended to escort the hundred-megaton star hive fighter carriers. "I take it they weren't here?"

"No," Lodovoch said. "We met them in the Dead Zone. I received intelligence that a Wendira battle group was operating in the Dead Zone, attempting to scout our positions or even attack if they saw a weak point.

"I took *Dreamer of Liberty* and her escorts out to chase them off," the Laian officer continued. "We arrived at the system we expected to find them and it was empty, so I was prepared to write it off as bad intel—and then the Wendira group *did* arrive."

Morgan concealed a shiver. If the Wendira had been told the same thing as the Laian commander, she could see how that had ended...

"We chased each other around the star system for a day or so," Lodovoch told them. "They were acting aggressively...but reconsidering the sands of time, so was I. We were both attempting to intimidate each other into fleeing."

"What happened?" Morgan asked.

"I opened fire," the Laian officer said bluntly. "That may count as provoking this war, Captain, I do not know. Honor demands honesty. I took their maneuvers for an attack on my ships and opened fire in what I regarded as self-defense.

"The engagement lasted less than an hour before we both withdrew. Once we had sufficient distance, they opened a hyper portal and retreated. We did the same. The system we fought in was valueless."

"And the answer to your question, Sword Lodovoch?"

"It seemed strange to me that our intelligence was so perfect," the Laian officer said grimly. "We arrived at the perfect time to find ourselves in a clash with a Wendira squadron that I now realize wasn't truly looking for a fight.

"I look at the sands that passed and I see a pattern, one that suggests that the Wendira were there for much the same reason I was —and they saw in me the threat I saw in them. I have asked questions, Captain Casimir, and I have failed to find any other source of that intelligence."

"Surely, your intelligence sources are classified," Awav asked.

"They are," Lodovoch agreed. "But when all I see says there was no confirmation, then I question what happened. What I did not see was a reason for any deception, so I was left with merely shifting ground beneath my feet.

"Until today."

"Sword?" Morgan said.

"If we are seen to provoke this war, will the Imperium abandon us?" Lodovoch asked.

"It depends on the circumstances," Awav told her. "But the treaties bind the Imperium to help *defend* the Republic, not support you in offensive wars. If the Empress believes you have deceived us, then she may well withdraw the Grand Fleet.

"The Kanzi civil war remains a concern, after all."

Awav even managed to say that with a straight face. Morgan was impressed. The general impression *she* had was that the High

Warlord and First Priestess of the Kanzi Theocracy were intentionally drawing out the civil war at this point, using it as an excuse to implement a program of social reform.

Normally, Morgan would find that distasteful...but on the other hand, the Kanzi leadership was trying to abolish slavery. Some ends justify some means, she supposed.

"I do not know the source of the intelligence that led to that battle, but I fear that my Wendira counterpart was as deceived as I was," Lodovoch told them. "We were intentionally put into a situation where both of us could report to our superiors that we were attacked.

"That has...disturbing suggestions, and yet..."

"And yet it fits neatly, doesn't it?" Morgan asked. "I appreciate your honesty, Sword Lodovoch. It will be reflected in my report to the Fleet Lord."

Lodovoch inclined her head.

"I do not know what answers you draw from this, Captain Casimir," she admitted. "I hope they are useful. My task here is to be the forward post of the Republic *without* provoking the Wendira. I now fear that I have failed at that."

"If you have, other currents were at play," Awav told her. "I would ask that you provide a detailed report on the battle that we can give the Fleet Lord. Our duty, above all else, is to avoid a war if possible."

"I will give you that," Lodovoch told them. "I have more selfish reasons than most to avoid any conflict with the Wendira." She chittered in bitter amusement. "These sands would see the first bloodshed of any grand conflict—and the blood would be of the Laians under my command. We are the farthest outpost of the Republic, after all."

And while a war-dreadnought could fight a star hive one-on-one with ease, even with the starfighters and the escorts, two war-dreadnoughts couldn't stop a *fleet*.

CHAPTER THIRTY

"Past-Seeker Rindunst, I apologize for the delay," the dull-colored Laian on the screen told Rin, slurring the archeologist's name together even with the translator.

"It is all right, Past-Seeker Lodokan," Rin replied with a chuckle. "We did arrive unexpectedly. The disadvantages of using a warship for transport. Does your work here progress?"

"It progresses, it progresses," Lodokan agreed. "We have not yet proceeded to actual digs, so I do not know how much of value we can provide to each other."

"I don't think I'm expected to provide world-shaking insight at every one of your dig sites, Past-Seeker Lodokan," Rin told the other scientist. "But your superiors didn't tell me much of anything about what I was looking at here. If you fill me in, I may be able to provide some small value."

"I have read your papers, Past-Seeker Rindunst," Lodokan told him. "Your insight on Those Who Came Before is impressive. Our own work here is far less galaxy-shaking in every way, but it has its purposes."

Rin blinked in surprise. He hadn't expected to encounter anyone in the Republic who was familiar with his work, let alone able to recognize that his focus was on the Alava.

"Every investigation into the past is intended to provide insight into the present or the future," he said slowly. "Very little of my work has shaken the galaxy, as you say. My trip here to the Republic is as much a sabbatical as a favor to your government on the part of my Institute."

"Of course, of course," Lodokan agreed. "Now. What do you know about the Kasad Pair and Moon Four?"

"I know the Kasad Pair is two gas giants of approximately fifty-thousand-kilometer diameters orbiting a shared center of gravity," Rin said. "My understanding is that they have, between them, twenty-six planetoids large enough to be considered moons.

"That's about it," he admitted.

"All right," Lodokan said with a mandible-clacking laugh. "The most important thing to realize, then, is that the Kasad Pair is just outside the liquid-water zone of Kasad. Given the additional reflected energy from the Pair themselves, the innermost half-dozen moons have liquid water and atmospheres. What does that imply to you?"

"That there's a xenoarcheology team here suggests that there is life," Rin noted. "That there is no colony here suggests that the ecosystems and planetoids in question are not particularly stable."

"Correct twice," Lodokan agreed. "Moons Two, Four and Six have all independently evolved complex life. Flora and fauna. The other three with atmospheres have minimally complex ecosystems, entirely microbial.

"Moon *Four*, however, we believe supported a late-industrial-age society before suffering a system stability collapse."

"A system stability collapse?" Rin asked.

"None of the theoretically life-supporting moons are far enough out from the Pair to completely avoid the tidal forces, debris fields or even the material flares from the gas giants," the Laian told him. "We believe that approximately twenty thousand A!Tol long-cycles ago, a jet of heated material impacted the Pair-ward hemisphere of Moon Four.

"While the overall ecosystem recovered, most of the high-complexity life died off. Flora and small fauna survived. The moon is currently extremely vegetation-dense, in recovery mode from the system collapse.

"The fauna will rapidly evolve to compensate and rebalance the system, but that takes somewhat more time than Moon Four has had."

Rin nodded his understanding. Moon Four had suffered an equivalent to Earth's dinosaur-killer ten thousand years earlier. The plants had survived and exploded, but most of the large land fauna was gone.

Including any intelligent species.

"But there were settlement sites?" he asked.

"Scans suggest dozens of metropolises of significant scale," Lodokan confirmed. "There are likely hundreds we are missing, where there wasn't enough concrete and metal to be detectable from orbit.

"A thousand thousand Past-Seekers could sink entire lifetimes into this world, Past-Seeker Rindunst. There are cities and continents and libraries and..." Lodokan ran out of breath. "We don't even know where to begin, I must admit."

"We have over thirty different potential sites. Without more information, we're basically picking at random."

"That's not the worst way to start," Rin said with a chuckle. "As you say, you need more information. Do we even know what they looked like?"

"Not yet," Lodokan admitted. "All of the sites are buried under vegetation, Rindunst. It will take vast effort to reach even one. The cost...must be justified, I am afraid."

"Beyond the knowledge gained, what justification is needed?" Rin asked. "Even if all you learn is how a world dies..."

He shivered.

"Even that can be worth something, sometimes," he murmured.

"I agree, but the work must be paid for. So, my superiors dither over which site to work at, and I sit in orbit and run a thousand thousand scans," Lodokan said. "I would be delighted to send you my data, Rindunst, but I fear you will not gain more than I did."

"I'll take a look anyway," Rin promised. "I'm here for a day or two no matter what; I may as well take the time."

LODOKAN HAD, if anything, been understating the scope of Moon Four's inhabitation. Several of the metropolises the Laians had identified were *megalopolises*, sprawling cities covering hundreds of square kilometers of what was now jungle.

Skyscrapers provided anchors for trees and vines to reach dozens of stories into the sky, creating an interwoven net of vegetation that made details even harder to identify than they would have been otherwise.

Without even knowing anything about the people who'd lived on the moon, Rin could envisage them a bit. What he could see of the cities looked closer to Earth's mid-twentieth century than a lot of non-Terran cities or dig sites he'd seen.

If that estimate was right... He checked for something and smiled as he saw something that Lodokan hadn't done.

Leaning back in the workshop chair, he opened the link he had to *Defiance*'s scanners.

"Commander Nguyen, can I beg a favor?" he asked the tactical officer. "I need to redirect one of our main passive arrays at one of the moons."

"Why?" Nguyen asked after a moment, it clearly taking her a second just to realize who was talking.

"I'm helping out the local archeologists, but I want a radiation scan, and I think our passive arrays might be better than the civilian sensors he's got," Rin told her.

"Well, it's not like I'm doing anything else with the sensors right now," the officer chuckled. "All right, Dr. Dunst. Which moon?"

"Moon Four," he told her. "If I can get a full scan of the surface over the next few hours?"

"We'll forward it once we've got it," Nguyen confirmed. "You've got access to that data?"

"I do. Thank you, Commander. I appreciate it."

"If you know what you're looking for, I can get my team to take a gander," she suggested. "It might be a good exercise."

Rin exhaled, looking at the data and then shaking his head.

"How's your team at finding nuclear power?" he asked. "I think any impact sites are probably long-eroded, but if someone was running a heavy-water fission plant, for example, we should still be able to pick it up ten thousand years after it went offline, right?"

"Probably," she agreed. She paused thoughtfully for a moment. "It depends on their safety measures, I suppose. Should still be detectable either way."

"I can give you a few places to start," Rin offered.

"Hold onto those for now," Nguyen told him, her voice wicked. "I want to see how my sensor techs do with 'find a ten-thousand-year-old nuke plant on a moon two-thirds the size of Earth' before we start giving them *clues*."

"PAST-SEEKER RINDUNST!" Lodokan greeted him as the com channel opened. "How can I assist you?"

"It turns out, Past-Seeker Lodokan, that I actually can assist *you*," Rin said. "I was looking at the scans of the ruins, and they reminded me of a particular part of my own people's past. I talked to the tactical officer of my ship, and she handed the question to her team as an exercise."

"What question, Rindunst?"

"Did you know that Moon Four's natives had fission power plants?" Rin asked.

The Laian froze. "They had what?" he finally said.

"We've confirmed the presence of eleven fission-pile nuclear plants at various locations," Rin told him. "Various types and we think we found the signs where a couple were decommissioned. But...in terms of your question of where to dig *first*, one of their megacities had four of the nuclear power plants in a grid around a particular location.

"When we checked that location out, it appears to have a buried fission plant that was operational well after the rest failed. I would guess an emergency bunker of some kind...which would be a good place to start, wouldn't it?"

Lodokan chittered in laughter.

"It would, Past-Seeker Rindunst. Our scans showed some radiation but not enough for me to consider the possibility of nuclear power plants or using one to locate a concealed facility."

"That last was one of our junior techs," Rin admitted. "I think they impressed their boss with that one."

"They impressed me with that one, though I doubt it matters," Lodokan told him. "That gives me something to pass on to my superiors. We might not start digging soon, but I'll make sure we tell you what we find."

He paused.

"Assuming we get to dig, I suppose."

"Why wouldn't you?" Rin asked.

"I'm not blind, Past-Seeker Rindunst," Lodokan said. "I can see the sands of war blowing in my direction. I hope what we have learned is not forgotten when fire burns through these stars once more!"

CHAPTER THIRTY-ONE

"THE PROBLEM WE NOW FACE IS THAT EVERYTHING WE HAVE provided to Fleet Lord Tan!Shallegh has implicated the Laians," Ki!Tana told Morgan and Rin as the three gathered in Morgan's office.

Defiance vibrated around them, the cruiser on her way out of the Kasad System toward her next destination.

"I know," Morgan conceded. "We have ten cycles left before Tan!Shallegh is supposed to leave for the peace summit. It should only take him five to reach the system they're meeting in.

"That means if we don't get him proof of a *two-sided* conspiracy in fifteen cycles, he may well have no choice but to cut the Laians off," she concluded. "If we can only provide evidence that the Laians are provoking this, the Imperium can't get involved."

"And if the Wendira and Laians fight each other without Imperial involvement, it will be another long, bloody mess," Ki!Tana told them. "They're very evenly matched."

Morgan grimaced. The A!Tol Imperium was still far short of the technology or numbers necessary to fight either of the two powers involved. They *did* have enough technology to make them match up ton-for-ton with either side, which meant the Grand Fleet could tip the balance.

Without the Grand Fleet, well. There was a reason the Wendira and the Laians had fought six wars over the last two thousand long-cycles and were *still* glaring at each other over the same stretch of dead stars. Industrially, economically, technologically...the two Core Powers were a near-even match for each other.

"Every location we've plugged into the model draws a tighter net," Rin told her. He sounded tired. He'd been helping Murtas and Ki!Tana model the apparent path of the survey fleet they were trying to find, but the mystery fleet had been everywhere.

"And that net seems to be drawing in on the Astoroko Nebula. I'd guess they're hunting clues and data based on information we don't have, but if they're narrowing the search pattern..." He shrugged his shoulders. "They're narrowing it in on the nebula, and the nebula makes sense as somewhere a fleet could have gone unnoticed for fifty thousand years."

"So does deep space," Morgan replied.

"Alavan jump technology would never have left them in deep space. It was instantaneous, or near-enough," Ki!Tana reminded her. "They would have been *somewhere*. A fueling station, a base, a colony...somewhere."

"The Mesharom knew where every fueling station in the Dead Zone was," Morgan countered. "So, they weren't at one of those. Which means they were somewhere else, chasing an unknown enemy into an unknown location. We don't know the parameters of their operations, which means we have no way to predict where they went."

"But our conspirators clearly *do* know more," Rin said. "We need to pin somebody fully in their loop down and ask them a bunch of questions."

"What about cracking open *Harvester*'s files?" Morgan asked. "Most of what Katavan knew should have been in those, right?"

"Murtas and his team are working on it," Rin admitted. "But the encrypted files are actively designed to resist exactly what we're doing. We've slagged a virtual machine with a copy of those files once already."

Morgan sighed. At least with the Mesharom data technology they were using, they could circumvent the copy protection on those files. Accessing them was an entirely different story.

"So, we head for the Tomarot System," she told them. "That's the plan anyway. If they put ships in for the attack on Ritchit, *somebody* there knows more than they're telling.

"If we have to go back to our Laian *associates* for authority to start arresting Laian officers, it's going to draw eyes...but even if I agree with their goals, I'm far more concerned about stopping this war than protecting this damn conspiracy."

"We're all secondary enough to it that I don't think anyone expects differently," Rin agreed. "We need those answers—and we'll get them, love."

"I think even Ki!Ron will understand if we risk exposure to stop a war," Ki!Tana said. "A trillion sentient beings died when the Dead Zone was created. I will sacrifice much to prevent that happening again."

"The answers are out here," Morgan said. "So, we find the bastard who has them and we beat the answers out of him. Not a great plan...just the only plan I've got."

ANY PLAN INVOLVING *ACQUIRING* potential people to beat answers out of was going to need *Defiance*'s Marines, which found Morgan in the training gym of Marine country an hour later. She stopped just inside the door as she saw Pierre Vichy standing in the middle of the padded sparring area, wearing knee-length shorts and a tight tank top.

While Rin's dramatically softer exterior was generally more to her taste, she had to admit that her Marine CO definitely made for an attractive sight. Enough of one that it took her a moment to realize there were four *other* Marines in the sparring area, two men and two women, wearing similar clothing.

"And...go!" someone announced.

The four junior Marines moved as one. To Morgan's half-trained eye, they were probably part of the same unit. They had trained together and had a clear situational awareness of each other's positions and movements.

To her, the Marines closed on their CO like a pack of pouncing wolves, grace and brutality combined into a speedy attack that could only end one way. Vichy didn't even start moving until the Marines reached him.

A moment later, two Marines who were fractions of a second faster than the others were on the ground, wrapped around each other in an awkward pretzel. A third was sliding across the padded floor, the momentum of their attack converted into the momentum of their exit, and the last was on the ground, one arm behind her back and the other pinned under Vichy's knee.

The dojo was silent, and then the original announcer—who Morgan now recognized as Defiance-Bravo Company Commander Oghenekaro Hunter—chuckled loudly, the Black man eyeing the wreckage.

"I think you can let Lance Robbin up, sir," Hunter told Vichy.

The young Marine NCO popped back up the moment her boss released her, rubbing her arm as the rest of her fire team slowly got back to their feet.

"What *was* that, sir?" she asked.

"The reason you train in more than one martial art, mes amis," Vichy replied. "Aikido is a purely defensive art, but having it to fall back on when a collection of Krav Maga–trained grunts come at you is handy."

"Sir, yes, sir!" the Marines chorused.

"Hunter, I see the Captain is looking for me," the Battalion

Commander continued. "Can you walk them through some basic Aikido fundamentals? It might come in handy."

He walked over to Morgan, clearly not having even worked up a sweat.

"How can I help you, Captain?"

"Do you need to hit the showers?" she asked. "I need to ask you some hopefully hypothetical questions."

"I'm fine, though I could probably do with a change. My office, sir?"

———

MORGAN WAS GOING over the latest assessments from Ki!Tana when Vichy stepped into his office. He was back in uniform, the tight-fitting shipsuit only slightly less flattering than the shorts and tank top, and took his seat behind his desk.

"I and *Defiance*'s Marines are at your disposal, mon capitaine," he told her. "How may we serve?"

"I assume you've been paying attention to your Laian counter-parts as we've been bouncing across their space?" she asked.

"Yes, sir," he confirmed. "We've only had a few exercises with them along the way, but they've let me observe some of their training, and I have some decent files on their equipment from the information Murtas is going through."

"Your opinion, Battalion Commander?"

"C'est très bien," Vichy said. "Their training is good; their equip-ment is better. Their armor is better than ours, their plasma rifles are better than ours. Trooper for trooper, they're more than a match for us, and they're better at team coordination than most Imperial races.

"I suspect we'd have an edge on the battlefield because we're better at individual initiative, but it would be a thin edge indeed."

"What, no spiel about how Imperial Marines are better than anyone else in the galaxy?" Morgan asked.

"I am not American, Captain," Vichy reminded her. "My job is to give you an accurate assessment of what my people can do. I would have no hesitation going into combat with Laian ground troops in support or at my side. Why?"

"You've seen the naval bases we've visited and their security measures," Morgan said. "If I ordered you to take the commander of one of those bases prisoner, would you be able to?"

Vichy was silent for a surprisingly long time, looking past Morgan to the decorative antique weapons on his office wall.

"No," he finally said flatly. "The diplomatic and political consequences of such an action are outside the scope of the question, though they're enough to terrify me, but even within *my* scope...no.

"I have a half-battalion of Marines, all human. With the best gear the Imperium has to offer, I still would not trust my stealth shuttles to permit a subtle boarding operation on a Laian military base.

"Even assuming that we somehow managed to succeed in *boarding* the station in the first place, my people would be outnumbered and outgunned. While I do not truly believe we would be out*classed*, even the most surgical of operations would face far more resistance than we would be able to overcome."

He shook his head.

"Je suis désolé, mon capitaine," he concluded. "But it cannot be done with the resources available to us. I could see, maybe, a joint operation using *Defiance*'s weapons to secure sections of the facility we were assaulting, but...that would require *Defiance* to have complete control of the space around the Laian base."

"Which, given these bases support war-dreadnoughts, is unlikely," Morgan agreed. "Damn."

"Were you expecting a different answer?"

"No, but I was hoping," she admitted. "We're coming up short on the intelligence front, Vichy. We're going to need prisoners to interrogate, prisoners we know are in the loop on this damn conspiracy.

"Right now, I have enough evidence to get the Imperium out of a war between the Wendira and the Laians—and not enough evidence to prove that a third party is trying to start one."

"Are we sure there is a third party?" Vichy asked. "This could be Laian agents using links into the Imperium to play a game of many layers."

"I..." Morgan shook her head. "I trust the people in the Imperium who briefed me on this, Vichy," she said. She couldn't tell him about Ki!Ron or the fact that the Empress clearly knew about all of it, but she could tell him that.

"Then I will sit down with my officers and present them with an impossible scenario," Vichy told her with a smile. "It will be good training for them to consider how to extract a base commander from a facility held by a Core Power. Even if we don't have to do it this time, then—"

An alert on Morgan's communicator interrupted him.

"Captain Casimir to the bridge, Captain Casimir to the bridge," Nguyen's voice rang out from the device in Morgan's hip pocket. "We have hyperspace contacts."

Morgan was still grabbing for the communicator when alert icons flashed up on the screens around them.

Nguyen had called the ship to Status One on her own initiative. It wasn't battle stations...but it was only one step below it.

CHAPTER THIRTY-TWO

MORGAN HAD BARELY REACHED THE ACCESS HATCH TO THE bridge when the warning icons on consoles vanished—replaced a moment later by the initial "wake 'em all up" klaxon of the battle stations alert.

She charged onto the bridge in time to hear Nguyen verbally announce what had made that decision.

"Hostiles have opened fire. Unknown number of interface-drive missiles incoming." The tactical officer looked over at the door and spotted Morgan with a visible sense of relief.

"Brief me," Morgan snapped, crossing the bridge at a brisk-but-not-hurried pace.

"Three anomaly contacts picked up at twenty light-seconds," Nguyen told her. "Contacts were still vague until they opened fire; I believe they're running stealth fields. We adjusted course to evade them, but..."

"That told them they'd been detected, and they opened fire," Morgan concluded. "Sword and Buckler?"

"Deploying. One hundred seconds to impact."

Defiance was now fleeing in front of the missiles, but the weapons had twenty-five percent of lightspeed on her. The ships that had launched them were the same as before, closing at point six two.

"Commander El-Amin, evasive maneuvers," Morgan said calmly as the navigator took his own seat. Icons on her repeater screens continued to flip to green as officers and crew reported to their stations. "Commander Rogers, get the CIC team on those scanners. I know distinguishing missile signatures isn't easy in this environment, but it's *critical* we know how many missiles are coming at us."

"Sir," the XO replied crisply.

There were three major anomalies on screen. Each had launched its own cluster of munitions, too close together to be resolved yet.

Morgan's visibility bubble was expanding toward them, too, as the Buckler drones spun outward from her ship. Two light-seconds of space to engage in wasn't much...but it was still twice as much as one light-second.

"Commander Nguyen." Morgan calmly turned back to her tactical officer. "Return fire. Pick one target, hit them with everything we've got."

Twenty-four new icons appeared on the screen moments later as *Defiance's* own missile launchers spoke. The cruiser's sublight weapons were a secondary system now, though, with her twelve hyperspace missile launchers acting as her true main battery.

A main battery she couldn't use there.

"They've got us at a disadvantage here, sir," Nguyen reminded her.

"I know. I want numbers on those missiles," Morgan said. "Hold your target and *keep firing.*"

"Impact in thirty seconds," Rogers's voice interjected calmly. "Estimated one hundred eighty missiles incoming, sixty per bandit."

"Understood," Morgan confirmed. "I mark the targets as Laian escort cruisers; do you confirm?"

"We're calling it ninety-plus percent here, sir," the XO replied. "Twenty seconds to impact. Bucklers engaging...now."

"El-Amin?" Morgan said.

"Engaging sprint mode," the navigator confirmed. "Buying the Bucklers time."

Relative velocity got ugly at these kinds of speeds. The interface drive negated the *time*-dilation effect of their speeds but not the other effects. An extra ten percent of lightspeed took the engagement time from four seconds to five and a half.

That second and a half could make all the difference.

Defiance had eight Buckler drones out in the direction of the incoming fire, but the drones relied on tachyon scanners and hyper-fold cannons almost as much as their mothership did. Their plasma and laser systems were effective enough...but they weren't *as* effective.

Almost a hundred missiles got through, and Morgan barely kept her concern off her face as her shield strength indicators flashed from green to orange in a single strike.

"Push the Bucklers out farther," she ordered calmly. "Maintain sprint velocity."

"Hostiles have also increased velocity to point seven *c*," Nguyen reported. "They aren't gaining on us, but they're holding the range at nineteen light-seconds."

Five point seven million kilometers. Well outside the range of *Defiance's* hyperspace-capable energy weapons. And their own missiles, well...

"It's hard to be sure, sir," Nguyen said quietly, "but I think they got all of our missiles. No impacts confirmed; I repeat, *zero* impacts confirmed."

"The good news is that they can't see much better than we can," Morgan replied, watching the second salvo of Laian missiles charge in. "Or communicate, for that matter."

Whatever happened out there, no one was ever going to know. Morgan and her crew would just...vanish.

It happened, after all. Hyperspace was only *mostly* safe. It wasn't common for ships to go missing, but it happened. There wasn't even a point in searching, not when a ship without an interface drive was only visible in the last few hundred thousand kilometers.

A ship without an interface drive was only visible in the last few hundred thousand kilometers.

A cold and evil smile spread across Morgan's face.

"All right, everyone," she snapped. "We can't fight three escort cruisers in hyperspace. They're down a chunk of their firepower, but we're down almost *all* of ours. But what they *can't* do is see any better in this mess than we can!

"El-Amin, when I give the order, you kill the drive."

"Sir, I..."

"Did this become a democracy while I wasn't looking?" Morgan snapped, her gaze locked on the timer for the incoming second salvo. Twenty seconds. "When I give the word, you throw the drive into emergency shutdown."

Fifteen seconds.

"Yes, sir!"

"Nguyen, when I give that command, send the Bucklers into autonomous mode."

"Yes, sir!" the tactical officer replied.

Ten seconds.

"What do I do, sir?" Rogers asked from CIC.

"Tell me we're going to survive this next salvo," Morgan said, looking at the shield-strength indicators. They'd cooled from orange to yellow, but that might well not be enough.

"Stand by," she continued.

Five seconds. The Bucklers opened fire; lasers and plasma hammered into the incoming missiles.

Three seconds. The Sword turrets joined the chaos. They had the missiles' number now, but the Laian missiles had incredible ECM, leaving *Defiance*'s scanners and computers barely able to resolve their locations normally let alone in the radiation soup that was hyperspace.

Impact.

"Shields are *down!*" Nguyen snapped. "Multiple hits on the armor; we have breaches. I repeat, *we have breaches.*"

"El-Amin, *now!*" Morgan barked.

The entire ship lurched as the emergency shutdown protocol kicked in. Normally, it took the same six seconds to shut the drive down as it did to boot it up. Emergency shutdown took all of the kinetic energy and vented it to space.

Most of it.

Lights flickered across the bridge and warning icons flared across Morgan's repeater displays—but a massive pulse of energy filled space around them, overwhelming the feeble attempts of the shield generators to come back online.

Silence.

"Status report," Morgan ordered.

"Damage control is on their way to multiple breaches in the CM armor," Trifonov said quietly, the logistics officer acting as Engineering's voice on the bridge. "Microbot substrate appears to have sealed the atmosphere loss, but we have multiple displaced plates."

Morgan nodded silently.

Defiance's final defense was a layer of armor made of hypercompressed matter, almost immovable and unbreachable. To be able to build a ship of it, though, it had to be done in plates, and the connections of those plates were vulnerable when hit by hammers traveling at eighty-five percent of the speed of light.

Those plates were suspended on a substrate made of compressed-matter-laced-microbots that absorbed impacts and moved to fill in breaches. The combination wasn't invulnerable, but it was actually tougher than the Laian equivalent.

"Seventeen direct hits," Nguyen reported quietly. "We've lost the entire Alpha-Five battery, sir. We're down four interface-missile launchers."

"I have only two questions, Commander Nguyen," Morgan replied. "What are the bastards doing...and do I still have my plasma lances?"

DEFIANCE HAD MOVED FAR ENOUGH AWAY from her last location that the next missile salvo missed her entirely, though many of the robotic minds aboard the weapons selected the Bucklers as acceptable secondary targets. The defensive drones were gone after that, leaving nothing to show where the cruiser was on the Laian scanners.

Hyperspace anomaly scanners were, thankfully, entirely passive. Morgan's ship wasn't doing *anything* that could be detected—but they could watch the three Laian ships.

The enemy let the two salvos they'd already launched fly through where *Defiance* had been before they made up their mind to do anything. They'd slowed to a halt fifteen light-seconds away while they presumably discussed their plans.

"They could just leave," Morgan muttered. "I'd take that, too."

Despite everything, both of *Defiance*'s wingtip plasma lances were intact. Their range was badly degraded in hyperspace, unfortunately. The Laian ships had stopped *inside* the normal-space range of the big near-lightspeed weapons.

"Enemy is back up to speed and heading our way," Nguyen reported as if she hadn't heard her Captain. She probably hadn't. "Velocity fifty percent of lightspeed."

"Dial them in as they close," Morgan ordered. "Plasma lances on one and two, missiles on three." She considered for a moment, then tapped a command key.

"Vichy, are your shuttles scrambled?"

"Yes," the Battalion Commander said instantly. "My Marines are in dam-con positions though. Your orders?"

"Get your people on your shuttles. I may have found an easier target for the mission we discussed."

Several seconds of silence followed.

"On it," Vichy finally said.

"Range is six light-seconds and dropping," Nguyen reported.

"Bandits have cut velocity to one-quarter light. They're spreading out to maximize their search, but I'm guessing they have a pattern in mind."

"Target Three is going to pass within our visibility bubble," Rogers said from CIC. "Twenty seconds from...now."

"Understood. Targeting orders remain," Morgan replied. "Shields?"

"Back up. Integrity is only at forty percent," Trifonov warned. "We can't take more than one serious salvo from their proton beams."

"I'm just glad the Laians decided the plasma lance was obsolete," Morgan said.

The Imperium had developed the technology based on samples and expertise provided by the Laian Exiles, upgrading it over time with their own expertise and then useful parts of the Mesharom Archive.

The main Laian Republic Fleet had discarded the plasma lance a century earlier in favor of their own version of the hyperfold cannon.

"Five seconds to visibility bubble," Nguyen said softly. "All targets in range and locked in via anomaly scanners."

Morgan exhaled, studying the three crimson dots.

"Fire at will, Commander Nguyen," she ordered.

Seconds passed in the blink of an eye, and icons flashed on Morgan's screen.

The plasma lances were near-lightspeed weapons. The two cruisers Nguyen had targeted with those beams never knew what had hit them before the magnetic channels had locked on and a dozen tons of superheated plasma had smashed into them.

Shields and armor alike vanished beneath the deadly stream of power that punched deep into the escort cruiser's hulls. *Defiance* only managed to hold the beams on-target for a second at most...but it was enough.

Both cruisers vanished from the anomaly scanners as engines and power plants failed, the ships almost certainly coming apart in the gray nothingness of hyperspace.

The third ship had time to realize she was under attack, but that was it. She shot down one of the twenty-four missiles Nguyen had fired, the other twenty-three hammering into her at point-blank range. A second salvo arrived moments latter, smashing into shields already wavering under the impacts.

The escort cruiser returned fire, her proton beams lashing across *Defiance*'s shields, but her own shields collapsed as Nguyen's third salvo struck.

"Vichy."

Morgan didn't even need to tell her Marine CO what the order was. A flock of assault shuttles blasted clear of *Defiance*, crossing the distance between the two ships in fractionally more time than the missiles, and stabbed into her sides like immense angry mosquitos.

"Hail them," Morgan ordered.

"Laian vessel, this is the A!Tol Imperial cruiser *Defiance*," she barked. "Your weapons have been crippled and my Marines are boarding your vessel. Surrender now and we can avoid further loss of life on both sides.

"Do not, and my Marines will take your ship by storm. We both know how ugly that will get. I don't know why you attacked my ship...but I am *going* to find out."

There was no response and Morgan grimly linked up the software that would show her Vichy's tactical displays on his repeater screens. The escort cruiser's compressed-matter armor was resisting the heavy plasma drills mounted on the assault shuttles' noses—but it was exactly what those drills were designed to break through.

"Shuttle four, pause the drill and send another nanite pulse," Vichy's voice ordered calmly, the repeater screen echoing it into Morgan's earbud. "You haven't weakened the armor enough yet, and it's costing you time we can't spare."

Looking at shuttle four's reports, even Morgan could see the problem. The assault shuttle was a full two centimeters behind the other spacecraft.

Four of the other shuttles broke through simultaneously, the plasma drills opening four-meter-wide holes in the warship's armor and clearing the path for the Marines to move forward.

"No resistance yet," one of the squad NCO's reported. "Establishing beachhead, standing by for contact."

"Sir!" Nystrom said, catching Morgan's attention. "We have an incoming transmission."

"Captain Casimir, this is Seven Thousand Five Hundred and Twenty-Third Sword of the Republic Kolotak," a translated voice told Morgan. "I have eyes on your Marines and I can see the sands of what will come to pass.

"I offer the surrender of my ship and crew on the condition that you guarantee our lives."

General galactic law would proclaim the Sword's actions piracy or terrorism, Morgan knew. Given the Republic's desperate need for the Imperium's assistance against the Wendira, the Laians might well turn a blind eye if Morgan summarily executed the cruiser's officers. She could certainly *justify* it under the standard "laws of open space."

On the other hand, she *really* needed answers from them.

"Am I on?" she asked Nystrom.

"On your order, sir."

Morgan made a go-ahead gesture and faced a recorder.

"Sword Kolotak, I will guarantee the lives of your people so long as you are in my custody," she promised. "I will also promise that if you cooperate fully and completely with our questions and investigation of this attack, you will be turned over to the Republic to face trial under Laian law with that evidence.

"If that is not sufficient, well..."

Kolotak's image reappeared as Morgan was speaking, Nystrom clearly setting up a live channel. He visibly winced at her demand for full cooperation but bowed his armored head.

"I accept your terms, Captain Casimir," he told her. "To spare the lives of the officers and crew under my command, I fully accept your terms and will provide what answers I can to your questions."

"Good," Morgan told him. "Have your crew and defenders lay down their arms and make contact with my Marines. They will be waiting for you."

"That will not be difficult," Kolotak admitted. "My Blades of the Republic refused to raise arms against the Republic's allies once they understood the situation."

His mandibles snapped in bitter amusement.

"You see, Captain Casimir, my own people leave me no choice but to accept your generous terms."

CHAPTER THIRTY-THREE

"I HAVE UNE NOUVELLE AMIE FOR YOU TO MEET, MON capitaine," Pierre Vichy told Morgan as he stepped out of the assault shuttle. A moment later, the smaller figure of a female Laian followed him, clad in unpowered body armor with an empty weapon harness.

"This is Spear of the Republic Amoko," Vichy continued, "the senior Blade officer aboard the Republic cruiser *Eternal Fall*."

Amoko clasped her upper arms to her chest and bowed.

"Captain Casimir, I hope that I speak for the entire Republic when I present our apologies for what has happened here," she told Morgan swiftly. "I was informed we were engaging an unknown pirate vessel, not an allied warship. I do not know where the deception began, though I must assume that Sword Kolotak was aware of the truth."

"I appreciate your apologies, Spear, but this remains an act of war on the part of the Laian Republic," Morgan reminded Amoko. "We were ambushed and attacked by *three* cruisers of the Republic Navy."

"I know," Amoko said quietly, her words in untranslated Laian that Morgan's own systems interpreted. Either the Blade hadn't been wearing a translator or Vichy had confiscated it. "And all I can say,

Captain Casimir, is that I do not believe the majority of the crews knew who we were fighting or that the ship commanders acted without proper authority.

"I will gladly provide your people with everything I have access to that could help resolve this betrayal," she continued. "If there is anything within my power that may assist in salvaging the relationship between our nations, it will be done."

Morgan nodded, though she had to swallow down a moment of feeling truly sick. Amoko was probably correct. Most likely, the crews of the three cruisers had had no idea what was going on...and with the standard complement of a Laian escort cruiser, she'd just killed over two thousand people who were effectively innocent.

"Sword Kolotak, I suppose, is my main concern," Morgan said grimly. "Where is he?"

"He remains aboard *Eternal Fall*, under guard by my Marines," Vichy told her, his translator turned off so Amoko couldn't follow him. "I felt it wise to divide our Blade prisoners between the two vessels. Spear Amoko appears to be telling the truth, but minimizing our immediate risks seemed sensible."

"Agreed. Well done, Battalion Commander," Morgan replied. "Is *Eternal Fall* secure?"

"She is," Vichy confirmed. "We have control of all armories and weapons, as well as Engineering and the bridge. Our tech teams aren't quite up to operating her, but she is no threat to anyone right now."

"And her damage?"

Defiance had thrown over seventy missiles into the cruiser at point-blank range, after all.

"Considérable," Vichy said calmly. "She can still fly, but I wouldn't want to take her into a fight."

"So long as she isn't going to explode on the people we have aboard, I'm happy," Morgan replied. She turned back to their prisoner.

"Spear Amoko, I will take you up on your offer of assistance," she told the Laian. "We have a lot of work to do, but I'm hoping that *Eternal Fall's* officers may provide some answers I've been looking for."

"I don't know what you seek, Captain, but I am at your disposal. This...mess is of my people's creation. I must do all I can to resolve it."

VICHY LOOKED MORE than a bit confused by the group debriefing him in Morgan's office later that day. He, Rogers and Morgan were the only actual officers in the room, with Rin and Ki!Tana both being inarguably civilians.

He took it in stride after a moment, especially after Rin passed him a large mug of steaming coffee.

"It's a mess," he told them bluntly, his accent suddenly fainter than usual. "Most of the junior officers, noncoms and enlisted are on much the same page as Spear Amoko; that was one of the reasons I brought her aboard.

"They didn't know what was going on and were falling over themselves to be helpful once they realized they'd attacked an Imperial warship. Most of them are furious at us for killing their friends, but they also realize that we were under attack."

"They left us no choice," Morgan said grimly. "I'll grieve their dead with them, but I won't regret what I had to do."

"Once the story leaks, a lot of people are going to be *very* impressed," her First Sword added, Rogers grinning. "One Imperial cruiser versus three Core Power ships? That's not a fight we should have won."

"In many ways, I'd have preferred it if they had retreated," Morgan told Rogers. "That they came in to finish the job tells me they *really* want us to stop asking questions, even risking their own operational security to take us out."

"I didn't think we'd really put together enough to be a threat," Rin admitted. "The patterns we were seeing were sending us in the right direction, but we had a long way to go. I guess the question is who on that ship *does* know anything."

"The captain at least," Vichy suggested. "The entire bridge crew is completely clammed up. We're not even getting names and serial numbers out of them. There's enough other officers and noncoms doing the same in the rest of the crew for me to buy that they could pull off attacking us without pushback."

"But those people aren't talking to us, are they?" Morgan asked.

"No." Vichy shook his head. "Murtas's teams are going aboard now to see what they can pull out of the computers. We've got a few sets of high-level access codes, thanks to Spear Amoko and others, but I suspect we'll run into barriers those can't get through."

"I have an answer for all of that," Ki!Tana said, the big A!Tol speaking for the first time. "Bring me Sword Kolotak."

"Ki!Tana?" Morgan asked carefully. "I cannot hand over a military prisoner to you. Not without a damn good reason."

"Then don't; I just need to interrogate him. I can do so with full supervision from your crew if you prefer," Ki!Tana told her. "One of the things the Exiles developed is a highly effective truth serum to use on their kindred.

"Like most such things, it's far from perfect, but it will definitely open the mouths of those determined to remain silent," the old alien told them. "They *will* answer your questions, Captain Casimir."

Morgan exhaled, considering.

"I don't like it," she admitted. "We're not supposed to use chemical interrogation without critical need. There are serious risks for all of them." She grimaced. "We're not pirates, Ki!Tana."

The Laian Exiles on Earth were double exiles. Their ancestors had fled the Republic after losing the civil war there, and then they had left the main Exile base, a mobile space station humanity had nicknamed Tortuga for its role in the Imperium and Theocracy's criminal underworlds.

"If we don't find this conspiracy, we are looking at a war that might kill billions," Ki!Tana pointed out. "We can have doctors on tentacle to make certain we do not hurt Sword Kolotak...but we need these answers, Morgan."

She concealed a shiver. Ki!Tana didn't use her first name much, though the old Ki!Tol definitely knew her well enough to justify it.

"Interstellar convention frowns on chemical interrogation except to avoid immediate threat to life," she repeated, then sighed again. "But I think this has to count. Vichy?"

"I'll have Sword Kolotak brought over," the Marine confirmed. He shook his head. "I'd really like to be able to prove to *Eternal Fall*'s crew that they were being used. Those people deserve some truth."

"Then let's hope Sword Kolotak has some to share," Morgan concluded. She shook her head. "If we're going to do this, let's do it."

CHAPTER THIRTY-FOUR

KOLOTAK WAS ESCORTED INTO THE INTERROGATION ROOM BY four of Vichy's Marines, the humans looming over the normally taller Laian in their heavy power armor.

He'd been stripped of anything resembling a weapon, leaving him in a plain tunic that covered his carapaced torso with only a handful of insignia that Morgan wasn't entirely familiar with. Medals, presumably, as the one insignia she *could* read was the two-centimeter-long gold sword pinned to the center of the tunic's collar.

"Sit," she instructed as the Marines stopped the Laian officer across from her. The room was larger than many interrogation chambers, since they'd need to fit Ki!Tana and a medical team in there, but the basic structure was standard: one metal table and two metal chairs, all fixed to the floor.

There was a one-way window along one wall where several other key members of Morgan's team would be observing, and cameras were rolling in each corner. The use of chemical interrogation was borderline enough that she was going to do it as aboveboard as physically possible.

For several seconds, Kolotak seemed to consider ignoring the order. Finally, though, he took a seat in the chair. It was designed for Laian physiques and shouldn't have been any more uncomfortable for him than Morgan's was for her.

Of course, the Marines manacled Kolotak to the chair a moment later, which probably changed the comfort level. With a nod, Morgan dismissed them and turned her attention back to the prisoner.

"From our conversation around your surrender, you realize that you are not, technically, a prisoner of war," she reminded him. "You are arguably a pirate or a terrorist. While I have not yet made contact with your government, I can't imagine they're going to validate and support your actions. Do you?"

Kolotak shook his head.

"You also promised that you would answer my questions," she continued. "So far, you have been surprisingly uncommunicative with my officers for someone who made that promise. So, Sword Kolotak, are you going to answer my questions?"

The room was silent, the quiet extending for long seconds before the Laian bowed his head.

"I will answer what I can," he finally conceded.

"That was not the deal," Morgan told him. "While I am now sufficiently certain that you lied to your crew to keep most of them safe, you remain in a legal status where my authority to summarily execute you is arguable...but very definitely real."

The Laian met her gaze levelly. Morgan could read the fear in his body language, but there was determination, too. This could get very messy.

"What do you want to know?" Kolotak asked.

"Someone sent three Laian cruisers to attack me," she told him. "I want to know who and why."

He stared back at her.

"Well?" she asked.

"I can't answer those questions," he told her.

"Fine, for now," Morgan said with a cold smile. "Then I want to know if you are directly or merely indirectly in contact with the organization arranging provocations on both sides of the Laian-Wendira border."

That struck home. Kolotak recovered quickly, but he had jerked as though struck when Morgan asked her question.

"I am not aware of any such organization," he finally said.

"All right, then do you know where that organization is basing the fleet they are using this mess as a cover for, or what operations that fleet is engaged in?" She held his gaze, staring harshly into the other captain's multifaceted eyes.

"If I don't know of the organization, what would I know of this fleet?" Kolotak demanded.

"Well, you were lying before, so I figured I'd ask," Morgan told him, still smiling coldly. "If you refuse to keep your word, Sword Kolotak, then the deal we made starts to look very fragile. Worse, I need those answers, Sword.

"You can give them to me freely, as you promised, or I can find other ways to extract them from you or your computers."

The room was silent for a long time as she held the other captain's gaze, but Kolotak finally clicked his mandibles in forced derision.

"I do not know what delusions you have been fostering," he told her. "Our ships were hunting pirates and mistook you for one, an error hardly defused by your opening fire."

"I see." Morgan studied the Laian for several more seconds. "You realize, of course, Sword Kolotak, that both your ship's records and my own show that your ships fired first? And, for that matter, that the files provided by the Republic show that *Eternal Fall* is supposed to be on the far side of Laian space?"

Kolotak shook his head in silence.

"Sword, there is an easy way out of this, and it is to tell me the truth," Morgan told him. "If you continue on this path, you possibly put the lives of millions or even billions at risk. Help me."

The room was silent again and Morgan sighed.

"Bring in the medical team and Ki!Tana," she ordered aloud. "I tried."

Ki!Tana led the way in, and Kolotak stared at the big Ki!Tol in dismay—almost ignoring the team of medics until they started swabbing his arm with a Laian disinfectant.

"What is this?" he demanded.

"It happens that my associate here spent a great deal of time with the Laian Exiles," Morgan told him. "It appears the Ascendancy's survivors followed a rather different path with regards to chemical science than the Republic's did. It does open some options."

"I am a prisoner of war; I have rights!" Kolotak snapped.

"You are a rogue officer taken in the act of an unauthorized attack in time of peace between our nations," Morgan replied. "I have grounds to believe that you are aware of an operation of critical danger to the Laian Republic. If you answer my questions, this will not be necessary."

Ki!Tana produced a small refrigerated case and passed it over to the doctor.

"Point zero three milligrams per kilogram of the subject's mass should suffice," she noted aloud.

The doctor nodded and began carefully filling a hypodermic.

Kolotak stared at it in fear for several long seconds, then exhaled in a horrific buzzing noise of distress Morgan had never heard from a Laian before as he seemed to sink into himself.

"We were told you were asking too many questions, that the plan was in danger," he gasped out before the needle ever reached him. "They judged that eliminating you would be to our overall benefit. My ship was sent to rendezvous with two vessels deployed from Salroduk to make sure you didn't complete your voyage."

"Who were *they*?" Morgan asked.

"A group of wealthy individuals in the Republic, executives and politicians. My core orders came down official channels, but most of the details were unofficial and came with large amounts of money."

Kolotak's gaze was fixated on the needle in the doctor's hand.

"Were these individuals conspiring with the Wendira?" Morgan said quietly.

"I don't know," he admitted. "I... Maybe. I know when I rendezvoused with our main control here, there were Wendira units present as well. I don't know what they're doing," he insisted before Morgan could ask, "but they have a mobile dockyard and several capital ships that shouldn't be here.

"I took...I took that as proof we were following real orders. Only the real Navy could have one of those ships."

Morgan had seen several of the mobile yards at Tohrohsail. Mobile and hyperspace-capable, they were designed to provide repairs to anything up to and including war-dreadnoughts without pulling them back from the front. The entire Republic only had thirteen of the ships, though. She could see Kolotak's point.

"Do you know where they are?" Morgan asked.

The Laian officer deflated.

"I know where they will be, yes," he admitted. "Just...don't drug me. I don't know what's in that...and I have critical medication allergies. Potentially *fatal* ones."

That explained the panic, at least. It would have made Morgan feel bad...except that the man in the chair across from her had just admitted to taking money to help start a war.

"How much of *the plan* did you know?" she asked.

"They were doing something here that they needed to be covered up, and my superiors felt that the alliance with the Imperium was enough to finally tip the balance against the Hive," Kolotak told them. "We were to start a war, make it look like the Wendira started it, and finally crush the bastards into the sands of forever."

"All right, Sword Kolotak," Morgan said, waving the medical team aside for the moment. "I'll need you to tell me where to find that dockyard and that fleet—and then I'll need you to give a formal recorded statement of the details of what you've just told me that we can send your fleet command.

"There won't be a war, Sword, especially not one where you feed the Imperial Fleet into the grinder for the Republic!"

CHAPTER THIRTY-FIVE

It was more than just Morgan's office now, and she'd gathered more than the key *associates* for this briefing. They had something solid to go on, and she waited for the last of her senior officers to grab coffee as Rin fiddled with a display at the head of the conference room.

"All right, people," she told them. "What was a vaguely supported and scary theory when it was first presented to me some weeks ago is now a strongly supported and terrifying fact. We now *know*, without much question, that a third party is attempting to start a war between the Laian Republic and the Wendira Grand Hive.

"That third party appears to have resources on both sides of the border. The core fleet we have confirmed from *Eternal Fall*'s files and Sword Kolotak's confessions is a Laian Navy mobile dockyard, two Laian war-dreadnoughts and a minimum of one Wendira star hive.

"It seems like Sword Kolotak was a relatively junior member of our hostile conspiracy—about as junior as someone who was actually part of their hunting fleet could be, in fact. He doesn't know what his superiors are hunting and doesn't know where they're planning on investigating next.

"What he does know is the intended movement pattern of the central base, that mobile dockyard. We know where she's going to be for the next twenty cycles."

Morgan waited for that to sink in and smiled.

"We will shortly be dropping out of hyperspace to transmit everything we have learned to Fleet Lord Tan!Shallegh. The confessions and files from *Eternal Fall* will hopefully be sufficient for the Fleet Lord to convince the Laians and Wendira to step back from the precipice of war.

"That means we will have achieved half of our objectives out here."

"But we still know nothing about the Alavan fleet," Rin noted.

"Exactly," Morgan confirmed. She gestured to the projectors. "Dr. Dunst?"

Rin nodded and brought a hologram alive with the map of the region, red icons marking each known location of the conspiracy fleet.

"The conspirator fleet does not appear to have been directly engaged in provocative incidents for the last twenty cycles or so," he told them. "That suggests to me that they're closing in on their target.

"Most of the hard work is likely being done by smaller survey ships, with the main fleet waiting in reserve. They've clearly been surveying systems along the Dead Zone for some time and have a lot more information on this fleet than we do. But everything we have learned brings us to one conclusion."

The Astoroko Nebula flashed in the hologram.

"They have concentrated their efforts around Astoroko for the last few weeks, and the schedule has the central fleet on the edge of the Nebula now," he told them. "It seems likely now that the Alava pursued their defeated foe into the stellar nursery, where their enemies expected the radiation and particle densities to cover their escape.

"It seems equally likely that that fleet never left the Nebula. We are, however, talking about a zone some fourteen light-years in diameter. Even if our conspirators had been searching for the last long-cycle, they still might not have found their target."

"How long do you figure it will take, Doctor?" Nguyen asked.

"It depends on how good their data is, but it seems to have taken them over a long-cycle to narrow it down to the Nebula," Rin pointed out. "I would guess their ability to narrow it down from here sucks. We're hunting dead ships, after all.

"At this point, it's down to luck. They could find the Alavan fleet tomorrow—or it could take them a dozen long-cycles. They're assuming the latter and that's why they're trying to start this bloody war."

"So, what do we do?" Rogers asked.

"Rin, Ki!Tana?" Morgan looked at her lover and her old family friend. "We can't fight that fleet, so I'm hoping one of you has an idea."

"We need their data," Rin said instantly. "I am one hundred percent certain I have data they don't—and it would strongly appear that they have data I don't. If I can get their data and combine it with everything we have from our...assorted sources, I think I have a decent chance of narrowing down the search."

Morgan trusted her officers with her life, but she still wasn't cleared to tell them about the Mesharom Archive and the Imperium's access to it. They didn't need to know—and thankfully, Rin was probably even better at managing that knowledge than she was.

"How are you planning on pulling that off?" Murtas asked. "Even with the scanners Ki!Tana has, we need to get within five hundred thousand kilometers to access Laian systems—and the data center on that mobile shipyard might be even more secure."

"I would assume that this conspiracy has access to Mesharom-level technology for key items like that," Rin admitted. "We will, even with Ki!Tana's tools, need to penetrate the shipyard and acquire direct physical access to their data center if we are to steal their files."

The briefing room was silent.

"*Eternal Fall,*" Vichy suggested quietly. Everyone turned to look at the Marine commander, and he shrugged. "She's one of theirs. She has the codes, she has the authorizations, they're expecting her back—she's even had the shit kicked out of her, so she has every reason to go straight to the repair ship.

"We fly her into the designated rendezvous coordinates and dock like we belong. My Marines board the ship and hit the data center while they're still confused. We fall back on *Fall*, board Ki!Tana's stealth ship, and blow the cruiser as we run."

The room was silent and Morgan gave her Marine CO a firm approving nod.

"That might just work," she noted. "Ki!Tana? It's your ship and your tools we're talking about using."

"It is doable," she confirmed. "But...you will need Laians. We can make another male Laian of approximately the right age look and sound like Kolotak, but we need a Laian at the core of the illusion.

"Plus, none of your people are truly up to flying a Laian warship. You will need a portion of *Eternal Fall*'s crew."

"Given how pissed some of them are, I believe we can do that," Vichy said.

"I have to go," Rin interjected. Morgan leveled a Look on her partner. "Are we going to have the time to download their entire database, Commander Vichy?"

The Marine grunted.

"We could *make* the time," he said slowly. "Mais on l'achète avec du sang."

But we buy it with blood.

Morgan could do the math. To hold the data center that long would mean they'd, at the very least, have to fight their way out. There'd be no quick smash and grab without someone who knew *exactly* what they were looking for and *exactly* how to find it in a database.

"I've been working on the Laian databases from *Harvester of Red*," Rin reminded her. "I can do it faster than anyone else."

"It's got to be you," Morgan conceded. She didn't *want* to, but she did it anyway.

Because he was right. There was only one person aboard *Defiance* who could get into a Laian database and find the right data in the amount of time they'd have.

"I'll need some of Murtas's people," Rin told her. "I'm good once I'm in the database, but some extra tools and hands breaking in won't go amiss."

"I'll need *all* of my Marines," Vichy said grimly. "And Ki!Tana and her ship—and you can't be far behind us, sir. That stealth ship isn't going to get away on her own!"

"We'll be waiting for the pickup," Morgan promised. "Let's sort out the details, people. This plan is nuts...which is why it might just work."

CHAPTER THIRTY-SIX

THE FIRST PROBLEM WITH THE PLAN FELL OUT OF THE DETAILS almost immediately.

"We need a hundred crew, minimum, to run the ship. The fewer of them are our Laian friends, the more hands we end up needing," Rogers estimated.

"And I want to bring the full Marine contingent. Three hundred Marines," Vichy continued.

"My ship will hold fifty at most," Ki!Tana warned them. "Using *Dark Eyes* to evacuate the entire contingent isn't possible."

Most of the officers who weren't required for the plan had returned to their other duties, leaving Rogers, Vichy, Morgan, Rin and Ki!Tana to sort out how they were going to hit the conspirators' shipyard.

"Don't Laian escorts have stealth fields of their own?" Morgan asked. "We should find out if it's still working. It won't cover them for the last few million kilometers, but surprise might get them that far."

Maybe. Morgan didn't like hanging the lives of hundreds of people under her command on that kind of *maybe*, but she didn't see a lot of other choices.

"Could we interface Ki!Tana's device with the emitters from *Eternal Fall* to increase their effectiveness?" Vichy asked.

"Unlikely," the Ki!Tol admitted, but a flash of thoughtful colors crossed her skin. "I will need to study the Laian system in more detail. I'm not as familiar with it as I would like. Potentially, if some of their key engineers cooperate, we might make that happen."

"It sounds like we need to talk to the Laians before we go much farther with this plan," Morgan said. "Do we think they're likely to help? Some of them are furious to realize how badly they were played, but it's a big step from being angry your boss lied to you to helping us in a covert op against one of their own ships, regardless of whose hands that ship is in."

"We could potentially lean on some associates of mine in the Republic to get orders to them from Laian authorities," Ki!Tana suggested. "The risk should be acceptable."

Morgan glanced at her officers, who weren't fully briefed on the existence of the *associates* in question but had to guess that Ki!Tana was linked to *something* deeper.

"Can we get *Eternal Fall* back into regular space with us so we can make hyperfold calls?" she asked.

"Her hyperdrive and emitters are intact enough," Rogers said. "Even without any assistance from the crew, we should be able to get her through a portal on her own. And if not..." She shrugged. "We can tow her, right?"

Morgan considered every aspect that would be involved in that task, and snorted.

"Theoretically, at least," she conceded. "I'd prefer to take her out under her own power. Vichy—I want you to talk to Spear Amoko. She seems like our best in to knowing who in the crew we can get on our side.

"I think we want to get formal orders for *Eternal Fall*'s crew regardless. If we do this on our own, *we're* violating a few interstellar conventions. If we get *permission*, it's all legit."

"But if we get permission, they might know we're coming,"

Rogers suggested softly. "How certain are you, Ki!Tana, that your associates won't betray our mission to the people we're hunting?"

"They should not," the Ki!Tol said. "But...it is possible. It depends on Captain Casimir's plan and desires. She is right that what we are discussing is...questionable at best. We might provoke a Core Power."

"I'm not as worried about that as I might be," Morgan said. "The Republic needs us more than we need them right now. And with the Wendira Grand Hive rattling sabers at the border, they're not going to pick a fight with the Imperium.

"The Empress *might* be forced to disavow our actions to keep the alliance," she said levelly. "If so, that is a duty I am willing to carry."

Her career with the Imperial Navy would be dead in the water at that point. If A!Shall disavowed Morgan's actions, she would almost certainly be forced to resign in disgrace.

That would be...hard. On the other hand, Morgan doubted that Ki!Ron or even A!Shall would let that be the be-all-and-end-all for her. Even if the Imperium and the association cut her completely loose, she could always go home. The Militia might be pressured to refuse her a commission, but the Imperium couldn't stop her parents employing her somewhere.

She was *far* more shielded from formal displeasure than the rest of her crew.

"Let's find out if we can get any of the Laians onside without formal orders," she decided aloud. "If we can do this below the radar, I think everyone ends up ahead."

Potential future consequences be damned, she wasn't going to risk her crew.

MORGAN WAS GOING over the still-rough reports of *Eternal Fall*'s damage some hours later when a chime sounded at her office door.

"Enter," she ordered.

Vichy led Spear of the Republic Amoko through the door, the Marine taking a moment to pull a Laian-style chair through after them so their not-quite-prisoner, not-quite-guest could sit.

"I've briefed Spear Amoko on as much of the situation as I feel comfortable sharing," the Battalion Commander said briskly. "She said she might be able to help us."

"I appreciate that, Spear Amoko," Morgan told the Laian. She'd looked up the woman in the files the Republic had given her and had discovered the reason why officers below the rank of Sword didn't usually give the number as part of their rank.

As of the last official update, Amoko was the One Hundred and Twenty Thousand Two Hundred and Thirty-Fifth Spear of the Republic. She was also almost a decade younger than Morgan, only ten years into her military career.

Laians matured faster than humans did but lived long enough that twenty-eight for a Laian wasn't *that* much more mature than twenty-eight for a human.

"Did Commander Vichy brief you on what we're hoping to do?" she asked.

"You want to use *Eternal Fall* as a gore-mother larva host," Amoko told her. "Because Sword Kolotak is one of theirs, they will not question her arrival at their shipyard or her request for repairs. We can deliver your Marines without suspicion until it is too late."

Morgan decided she did *not* want to know what a gore-mother was. The metaphor appeared to be equivalent to trojan horse, though, so that covered her bases.

"Exactly," she agreed. "We need access to their data files to try and find their objective before they do—and to prove to both the Hive and the Republic that they are being played for fools...and hopefully avoid the war."

Regardless of whether she asked for official Laian orders to cover the use of a friendly warship as a trojan horse, she still needed to take

Defiance out of hyperspace and update Fleet Lord Tan!Shallegh on all they'd learned from Kolotak.

She hoped that would be enough to avoid the war, but she was going to keep finding anything she could use for that objective, too.

"You will need engineers and pilots at a minimum," Amoko told her. "We will also want to transfer all *non*-volunteers to *Defiance*... where they will require guarding. If you send all of your Marines on *Eternal Hope*, will you be safe from the conspirators among my own crew?"

"I have other security personnel who will take on that task," Morgan assured the Laian. She wasn't sure that Speaker Susskind's military police had the numbers for the task, but they'd make it work.

"Of course," Amoko agreed. She clicked her mandibles thought-fully. "But the sands of time suggest to me that my former Sword's allies may be more dangerous than we expect. The vision of security is often as important as the truth."

"It happens," Morgan admitted. "What are you thinking, Spear?"

"I am certain as rock becomes sand that I can find one hundred of my Blades who I can trust without question," the Laian Blade officer told them. "There are a dozen officers and noncoms I trust as far, as well. If we lean on them, I believe we can provide a skeleton crew for *Eternal Fall*.

"I suggest that I and one hundred of my Blades accompany Battalion Commander Vichy on this mission," she concluded. "Even with the crew, his Marines will still outnumber the Laians aboard *Fall*, to provide both vision and truth of security, while you will retain one hundred of his Marines to secure the prisoners aboard *Defiance*."

Morgan leaned back in her chair, surprised by the offer.

"Crewing the ship is one thing," she noted. "But you are offering to join Commander Vichy in the boarding operation."

"If only humans board the shipyard, there will be a battle almost instantly," Amoko pointed out. "If the lead elements of our assault are Laian, the confusion will buy us time."

"It buys us a chance to maybe get the data and get out without a major firefight," Vichy agreed. "I...didn't dare suggest it, mon capitaine."

"Are you certain, Spear Amoko?" Morgan asked. "You are taking a significant personal risk."

"Sword Kolotak is guilty of treason," Amoko replied. "That leaves an open question as to who is in command of *Eternal Fall*. Given the likelihood that other senior officers have also walked in tainted winds, there is arguably no command authority over me.

"I must therefore act as I see best for the good of the Republic. The Republic does not need this war and does not need shadowy conspiracies playing games on our borders. Therefore, your mission is very much in line with said good of the Republic."

The Laian shook her armored head.

"I see no alternative but to act to save my Republic," she told them. "Your plan serves us as well as your own. We will find your answer and we will crack open this conspiracy.

"You may have your own reasons to fight this battle, Captain Casimir, Commander Vichy, but let us be clear as to why I join your winds: I am fighting to save my Republic."

"Fair enough," Morgan conceded. "I think that works just fine for us."

After all, Morgan might arguably be part of a shadowy conspiracy these days, but her associates wanted to protect the Republic, not drag it into a pointless war.

CHAPTER THIRTY-SEVEN

Both ships emerged into regular space in neatly matching flashes of blue-white light. Morgan had debated leaving *Eternal Fall* in hyperspace to prevent anyone aboard reporting in, but Vichy assured her the Marines were in full control of the Laian ship's hyperfold communicator.

She stared at the recorder in her office, trying to muster the words to tell Tan!Shallegh what he needed to know without breaking confidences. Finally, she sighed and started at the beginning.

"Fleet Lord, I hope this message intercepts you before you reach your rendezvous with the Wendira and Laian representatives," she began. That seemed likely. There were still three cycles left before he was supposed to leave, another five after that before the Fleet Lord arrived.

Even with hyperspace variability, it was still at least seven cycles before the peace conference began.

"While we were engaging in the surveys for Envoy Awav, we were attacked by a trio of Laian warships without warning," she reported. The Envoy was currently spending his time very much out of the way. He appeared to have decided that the best way for him to accept Morgan's diversions was to stay out of them entirely.

"Given what I learned later, I regret to report that two of those ships were destroyed. We captured the third mostly intact and have interrogated her senior officers."

She sighed.

"They appear to have been working with a third party that is manipulating official and unofficial military units on both sides of the border to provoke a war. Only the willingness of officers and politicians on both sides to extend the benefit of the doubt has kept them from succeeding.

"I am attaching everything we learned from Sword Kolotak as to the nature of his command and mission—including that most of his crew had no idea what was going on. I hope that this information is sufficient for you to convince both sides to step back from the precipice."

For several seconds, Morgan considered leaving it at that, but... she was about to do something incredibly risky. She was also going to send an update to Ki!Ron, but Tan!Shallegh was the being in a position to potentially save her crew if something went wrong.

"It is no surprise to you, I suspect, that I am operating under covert orders from Empress A!Shall herself," she admitted. "I cannot give you details still, but you need to know that *Defiance* is moving on the central fleet of these conspirators.

"In combination with several officers from *Eternal Fall*, the captured cruiser, we believe we can infiltrate the conspiracy's ships and acquire information critical to my mission. It is likely that we will learn more information with regards to the attempt to trigger a war, as well. Any information I can find will be forwarded."

She paused, then swallowed.

"I am including the information we received with regards to the fleet's location under a timed encryption," she finally said. "I need the opportunity to move without interruption, but if you have not heard from me by the time the encryption expires, I think we both know what will have happened to me.

"I leave what to do with that data then to you."

She ended the message and dropped it into the queue. She stared at the recorder blankly for a few more seconds, then started a message to Ki!Ron.

"Ki!Ron, this message is attached with a large pile of information I don't know if I should be giving you," she said bluntly. "We have been engaged by several ships I now know to have been operated by officers involved in the conspiracy. They were lying to their crews, which has provided an opening for us.

"I have one of their ships and we plan to take it to their central command ship shortly. Dr. Dunst believes that if he can get his hands on their data with regards to the Alavan fleet, combined with our own information, he can do a better job of locating the target.

"Six cycles after we arrive at the conspiracy fleet, Fleet Lord Tan!Shallegh will receive its location. If we have not already retrieved the data, it will likely be lost when *someone* blows them to hell.

"At that point, I'm unlikely to be in a position to give a shit," Morgan concluded dryly. "If you have any other associates in a position to intervene at that point, it might be wise to bring them up to speed.

"I'm going hunting. Hopefully, we'll speak in person soon enough."

She slotted that message into the queue as well, then considered the situation silently for a long time. Most of it, though, was working out what components of what was going on that she *could* tell Victoria.

Once she had that sorted, she started the recorder for a third time. She wasn't going off on a mission against insane odds without telling *both* of her lovers that she loved them.

And Rin was far easier to access.

CHAPTER THIRTY-EIGHT

"THAT IS QUITE THE BOX MY PEOPLE ARE HAULING," VICHY observed with a chuckle as Rin and three Marines hauled the container out of the workshop.

"I don't want to interface any of my work with the Laian computers," Rin admitted. "So, I'm borrowing a setup from *Defiance*. I checked with Commander Liepins," he assured the Marine. "We're good."

"All right." Vichy gestured for the Marines to keep the container moving. "Seriously, though, are you sure you have everything?"

"I am," Rin told him. "I'm just cargo, Pierre. All the way to the data center."

The Marine winced.

"Is there any way I can convince you that you don't need to go *quite* that far?" he asked.

"Since all of us, including Captain Casimir, know that I *do* need to go that far, no," Rin said. He patted his friend on the shoulder. It wasn't *quite* a stretch, but Vichy was much taller and leaner than he was. "If we'd brought some other Alava experts along, maybe, but we didn't. We barely had the excuse to bring me."

"Because knowing *that* makes me so happy," Vichy said. "Il y a trop de mensonges, mon ami."

That took Rin a moment to process, but he shook his head.

"No lies, as best as we can," he told the Marine. "Secrets, yes, but no lies, I don't think. You know the mission. You know why I'm actually here."

"Je sais," Vichy agreed. "Still. All seems rather shadowy to me."

"That's because it is," Rin agreed. He wasn't entirely comfortable with it himself, but he was used to secrecy by now. That was part of the job of a man who had large chunks of the Mesharom Archive stored in a computer embedded in his spine.

"So, how do you think this is going to go wrong?" he asked the Marine as they made their way toward the shuttle.

"In ways I have not foreseen, I suspect," Vichy told him. "The ones I can foresee, we will have a plan for. It's the *other* ways I'm worried about."

"So, we have a general fallback plan?" Rin asked. He realized even as he said it what that plan had to be, and shivered.

"Shoot our way in, shoot our way out, buy the time you need with blood and fire," the Marine said calmly. "I'd *prefer* that this goes quietly, but...je suis réaliste."

Rin snorted.

"Fair."

"For example, I did not expect to get you off the ship without running into mon capitaine," Vichy told him, elbowing Rin gently and pointed to where Morgan was standing next to the shuttlebay entrance, looking coolly professional as usual.

"I'll wait for you on the shuttle," the Marine continued. "Side room there should be quiet for a few minutes."

The Marine pointed and Rin nodded his understanding.

"Thank you."

"IT'S a little late to talk me out of this, you know," Rin told Morgan as the door slid shut behind them.

"Given everything I do on a day-to-day basis, talking you out of risking yourself would be hypocritical," she admitted. "Just being on this ship is putting you at risk, really. We managed to get shot at doing what's supposed to be an *inspection tour*."

Rin chuckled. That was true enough, though he wouldn't have expected Morgan to pick up on that part. He honestly figured he wasn't in an increased amount of danger until he followed the Marines onto the enemy ship.

"We certainly don't seem to be making friends out here," he told her. "I hope that trend ends sooner rather than later."

"You're just here for fascinating dead things. I have a few more immediate concerns," she replied with a smile.

"If only the people I studied had been dead for long enough for people not to be fighting wars over their wreckage," Rin said. "The Alava are fascinating, but they did so much that has come back to haunt us."

"I know." Morgan pulled him into her embrace and he leaned his head against hers. "You stay safe, okay? I don't want to lose you."

"I'm not planning on it," he murmured in her ear. "*You* stay safe too, okay? I don't quite follow how dangerous 'two war-dreadnoughts and a star hive' is, but I'm guessing it's enough to eat *Defiance* alive."

"Without chewing," Morgan admitted. "But this is the job I signed on for. Not so much you."

"I knew what I was getting into when I agreed to come with you out here," he said. "Ki!Ron's mission was never not going to be...hrm... combat archeology?"

That got a laugh from her, an interruption that allowed him to kiss her.

When they came up for air a moment later, Morgan stepped back and studied him.

"I love you," she said, her voice suddenly entirely serious. "I love Victoria, too, don't get me wrong, but I love you. Don't... Just..."

"I know," he promised. "I love you. We'll all be fine, I promise."

It was the first time *that* particular word had been used between them, but it felt right. And Rin was certain in what he was saying, too. They were going to be fine.

And if they weren't, well...the odds were that whatever happened would happen to both of them regardless!

CHAPTER THIRTY-NINE

RIN'S SHUTTLE WASN'T THE FIRST TO RETURN TO *ETERNAL FALL*. A calmly ordered phalanx of Marines filled the Laian cruiser's boat bay, a squad Lance passing out flimsy tablets to each person as they left the spacecraft.

"Here you go, Doctor," the scarred woman said, passing him his own tablet. "None of us Imperials know the ship layout at all, so we rigged up a map and guide for where we're putting you.

"You're near the bridge, with Ki!Tana," she told him. "Two of my Marines will escort you." She glanced around the bay, her gaze resting on where a squad of Laian Blades were exiting their spacecraft.

"You don't go anywhere without at least two Marines; am I clear, Doctor?" she said. "The Laians aboard are people we trust, but still... you're a Category Two asset. We're keeping a close eye on you."

"Of course, Lance," Rin agreed genially. He'd survived a handful of gunfights since pirates had overrun his dig site near the Kosha System, but he didn't think he was worth much in one. "Do I have space for my equipment?"

"You should," the Lance confirmed. "I didn't pick the spaces, but

I've orders to send your boxes up to the same place as you. Command crew wants you to meet them as soon as you have a minute; ping one of the Commanders when you're ready."

"Thank you, Lance." He turned an eyebrow back at Vichy, the Marine officer disembarking behind him.

"Give *me* a twentieth-cycle, if you'd be so kind, monsieur," Vichy told him with a chuckle, confirming the suspicion that the Battalion Commander was one of the "Commanders". "Rogers should be on the bridge, getting used to running a ship in Laian. She speaks fluent warship, but this should be an experience for us all."

Rin gave his friend a nod.

"I'll give you that twentieth-cycle," he promised. "I'll need it myself."

A bit over an hour; that might not even be enough time for him to get everything sorted out in his new lab. He wasn't going to link in to *Fall*'s computer systems but he needed a data feed *from* them. That kind of one-way connection took some doing, but he had the tools.

"If I could get you to keep moving, Doctor, sir?" the Lance asked. "We've got over four hundred sentients coming aboard and we're barely halfway through. The other boat bay is out of commission, so we can only process two shuttles at a time."

"Moving on, Lance, moving on," Rin promised, his two escorts falling in with him and Vichy as they obeyed the noncom's request.

The interior of the ship was odd, but the first humans aboard had laid holographic tape around the exit from the boat bay. It glittered in the light, an easy guide for the humans on a ship lit for people who saw well into the infrared.

"We've rigged lights in most of the key corridors and the rooms we've assigned Imperials," Vichy told him as they stepped out of the boat bay and Rin could finally properly see. The boat bay hadn't been dark, per se, but it had all seemed fuzzy.

The corridor had a neat row of light disks, sticky pucks that could be found for cheap in any corner store on any Imperial world, stuck at head height. They provided light that was far easier on Rin's eyes than the normal lighting.

The ship still seemed dark, a strange mottled mix of red and black that told Rin that most decoration and signage was written in colors outside his perception.

He studied the tablet he'd been given, aligning its *YOU ARE HERE* dot with his position and checking its directions. His Marines were double-checking their own tablets, in case he managed to get lost.

"All right, Pierre, I think I'm good," he told the Marine. "I guess we're having a command crew meeting shortly?"

"Rogers at least told *me* that in advance," Vichy chuckled. "Allons-y, Rin. Allons-y!"

THE LIGHT DISKS in the set of quarters given to Rin shone down on empty floors and alien hygiene facilities. He figured out the Laian toilet quickly enough—the water was mixed with just enough sand to be abrasive and not require much soap for cleaning—and he figured the lack of furniture was someone anticipating his needs.

Everything he needed was in the crates the Marines had delivered, which meant what he needed from his quarters was space. He'd set up impromptu computer consoles before, too. Xenoarcheological dig sites rarely came with handy military-grade computing equipment.

And this time, he had two willing Marines to help out!

His screens went up first, followed by the boxes of concealed molecular circuitry borrowed from *Defiance*. A folding workbench gave him space to set up his limited artifact-analysis tools—he didn't expect to need them, but better to have them and not need them than the other way around—and another bench became the base for the screens and computers.

A secondary box, a specially designed tool Murtas had loaned him, linked in to the data ports in the mottled walls of the Laian ship. The box acted as a one-way firewall. He could pull data from the Laian ship, but the ship's computers had no access to his system.

Once it was all set up, he made sure the connection to *Eternal Fall* was offline, then brought his systems up. A few moments of focused meditation unlocked the storage drive at the base of his spine, and he took a long look at the information he'd collated about the Alavan fleet.

The Mesharom tablets on their former rulers had been of variable detail at the best of times, but they'd known where the vast majority of the Alava's key fleet anchorages were. Based on what they'd found at some of the other anchorages, the one by the Dead Zone should have been home to thousands of ships.

They had a solid idea of how many were missing, and the numbers—and the data on what an Alavan warship looked like— were bone-chilling to Rin. A thousand ships, give or take, a hundred of them full-size motherships over a thousand kilometers in diameter.

If someone tried to turn on their engines, they'd die. That lesson had been learned the hard way too many times over the last thousand years. But even the files that the Imperium had on the Alavan motherships didn't include much of what the ships had been armed with or had carried for other systems.

They had guesses. They'd run into refurbished Alavan defensive platforms when they'd fought the Taljzi, after all—but the Taljzi had shown an astonishing gift for judging what could and couldn't be reactivated of Alavan technology.

Rin suspected some of that was due to the fact that every living Taljzi for several hundred years had been a product of an Alavan biotech cloner. Enough memories had been passed down that the people working on Alavan tech for the rogue Kanzi sect had a *lot* of experience.

He'd interviewed some of those people. It had been a strange experience, sitting in a room with someone who was physically about twenty-five years old but had memories stretching back half a millennium.

But while the Taljzi had learned a lot about Alavan technology, they knew almost nothing about the Precursors themselves. They'd wrapped lack of information in myth and practical experimentation —and with the ability to mass-produce more of themselves, they'd been more cavalier with their lives than any other species Rin had met.

He knew there'd been *something* going on in the extremities of the Alava Hegemony now. They'd encountered an entire rogue province, building biotech the Hegemony would have burned on sight, out in the Kosha Sector. The systems around Arjtal had been a more obedient province, but even they had experimented with biotech like the cloner.

And yet the Hegemony had officially banned any experimentation with biotech like that. Rin didn't know why, but it had clearly been a ban more often ignored than obeyed.

He shook his head.

He had about two-thirds of the picture. Some of the answer, he hoped, was aboard the conspirators' ship.

The rest was either aboard the Alavan fleet or lost to the mists of time.

───────

TWO LAIANS, a Ki!Tol and three humans made up the new "command crew" of *Eternal Fall*. Rin knew everyone except one of the Laians, nodding to them all as he took his own seat in the conference room.

The purpose of the space was clear enough, even if the table was an asymmetrical solid block unlike anything Rin had seen in the Imperium. Light disks had been stuck around the room for the sake of the Imperials' eyes, and both human- and A!Tol-style seats had been brought in.

"All right, everyone," Rogers told them. "I think I'm the only person here who has actually met everyone, so I'm going to handle the introductions."

The petite redhead grinned.

"I am, for the moment, the senior officer and captain of *Eternal Fall*," she told them. "That's obviously a temporary situation at best, as we have every intention of returning *Fall* to the Republic Navy when this is done, but the situation is such that we can't trust any of the senior Laian officers to lead this mission."

She gestured to the two Laians.

"This is Spear Amoko, the commander of *Eternal Fall*'s Blades of the Republic, and Spear Notulik, one of her junior engineers. Spear Notulik is the senior officer of *Fall*'s original crew that we believe we can trust, and will be acting as my executive officer, managing the Laian crew."

Rogers continued on with another gesture to Rin and Vichy.

"Battalion Commander Pierre Vichy is the commander of *Defiance*'s Imperial Marines and will be leading the boarding action that is the primary purpose of our mission here. He and I share overall command of the mission. Dr. Rin Dunst is our civilian specialist on the Alava. He'll be joining the boarding operation because he has the best knowledge of just what we're looking for.

"Lastly, this is Ki!Tana, another civilian specialist on our high-level stealth and cyberwarfare systems," Rogers concluded.

Rin hid a grin. That was *one* description for why Ki!Tana was there—an easier one to give the Laians than "the Imperium tends not to argue with Ki!Tol who decide they want to come along" or her being sent directly by the Empress.

"At final count, we have thirty-two Imperial Navy crew aboard, supporting one hundred and eleven Republican Navy crew," Rogers continued. "Our job, basically, is to get the assault force onto our target: two hundred Imperial Marines and one hundred Laian Blades."

"Both myself and Ki!Tana will be accompanying the boarding action," Rin told her.

"I know," Rogers conceded. "I think that's insane, but it's not my call."

"It's necessary," Ki!Tana told them, determination flashing over her skin.

"We'll be cruising most of the way to the rendezvous point in company with *Defiance*," Rogers continued. "Approximately one light-year short of the destination, we will break off and proceed on our own to keep *Defiance* off their anomaly scanners."

Anomaly scanners in realspace picked up targets farther away than if they were relying on speed-of-light data, but they were still far short of instantaneous. From a light-year away, *Defiance*'s signature wouldn't be picked up for a few months at least.

"We have rigged up a software program to map Spear Notulik's face to a simulacrum of Sword Kolotak," she told them. "Given our very real damage and Sword Kolotak's involvement in the conspiracy, we have every reason to believe we will be allowed to dock without much question."

"From there, we board as rapidly and quietly as possible," Vichy said, picking up the briefing. "The Blades lead the way, stunners first. We want to kill as few as possible at this point. If we can manage to get Dr. Dunst and Ki!Tana to and from the data center without engaging in open warfare, everyone wins."

"What are the odds of that?" Rin asked.

"Ice in the desert," Spear Amoko said bluntly. "Security systems will likely pick up our moving in a block before we even engage with any on-board teams.

"If we neutralize cameras as we go, hopefully they will not realize there are Imperials aboard. That confusion will buy us some time, but I do not expect to reach the data center before we begin to face significant resistance."

"We do believe that between the Blades and the Marines, we can complete the mission," Vichy told the rest of the command crew.

A chill ran down Rin's spine. He couldn't help but note that Vichy had not said they could complete the mission *without losses*. His incursion into a conspiracy data center was going to cost lives on both sides.

It had better be worth it.

"How do we get out when it's over?" Notulik asked. "Our stealth field is damaged and wouldn't function at close range in any case. I agreed to the mission presuming there was an escape plan."

"There is," Ki!Tana agreed. "You and I and whoever else in your team has experience with the stealth field will be working on your system for the entire trip. We should be able to repair it at least, and I have some ideas of how to upgrade it.

"I am familiar with Laian technology as well as Mesharom stealth systems," she told the Spear. "We will be fine."

"We will also be relying on surprise to get us at least some distance from the conspirators," Rogers admitted. "Once we break away and lose the pursuit, we will rendezvous with *Defiance* and take both ships to our final destination."

"Which is?" Notulik asked.

"An Alavan ship graveyard," Rin said flatly. "We will then either destroy the ships ourselves or make contact with trusted individuals in the Laian government to see them properly handled.

"If we can steal the graveyard out from under these bastards' noses while sending the Laian fleet after them, they will have failed in every way." He smiled. "I like the sound of that myself, and they haven't directly betrayed *me*."

He'd never heard an angry Laian growl before. Now he heard it from two of them at once...and somehow the fact that both Amoko and Notulik were females and smaller than their brothers did *not* make the sound less intimidating.

CHAPTER FORTY

MORGAN WATCHED THE ICON MARKING *ETERNAL FALL* accelerate away from *Defiance* with a chill lump in her stomach. She couldn't bring the Imperial cruiser any closer, which meant that her lover, her executive officer and so many others were now on their own.

"Captain Casimir?" a calm translated voice asked behind her.

She turned her seat to see Envoy Awav making his way across the bridge toward her. The Ivida looked out of place on *Defiance*'s bridge, his dark red skin and civilian clothes marking him out against the uniformed human crew.

He also looked uncomfortable, clearly unsure how to stay out of the way amongst the working crew.

"Envoy, welcome." She gestured him to an observer chair next to her. "I can use a distraction. What's on your mind?"

"Do we know if we will be able to resume my mission eventually?" he asked as he took the seat. The chair scanned him on approach and adjusted its design to fit an Ivida. The transition from human-comfortable to Ivida-comfortable was less drastic than some changes Morgan had seen the bridge furniture make.

"I have no idea," Morgan admitted. "Your mission is important, Envoy, and we'll see what we can do. We may have to transfer you to another ship eventually, depending on what we find on this mission."

"I appreciate your honesty," the diplomat said...diplomatically. "I must admit relief that the Empress advised me of these currents before we were sent here. If I had seen my mission so abruptly discarded without warning, I might have been...upset."

"I appreciate your patience," Morgan told him. "Your mission *is* important, Envoy. Despite what it may look like, I do believe that. Hopefully, this cold war will be cooled back down by the evidence we've provided, but even if it isn't..."

"We need to know if we can trust the Laians in the future as well," Awav said. "But this conspiracy you have uncovered..."

The Ivida twisted his arms in an odd gesture no human could duplicate. The equivalent of a headshake, Morgan believed.

"I know it was what you were looking for," he admitted. "But the scope and depth of their power and their...evil...it frightens me, Captain Casimir. Are we ready for this battle?"

"No," Morgan said with blunt honesty. The envoy deserved that much from her. "*Defiance* can't fight these people, Envoy. We're badly outgunned. Trickery and surprise will carry us a long way, though. If Rin, Vichy and Ki!Tana can learn what they need, we might be able to find this graveyard in time."

"And what do we do when *we* find it, Captain?" Awav asked.

Morgan glanced around the bridge. There was no one present who wasn't cleared for this. She'd filled her bridge crew in on most of this already.

"Not that long ago, we'd have called in the Mesharom Frontier Fleet," she told him. "For a discovery of the scale we fear we're facing...there are assets in the Imperium and the Republic that can and will be deployed to make certain the wrecks are handled safely. Studied but not turned on."

She shook her head.

"There are too many dangers in old Alavan technology, Envoy. I have seen entire star systems harnessed to their designs, and the power they commanded is all the more dangerous for a hundred thousand long-cycles of neglect."

Awav was probably cleared for the nature of the Alava's fall, but not everyone on Morgan's bridge was. The details of what they faced today were one thing. The terrifying nature of how the Alava had died...that was something even the Imperium kept secret.

"What do you expect to learn from these conspirators?" he finally asked.

"I don't know," Morgan conceded. "Rin and Ki!Tana tell me that the information we have wouldn't have led to the places the conspirators have searched, though. So, they clearly have data we don't have— we're hoping *we* have data they don't.

"With our data and theirs combined, Rin thinks he has a better chance of finding the Alavan graveyard fleet than they do. That's all we have to go on...but right now, we've narrowed it down to a nebula light-years across.

"We don't have the time to search that," she admitted. "We need an answer *now*. The sooner we have that answer, after all, the sooner we can continue your mission, Envoy."

"If I or my team can be of any use at all, let me know," Awav asked. "We may be mostly diplomats, but that skillset may yet come in handy—and my people are also trained as military analysts.

"We were, after all, assessing the military readiness of an entire border!"

———————

MORGAN TOOK a moment after returning to her office to touch the rock Rin had given her, drawing strength from the symbol of connection to both her lover and her homeworld.

That was *all* she could spare time for. Sending the executive officer away, even for what was only supposed to be a few days, drastically expanded the Captain's workload. Her messages were already clamoring for her attention to a dozen different minor crises, the inevitable working disasters of a warship of a thousand souls.

Clearing through the first wave of issues took over an hour, though it thankfully didn't require any actual meetings. Most of them just needed someone outside the departments in question to provide a decision.

It was amazing how quickly arguments ended once the Captain gave direction.

That, unfortunately, was only one hour of the almost seventy she expected to have to wait before Rin returned. Worse, in many ways, was that everyone she would normally talk to about her concerns and stress was aboard *Eternal Fall.*

There were only so many people a Captain could show weakness to. Civilian advisors she trusted, her XO, and *maybe* her Marine commander, who sat outside the normal chains of command. Somehow, even Pierre Vichy, the pompous Frenchman, had managed to end up as a friend she trusted.

Everyone serving aboard *Defiance* that Morgan Casimir would have called a friend was on board the Laian warship, pushing ever deeper into hyperspace that showed a thousand signs of the dispersed but present mass on the other side of the interface.

Defiance was inside the Astoroko Nebula now. Morgan suspected the answers to her questions and her final destination were also inside the Nebula. No one was coming out until someone found the Alavan graveyard; she was certain of that.

She could, she supposed, take *Defiance* into normal space...but so long as she was incommunicado, no one could order her to release the Laian warship she'd taken captive. It was too late now, but it was better that *all* of this was over before anyone could send her orders to do something else.

That way, if the Empress had to disavow her actions, there was no argument over the fact that she'd operated alone.

Morgan sighed and brought up a navigation program on her console, one that projected *Eternal Fall*'s estimated current location to the main wallscreen of her office. More messages were starting to fill her inbox again, but she'd get to those in a moment.

For that moment, she looked at the three icons on the map on her wall: *Defiance*. The scheduled location of the central conspirator fleet...and *Eternal Fall*, a stolen, battered warship carrying the only people she loved within five hundred light-years of her.

CHAPTER FORTY-ONE

"EMERGENCE IN ONE HUNDREDTH-CYCLE."

Captain Rogers's voice echoed through the corridors of their borrowed warship, and Rin took one final look through everything he'd packaged into his portable kit. Some of what he was carrying was fragile and almost irreplaceable, among the few pieces of Mesharom-grade computing hardware the Imperium had built.

It was also absolutely necessary if he was going to tear into a Laian data center and extract the information he needed in minutes instead of days or hours.

A sharp rap on the door of his workshop drew his attention.

"Come in," he shouted. The Marines outside his door should have turned away anyone who *wasn't* supposed to be there, after all.

The door slid open and three Marines in power armor stepped through, hauling a man-sized casket with an ease that belied its weight. The lead Marine's helmet was down, showing Pierre Vichy's face as the French officer grinned at him.

"Tu sais, when I ask you to meet me for something, I usually have a purpose," Vichy told Rin. "Come here."

The other two Marines stood the casket up as a woman in the

under-armor bodysuit stepped into the room as well, a tray of tools following her on an automated trolley.

"What's going on?" Rin asked. "I don't remember a message."

"I sent it an hour after that first meeting," Vichy told him. "You're ready to go?"

"Yeah." Rin was distracted now, looking for the communicator he'd clearly tossed aside a bit too readily.

"No time for that, Doctor," Vichy said. "Cameron!"

Rin wasn't sure what was going on, but the unarmored Marine stepped up to him with the trolley, eyeing him up and down with a look that made him aware of the extra weight he carried compared to the Marines.

"Doable," they said grimly. "Would have been better with more time."

The Marine had several tools in their hands Rin would have sworn they hadn't had a moment earlier.

"Hold still," they continued sharply. One tool was now pointed at the top of Rin's head and another at his shoulder. "Jonas, hook up the processor to the coffin."

One of the armored Marines took a device from the trolley and plugged it into the casket as Rin began to catch up with what was going on.

"You can't fit me for armor in the time we have left," he protested.

"Would have been better with more time," Cameron agreed. "Now hold still."

The tools began to emit flashing pulses of light as the Marine armorer ran them over Rin's entire body. Different devices appeared and vanished with a speed and smoothness that Rin had to respect, but the whole process still took the entire time before emergence.

The cruiser shivered around them as they plunged out of hyperspace, and Rin's earbud chirped.

"Dr. Dunst, did Vichy manage to pin you down for the sizing?" Rogers asked.

"I think it's currently ongoing," Rin admitted. "I didn't think about armor."

"The Marines were *not* letting you aboard a Laian starbase without power armor," Rogers told him. "And I agree with them one hundred percent, Dr. Dunst. Cooperate with the Marines; I'll link you to the channel we're opening with the locals."

"They're here?" Rin asked.

"They're here. We had the right data."

The channel went into passive mode. Rin took a moment to be sure it was okay if he moved, and then he stepped over to some of the equipment he *wasn't* taking with him. A few moments later, a projection of *Eternal Fall*'s scan data appeared on the wall.

"There's the shipyard," he said aloud. It was hard to miss. A war-dreadnought was several kilometers long. The mobile shipyard meant to repair one was six kilometers long and two in diameter. Rin wasn't even sure how they got the immense vessel to move—but he wasn't a hyperspatial interface engineer.

"Strip," Cameron ordered.

"What?" he demanded.

"Strip," the armorer repeated. They'd produced a duplicate of the under-armor shipsuit from somewhere, one that looked like it might even be Rin's size. "We need to link the suit to you and to the armor. Your clothes will get in the way."

Flushing, Rin obeyed—focusing his attention on the wallscreen to help stay composed.

Two images added themselves to the feed without his doing anything. Someone on the bridge had realized what he was doing and being helpful. One was the video feed of Spear Notulik, sitting in the central command seat on the cruiser's bridge, with Amoko and Rogers easily visible.

The second was a video feed of Sword Kolotak on a bridge full of busily working Laian staff. The only marker telling Rin that that feed was an edit of the first feed was that the visible damage was the same.

"Shipyard *Builder of Tomorrows*, this is Sword Kolotak aboard

Eternal Fall," the central Laian on both feeds said, giving Rin a moment of disorientation.

It was, of course, in that moment that Cameron and their team started dressing him in the bodysuit. He shivered under the cold fabric, adjusting to help as best as he could.

"We have completed our objective but have taken severe damage. I am requesting a docking slot and repairs ASAP. Authentication code..."

What followed wasn't translated for Rin, making it a collection of buzzes and clicks he didn't understand. Presumably, those were letters and numbers in the Laian main language.

"Raise your arms," Cameron ordered as the message ended. Something buzzed in his armpit, biting against his skin. As the same moment, the bodysuit's plumbing attachments clicked into place with an equal bite.

"Good, bodysuit is live and mapped to you," the armorer confirmed. "Armor interface online. Adjustments from initial scan complete."

They stepped back and grinned.

"Moment of truth, Doctor. If you'd do the honors, sir?"

Vichy had apparently been standing there the whole time, a realization that made Rin flush again. The Marine didn't seem to be bothered by, well, anything, and tapped a command on the side of the casket.

The tall metal container slid open, revealing the suit of power armor inside. The microbot sludge that both protected and maintained the armor retreated into the casket as Rin watched, and the armor popped open.

"Face first, Doctor," Vichy told him with a grin. "Don't worry; it was nerve-wracking for us at first, too!"

Rin snorted in disbelief and obeyed. There were no visible screens or anything, and it very much felt like he was stepping into a him-shaped coffin. Nonetheless, he leaned into the armor, closing his eyes against the moment of claustrophobia as the rest of the armor closed behind him.

"You will feel some slight discomfort," Cameron's voice warned in his ear—right before several bits of the armor proceeded to repeatedly hammer into his sides with varying force.

"All right, adjustment complete, bringing the armor online," the armorer continued.

Light against his closed eyelids told Rin he could open his eyes. He could now see all around him, as clearly as if he weren't wearing anything. He took a delicate step backward and the armor smoothly moved with him.

"You're in tutorial mode," Cameron told him. "We're not taking you *out* of tutorial mode. That means you're not carrying weapons and your onboard weapons are disabled. The suit will move with you and do most of the work for you without overcompensating.

"We use this mode to get trainees used to moving in it before we give them full control of the suit," the armorer continued. "It handles a lot of the work for you in terms of maneuvering the mass and muscles of the armor.

"The price is that every Marine around you will be faster, stronger and more flexible than you in every sense," they noted. "You're getting maybe ten percent of the benefit from the armor except in one way: you're actually wearing armor."

Rin nodded, then realized that probably wasn't visible outside the suit.

"That makes sense. Um. Can I use my tools?"

"I have increased the sensitivity of your gauntlets slightly from the default tutorial," Cameron told him. "You should be able to do everything you'd be able to do unarmored. If you can't, you can verbally order the suit to retract the gauntlets."

"Suit, retract gauntlets," Rin said hesitantly. He *felt* the armor fold up around his hands, a mix of plates and microbot support moving back into the forearm bracers. Warm air rippled around his bare fingers and he looked down at them, now shockingly small against the bulk of the power armor.

"Suit, restore gauntlets," he ordered. This time, he watched the armor flow out over his hands and take form. "Any other pieces I can do that with?"

"Yes, but they're all disabled," Cameron told him. "Priority is keeping you alive, Dr. Dunst."

"I understand," he said aloud, then noticed new activity on the image of the bridge on the wallscreen.

"We understand, *Builder of Tomorrows*," the simulacrum of Sword Kolotak replied to a message Rin hadn't heard. "My navigator is proceeding on the assigned course. We will arrive at our assigned dock in seventeen minutes."

Eternal Fall was moving again, heading toward the shipyard, and Rin finally paid attention to the rest of the icons on the screen. There were three large icons, though none approached the size of the ship-yard itself, ten mid-sized ones and fifteen small ones. Several icons marked the presence of entire groups of very small ships as Rin stared blankly at the codes.

"Vichy, can you read the icons?" he asked.

"A star hive, two war-dreadnoughts, ten Wendira star shields, fifteen escort cruisers and a few hundred starfighters," the Marine reeled off instantly. "We better hope the clever parts of this plan work, mon ami. We can't fight that without Fleet Lord Tan!Shallegh."

"Well, we have docking clearance," Rin told the Marine. "That's the first step, right?"

"That it is. You ready to move in that gear?"

"I am," Rin confirmed. He took extra care anyway as he crossed the room to his bag of gear. "What now?"

"We meet Ki!Tana and Amoko and board a hostile starship with a standard crew of twenty-five thousand," Vichy said brightly. "C'est facile, pas de problème."

CHAPTER FORTY-TWO

THE STANDARDIZED DOCKING TUBES WERE DESIGNED TO HANDLE normal ship-to-station traffic, not to offload a half-battalion of Marines in one shot. They were what the infiltrators had, though, and it looked like they were making do.

"The Blades go first," Vichy's voice murmured in Rin's ear as the tubes connected and airlocks hissed open. "They're at least the right species."

It looked like only four or five suits of power armor could march abreast in the docking tubes, but this was only one of three connections. The thirty Laian Blades there were into the tubes in seconds, followed by the first Marine squads moments later.

"Lance Aniston, you're on the doctor," Vichy ordered.

Four Marines were around Rin before the Commander even finished speaking. Rin suspected the fire team had already known that and the verbal order had been for his benefit.

"Come on, Dr. Dunst," Lance Emily Aniston told him with a chuckle. "We're not the end of the line; someone has to make sure we don't get shot in the back.

"Let's move."

Another dozen Marines were behind Rin and his escorts as they entered the docking tubes.

"Initial contact on emergence," a translated voice reported, and Rin realized Vichy had him copied on the main command channel. "Welcoming party, no suspicions until they saw the armor. Everyone was stunned before they hit an alarm; localized disruptors have the cameras down."

A tiny map popped up the lower left corner of Rin's vision, filled with the schematics of the ship.

"No guarantee the maps are right," Aniston told him. "But that's what Spear Amoko gave us."

A dotted white line twisted its way through the schematics, and Rin smiled calmly.

"And we follow the yellow brick road?" he asked her.

"Dotted white line, same diff," the Marine replied. "Or the armor in front of you, whichever makes you happy, Doctor."

"Contact on team three," another voice said. Still Laian, the translation came over the original alien speech instead of replacing it. "No difficulties, seven more stunned and tucked out of the way."

"We should be seeing more than this, shouldn't we?" Vichy asked.

"Yes," Spear Amoko agreed. "But that would require them to have thousands of Republic Navy officers and crew they could trust not to betray them when they saw Wendira ships outside. The starbase may be on a minimal crew."

"Lucky us," the Marine said. "All right, all teams, step up the pace. So far, so good, but we need to converge before people in security sections start asking questions."

Rin wasn't even sure how they'd made it this far without triggering an alarm, even with the localized jammers the lead units were using to disrupt cameras. The data center was a kilometer away from their entry point and they were almost halfway...

"Contact!" someone snapped. "Armored security team on the

approach to the data center, ten suits." Pause. "Neutralized, but they had time to trigger an alarm."

There was nothing audible or visual, but Rin knew every communicator aboard the massive starship was probably lighting up.

"Move in and secure the data center *now*," Vichy snapped. "Get the data team on site ASAP. This just turned into a race against the clock, so let's make that timer as big as we can!"

KI!TANA had her own power armor and was far more familiar with it than Rin was. He wasn't surprised to find her waiting when they reached the big security doors sealing off the main entrance to *Builder of Tomorrow*'s data center.

She had her own tools out and had opened the door control panel. The doors would withstand most of the tools available to the Marines...and the ones that could breach the door, as Rin understood it, would destroy the data center.

"Your timing is impeccable, Dr. Dunst," the Ki!Tol told him, extracting data probes from the panel as she lifted herself off the ground. The doors slid open behind her as her armored bullet-like torso faced him.

"We are in, which means you are up."

"I'm not going to turn down your help," Rin told Ki!Tana, shivering as another contact report echoed in his ears.

"Of course not. Let's get to work."

Rin followed her in, poking at various controls until he'd muted non-urgent messages on the command channel. He didn't need the updates now. He needed to focus on the task at hand. His bag of tricks gently dropped next to the central console and he opened it.

"I have a portable holographic data scanner with me," Ki!Tana told him. "I will start copying everything. You see if you can access the system and be more specific."

"Good plan," he agreed, probes and wires assembling rapidly

under his hands as he linked himself into the starbase's computers. The gauntlets weren't *much* of an impediment, but he quickly retracted them anyway,

Anything in the way of his muscle memory slowed him down, and every second he lost was a second a Marine might have to die to buy him.

He started with the codes they'd acquired on *Harvester of Red*. Those didn't get him anywhere, but the system's reaction to them told him useful things. The codes from *Eternal Fall* had similar results.

Both sets of codes were *valid*, he concluded; they just weren't authorized for the access he was trying for. That gave him an interesting starting point, and he linked another module in as he fed *Eternal Fall*'s command codes in again.

They weren't giving him access, but they *were* showing him how access worked—and with the Mesharom-grade decryption module he'd just plugged in...

"There we go," he said aloud. "I'm into the system, commencing searches."

"That was fast," Aniston told him.

"Practice," Rin replied, then sighed as the indices began to flow across his screen. "Practice and stolen Mesharom tech. I'm setting up data searches now, but there's a lot of information here. It's going to take time."

"Well, we just blew the closest elevator to merde," Vichy told him cheerfully, the Marine apparently listening in on all of Rin's channels —which Rin thought was fair enough! "That'll buy us at least a few minutes. Amoko has a team sweeping the nearest security stations and armories, but that elevator was the first response we'd seen yet.

"I think these people are *way* understrength...but I'll remind you, Doctor, that *still* almost certainly means they have more troops aboard than we do.

"And *they* have a fleet to borrow more troops from right here. We don't."

Rin fed another round of parameters into the system in front of him, testing to see how many parallel searches his hacked access would give him.

"I'm on it," he promised. "But...I can't say how long this will take. It depends on how much data there is, how much of it we want, and how fast these computers are."

"I'd say you've got at least ten minutes," Vichy noted. "Everything after that...well. It might start getting expensive."

BY THE TIME Rin could hear plasma fire crackling in the distance, he was reasonably sure he'd found what he needed. It wasn't as easy as there being a single archive labeled *All Secret Alavan Data No One Else Has Is Here*, of course. There were six different sets of files with different bits of information that seemed relevant, and bits scattered through much of the rest of the database.

The six primary archives were all copying when Ki!Tana's tentacle tapped his shoulder.

"We've got about twenty percent of the entire database," she told him. "How are you swimming?"

"I think I've located everything I need and it's copying," Rin replied. "Another minute. Vichy?"

"We're intact so far," the Marine said grimly. "Positions are holding; they haven't thrown a hard push at us yet. They're getting more organized and better equipped. That ten minutes is up, Doctor. Can we move?"

"Not yet," Rin admitted. His console chirped at him and he checked. Two out of the six archives were on his disks. "Each of these archives is multiple petabytes of data, Pierre. They're not copying quickly."

The deck shivered underneath them, a sensation everyone *around* Rin clearly recognized.

"You just ran out of time," Vichy told him. "They just blasted through the deck well away from our defensive positions. I'm pulling my people back, but they are *between* us and you."

"I will take care of it," Ki!Tana said. Rin blinked as the A!Tol produced one of the larger plasma weapons he'd ever seen from somewhere in her mess of tentacles. "The holo-scanner is running. Grab it when you leave, Dr. Dunst. It will shut off automatically."

"All right."

Rin swallowed hard as everyone else in the room drew weapons and headed back to the entrance. Three archives were copied. The other three were all halfway done, but...

Plasma rifles cracked all too near to him as the Marines in the corridor engaged the Laians heading their way. Ki!Tana's weapon joined the chaos a moment later, recognizable by the sheer speed it fired at.

Normal plasma rifles fired every few seconds. Whatever the big Ki!Tol was carrying, it was firing multiple times a second, creating an unending crackle that Rin knew told a tale of fire and death.

Five archives done. He watched the progress bar on the last one and checked on the spider that was grabbing the local context for the rest of the mentions. The spider didn't have everything—it was barely half-done—but it would have to be enough.

The last archive chimed complete. He folded his computer back into the armored carrying case and looked around for Ki!Tana's gear. The odd-looking pocked ovoid of the Mesharom holo-scanner went back in its own carrying case, the extra "muscles" of the power armor helping him sling both cases over his back.

"We're done," he announced on the channel he shared with Ki!Tana and Vichy. "Can we move?"

"Corridor is held by hostile Blades," Ki!Tana said calmly. "Aniston's team and I are keeping them back, but they have us surrounded. We have ourselves a blocked tide."

"We're on our way," Vichy promised. "Keep their attention on you. I doubt they're stupid enough to completely miss us, but every little bit helps."

The rapid *crackcrackcrack* of Ki!Tana's weapon echoed in the station again as Rin approached the data center exit.

"Oh, we most definitely have their attention," the Ki!Tol said with a beak snap. "Everyone is very, very confused."

One of the Marines stopped Rin from going far out into the corridor. He didn't catch which one as he obeyed the gestured command and checked on the situation. Barrier grenades had been thrown into the hallway, sprouting up chest-high walls of plasma-resistant foam to give the Marines cover.

Ki!Tana was behind one of the barriers, demonstrating just how low a being whose height was *all* tentacles could shrink as she waited for a moment. Then she popped back up to her full height, leveling the plasma minigun down the hallway and firing.

A spray of plasma bolts walked along the corridor, burning holes through walls and power armor alike. A desultory salvo answered her fire, the Laians more concerned with staying alive than shooting back.

"Hold position," Aniston snapped as one of her Marines began to move forward. "The barrier grenades are the only thing keeping us safe. Nobody make a dumb move until the Commander gets he—"

The cascade of gunfire that cut her off answered the question of *when* Vichy would arrive. Chaos overwhelmed the Laian positions, and the Marine fire team leader chuckled.

"All right, *now* we go!"

Rin was at the tail of the movement, letting Ki!Tana and a dozen Marines lead the way in a hail of plasma bolts. As they reached the corner, he had to swallow as he reached the consequences of holding the line outside the data center.

All of the Marines were still with him, but there were at least a dozen Laians sprawled in the hallways, wrecked armor still sparking around lethal wounds. More were falling as his escort collided with the rest of the defenders in a clash that ended before Rin could follow what was going on.

The first wave of friends they ran into were Laians of their own,

Imperial-provided IFF codes blinking their silhouettes in green as he came around the corner.

"They had to know there were Blades of ours on the ship, but they hesitated anyway," Amoko told them as she linked to their radio network. "They won't mistake those sands again. We must move."

"And quickly," Vichy added. "One of the war-dreadnoughts is moving into position to block *Eternal Fall*'s escape routes, and the rest of the ships—including the Wendira—are sending shuttles toward *Builder*. We are almost out of time."

"We have everything we need," Rin said. "And if we don't...I wasn't going to find it anyway."

"Right. Allons-y!" Vichy barked. "Everybody *move!*"

CHAPTER FORTY-THREE

WHOEVER WAS IN CHARGE OF THE DEFENDERS WAS CLEARLY waiting for their reinforcements to arrive from the conspirator warships. No one got in the way of their flight back to the stolen cruiser—at which point they found that the interior side of all of the docking tubes had been sealed.

Rin was concerned for a moment...and then Vichy started laughing.

"They expected this to slow us down?" he asked. "Lead squad —*blades.*"

In answer to the chuckled command, the lead Marines extended long blades of some kind from their right—left in some cases— gauntlets and stabbed them directly into the airlocks.

Whatever the airlocks were made of, it was inferior to the vault doors on the data center and gave way easily before the Marine's close-combat weapons. The docking tubes were open in under a minute, and Rin found himself rushed aboard by the Marines.

"Our part in this is done," Vichy said quietly as the last Marines and Blades rushed past them. "We lost six people. Was it worth it, Rin?"

The archeologist winced.

"I don't know," he admitted. "Not yet. I need time to go through everything. Preferably without getting shot at."

"Well, get started, then," his friend said sharply. "My part is done, but yours has a few steps, doesn't it?"

"First, can you help me out of this armor?" Rin asked. "I can't work well in it."

He looked around.

"Where's Ki!Tana?" he asked.

"Probably headed straight to Engineering," Vichy said as he stepped up next to Rin. "The next stage of this is her baby."

A gauntleted hand descended on his shoulder.

"I can't give the suit orders," the Marine continued. "Command is Exit Protocol Bravo-One."

Rin repeated the order and the back of the suit hissed open, letting cooler air wash in over his back as Vichy's armored hands gripped him and gently guided him out of the suit.

"You did okay, Rin," Vichy told him. "But I don't like my people dying. Make sure it was worth it."

"Everything in my power, Pierre," Rin replied. "You know that. We just have to live through the next few minutes."

Eternal Fall vibrated around them, a familiar sensation unchanged by the different colors and design of the warship versus the ones Rin was used to.

"We're moving," he noted. "Guess we'll find out if the stealth field works or not."

NOTHING HAD HIT *Eternal Fall* by the time Rin was back in his workshop and had access to the display showing him the area surrounding the ship again. That two-minute trip coincided with the most dangerous part of their journey, the part where if they were using *Fall*'s original Laian stealth field, they *would* have been visible to the conspirators.

"Ki!Tana, we owe you thanks," Rogers was saying as Rin brought the bridge display back up again. "They knew we were there, but they didn't localize us enough to do more than hit the shield. I didn't think that was possible."

"It isn't," the Ki!Tol said bluntly. "But because they *knew* that *Eternal Fall* had a Laian stealth field, that's what they were looking for. By the time they realized they were focusing on the wrong wavelengths, well... They couldn't hit you."

There were cruisers coming after them now, Rin could see, but the ships were out of range.

"I see we have friends," he said. "Captain, can we escape them?"

"We can get into hyperspace ahead of them," Rogers confirmed. "The odds are in our favor after that. Worst-case scenario, they follow us back to the rendezvous and, well, *Defiance*'s interface drive is down."

Rin remembered the fate of the cruisers who'd ambushed them earlier, and shivered. If they were pursued, the ships would never even know *Defiance* was there before they died.

He didn't like any of this, really, but he knew he was getting disturbingly used to being this close to violence.

"I think I have the data we need," he told Rogers. "It's going to take some time to go through it all."

"We're a full cycle from making rendezvous with *Defiance*," the acting captain told him. "I suggest you get started?"

"Keep us alive, Commander Rogers, and I'll do just that," Rin replied.

He turned his attention back to his computers. The security box protecting his setup from *Eternal Fall*'s would also help him load the archive data into his systems without bringing any executable code with it.

There was a tremor through the ship as they plunged through a hyperspace portal, and he allowed himself a nod of satisfaction. The people his lover commanded were spectacularly competent. He could trust Rogers and Ki!Tana to get him safely back to Morgan Casimir.

He needed to see if he could find the answer to how the conspiracy was tracking down the dead Alavan fleet. They knew something he didn't know, something that hadn't been in the archives of a Mesharom war-sphere.

And maybe, just maybe, when he put everything together, he'd answer a few more questions along the way.

CHAPTER FORTY-FOUR

Rin leaned against the wall in the conference room on *Defiance* in exhaustion. He hadn't slept since before the raid on *Builder of Tomorrows* but he now knew the answers he needed. He didn't *like* the answers, and a sick feeling nestled in his stomach as Morgan entered the room, joining the collection of officers and civilian associates leading this mission.

"How are you doing?" Morgan asked.

"I'm going to sleep for a dozen hours after this is over," he told her. "But right now, you all need to know what I know. I have some data to feed into Ki!Tana's model to give us new places to investigate, but...there's some background that's key, I think."

"All right, everyone," Morgan said with a nod to him. "Let's all hear just what the professor has to brief us on."

She took her own seat and Rin faced the officers. This was purely an Imperial crew now. He hadn't been involved in the discussion of what happened to *Eternal Fall* now, but only the Imperial officers remained.

He and Ki!Tana were the only civilians in the room, and Morgan had kept the rest to the cruiser's most senior officers, people that were cleared to know just how the Alava had died.

"I've gone through the key points of the data the conspirators had," he told them. "I've cross-referenced everything we had from our own archives, everything we learned from the Taljzi and everything we learned out at Kosha...and I have discovered a fundamental misunderstanding on our part of why the Alava fell."

He smiled grimly.

"They did not attempt to change the rules of physics to make their ships more efficient because they could. They did so because they were at war," he told them. "We think of the Alava as godlike, their technology still far beyond anything we could duplicate now, but they were facing an enemy that truly terrified them.

"By the time of their fall, the Alava didn't have much concept of physical text versus digital information transfer with computers and neural implants," he noted. "It appears that some of them kept up the concept much as some people now have typewriters. One of those Alava was the commander of the fleet base we know the fleet we're hunting launched from—and the conspirators appear to have acquired their journal at some point."

He had everyone's attention now. Even the military officers understood the value of having an actual *document* from the Hegemony.

"The journal appears to have been badly damaged by age, and not all of its contents were loaded into the database I could access on *Builder of Tomorrows*," he told them. "But the base commander spoke of 'The Enemy.' They didn't include much detail on what they were fighting, only that worlds and even sectors had been lost.

"There are a few references to 'scientists and traitors' experimenting with the technology of their enemy, which I think is what we saw at Kosha and Arjtal," Rin said. "This enemy appears to have been using biotech on a scale that allowed them to face the Alava on an even level. What we saw in Kosha was an Alavan faction that had either betrayed the Hegemony and joined this Enemy or that was experimenting with the Enemy's technology—creating things like the stellarvore."

"They broke the galaxy because they were afraid?" Nguyen asked, the tactical officer sounded stunned.

"Exactly," Rin agreed. "I don't know if this Enemy was actually a threat, given the scale and power of the Alava Hegemony, but it was more so than anything else they'd ever encountered. I'd guess the project was already ongoing and they either rushed it or turned it on because of this war.

"We all know what happened then."

"So, we know why the Alavan fleet was sent out," Morgan said. "Does that help us?"

"Thanks to the conspirators, we now know their official course," Rin noted. "The conspirators have investigated every point on it, so we know they detoured from it. Our opponents are operating on the assumption that the fleet pursued an Enemy force into the Nebula, which I believe is a fundamentally sound assumption.

"Hence us all being here."

"Does that help us find them?" Ki!Tana asked. "We don't know where the battle was, so that doesn't narrow down any locations."

"We know a few things the conspirators don't," Rin told the old alien. "We know about the Kosha Sector and the traitors there...and while the Kosha Sector may have been experimenting with the Enemy's tech, they weren't the Enemy. That means I have several solid regions of space that we know the Enemy *didn't* come from.

"Along with that, though," he smiled sadly, "is that one of the sites I visited for the Laians didn't feel very Alavan. It felt like someone had carried out high-intensity resource-extraction operations using complex biotech.

"If we assume that site was a temporary resupply post for this Enemy, then that *does* give us an angle of approach for them. Plugging that into Ki!Tana's models gives us a few locations for the *battle* to have taken place, at least.

"While those are no guarantee of finding the Alavan fleet, they are definitely a starting point."

He tapped a command, popping up a map of the Astoroko Nebula on the wall next to him. Four new glowing icons appeared on the projection.

"I don't know if we can detect much of a fifty-thousand-year-old battle," he admitted, "but...it's a starting point."

"Depending on how dramatic the battle was, in terms of debris and energy levels, it's actually possible we might be able to find some signs still," Nguyen suggested softly, the tactical officer looking at Rogers for support.

The First Sword nodded her agreement.

"We wouldn't in regular space, but this is a pretty dense nebula," Rogers said. "The signs might be pretty sparse and subtle, but we might just find something."

"Then that gives us some work to do," Morgan stated. "Thank you, Dr. Dunst. I think our little side trip just proved worth it."

He nodded and slumped into a seat, surrendering the floor to *Defiance*'s Captain.

"*Eternal Fall* will be leaving for the Tohrohsail System shortly, carrying a full encrypted copy of everything Dr. Dunst found," she told them all. "We'll send our own reports via hyperfold com at our first investigation point.

"Now that we have more information than the conspirators, we might manage to track this fleet down before them. If we manage that, we will be calling for backup ASAP," she continued. "Hopefully by then, Fleet Lord Tan!Shallegh will have managed to get the Wendira and Laians to step back from the precipice, because the more I hear about everything, the more I want to make sure Alavan warships don't fall into these people's hands."

"If their Enemy was using the same kind of biotech as we saw out at Kosha and Arjtal, there's something else we need to worry about," Rogers pointed out. "We know Alavan tech doesn't work...but we keep running into fully functional biotech from the same time period.

"The ships their Enemy was using might be intact enough to be salvageable."

"And the last thing we need is a bunch of war profiteers getting their hands on intact biotech warships," Morgan agreed. "Rin, what are the odds?"

He shrugged, struggling against exhaustion to organize his thoughts.

"I don't know," he admitted. "Everything suggests that's the tech this Enemy was using. And...yeah, we've seen working Alavan biotech again and again; and it looks like all of that tech was derivative."

"That makes getting there first even more important," Morgan said with a sigh. "We need to get underway. Rin, can you send El-Amin your coordinates?"

"Of course."

"Everyone else, make sure your departments are all on the ball and realize as much of the importance of this situation as we can afford to share," she told the officers.

"El Dorado, a graveyard, a fleet...whatever we want to call the objective, we have to find it first. The last thing anyone needs is for that tech to fall into the hands of the kind of people who tried to start a *war* to cover their tracks."

CHAPTER FORTY-FIVE

MORGAN WATCHED *ETERNAL FALL* BLAZE AWAY THROUGH hyperspace thoughtfully. With everything Rin had dropped on her senior officers, their problem was now very clear. They were facing a collection of war profiteers who might, if she failed, end up in possession of *functioning* technology that had given the Alava a run for their money.

"Ki!Tana." She opened a private channel to her stepmother's friend. "Did you take your stealth-field upgrades out of *Eternal Fall*? She's going right back to the Laian fleet, after all."

"Didn't need to," Ki!Tana replied. "I just wired my generators into her projectors. With *Dark Eyes* back aboard *Defiance*, *Fall* doesn't even have a stealth-field generator now. Not until hers is fixed."

"Handy," Morgan murmured. "Thank you."

Defiance was moving as she spoke to Ki!Tana, El-Amin bringing the interface drive online and sending them hurtling toward the first of their new waypoints at sixty percent of lightspeed.

"We're here to deal with this together," the A!Tol replied.

"Does Rin's theory make sense to you?" Morgan asked.

There was a long silence on the call.

"It fits the data he found and that we have," Ki!Tana finally said. "I...I find the waters questionable that lead to even the existence of handwritten Alavan documents. If such existed, I would have expected the Mesharom to be aware of the possibility and far too careful to allow one to fall into hands this untrustworthy."

"But?"

"But it fits what we know," Ki!Tana repeated. "It fits the pattern. It explains why an entire pocket empire existed out at the Kosha Sector that wasn't mentioned in the old Mesharom tablets.

"The only things that the Mesharom could write down were what they knew," the Ki!Tol reminded Morgan. "I doubt the Hegemony told their subject races they were even fighting a war, let alone losing one. The Mesharom and their other subjects helped build their warships, but only Alava served on them."

Morgan swallowed a sigh. They were half a cycle—about eleven and a half hours—from the first possible battle location. She couldn't show her crew that she was hesitant about all of this.

"So, the Mesharom never knew about the war, so they couldn't include it when they wrote down everything they could remember of the Alava," she finished the thought. "Which leaves us running on guesses and fragments as we search for the wreckage of a battle where we know nothing about one side except that they existed.

"We're not even sure who won. Only that the Alavan ships shut down when they triggered their core device."

"Exactly," Ki!Tana agreed. "Your partner has found an ugly hidden tide, Morgan. I hope we can dodge its worst pulls."

"We can only wait and see," Morgan said. "I'm not sure we're going to find any more answers out here. Just a bunch of wrecks that can't fall into the wrong hands."

"You need to be prepared to destroy them," Ki!Tana warned. "We both know what the best option is when it comes to that, much as I hate to even consider it."

"I do," Morgan said levelly. "I will do what I must."

She looked around the bridge and sighed.

"Rogers, I'm going to get some rest before we reach the waypoint," she told her XO. "You have the bridge."

MORGAN DIDN'T GO to her quarters first. She would soon enough—she had an extremely cuddle-able lover in her bed and she wasn't going let that go to waste, even if she doubted the exhausted archeologist had energy for more than cuddling—but there was something else part of her needed to do.

The guards on *Defiance*'s magazines, an omnipresent force no matter where she was, let Morgan pass without question. They knew their Captain—and that no one without proper authorizations would make it far, even if they didn't stop them.

The magazines for the rear batteries of the ship were attached to a corridor that ran through the carefully designed and baffled armored sections. Each door was labeled with its battery and launcher, the storage spaces behind them containing interface-drive missiles and single-portal hyperspace missiles in neatly organized racks.

At the end of the corridor was what looked like a solid wall, one that Morgan had only inspected in person once. She placed her hand on a seemingly unmarked section of it and winced at the prick as the concealed scanner took a DNA sample.

She stated her authorization codes aloud as it confirmed her DNA and palm print, and then the entire bulkhead slid aside to let her in.

The magazine on the far side was smaller than the cavernous spaces that held her cruiser's missile armament, but it only held three individual weapons. Each was nestled in a cradle, ready to be delivered to the concealed launcher that would fire the oversized munitions.

Morgan crossed to the closest of her starkillers and ran her fingers along the smooth white shell of the spherical weapon. They didn't *look* like the most powerful weapons in existence. They looked like weirdly shaped shuttles.

But each of those prosaic-looking spheres contained the ability to destroy an entire star system. In a place like Astoroko Nebula, where a dozen blue dwarfs were in the process of being birthed, she wasn't even sure what the consequences of firing a starkiller would be.

She was only sure that Ki!Tana was right. Morgan Casimir was the only living officer of the A!Tol Imperial Navy who'd fired a starkiller...and if it looked like the conspirators were going to get their hands on the Alavan fleet, she might well become possibly the only living officer to have fired starkillers *twice*.

Defiance certainly couldn't defeat the conspirators' fleet. She'd already told Tan!Shallegh everything she'd known before she'd sent *Eternal Fall* to *Builder of Tomorrows*.

Now she had to call for help and hope that the timing worked out.

She didn't regret what she'd done in the slightest, but she also never wanted to see a star blown up by her orders ever again.

CHAPTER FORTY-SIX

Defiance's bridge was silent as the cruiser flashed through the emergence portal to their first waypoint. Morgan wasn't sure what she expected to find, but the most likely scenario was, well, nothing.

And that was what they found.

"We're scanning for anomalies," Nguyen reported after a few more seconds of silence. "There's nothing immediately obvious, but we're looking for signs of an ancient battle. It may take a while."

Morgan nodded silently, studying the space around them. One of the Astoroko Nebula's protostars filled an entire side of her view, the still-growing giant a brilliant beacon less than a dozen light-minutes away.

"Nystrom," she turned to her communications officer. "Ping the nearest hyperfold relay and make sure we pick up any messages waiting for us. We can wait a cycle here if that helps us get our messages."

There would be a thousand messages somewhere in the pipeline for *Defiance*, but without some notice of where she'd been going, there was no way they'd arrive without Morgan's ship looking for them.

Morgan was waiting on personal messages, like the rest of her crew, but the important one would be the response from Fleet Lord Tan!Shallegh to her earlier messages. The hyperfold was faster than light, but it wasn't instantaneous.

She'd abused its limitations to protect her crew and herself from an order to stand down—an order her Tsunami-level orders would require her to disobey.

"Even with the relays, sir, it'll still be an entire cycle before our ping reaches a starcom," Nystrom warned her. "We'll get anything that's already in the local network, but there's no guarantee our messages are."

"I know," Morgan conceded. "Include all coordinates of our sweep under Dragon Protocol encryptions. The Fleet Lord will be able to read them and make sure we get our mail at one of the stops."

She looked at the screen again. Other than the incipient blue giant, there was nothing there but *Defiance*. She didn't think Nguyen's team was going to find much, either.

The odds were decent that *one* of the new waypoints Rin and Ki!Tana had worked up would be their destination—but the odds of any particular waypoint weren't great. Morgan hadn't expected to get lucky the first time.

"Let me know if anything pings our sensors," she ordered. "I'll be in my office."

MORGAN HAD BEEN RUNNING through paperwork for about half an hour when the door chimed and opened to reveal her XO.

"First Sword, how can I help you?" she asked.

Rogers took a seat thoughtfully.

"Not sure, sir," she admitted. "Still...wrapping my head around losing people, I guess. They were Vichy's Marines, but they were under my command. No one above me, no one else to stop the buck with.

"My command. My responsibility."

"Yes," Morgan agreed softly, eyeing the younger woman. "Hurts?"

"I barely knew any of them, but...yeah. And yet...it feels like it should hurt more?" Rogers said.

"Both will be true for a long time," Morgan told her. "I remember every name, every face, of the people we lost to the Mother and its cultists. A quarter of the crew died."

"That hurts too," her subordinate conceded. "But...I wasn't responsible then."

"I was," Morgan said. "And I'll carry those names to my own grave. And I'll carry the names of the Marines you lost at *Builder of Tomorrows*, too. I sent you all out there. They died at my orders."

"And mine."

"And yours," Morgan agreed. "We can't change what happened, Commander Rogers. We can only make certain that we learn from it —and make certain that the mission they died to achieve is completed."

"We got the information; we're using it as we speak," Rogers concluded. "So, we're doing what we can?"

"We are," Morgan said. "And you're still going to feel like you're failing your dead."

She still had dreams—not really nightmares anymore; familiarity and therapy had smoothed the edges—about the pilot who'd rammed his shuttle into the Alavan cloner the Taljzi had used to fuel their expansion. Morgan had drawn up the mission brief and made the attack possible, but it had been Lesser Speaker Kenneth Donnelly who'd given his life to end that war.

He'd been posthumously promoted to Fleet Lord, the pension for that rank handily supporting a widow and disabled sister.

Morgan still felt she'd failed him some days.

"I get it, I think," Rogers said. "Better to feel this than not, I suppose?"

"Exactly," Morgan told her. "We grow calluses, we have to, to survive. But we can never *stop* feeling it. The officers and spacers under our command put their lives in our hands. Regardless of species or creed, they follow us into the fire.

"Not all of them make it out. Not all of them ever could. We owe it to them to finish the mission and to make sure as many of them make it as possible."

She shook her head.

"There are very few good parts to this job, Beth," she told her First Sword. "We don't do it because it's easy or because it's fun. We do this job because someone has to, because we're good at it...and because someone else might get it wrong."

Rogers bowed her head and exhaled a long sigh.

"Thank you, sir," she said. "I appreciate it."

"Tan!Stalla gave me about the same lecture," Morgan told her subordinate. "She commanded *Jean Villeneuve* when we went into the hell storm that was the battle of Arjtal. Some day, you'll give the same lecture to officers under your own command. It's part of the tradition and history of the Imperium."

"It helps to know we all struggle with the same demons," Rogers admitted.

"It does. And, Commander Rogers?"

"Sir?"

"If the struggle ever seems too hard, ever seems like you're facing it alone, remember that it *is* hard but you *don't* face it alone," Morgan told the younger woman. "This ship has three fully trained counselors aboard. They know this dance better than I do. I can tell you what worked for me. They can help you find what will work for you.

"That's their job. Part of *your* job is to know when you need to use them and to do so. You understand?"

"Yes, sir."

CHAPTER FORTY-SEVEN

MORGAN WAS ABOUT TO HEAD BACK TO THE BRIDGE WHEN Nystrom commed her.

"Captain, it looks like there was a package for us in the local network," the coms officer reported. "It's not a full mail delivery, just a limited drop of encrypted messages under a code I'm not familiar with. Flagged for you, your eyes only."

"Send them over," Morgan ordered.

Her inbox flickered at her as the messages downloaded and Morgan opened the most recent. She'd been expecting a message under top-tier Dragon Protocol or even standard Navy encryption.

Instead, the message confirmed who she was and then asked for her *Tsunami* clearance.

Hesitatingly, Morgan plugged in that series of numbers and watched the message slowly decrypt. The last person she was expecting to see when it finished was Empress A!Shall, though she supposed that fit with everything.

"Captain Casimir," the Empress told her calmly. "I have been reviewing everything that has come out of your mission as you report it. I have no useful information to contribute to your task. As of the last update I received, you were out of communication as you used a borrowed Laian cruiser to infiltrate our mysterious third party.

"I want you to know that I have already discussed this and the attack on your vessel with the Grand Parliament of the Laian Republic. Your actions of self-defense have been approved and endorsed by the highest levels of both nations. So, Captain Casimir, has your ploy to learn what information you can about *Builder of Tomorrows*.

"Be advised that no such mobile shipyard is on the lists for the Laian Navy. The Republic is going to investigate her existence in great detail and would appreciate any information your mission brings up."

The Empress fluttered her tentacles, the dull gray of her iron control somewhat off-putting to anyone familiar with A!Tol emotional coloring.

"The situation remains highly concerning. Fleet Lord Tan!Shallegh is scheduled to arrive at his meeting with the Laians and the Wendira in the next few cycles as I record this message. War may still be averted, not least thanks to your efforts, but the presence of the Alavan graveyard is worrying.

"A task force has been dispatched under Squadron Lord Tan!Stalla. You are authorized and required to bring her into the loop on Tsunami matters, but only in person. No electronic briefing can be provided.

"If..." A!Shall paused for several seconds, then continued again.

"If, in your judgment, Tan!Stalla's task force will not arrive in advance of the conspirators and you are unable to prevent the conspirators' locating the graveyard fleet, you are to destroy the Alavan vessels by any means available.

"You are explicitly ordered to deploy Final Dragon–class strategic weapons to eliminate the Alavan fleet."

The Empress was silent again for several more seconds.

"The currents of your prior actions suggest that your judgment in this matter is beyond reproach and that my Fleet Lords selected well for the Captains of our new strategic weapons platforms. Do not taint these waters, Captain Casimir.

"May the tide speed you."

The message ended and Morgan stared at the screen for several seconds in shocked silence.

After a few seconds, she tapped the second message. That one *merely* called for her Dragon security codes, what she had believed were the highest codes until very recently.

The image of her old Captain appeared on the screen, Tan!Stalla looking at the recorder with the purplish-red of warm concern flashing across her skin.

"Captain Casimir, I have been briefed on some of the current situation," the A!Tol said calmly. "I am advised that we are moving against an unknown third party that appears to be trying to instigate a war between the Laians and Wendira.

"I have vague but worrying assessments of their strength, but that has been factored into the forces under my command. I am en route to the Astoroko Nebula with sixteen *Galileo*-class superbattleships, sixteen *Bellerophon*-C-class battleships, and an escort of forty-eight *Thunderstorms* of various types.

"My understanding is that my force should suffice against any threat short of a major Laian or Wendira fleet deployment. My ETA is thirteen to sixteen cycles from my transmission of this message, but I don't know exactly where you are.

"If you can relay updated coordinates ASAP, we will make certain we are in position to support you.

"Tan!Stalla aboard *Jean Villeneuve*, out."

Morgan considered the two messages as she struggled with an overwhelming sense of relief. Not only was she not at risk of being disavowed for the actions she'd known were needed, reinforcements were on their way.

She checked the time stamps on the messages. Tan!Shallegh should have arrived at the peace summit already. Tan!Stalla was still at least nine cycles away.

She shivered.

By the time they hit the fourth of the new waypoints, their backup would still be five cycles away. A hundred and fifteen hours, minimum...more than enough time for their enemies to do something spectacularly stupid.

CHAPTER FORTY-EIGHT

"So, can someone tell me, please, that our next stop is *farther* from that...thing?" Nguyen asked.

Her question, said loudly and somewhat plaintively as the entire cruiser's bridge crew stared at the stellar formation in question, earned her several chuckles.

"That's, what, six hyper-giants in a natural mutual orbit?" Morgan replied. "I was wondering what was making such a dent in hyperspace."

"None of them have accumulated enough mass to quite qualify as hyper-giants," El-Amin corrected. "There's only about the mass of three blue giants in that mess."

"And your point?" Morgan said, to another series of quiet chuckles.

"It's an unstable formation that's sucking up a good chunk of the nebula's mass in this region," the navigator replied. "It will only last another hundred thousand years or so before the imbalances mean that one of them gets eaten by the others and the whole tableau collapses."

The *tableau* in question stretched over a full light-year of normal space. It matched up to a section of heavily distorted hyperspace that had been showing up on their anomaly scanners on the last trip, too.

"But, to answer Commander Nguyen's question, our next stop is actually closer," El-Amin continued. "Unless she finds our mystery fleet there, I think we are continuing toward the cluster."

Morgan nodded, studying the monster of a mutual birth through the scanners.

"Is hyperspace going to get as bad heading toward it as I think it is?" she asked.

"We can navigate reliably," El-Amin replied. "But...yes."

"Nguyen, once your team is done analyzing this region for signs of the battle, see if you can do some modeling for how bad our scanners are going to be affected as we get closer to the cluster," Morgan ordered.

"I can tell you right now it's going to cut the range on our anomaly scanners pretty significantly," Nguyen told her. "If our *friends* are out ahead of us, we won't have seen them."

"That's what I figured," Morgan replied. "See if we can model just how bad our eyes are going to be. I want to avoid surprises if we can."

"Understood, sir."

The bridge was silent again for a few minutes, until the most damning and hopeful phrase in the human language drifted out of the tactical consoles.

"Huh. That's funny."

"Initiate?" Nguyen said calmly. "Would you care to share with the class?"

"I don't think I'm looking at something that happened *here*, but there's some really screwed-up trails in the nebula that, if I'm calculating right, are from the right time period," the most junior officer in the tactical department, a shaven-headed South African woman barely out of the Academy, said slowly.

"Take a look, sir."

"Send it to my screen as well," Morgan ordered.

The scans appeared on her repeaters a moment later. For a moment, she couldn't see anything—but then Initiate Patience Mugabe highlighted what she'd seen.

"Those are gravity wakes," Nguyen said. "Like something heavy and fast cut through the nebula, creating a gap that's been drifting this way and expanding for millennia. Can we identify the source?"

"Nothing in our records would do anything like this," Morgan told her tactical officer. "But..."

She trailed off as she considered some of the studies she'd seen.

"Sir?" Nguyen asked. "I'm with you. Nothing I know of would do this."

"One of our ships running a singularity-mass-conversion power plant has the mass impact shielded by the interface drive," Morgan pointed out. The gravitational-hyperspatial interface momentum engine used the interface between realspace and hyperspace to create its impossible velocities, but it also neutralized a lot of gravitational impacts along with the relativistic issues.

"But we know the Alava used singularity power plants, and we *don't* know what they used for sublight maneuvering," she continued. "Their ships might just have had this effect. Can we *locate* the source?"

"It depends on if the drift velocity is— Thank you, Initiate Mugabe," Nguyen cut herself off as Mugabe put new data on her screen. "*If* this pattern is from around the fall of the Alava, we know when the fall happened to within a few cycles at this point.

"That would put the origin point of the patterns *here*."

A new blinking icon appeared on their main chart. Fifty thousand years was a long time for a pattern to travel, but it wasn't like nebula dust moved all that quickly on its own. Seven light-years. Roughly...

"That's directly between Rin and Ki!Tana's points three and four, isn't it?" Morgan asked.

"It's a probabilistic projection, sir," Mugabe said hesitantly.

"That's the ninety-percent zone, but both waypoint three and four are inside the fifty-percent zone."

"Nguyen, is there anything else here?" Morgan said quietly.

"I think this is the most we're going to find, sir," her tactical officer conceded. "It's a giant red arrow, better evidence than I was expecting to find short of wrecked Alavan ships. It's a question mark, we don't know what caused the pattern, but..."

"We don't have much else to go for, either," Morgan said. "El-Amin, plug in Initiate Mugabe's ninety-percent zone and set a course."

"Apologies, Commander Nguyen," the navigator said slowly. "But that's actually even closer to the cluster than the waypoints are."

"We're going to have severely limited visibility in hyperspace," Nguyen agreed. "It's going to be a lot easier to sneak up on us than usual."

"We'll have to live with it," Morgan replied. "It's the only clue we've got, which means we are following that trail, people."

MORGAN FOUND Rin in the workshop, with everything set up to allow him to follow *Defiance*'s sensor feeds.

"You saw what we saw?" she asked after stepping into the room.

He started and turned around.

"Knock, please?" he said. "I...get focused when I'm working."

"Sorry," she conceded. "The door was open."

"Fair, fair," Rin replied, chuckling. "What did you ask?"

She laughed.

"I asked if you saw what we saw on the bridge. The pattern in the nebula."

"I did," he confirmed. "And I'm comparing it to what we've seen at other sites. We don't have a lot of data on places where Alavan ships passed through nebulas, though."

"But you sound like you have an idea?" Morgan asked.

"Yeah." He shook his head. "We haven't seen anything like this associated with Alavan ships, Morgan. It's strange and new and it's making me nervous. I think you're right to follow it...but I'm not sure it's from the Alava."

"From their Enemy?" she said.

"Possible," he agreed. "From one of them, certainly. The time-space analysis Mugabe did puts it in the right place. I'm not sure what caused it, but I can't see any ship using a singularity as a power source allowing that much of the mass effect to reach beyond the hull. The tidal forces *inside* a ship having this much effect on the nebula would be...bad."

"I know," Morgan said. She'd realized that as soon as the initial excitement had passed. "But it's weird and it's in the right place, so we'll check it out."

"Oh, I agree," her lover said. "And I'm going to be right here, going over *everything*, when we get there. I hope I'll find some answers for you. If nothing else, I'm curious."

"Curiosity could get us all killed, but I'm with you," she told him. "Any ideas to look for?"

"The other thing that comes to mind is to look for the singularity itself," Rin pointed out. "Can we calculate its velocity from what we can detect?"

Morgan shook her head.

"Not easily," she admitted. "A direction, yeah, but any velocity calculation would be so vague as to be useless."

"Then I guess we go poke things with a stick and see what we find. Something fascinating, I suspect."

"Something dangerous, I suspect," Morgan told him, but she smiled as she said it. "But that's why you and I are here together. One of us to deal with the danger, the other to find the answers in the fascinating parts."

"I'll find you the answers, Morgan," Rin promised. "You just keep us all alive."

She stepped over to kiss the top of his head.

"I'm planning on it," she told him. "No matter what it takes."

She'd told him about the Empress's message. He put his hand on hers and squeezed.

"Any help I can give through the answers I find, I will," he promised. "We're close, Morgan. I can feel it."

"I hope so." She chuckled. "Though I wouldn't mind delaying anyone finding it until *after* Tan!Stalla arrives with our backup fleet!"

CHAPTER FORTY-NINE

MORGAN WATCHED HER SENSOR DISPLAYS WITH A CAREFUL EYE as *Defiance* drew closer to their destination—and to the swirling, chaotic pattern of the protostar cluster. Her hyperspatial anomaly scanners usually had effective ranges measured in hyperspace light-months—realspace distances of up to a light-century, though the time delay and detail made longer-range data useless for tracking.

Here, that range shrank to a handful of hyperspace light-minutes —realspace light-months at best. Hyperspace's normal gray void was disturbed, a twisting intermix of shades of gray that impeded even the normal one-light-second visibility bubble.

"I feel blind," Nguyen told her. "There could be an entire fleet out here and we wouldn't see them."

"And they wouldn't see us, either," Morgan replied. "That blade cuts both ways. For that matter, one of the fleets that might be out there is friendly."

Tan!Stalla's fleet probably wasn't close yet, but hyperspace had been known to do stranger things. The Imperial task force had hope-fully received the update on *Defiance*'s new destination and changed their course, too.

Unlike *Defiance*, after all, *Jean Villeneuve* had a starcom receiver. FTL messages could be sent to the capital ships of the relief fleet.

"Emergence at waypoint five in a hundredth-cycle," El-Amin reported, his left hand twisting the fabric of his headscarf as he validated his numbers.

"Everything around is clear, so far as I can tell," Nguyen said. "We wouldn't see the Alavan wreckage from hyperspace, anyway."

"Keep your eyes and sensors peeled," Morgan replied. "Even if this was the exact location of the battle, the wreckage has probably moved—but we *should* be able to detect it from there."

"Yes, sir." Nguyen's tone was dry enough to remind Morgan that she was repeating basic concepts from the academy, and she shook her head reprovingly at her tactical officer.

"Weapons status, tactical?" she asked.

"All batteries are online; ready capacitors and magazines are full," Nguyen said crisply. "Internal hyperspace portals are offline but everything is ready to bring them online in under sixty seconds."

That put *Defiance* at Status Three. Morgan considered bringing the ship to battle stations as the timer ticked down toward emergence. There *shouldn't* be anything out there but the dead and the nebula, but the conspirator fleet *was* looking for them.

She sighed.

"Take the ship to Status One," she ordered. Battle stations was *probably* a step too far, but putting a second shift on every duty station and having the Bucklers ready to launch seemed a reasonable precaution.

Her readiness display changed colors, from the green indicators of *station at current status* to the yellow of *station manned but not at current status*. Across the kilometer-long bulk of Morgan's command, her crew would be receiving alert notifications, calling the bravo shift to their duty stations.

Yellow indicators edged toward green with respectable speed as her people reported to their positions. Morgan watched two timers and nodded in satisfaction as the last station checked in.

Two point six thousandth-cycles—two hundred and twenty seconds. Entirely acceptable and, more importantly, completed a full thousandth-cycle before emergence.

"We're ready," she said aloud. "Translate on schedule, Commander El-Amin."

"Portal creation in thirty seconds," the navigator replied. "Stand by."

———

IT WAS obvious within seconds that Initiate's Mugabe's moment of confusion at an odd pattern in the nebula had brought them to exactly the right place. There would almost certainly be other wreckage scattered throughout the surrounding area, but at least one mothership's final resting point was only a light-minute or so from where *Defiance* emerged.

Even dark and dead, it was what they were looking for, and the fifteen-hundred-kilometer sphere drew the attention of Morgan's crew for a critical handful of seconds. Even the five-hundred-kilometer superfortresses the Taljzi had assembled from the wrecks of lighter Alavan warships paled against the scale of a true Alavan mothership.

Its scale distracted Morgan and her people for long enough that it took them a moment to realize they'd missed the damage. At some point, *something* had physically crushed a circular line a hundred meters across one hemisphere of the ship, smashing even compressed-matter armor into a trench of broken debris.

Once she'd realized there was damage, Morgan turned her eye on the rest of the data. Massive holes had been torn through the ancient hulk. There was *more than one* immense trench where something had struck the ship with unimaginable force. This mothership had been dead before the Alava had killed themselves.

It took a moment for Morgan to even recognize the flashing red icons of *other* ships emerging from behind the mothership.

"Vampire, vampire!" Nguyen chanted. "Hostiles detected. They were either inside or *behind* the mothership wreck. I'm picking up Wendira starfighters, at least a hundred of them."

Morgan swallowed a curse.

"Evasive maneuvers, battle stations," she barked. "Get me ID and number on those bastards."

Larger icons were emerging now as well. Even Morgan had failed to consider that the kind of trail *they'd* followed there would have been found by others—and the conspirators had been searching the same region of the nebula.

"I've got a war-dreadnought and two Wendira star nests," Nguyen reported after a few moments. "Secondary carriers, stealth ships."

"I know what a star nest is," Morgan replied. "Escorts?"

"Looks like four star shields and ten cruisers. It's a pocket task force, sir."

"Understood," Morgan said grimly.

The starfighters were blazing toward her ship at eighty percent of lightspeed. No living being could survive that for long...but the Wendira drones piloting those ships didn't *care*. Short-lived beings with genetic memories, their only hope of being remembered was to perform some great act.

"Take us back, full sprint," she ordered El-Amin. "Buy me time, Commander. Nguyen, get me as much data on that wreck as you can."

It *looked* like the wreck was truly that: a complete wreck of minimal value to the conspirators. Morgan could leave that be for the moment, but if there were more intact Alavan ships around...

"The cruisers are matching our velocity," Nguyen warned. "Everything else is moving at sixty-five percent of light. The fighters are gaining; estimate range in sixty seconds."

Morgan nodded. The starfighters' missiles weren't the problem. The problem was their close-range heavy plasma cannons. Individually weaker than her plasma lances, several hundred of them would tear *Defiance* apart.

And these fighters weren't underestimating her people, either. Rapid evasive maneuvers, cycling formations, randomized motions. Her missiles didn't have a chance of taking down more than a tithe of them, and her hyperfold cannons wouldn't do much better.

"That ship is a complete wreck, sir," Nguyen reported after a few more seconds. "The hull is probably the most intact part from what I can see and, well, the hull is shredded."

"All right," Morgan said calmly. "El-Amin, get us out of here. I'm not taking one cruiser against a dreadnought battle group."

Let alone a dreadnought battle group with support from the Laians' ancient enemies.

"Portal opening," her navigator replied. "We are entering hyper-space...*now*."

CHAPTER FIFTY

Hyperspace kept them safe from the starfighters, but that was the only thing their flight was guaranteed to keep away.

"Contact," Nguyen reported a few seconds after their own portal closed behind them. "We have portals opening behind us. Orders, sir?"

The anomaly scanners were a mess, but it was already too late to kill the interface drive and hide. Four anomalies were on the screens now and Morgan glared at them.

"Missile range?" she asked grimly.

"Anomaly-scanner traces aren't good enough for us to hit them at any range in this mess," Nguyen replied. "And vice versa. But if we head away from the cluster..."

"The range they can *hit* us at increases, even if we keep the actual range the same," Morgan finished grimly.

She hadn't given any orders, but El-Amin already had them flying away from the enemy ships at seventy percent of lightspeed. They couldn't hold that up for long. Morgan wasn't sure how long the Laian and Wendira ships chasing them could keep up *their* sprint modes, but she couldn't bet her ship that it would be less than she could.

There really was only one option.

"El-Amin. Set your course for the protostar cluster," she ordered calmly. "Take us right into the middle and pop a portal when you think we're covered by the gravitational disturbances."

The bridge was silent but Morgan could see the indicators change as El-Amin followed her orders.

"That's risky, sir," he finally told her. "We're probably safe in hyperspace, but if we drop out in the middle of it..."

"Eye of the storm, Commander," Morgan replied. "The cluster will have swept up all of the debris and gases inside itself millennia ago, and they mostly cancel out each other's gravitational forces, too. If we can get all the way in, it's a safe place to hide from anybody."

"We won't be able to send hyperfold transmissions from in there, sir," Nystrom warned. "We might have been able to from waypoint five, but the disruption will be too dense inside the cluster."

"We'll see if they're crazy enough to follow us," Morgan said grimly. "Worst-case scenario, we lead them on a merry chase through the hellstorm and lose them. I trust this ship's crew and engines over theirs."

Her bridge crew didn't argue, setting to their tasks with a grimmer tone to the silence.

"Enemy is splitting up," Nguyen reported. "One ship is keeping pace with us, approximately fifty hyperspace light-seconds back. The others are falling back."

"Your guess, Commander?" Morgan asked.

"They're chaining their positions to make sure each of them can be seen by at least one other ship as they follow us. They know we're headed toward the cluster, if nothing else."

Morgan nodded.

"It will be what it will be," she said. "At the end of the day, I'm confident we can kill any one of their ships except the damn dreadnought. If they want to follow us into realspace alone, with a chain of friends to tell them where they died, I'm fine with that!"

———————

IN NINETEEN YEARS of military training and service and dozens of hyperspace flights as the child of Earth's ruling couple, Morgan had thought she'd learned everything hyperspace could do and be. It was usually visibly bland, though the currents that made travel times so unpredictable were often gorgeous in their own grayscale way.

It was never *noisy*.

Except that here, it was. It started as a soft, whining buzz that Morgan had thought was just one of the many, *many* electronic circuits on the bridge going slightly out of alignment. But it got louder and higher-pitched as the seconds ticked on, and she watched her bridge crew twitch and wince or tentatively try to cover their ears.

"So, is this on record as a hyperspace phenomenon anywhere else?" Morgan finally asked, as much to make sure her people knew they weren't crazy as anything else.

"One of my juniors is looking into it," El-Amin told her. "There we go...yes. A milder form is on record on ships that flew through trinary systems in hyperspace."

"And that is why we go around star systems, even in hyperspace," Morgan replied with a forced chuckle. "Nobody is crazy, people. This is apparently just what hyperspace does when you're flying into a rosette of half a dozen stars."

"We are now inside the perimeter of the cluster," the navigator reported. "Stars all around us. The gravity metrics are weird. I'm watching for a spot where I can be a hundred percent certain we can *reenter* hyperspace after we exit."

It was easier to leave hyperspace than enter it. The gravity wells of planets and stars created areas where a ship couldn't do either, but a hyperspace exit portal could be created closer to a planet or star than an entrance portal.

"You have the call, Commander El-Amin," Morgan confirmed. "Nguyen, our friends?"

"We can see one of them," Nguyen reported. "I'm assuming her friends can see her, but we can't see them. Best guess is we're looking at a Laian cruiser, but she's still twelve million klicks back. This deep into the cluster, we can barely see the anomaly for *her*."

"Keep an eye on them," Morgan ordered. She took a long breath, managing to keep it steady for the benefit of her crew as she looked at the gravimetric data.

What a mess. There had to be an eye to this storm somewhere, the center point the protostars orbited. Where was it?

"Oh, you sneaky..." El-Amin cut off an unspoken curse in mid-sentence.

"Commander?" Morgan demanded.

"There's either a super-Jovian or a sub-dwarf at the center of this mess," the navigator replied. "We couldn't see it past the big guys on the perimeter, so it wasn't factored into my mass calculations. We're looking for the eye in the wrong damned spot."

"And?" Morgan asked, her voice surprisingly calm to her ears.

"We've got it. There's basically a giant Lagrange point right next to the central mass. Hold on. Portal in thirty seconds!"

"Understood," *Defiance*'s Captain said levelly. "Prepare to engage the enemy."

DEFIANCE PLUNGED BACK into reality like a screaming comet, tearing through a portal created only a few hundred meters ahead of her hull. El-Amin kept her leaping forward at seventy percent of lightspeed, opening up the distance between her emergence point and her current location while Nguyen plugged in new targeting data.

"Internal hyperspace portals online," the tactical officer reported calmly. "I'm assuming we have range degradation, but I can't confirm without test-firing."

"Understood," Morgan confirmed. "Do we have hostile portals?"

Silence. A moment. Then another.

"Confirmed," Nguyen said. "Hostile portal at seventy light-seconds; targeting with hyperspace missiles."

"Fire at will," Morgan ordered.

The Laian escort cruiser had guessed what was coming. Their Buckler-equivalent drones came through the portal first, a dozen billion-crown drones freely expended to buy the cruiser time against the FTL missiles that arrived at the same time as the cruiser.

The defensive drones did their job, shooting down half of *Defiance*'s salvos in the critical final second after they returned to regular space. The other half slammed into the cruiser's shield, multi-gigaton antimatter warheads smashing into the energy field like the hammers of an angry god.

A second salvo was already on its way and Morgan held the tip of her tongue between her teeth as she tried to assess the balance. The cruiser had them dialed in now, charging toward *Defiance* as the two ships focused entirely on each other.

Morgan's ship had the range advantage, but not by as much as normal. The disrupted state of hyperspace was costing them their accuracy, and too many of the second salvo went wide.

A new slate of defensive drones was out, and the cruiser continued to hurtle toward *Defiance*, both ships now blazing along at seventy percent of lightspeed as they dodged around the eye of the storm.

More missiles hammered home, the explosions lighting up empty space as the Laian ship's shields flickered.

"Sir."

Morgan barely heard Initiate Mugabe's voice, her focus entirely on the battle.

"*Sir*." The Initiate wasn't pinging Morgan. She was hitting an emergency channel that would ping Nguyen, Rogers and Morgan... all of whom were entirely focused on the enemy ship taking them.

"What is it, Initiate?" Rogers finally asked as another HSM salvo battered the Laian ship desperately trying to close the range.

"Look at the wide scans, sirs," Mugabe asked desperately. "We weren't the first people to try to hide here!"

Morgan was paying enough attention to yank her attention to the wide scans as the most junior tactical officer on her ship suggested. She inhaled sharply, any attempt to hide her surprise from her crew forgotten as she saw what Mugabe had seen.

She'd known they were being pursued, and she'd forgotten to do more than look for active enemy signatures in the area they'd arrived in. She'd dismissed the icons on her display as asteroids and planetoids...and missed the dozens upon dozens of Alavan motherships in cold orbits around the star at the eye of the storm.

CHAPTER FIFTY-ONE

DEFIANCE'S PURSUER PROBABLY DIDN'T RECOGNIZE THE DEAD ships until after Morgan and her crew did. They had, after all, emerged into a hail of antimatter explosions.

It was now even more critical that ship didn't survive.

"El-Amin, bring us about," Morgan snapped. "Nguyen, maximum rate of fire. Throw everything we have at that bandit. She does *not* get out."

"Sir!" both officers chorused, turning their attention to her orders.

"Rogers, work with Mugabe," Morgan continued. "ID those ships. I want numbers, types, status—and if there's anything else out there we tunnel-visioned past, let me know ASAP!"

"On it," her First Sword confirmed. "Mugabe, private channel."

New blue icons now marked the presence of the identified ships, but there was a lot of debris out there, now that Morgan was looking at it—more than she'd have expected at the eye of the protostar cluster. The super-Jovian gas giant didn't appear to have any moons, but there was a definite ring of midsized debris, some of which was *definitely* Alavan ships.

Morgan had to focus on the immediate problem. The Laian ship had initially accepted *Defiance's* challenge, both ships accelerating toward each other at seventy percent of lightspeed, but now she'd clearly seen what *Defiance's* crew had seen.

Both of them were there for the graveyard, and they'd finally found it. From what little Morgan had already seen, this was where the Alavan fleet had been when their compatriots had turned on the device at the galactic core...and, among other things, blown out every set of neural implants the Alava had ever installed.

Those ships were far more intact than the wreck the conspirators had already found. The wreck was bad enough, but *these* represented intact, if almost certainly nonfunctional, Alavan technology.

The type of technology that the Mesharom and their allies had done everything in their power to keep out of irresponsible hands for *fifty thousand years.* Even the Imperium's experimentation, based on the scan data of a wrecked Alavan ship, had drawn Mesharom ire on occasion.

It was that same experimentation that gave *Defiance* the weapons to go toe-to-toe with a Laian ship half again her size—but the Laian ship was running now. Their speeds were matched, but now it was the escort cruiser trying to keep the range open.

Mostly.

"We're in their missile range," Nguyen reported. A storm of incoming fire from the Laian ship made the report redundant to Morgan, but it was still relevant.

"Estimate six zero missiles inbound," the tactical officer continued. "I think she's trying to push for a clear zone to enter hyperspace, but she's not going to get it."

Twelve more hyperspace missiles erupted from their own tiny portals around the Laian ship, glittering explosions battering the target's shields. Unfortunately for Morgan's command, the Laians were aware of the existence of HSMs and had prepared for them.

Even with tachyon scanners providing real-time targeting data, the enemy ship's jammers and maneuvers were preventing the one-shot kill of interior detonations—but Nguyen had thrown over a hundred and sixty ten-gigaton warheads at the ship.

The shields couldn't take any more. They flickered and three missiles made contact.

"Target is damaged," Nguyen reported. "Interface-drive envelope is flickering; they've lost point two *c* and are continuing to slow."

"Close the range and finish her," Morgan ordered flatly. If the hostile ship tried to surrender, she'd let them, but...

"They're turning!" Nguyen snapped—but her own interface-drive missiles were launching now, spreads of twenty-four missiles blazing out every ten seconds. "Hyperfold cannon range in ten seconds!"

"Fire at will," Morgan said quietly. This was the moment of truth. The Laians had been using hyperfold cannons as their main energy weapon for far longer than the Imperium—but the Imperium had built *their* hyperfold cannons based on hyperfold communicators provided by the Mesharom.

No one was actually sure whose guns were longer-ranged...and whether *Defiance* survived the next few seconds would be decided by that critical factor.

"Firing!"

"Evading!"

Defiance's hyperfold cannons flung a massive amount of energy across deep space half a second before El-Amin twisted the ship through a spiral no reaction-drive ship could have matched. Incoming hyperfold cannon fire blistered through a dozen locations the cruiser could have been, but only two blasts hit her shields.

There was no follow-up salvo, as Nguyen's shots *did* hit home. The Laian cruiser started dodging a second too late, and the first blasts crippled her engines.

The second and third salvos finished the job, scattering pieces of the hostile ship across several thousand kilometers of space.

"Target destroyed," Nguyen reported as a shared sigh of relief filled the bridge. "Scanning for new contacts."

CHAPTER FIFTY-TWO

EVEN AS THE TWO CRUISERS WERE LOCKED IN THEIR DANCE OF death, Rin's focus was on the ancient starships orbiting the massive gas giant. From the moment he'd begun his study of the Alava, the Imperium had known that the Mesharom had retrieved and destroyed every one of the Precursor race's warships.

The Taljzi had refitted the hulls of a handful of midsized Alavan ships into superfortresses, but study of the fortresses' plans and wreckage had shown that everything except the hulls had been stripped out. There'd been little to learn from the Alavan ruins in the Arjtal sector, not least due to the Mesharom doing all they could to eliminate significant structures.

But now he had an entire *fleet* to study. Frozen at the moment of the Alava's fall, their crews murdered by their people's hubris, the ships were completely intact.

Enough of *Defiance*'s sensors were focused on the orbitals of the eye of the storm for him to keep learning more, with the XO and several members of the tactical team digging into the data next to him.

"I make it sixty-five intact motherships," Initiate Mugabe told him. "How many should there be?"

"We have no idea, really," Rin replied. "The data suggests they sent out a third of the sector fleet, which was probably a hundred ships. We saw one wreck, which means...well. It's entirely possible this is all that was left."

"Somebody killed thirty of these things?" Rogers asked.

"This 'Enemy' of theirs terrified the Alava," Rin said. "It wouldn't have if they weren't a real threat, one capable of taking down Alavan warships. That said, I'd believe that fifty millennia in this place would wreck even Alavan motherships."

He ran another search parameter over the wreckage and nodded to himself.

"There's at least a few hundred smaller ships out here, too," he told the sensor teams. "Though *smaller* is...relative."

The Imperium had found one Alavan ship in Alpha Centauri, but the courier ship had been tiny by Alavan standards. The geometries of their FTL technology had appeared to favor much larger vessels for efficiency. Even the smallest ships he could see here were a hundred kilometers across.

"These make even the Mesharom war-spheres look like toys," Rogers noted. "How did they even build these?"

"You've seen the data from the Arjtal campaigns," Rin said. "They carved up entire star systems' worth of planets into raw materials to feed into shipyards and foundries that filled the orbitals of super-Jovian gas giants.

"Even Mesharom technology isn't up to doing that today—and the Mesharom don't think in that kind of scale, either."

He shook his head.

"Can we get drones on the closest mothership?" he asked Rogers.

"Our pursuer is finally gone, so probably," the First Sword agreed. "We're clear for the moment, but we don't know how long."

"Fine, that's fine," Rin replied. "I know Casimir's orders, Commander Rogers. I need every piece of data we can get."

Rogers chuckled sadly.

"Understood. I've got a sweep in space; turning control over to Mugabe. Tell her where you need them, Dr. Dunst."

"Here," Rin replied, tagging the closest of the motherships—still some ten million kilometers away.

"Commander Rogers," he said consideringly as Mugabe expertly drove the robotic spies across the space at the heart of the cluster. "Do you see anything else out there?"

"Define *anything else*, Doctor?" the XO asked.

"We know they were fighting somebody," Rin pointed out. "We're assuming they pursued their enemy here, the enemy trying to hide here much as we are. We're picking up Alavan ships, but it seems likely that their enemy used a similar FTL to them."

"So, did they escape or are their wrecks here too?"

Rogers grunted.

"I'm not seeing anything else our sensors register as a ship," she admitted. "Asteroids, miscellaneous astrographic debris. Ice chunks... the kind of things that get caught in a gravity well."

"Commander...*this* gravity well is surrounded by six protostars that have been sweeping up every piece of mass in the region for a quarter-million years at least," Rin pointed out. "Do me a favor. Run the scan data past the metrics you drew up for the Servants and the Mother."

"On it," she said instantly. "That's a terrifying thought, Doctor."

"I think the Alavan stole these people's biotech. I imagine we're looking at the same kind of thing as the Alava, long-dead ships, but... we've seen pieces of Alavan biotech that survived fifty thousand years."

"Doctor, the drones are coming in for a first pass at the mothership," Mugabe told him. "Range is one million kilometers. I've slowed them down, but how close do you want to get?"

"All the way in, Initiate," Rin replied. "Stagger them if you can, I want as many views and angles of the ship as possible, but if we can get material samples from the surface, that's perfect."

A flashing light on his screen told him a call was incoming. He muted his recorder for the channel with Mugabe and Rogers and switched to Morgan.

"Morgan, we're making progress but there's a lot here to look at," he told her.

"I figured," his lover said calmly. "But we have a problem."

"Our conspirator friends know where we are?" He'd been paying that much attention to the assumptions the bridge crew were making. The ship chasing them had almost certainly had a tail watching her.

"I'm assuming our closest pursuer is going back for reinforcements, since the ship that *caught* us doesn't exist anymore," Morgan told him. "But we didn't go that far. I make it at most half a cycle before an entire fleet shows up."

Rin was silent for several seconds as he processed that, then sighed.

"How much time do you need for the starkillers?" he asked.

"Nguyen is running the numbers now, but it doesn't look like the eye is big enough to detonate," Morgan said. "On the other hand, hitting any three of the stars in the cluster is going to wreck the entire natural balance that creates this calm spot in the storm. But...the closest of those is two light-days away."

"The starkillers don't have that kind of endurance. I need to do hyperspace hops through the worst zone I've ever seen and drop timed weapons. I need at least four tenth-cycles to make sure we hit them all."

"That leaves you *one* tenth-cycle. Two hours and twenty minutes," she said flatly.

Rin knew that tone of voice. He was a civilian expert, the best person in the Imperium to be looking at this particular find, and there were arguments she'd concede because of that...but that was *command voice*.

His lover was also the captain of a starship of the A!Tol Imperial Navy, and some things could not be denied.

"I hate that we have to destroy all this," he told her. "But I understand. I'll get what I can in two hours."

"For what it's worth, I'm sorry," Morgan said.

"Don't be. It has to be done."

He muted the recorders for all of his calls and took a long, ragged breath. A cornucopia of knowledge lay in front of him. Potential technological insights aside, no Imperial archeological team had ever been able to go through an untouched Alavan vessel or site. What they could learn...

But the danger of the ships falling into hands of war profiteers was unacceptable. They'd do what they had to do.

He opened the channels again.

"Mugabe, where are we at?" he asked.

"Closest drone is at one hundred thousand kilometers," she told him. "The ship is big enough that it's causing problems with their navigation. Gravitational anomalies like crazy."

"That's not the size of the ship," Rin said. "They used singularity power plants in a way we don't understand. Each of those motherships was hauling around the mass of an Earth-size planet as a fuel supply. The containment systems were passive in some ways, which means they're having less impact than they should, but there are still several black holes trapped in each of those hulks."

The Imperium's prototype singularity power cores, scheduled for installation in the new leviathan-type ships, combined a captive singularity and a mass-conversion system for power. For them, the singularity was mostly a convenient way to store mass to feed into the converter later on.

The Alava had drawn power directly from the singularities in a way no Imperial scientist had worked out yet—and if the Mesharom knew, that information hadn't been in the databases the Imperium had acquired.

"Give me a live feed," he told Mugabe. "We're on a time limit; let's see what we see."

The data from the drone was coming in by hyperfold coms. They couldn't communicate outside the cluster, but the short-ranged communicators were still functioning well enough for the telemetry to come through clearly and in real-time.

The sheer size of the Alavan mothership was even more awe-inspiring at this distance. At fifty thousand kilometers and dropping, he didn't even need magnification to see it. This was a larger unit, probably a squadron flagship, some fifteen hundred kilometers in diameter.

None of the surface installations he could see in the magnified view were familiar to him at all. He knew what the surface components were of proton beams, plasma lances, battle lasers ...all of those, he could identify.

Unless he was mistaken, the primary weapon of the mothership was a series of concave dishes, each fifty kilometers in diameter. As the distance closed, they visibly dimpled the silhouette of the starship. There had to be at least a hundred of the dishes, which supported his theory that they were a weapon.

Even if Rin had no idea what *kind* of weapon.

He was looking at one of the dishes when he *swore* he saw something move...but that was impossible.

"Mugabe, run the footage back five seconds and see if you can get another drone on that section," he told her. "I saw something."

"It's dead, Doctor."

"I know," he replied, watching the footage run back and pausing it. That was impossible. An organic-looking tentacle, color indeterminate at this range, was waving out through a crack in the compressed-matter dish.

"Drone six has a new line of— *What the fuck?*"

Mugabe's curse echoed sharply on the radio as Rin flipped his view. The tendril had pulled farther out from the ship and was twisting to *look at the drone?*

"Drone six just got pulsed by some kind of sensor," Mugabe snapped. "What the hell?"

"Pull the infrared," Rogers ordered as she rejoined the channel.

New colors snapped across the displays as the drones switched to a scan for heat sources on the mothership.

"Not just on the mothership," the First Sword continued. "All sensors, all drones, full IR scan of the debris field!"

Rin stared at the mothership as the faded oranges and reds of the infrared scan lit up. The scan had always been running, but neither he nor Mugabe had looked at it since the beginning. From a distance, though, the compressed-matter armor of the mothership had concealed the truth.

Now...now he saw what the armor had hidden. The entire ship was alive. Not still carrying a crew. Not host to an ecosystem. *Alive.* Something had moved into the hull and *filled* it with a fifteen-hundred-kilometer mass of biomatter that now turned and unleashed a thousand tendrils through cracks in the hull.

Each tendril was turning, tracing routes through space as they filled the void above the eye of the storm with beams of a thousand sensors.

"Look at the rest of the 'debris,'" Rogers's voice ground out in his ear, and he hit a button to expand his view.

The drones were farther from the other motherships but still far closer than *Defiance* was. Spots of infrared heat flared on the scanners, visible from thousands of kilometers away if not millions.

The Alavan fleet was coming alive once more...and so was what they'd written off as ice and debris. Frozen creatures shook away the coating of fifty thousand years of hibernation, and plasma rockets flared to life on a thousand entities.

"They match the general bio signature of the Mother and the Servants," Rogers said, her voice toneless. "Every ship has been infested, Doctor. Every asteroid was actually a creature. We're not looking at abandoned bioships."

CHAPTER FIFTY-THREE

"We're looking at *living beings* that can act as starships."

Rogers's words echoed on the bridge, and Morgan looked at the ever-growing numbers of flashing orange icons on her displays. The Alavan motherships were bad enough, but some of what they'd *thought* were asteroids were living beings ten thousand kilometers long.

They paled in comparison to the size of the Great Mother, the stellarvore *Defiance* had fought and killed near the Kosha System—but the Mother had been a rogue Alavan construct. So far as she knew, the Alava had made the Mother a sun eater.

But the cells they'd started with, the living things they'd cloned... those had been the creatures she was looking at. When the Alavan computerized control system had failed, the Mother had grown to intelligence over fifty thousand years.

These...who knew?

"Nystrom, hail them," she ordered softly.

"Sir?"

"The Mother was intelligent and could speak to her cultists,"

Morgan said grimly. "We've never seen anything like this, which means these well may be the only part of their...kind to still exist.

"I won't kill them without *trying*."

"Pulsing the first-contact package," Nystrom replied.

"El-Amin, open the range," Morgan ordered. "Let's see if they'll talk to us, but let's not take any chances, either."

Defiance's interface drive returned to full power, dragging her away from the unknowns at sixty percent of lightspeed—and the unknowns' reaction told Morgan that she'd done *something* wrong.

"Contacts are accelerating toward us," Nguyen reported. "Multiple contacts accelerating in excess of three thousand kilometers per second squared. I am not detecting interface drives, but I am not picking up reaction mass, either."

"Any response to our hails?" Morgan asked. She was opening the range fast, but the contacts were accelerating at one percent of lightspeed every second. Some of the bioship Servants had been able to more than match *Defiance*'s velocity, though it had taken them longer to get up to that speed.

"Negative," Nystrom replied.

"We're being pulsed with what I would call lidar, radar and tachyon scanners," Nguyen said grimly. "Request permission to engage with hyperspace missiles."

"Denied," Morgan snapped. "We know *nothing* about these things.

"We know they ate an Alavan fleet," Rin's voice said grimly in her ear. "Morgan, I think we had the battle the wrong way around."

"What do you mean?" she demanded.

"The motherships were closer in to the eye than most of these bioships. I think..." he paused, swallowing. "I don't think the Enemy ran from the battle with the Alava. I think the Alava ran—and the fall just cut short this fleet's final stand."

A chill ran down Morgan's spine. She could imagine it all too well. The Alava had lost a third of their capital ships in a single action—and the Hegemony's fleets had probably been convinced of their invulnerability.

They'd broken. They'd run for cover in the protostar cluster, and the creatures had pursued them. There were *still* new contacts appearing on her screen, and she began to realize how pale an imitation the Servants had been of their true progenitors.

"El-Amin, Nguyen," she said quietly. "We have the course set for the starkiller deployment?"

"Yes, sir," her subordinates confirmed.

"Nystrom?"

"Still no response, sir. Wait." The coms officer held up a hand. "I have new modulated signatures incoming from one of the targets."

"Which one?" Morgan asked.

The creature was highlighted in the screen, and the cruiser's captain swallowed hard. The creature transmitting was swimming *out* of the super-Jovian gas giant at an impossible speed, rising from depths that had concealed a bulk Morgan wouldn't have believed before she'd seen the Mother.

"Can we translate?" she demanded as she stared at the hundred-thousand-kilometer body of the beast.

"Dr. Dunst?" Nystrom asked. "I think this might be as much your field as mine."

"Give me a moment." The archeologist paused. "I'm running it into some programs we use for Alavan symbols and code on a stand-alone machine. I've got...something."

"Play it for me," Morgan ordered.

"*SPEAK.*"

The translated word echoed around the bridge in the same way the Mother's voice had.

"We're just getting basic concepts through," Rin warned. "It's transmitting in what I *think* is an Alavan audio-compression format, but we barely know what the Alavan language sounds like. I don't think it's speaking its native language and—"

"Can we talk to it, Rin?" Morgan demanded.

"Yes," he said after a moment's hesitation. "But it isn't going to be a particularly...philosophical discussion?"

"Nystrom?" Morgan turned to her coms officer.

"As ready as we can be," Nystrom said in a swift exhalation.

"I am Captain Casimir of the Imperial starship *Defiance*," Morgan told the recorder. "We are not your enemies. Who are you?"

She glanced at Nystrom.

"Well?"

"We got across *something*." The half-Tibetan woman studied her screens. "Another modulated pulse. It's trying to talk to us, at least."

"CAPTIVE. LOST. MUST LEAVE. MUST FEED. KEY?"

Morgan had a transcription on her screens and shivered again.

"Rin? Your guess?"

"My guess is that whatever they use for FTL broke when the Alava shattered the universe," Rin told her. "The Alava were careful to avoid most biological processes, so these creatures survived, but they couldn't leave the protostar cluster. There was enough energy and material here for them to survive and enter hibernation, but..."

"They've been trapped here for fifty thousand years," Morgan concluded. She looked at the icons blazing toward her. "Range to closest unknowns?"

"Fifteen million kilometers. They have matched our velocity and several have exceeded it," Nguyen reported. "Sir..."

"El-Amin, stand by on the hyper emitters," Morgan ordered. "Nguyen, stand by on all weapons. Maintain passive targeting only, but make sure we have Bucklers out between us and them."

If they threw something at her she could shoot down, she was by god going to shoot it down.

She gestured for Nystrom to record again.

"We don't know you," she told the aliens. "Who are you?"

It took a minute for a round-trip message, but the big creature was pushing hard now. Several of the infested Alavan motherships had moved closer, allowing the being to latch on to them with immense tentacles, each thousands of kilometers long, and lever itself out faster.

"*WE INFINITE. WE FEED. KEY.*"

"What key?" Morgan sent back.

"*YOU ARRIVE. YOU LEAVE. INFINITE LEAVE WITH YOU.*"

Morgan exhaled a long sigh. That was what she had been afraid of.

"We can't do that," she told the presumably ancient being. "We can help you, but we can't take you from here."

Even if she could figure out a way to open a hyper portal big enough for the central Infinite ship, she wouldn't. Not without knowing a *lot* more about them.

"No response," Nystrom said grimly. "We're past the turnaround time of the last few messages."

"It's thinking?" Morgan guessed. "Who knows how a creature the size of a *fucking planet* takes a request for time?"

"Wait, I have..."

Defiance leapt in space and Morgan *heard* the impossible sound of the keel of the ship tearing around her. Gravitational tidal forces almost yanked her from her chair feet-first, forces that should never have made it through the ship's defenses.

"*GIVE. OR TAKE. INFINITE NEEDS KEY.*"

"What the hell was that?" Morgan demanded.

"That was a multi-teraton microsingularity passing through our shields like they didn't fucking *exist*," Nguyen snapped. "Velocity estimated at eleven nines of lightspeed. Missed the hull by about two hundred meters."

"We have critical damage to multiple systems and have casualties throughout the ship," Rogers reported. "Sir?"

"El-Amin, maximum evasive maneuvers," Morgan barked. "Full spri—"

How exactly the "Infinite" managed to land even a lightspeed ballistic-weapon hit at nearly a full light-minute was a question for another time, a question Morgan couldn't even consider as a minia-ture black hole tore through the entire length of her command.

Lights flickered on *Defiance*'s bridge for several seconds, and Morgan couldn't swallow a groan as the tidal forces tried to tear her body into a dozen pieces.

"El-Amin," she ground out. "Get us *out of here.*"

"I can't," the navigator replied. "I don't have control—I don't have power to the emitters."

"Liepins," Morgan shouted at her engineer. "I don't care what we give up, I need a hyper portal *now.*"

She wasn't even getting automated damage reports, and she could guess what that meant!

"I don't have hands or remotes to spare," her engineer snapped back. "If I get you emitters, I have to eject antimatter B...and all the sectors between it and the hull. That'll kill at least twenty people—and eject the starkillers!"

Morgan froze, staring at her repeater screens as basic reports started to come online. The drive was down to barely half-velocity. The shields were offline, useless as they'd proven today. Forty percent of the emitters were down...and one of the cruiser's two antimatter power plants was in critical overload.

And while she couldn't be sure of Liepins's numbers, they'd be blowing a full five percent of *Defiance*'s volume into space to emer-gency-eject the antimatter core. There would be at *least* twenty people in that space, even with the casualties they'd already taken.

Only one person on *Defiance* could make that call...and there was no other decision she could make.

"If we don't get out of here, we all die," she told Liepins, her voice frozen. "Eject the core and get me those damn emitters."

A third singularity missed them by ten thousand kilometers as she spoke, El-Amin's maneuvers buying them enough space that the ship's systems prevented further damage.

"Yes, sir," Liepins finally ground out. Red icons on Morgan's screen turned void-black as an emergency system no Captain ever wanted to use activated.

There were three different ejection systems for the antimatter core, but the singularity strike had shredded two of them. The remaining one was an act of desperation, one that used shaped charges to cut a massive hole in the side of the cruiser and blast everything from armor to the carefully concealed starkiller magazine into the void.

"Antimatter B is gone," Liepins said flatly as the entire cruiser lurched under the force of the ejection. "Drones and engineers are moving on the emitters. I need five minutes, Captain."

"You have until those things rip us to pieces, Commander," Morgan told him. "And they are now gaining on us at thirty percent of lightspeed."

The biggest fear they'd had about the Mother was that the sun eater could have duplicated *Defiance*'s matter-conversion power plant and hyperdrive. Morgan had the same fear with this "Infinite"... with the added certainty that the *Infinite* certainly seemed to think they could duplicate the hyperdrive systems.

"Any further messages from our large friend?" Morgan asked.

"No, unless the singularities count," Nystrom replied.

"Nguyen, report!"

"You're not going to like it," the tactical officer said.

"Report," Morgan repeated, her voice flat.

"I've identified the energy signature of the singularity cannon," Nguyen told her grimly. "It's not the big one shooting at us. It's one of the bigger ones in orbit...and four of her sisters are warming up their own big guns.

"And unless I miss my guess, the *really* big one has half a dozen singularity cannons of her own."

"Not to mention somebody wrapped a tentacle around the mothership the conspirators found and *crushed its hull*," Morgan pointed out. "Keep us moving, El-Amin."

"I have no idea what the closer units are armed with, but they're at ten million klicks and closing." The tactical officer paused. "With our damage, all I have is the ready magazines for the interface launchers. HSM internal portals are down and the missile-transfer tubes are *fucked*."

This time, *two* singularities appeared on the screen, and for a seemingly eternal instant, Morgan thought one of them was going to hit *Defiance*. Somehow, a last-second velocity change from El-Amin tore the cruiser out of the path of the incoming black hole.

Almost. The entire *port* wing assembly went with it—along with Morgan's only remaining plasma lance and probably another fifty of her crew.

"Liepins," she barked. "Time?"

"Now," he replied. "Fifty-fifty, sir. We can *generate* a portal. I can't guarantee it will hold long enough for us to get through, not without a few hours of work."

"El-Amin, you hear him?"

"I hear him," the navigator said, his voice as frozen as Morgan's own.

"Get us out of here!"

"Understood. Portal close!"

Icons flared blood-red warnings across Morgan's screens...and then the emitters came to life, tearing a hole in reality almost *on top* of *Defiance*.

New tidal forces ripped through the ship, the usual compensators clearly abused beyond their tolerances...and then suddenly there was quiet.

"Portal held," El-Amin reported, his voice utterly exhausted. "Portal is closed. We are clear."

He swallowed, the sound audible in the silence of the bridge.

"Course, sir?"

CHAPTER FIFTY-FOUR

"GET US AWAY FROM HERE," MORGAN ORDERED.

Her repeater screens were starting to update, and she wasn't sure she could say more yet. Formal status reports would follow, but *Defiance*'s automated damage-reporting and crew-tracking software told her the formal reports would be bad.

A lost connection to a personal communicator didn't mean the owner was dead, but it was a bad sign. Out of the thirteen hundred–odd souls aboard Morgan's command, three hundred and eighty-six had lost connection to the main network.

Most of those people were probably dead.

Morgan coughed softly, trying to clear her throat so she could speak clearly.

"Liepins, get me an update as soon as you can," she ordered. "Priority is life support, then the hyperspace and interface drives."

There was no acknowledgement. There didn't need to be. She knew how much work the engineer had in front of him.

Defiance had been built with two arching double wings covering the back third of her hull, delicate-looking but tough structures that held her plasma lances and a significant portion of her other weapons.

Those structures were gone now, torn away by the violence of the singularity strikes. Massive gouges had been torn in the cruiser's hull, entire sections of compressed-matter plating ripped away. The active microbot layer under the armor was holding in the atmosphere, but those robots were the *only* thing keeping the crew breathing.

"Sir, we're alone here for the moment," Nguyen told her. "But... we know we were being hunted by the conspirators. We have to move or we're going to get jumped here in hyperspace."

"What's our weapon status?" Morgan asked, hoping her voice sounded less hoarse to her people than it did to her.

"We have sixteen interface-missile launchers, but all we have is the ready magazines," her tactical officer said grimly. "That's five rounds per weapon. The other launchers are...gone. Plasma lances are gone. One of the HSM batteries is gone. The portal on the other is offline. Might be repairable, but the tidal forces tore it to pieces."

Morgan nodded silently.

An Imperial warship could accelerate from a standstill to sixty percent of lightspeed in a handful of seconds. That process was entirely inertialess, but the drive field created a shield against gravitational effects. The designers had layered in an entire system of gravitic and inertial compensators as well, to provide artificial gravity and protect against impacts.

Gravitational tidal forces weren't something the weapons systems were designed to deal with, not on the scale the Infinite's weapons had inflicted. The internal portals were among the most protected parts of the starship, which made their fragility a non-issue.

Normally. Today they'd learned something new.

"We can't fight our pursuers," she agreed quietly. "El-Amin, what's our velocity?"

"Thirty-two," the navigator replied. "That's with a decent safety margin, but...if I pushed to the edge of what I think the drive can take, we might get to forty-five percent of lightspeed."

"Which won't get us away from anyone," Morgan said. "Good call. Set your course out the opposite side of the cluster and then for rendezvous with Squadron Lord Tan!Stalla."

She wasn't sure what came next, but she knew her crippled cruiser wasn't going to be having an impact. Tan!Stalla had two full battle squadrons of the A!Tol Imperial Navy—but that was intended to be overwhelming force against the conspirator fleet.

Not against whatever the hell *Defiance* had woken up at the heart of the Astoroko Nebula.

"Nguyen, I need a threat analysis of those things as soon as you can," she continued. "Numbers, mass, energy levels...I need to know how they stack up to modern warships overall. Only the biggest ones seemed to have the singularity launchers, so I need a guess on what the hell the rest carried."

"Do..." The tactical officer swallowed. "Do we think they can duplicate the hyperdrive? That was a fear with the Mother, wasn't it?"

"The one talking to us certainly seemed to think it could," Morgan told her subordinates. "They probably can't just from sensor data of us opening a portal, but...if they get their hands on a ship, they almost certainly can."

"The conspirators are going to go exactly where we were, aren't they?" Nguyen asked.

The bridge was silent again and Morgan stared at the red icons marking her ship. *Defiance* was dying. They were now up to two of their five life-support plants online, so they'd probably make it out safely, but Morgan's ship was irreparable. She could *feel* that.

And where she'd failed, she didn't believe the Laian and Wendira fleet that had been chasing her was going to succeed.

"They are," Morgan replied levelly. "And while I'd rather wish them the curse of what they did so much damage hunting, they'd give the Infinite exactly what it wants."

She stared at the damage icons for a few more seconds.

"Nystrom." She turned to her communications officer. "We have relay drones, yes? Probes we can surround the area in hyperspace with to transmit a warning?"

"With the visibility bubble, we can't guarantee they'll get it," Nystrom warned, her words slow as she thought about the request. "But we can probably rig a few things up and put out a hundred or so beacons? We'd cover the most likely approaches."

"Do it," Morgan ordered. "I'll record a message."

She had no idea what she was going to say, but it was a momentary distraction from the crushing realization of how terrible her ship's condition was. She brought up the recording system and stared blankly at it for a moment before initializing it.

"To anyone entering the protostar cluster at the heart of the Astoroko Nebula," she said. "This is Captain Morgan Casimir of the A!Tol Imperial Navy. Do not, under any circumstances, enter normal space in this region. An unknown and apparently hostile sentient presence is trapped here and looking for escape.

"It engaged and crippled my ship in an attempt to capture our hyperdrive and will likely do the same to any ship that enters the eye of the protostar cluster.

"I know what treasures you think you are seeking—but all that remains is death."

She cut the recording.

"Nystrom, get that onto the beacons and get them out there," she ordered. "We want to get well clear of here before they arrive, but... we owe it to everyone to warn them. They might deserve their fate, but I don't want to find out how dangerous the people the Alava broke the galaxy to stop actually are!"

"WE'RE ready to brief you, Captain," Liepins's voice finally said in her ear. "I...suggest you take this in private."

Morgan considered that for a moment, then nodded. She activated her privacy shield, a vertical column of one-way material that descended around the Captain's chair. She could still see the bridge, but no one could see or hear her.

"I suspect we'll have to share the news with everyone, but I'll give you that," she told her engineer. "Lay it out, Commander."

"*Defiance* is doomed," Lesser Commander Gary Liepins said flatly. "All of our fusion cores were taken down by the impacts, and none are safe to reinitiate. Antimatter A is running, but..."

He sighed.

"I *want* to shut A down for repair and maintenance, but scans suggest that the only thing holding it together is the active force fields," he admitted. "I can't do the work I need to do without shutting down the force fields, and if I shut down the force fields, I think Antimatter A is just going to fall apart on us.

"The matter-conversion core had enough safety precautions built into it out of fear of a Little Doctor reaction that it's intact and operational."

Morgan wasn't entirely sure of the source of the naming for a runaway matter-disruption reaction, but the fear of a matter converter creating a self-sustaining field was factored into the design of Imperial power plants.

"So, we have the primary plant and one secondary until we shut that secondary down?" she asked.

"Exactly," he confirmed. "Worse, Life Support B and E are done. Too much damage to too many critical components. C is hanging on by a thread. We are holding our ground keeping the air breathable for now, but when—*not* if—C fails again, we'll start losing air quality.

"Slowly but surely, we will run out of oxygen. It'll be a matter of cycles, not tenth-cycles, but we won't have long."

"I understand," Morgan confirmed. She'd guessed it was bad, but she hadn't expected it to be *that* bad. "I'm guessing that's the worst news? After the casualties, that is."

She didn't have official numbers from the ship's surgeon, but there were still over three hundred crew listed as missing on her systems—and the medical bay automated systems were reporting another hundred and fifty wounded.

"Yeah. Unlike our encounter with the sun eater, we still have hyperspace emitters," Liepins told her. "We have the power to run what weapons we have left, if that ever matters. I've got teams working on the interface drive, but we're not getting her up to full speed, either."

"Understood. Keep working on it," Morgan ordered her engineer. "But...your judgment is that she's irreparable, yes?"

That was a question no captain ever wanted to ask her chief engineer, but Morgan needed to know. That was her duty.

"She's too new and too young for me to say it easily, sir, but...yes," Liepins admitted. "The damage is too deep, and the tidal forces of being that close to c-fractional singularities will have left structural damage I can't even detect."

"Understood. We're on way to rendezvous with Lord Tan!Stalla's task force," Morgan told him. "Should be...six to eight cycles or so. Less if you can give El-Amin more speed."

"I can probably get us to a safe half-lightspeed," the engineer promised. "In all truth, I don't think there's much else worth fixing on her. We're not going to make it back to Tohrohsail, sir, let alone the Imperium."

"Understood, Commander. Thank you," Morgan said.

"For what?" Liepins laughed bitterly.

"For doing what you can," she told him. "And for the work I know you're going to do keeping us all alive until we reach the fleet. We've made it this far, Gary. She'll take us where we need to go."

"That she will, sir. That she will."

CHAPTER FIFTY-FIVE

RIN AND KI!TANA SHARED HIS WORKSPACE IN SILENCE, watching as the robotic beacons spilled out of *Defiance's* probe bays. He hadn't been briefed on what the tiny spacecraft were supposed to be doing, but he could guess.

He just didn't think it was going to work. The people chasing them had attempted to start a war between two Core Powers to cover their search. They weren't going to turn back now, not on the warning of a woman they could only see as an enemy.

"What do we do?" he asked the Ki!Tol.

"We communicate with our associates as best as we can," she told him. "We make certain the Republic and the Grand Hive know what we found. And we warn them."

"I should have guessed," Rin admitted. "The moment we realized the Alava's enemy was using biotech ships, I should have put that together with the Mother being sentient."

"It wouldn't have changed what we did," Ki!Tana told him. "We would have assumed that spaceborne creatures would have died as much as we assumed living ships would have."

"Except we thought the ships might still be alive, based on the

Mother's endurance," Rin argued. "We just thought their *crews* would be dead. The thought that they didn't even *have* crews..."

"The Alava never recorded anything about their Enemy in a way we could access," Ki!Tana said, her fear-marked purple-black skin belying the calmness of her words. "We did not know who they fought; we knew nothing of what to expect."

"If this was the enemy the Alava fought, where the hell are the *rest* of them?" Rin asked. "The Alava wouldn't have panicked over a single fleet, however dangerous."

"I do not know," Ki!Tana admitted. "There are questions yet to be answered, questions we can't even see yet. We will learn more of this 'Infinite,' I have no doubt."

"That's what I'm afraid of," he said. "My curiosity, my failure... we've unleashed something, Ki!Tana. I don't know if we can stop it."

"This ship can't," she told him. "I'm not certain even the fleet we head to rendezvous with can. But the forces of two Core Powers and the A!Tol Imperium have been mustered in this region. There are few things that can stand against the fleets that were here, ready for war.

"We must make certain those fleets face the same enemy."

"Especially if the conspirators hand the Infinite a hyperdrive." Rin stared at his data. "These things terrify me, Ki!Tana. They'd fascinate me if I thought they would *talk* to us, but the same things that fascinate me scare me."

"Cooperation with the Infinite would lead to many discoveries," Ki!Tana said. He *thought* she was agreeing with him, but he couldn't be sure.

"A new form of inertialess engine. Some form of generating or concentrating mass reliably enough to use singularities as *weapons*?" Rin shook his head. "The scan data suggests that many of the smaller Infinite creatures had similar weaponry to the Servants—no real surprise there—but I somehow doubt that's all they have."

"The Servants were a clear attempt to imitate them, to duplicate the Infinite's tools via a very Alavan megastructure version of whatever breeder the Infinite have," Ki!Tana agreed. "Presumably, they had a computer control system...one that their folly destroyed."

"And so, the Mother became sentient because the samples they based her on were sentient," Morgan said from behind them.

Rin looked up at his lover's voice and his heart fell at the sight of her. She was still perfectly turned out, her uniform impeccable, her hair locked in place...but her eyes told him everything.

Ignoring Ki!Tana, he crossed to her and embraced her tightly.

"*Defiance?*" he asked.

"She'll get us to Tan!Stalla's fleet," Morgan replied. "After that...I don't know, but the prognosis isn't good. Three hundred dead. Over two hundred wounded. Half my crew..."

Rin squeezed gently.

"What now?" he asked softly.

"We get to our reinforcements and we warn them about what we've seen," Morgan told him. "We hope that Tan!Stalla can intercept the conspirators, but...it's almost certainly already too late."

"Then we must prepare for the Infinite to awaken and leave the Astoroko Nebula," Ki!Tana said.

"There have to be other pockets of it left," Rin warned. "The Alava wouldn't have feared one fleet. I don't know where they might be hiding, but I'm not going to bet against the fleet that gets a hyperdrive not being able to find the rest."

"We've woken up something terrible, love."

"I know," Morgan said softly. "And I see a step we can take, but I don't like it."

"*Dark Eyes,*" Ki!Tana murmured.

"Exactly. Your ship is undamaged," Morgan told the Ki!Tol while Rin was catching up. "I'm guessing no one except you can fly her?"

"She may have been built by the A!Tol, but she's fundamentally Mesharom," Ki!Tana agreed. "The robots and computers are designed for a crew of one. Me."

"I need someone to brief Tan!Shallegh. You can't even talk to him on a video screen," Morgan said flatly.

Rin finally fully caught up. There was no way *Morgan* could abandon her command, however crippled the cruiser was. Ki!Tana couldn't be around male A!Tol—as Morgan said, even a video-call could be dangerous for her.

"You need me to go with her," he said. "Morgan, I..."

"You're the only one I can spare," she said bluntly. "I need every one of my senior officers keeping the damn ship together until we get to Tan!Stalla. I need you to go to the peace talks and convince everyone that the shit is going to hit the fan and they need to stand together."

"The Laians and the Wendira have hated each other since before your people developed gunpowder," Ki!Tana warned. "Convincing them not to fight each other is one thing. Convincing them to face an enemy *together*?"

"The conspirators did it," Rin said grimly. "If they managed to convince Wendira and Laians to work together for money and profit —and to damn their own peoples to war in the process!—I think we can convince them to work together for their very survival."

"I want to say it's not going to be that bad," Morgan murmured, "but...it might be."

Rin's heart crumpled as she leaned against him.

"You have to go," she told him. "And you have to go *now*. Every minute we argue is another minute closer the conspirators get to handing the Infinite the key to the galaxy.

"My place is here. Someone has to talk to Tan!Shallegh...and fortunately, we know where he is."

"*Dark Eyes* has the density generators of a Mesharom courier," Ki!Tana admitted. "If I push her, we should reach the Fleet Lord shortly after you reach Tan!Stalla."

"I have Nguyen's people downloading everything we know onto a data folio for you. You'll have a few copies and I assume you'll load it into *Dark Eyes'* systems, but...it is absolutely critical that information reach Tan!Shallegh as soon as possible."

"I understand," Rin murmured. "I'll do it. For you...and because it has to be done."

He kissed her and she leaned into it fiercely, almost desperately.

"We'll be fine," she insisted. "But you have to go," she repeated. "You have to go now."

CHAPTER FIFTY-SIX

DEFIANCE LIMPED THROUGH THE HYPERSPACE PORTAL LIKE THE wounded animal she was. Morgan could feel every gash, every breach, like it was on her own skin. Her ship didn't even *look* right without the wings.

Life Support C had failed a full cycle before, and a ticking red number on her repeater screens warned her of the biggest problem—an estimate of the time before the average oxygen level on the ship dropped below nineteen point five percent.

Some areas of the ship would be dangerous before that. Some would be safe after that. But at that point, the average area in her ship would be actively dangerous for her crew.

"Sir, we have contacts on the scopes," Nguyen reported. "We're being pinged by tachyon scanners—I have multiple Imperial cruisers inbound."

"Hail them, hyperfold coms," Morgan ordered. "I need to talk to Squadron Lord Tan!Stalla immediately."

A minute passed as the back-and-forth handshakes passed between her ship and the other Imperial vessels. Morgan took the time to check the status of the fleet waiting for her.

It was either Tan!Stalla's task force or another force of sixteen superbattleships and an equal number of battleships flying Imperial IFFs was in the area.

Unfortunately, this was also the last place she'd seen *Builder of Tomorrows*, and there was no sign of the rogue shipyard. That hopefully only meant that the mobile starbase had moved to a different location and not...the worst-case scenario.

"Sir, I have the Squadron Lord for you," Nystrom told her. "Linking through now."

Morgan focused on the recorder in front of her as a holographic image of the Empress's niece—the closest English description to the relationship, anyway—appeared in front of her.

"Captain Casimir, we didn't even recognize your ship," the A!Tol told Morgan, her skin flushing dark blue with concern. "What happened?"

"We found the Alavan fleet," Morgan told her superior. "And we found the enemy they were fighting. The eye of the Astoroko Nebula is home to a fleet of intelligent biological starships. They lack a functioning FTL drive and tried to capture ours.

"My tactical department will forward you all of our sensor data, but we were badly outnumbered, outmassed...and outmatched," Morgan admitted levelly. "*Defiance* is crippled. I have insufficient life support to keep my crew safe.

"I have to request a full evacuation."

The hyperfold channel was instantaneous, but it still took at least thirty seconds for Tan!Stalla to reply.

"We have no capacity for an engineering survey or repairs here, Captain," the A!Tol said levelly. "If we evacuate *Defiance*, we have to scuttle her."

"I know, sir."

"Understood," Tan!Stalla said. "And the status of the conspirators?"

"At least one cruiser was destroyed when they followed us into the eye," Morgan reported. "I believe they know where, and follow-up ships would have been en route. I am afraid that the hostiles in the Nebula may attempt to capture an intact ship to reverse-engineer our technology—specifically our hyperdrives."

"It's worse than you think," the Squadron Lord said calmly, her skin darkening. "We chased off a force I presume to be your conspirators when we arrived a cycle and a half ago. One of the units was definitely large enough to be the shipyard you reported...and they all headed toward the protostar cluster.

"My orders were to rendezvous with you for a full update, so I pulled my escorts back to keep them safe."

Morgan stared at the hologram and recorder in shock.

"The...the *shipyard* might have gone into the eye?" she whispered.

"We don't have data to be certain," Tan!Stalla replied. "Given this data, I will need to confer with the Fleet Lord—but I think we will need ships in immediately to confirm what we're looking at.

"We'll be careful," she promised, holding up a manipulator tentacle before Morgan could say a word. "We'll see if we can identify a safe distance to scan these unknowns before we send anyone in."

"There's a limited safe zone to exit hyperspace in the center of the cluster," Morgan warned. "We may not be able to get safe updates."

"I'll review the data. You and your senior officers will oversee the evacuation and report aboard *Jean Villeneuve* when it's complete." Tan!Stalla shivered. "I leave setting the scuttling charges to you, Captain Casimir.

"That is, traditionally, the task of the ship's final captain."

CHAPTER FIFTY-SEVEN

SOMEHOW, RIN HAD EXPECTED TO FIND IMMENSE FLEETS gathered at the empty system picked for the peace conference. Instead, *Dark Eyes* had arrived to a mere handful of ships—only three, in fact. One star hive. One war-dreadnought. One *Galileo*-class superbattleship, *Va!Tola*.

Rin was only vaguely familiar with Va!Tola. *Va* was a rare prefix, usually awarded extremely late in life for scientists and leaders who had made massive advances for the benefit of the entire race. Va!Tola was, if he recalled correctly, the A!Tol who'd invented their version of the hyperdrive.

It was a fitting name for a *Galileo*-class ship, a class named for one of Earth's most famous historical scientists by the human-led development team.

"*Va!Tola*, this is Dr. Rin Dunst," he transmitted to the A!Tol capital ship. "I need to speak with Fleet Lord Tan!Shallegh immediately. Code Tsunami. I repeat, Code Tsunami."

Invasion imminent. Rin didn't think that the Imperium was going to be invaded, but the Infinite were about to spill out of the Astoroko

Nebula, which edged on the space of both the Grand Hive and the Republic.

Hopefully, Morgan had managed to reach Tan!Stalla by now, but only so much information could be sent by hyperfold. The most secure and complete transmission of the data they had was via the data folios Rin was carrying.

"Dr. Dunst, this is Commander !Vaon," an A!Tol greeted him. "I am the Fleet Lord's communications officer. He is in conference with the Laian and Wendira representatives aboard *Va!Tola*.

"We are acting as neutral waters for critical negotiations, but Code Tsunami opens doors. What is going on, Doctor?"

"An outside-context problem, Commander," Rin told the officer. "Have you received any communication from Captain Casimir yet?"

"The intelligence from Captain Casimir is what's allowing the Fleet Lord to keep these negotiations open, Dr. Dunst. We have no recent messages from her, however, since the confirmation of *Builder of Tomorrows'* existence."

Faster-than-light communications weren't necessarily instantaneous. Morgan *had* to have reached Tan!Stalla's fleet by now, but it could take as much as four or five cycles for her message to reach the Fleet Lord.

"Commander...I *need* to speak to the Fleet Lord," Rin finally said. "I'm not sure what codes or authorizations I can give you to make that possible, but the very existence of the Republic and the Hive may be at risk here."

The channel was silent.

"Then, Dr. Dunst, may I suggest that you speak with *everyone*?"

A!TOL females were immense beings normally, at least two meters tall when moving on their main locomotive tentacles. Wrapped in power armor, the A!Tol Marines that guided Rin through the corridors of the superbattleship loomed like angry goddesses.

Their destination was guarded by more of the A!Tol Marines, though this set wasn't alone. They were very carefully positioned as the middle of three protective contingents, separating the Wendira Warrior-caste soldiers from the Laian Blades.

Armor and cross-species differences obscured a lot of body language, but the glaring was still very clear to Rin.

"I am invoking the right of the host to interrupt," Commander !Vaon told the guards calmly. "Dr. Dunst possesses critical information relevant to both the peace conference and all three of our nations. Stand aside."

The A!Tol contingent split immediately, not *quite* bodily pushing the Wendira and Laian guards aside to allow Rin and his communications officer escort to approach the doors.

"Ready?" !Vaon asked softly.

Rin nodded firmly, swallowing hard as the A!Tol plugged a code into the door's control panel.

The security hatch swung open with enough noise to draw attention from the room's three occupants and Rin felt their eyes on him as he walked in. !Vaon remained at the door, leaving him alone as he faced the three senior fleet commanders and politicians charged to prevent a war.

"Dr. Dunst, this is unexpected," Fleet Lord Tan!Shallegh said calmly. The A!Tol didn't seem bothered or even overly surprised by the interruption. Rin presumed !Vaon had told him in advance.

"Who is this?" Princess Oxtashah demanded. The Wendira Royal spread her iridescent wings in aggravation, a gesture that made the already-large being expand intimidatingly.

"Dr. Dunst is one of the Imperium's leading xenoarcheologists," Eleventh Voice of the Republic Tidirok said slowly, the Laian turning dark multifaceted eyes on Rin. "I am not certain why he is here."

"I bear warning," Rin told them. He stepped into the room and laid the three data folios he was carrying on the small table in between the three representatives.

"You already know you've been played for fools," he continued.

"Industrialists and traitors on both sides of the Dead Zone tried to lure you into a war for their own profit and to help conceal their operations in this region.

"I *hope* that your presence means they failed at the first part, but they have succeeded at the second," Rin said. "They were hunting something very specific and they have found it."

"They were hunting a myth based on a lie," Voice Tidirok said flatly.

Rin met the Voice's gaze levelly.

"So, you know about the Alavan officer's diary?" he asked.

"It was proven a falsification dozens of turnings ago," Tidirok replied. "A fraud intended to lure fools into the pursuit of treasure in empty sands. I know what they thought they were looking for, but it does not exist."

"It was not false," Rin told the Republic officer.

Laians couldn't lose color in the same way a shocked human would. They lost active control of their mandibles, the claw-like portions of their mouths slumping downward in a nearly relaxed position.

"Following their information, Captain Casimir and I managed to get *Defiance* to the wrecked Alavan fleet ahead of them," Rin continued. "Doing so was...a mistake."

"What do you mean?" Tan!Shallegh asked. "I do not doubt that Casimir did whatever was necessary."

"The Alavan fleet was sent out to face an enemy," Rin reminded them. "Neither your traitors nor Casimir and I gave that enemy a second thought until it was too late. But they survived where the Alava died."

"That was fifty thousand years ago," Oxtashah said. "They cannot have..."

To explain everything, Rin had to betray things the Imperium was *trying* to keep secret. He didn't have a choice, though. He gave Tan!Shallegh the barest of glances before he breached Imperial classifications.

"Last long-cycle, the Imperium encountered an Alavan biotechnological megastructure that had survived since their fall," Rin told them. "It was alive, functional and sentient. It was determined at that point to consume an Imperial colony for energy and mass—and to steal our technology.

"We now know that creature was based on stolen samples from the Alava's Enemy, a group of entities that call themselves the Infinite. The Infinite trapped at the heart of the Astoroko Nebula consumed the Alavan fleet and much of a super-Jovian gas giant to survive fifty thousand years of isolation.

"I do not know what they were when the Alava fought, but that isolation appears to have driven them mad," Rin said flatly. "They attacked *Defiance* the moment we refused to hand over our hyperspace-portal emitters. We barely escaped the system, and I understand *Defiance* to have been permanently crippled."

He gestured at the data folios.

"Those folios contain the complete sensor information of *Defiance*'s encounter with the Infinite...but what we saw is not the worst."

"Those fools," Princess Oxtashah whispered.

"I must review this data," Voice Tidirok said levelly. "But... Doctor...please tell me that my traitors were not so foolish as to deliver *Builder of Tomorrows* into these claws."

"I don't know," Rin admitted. "That would be..." He grimaced. "We know that the creature we encountered out at Kosha reverse-engineered interface drives and hyper portals from technology provided by fools who believed it a god.

"It lacked the power to operate either system at a scale useful for itself, but it recreated the technology with relative ease. I now recognize it as a larger but otherwise inferior version of the true Infinite."

He shook his head.

"In possession of even an intact starship, the Infinite will escape their trap within a long-cycle," he told them. "If *Builder of Tomorrows* has fallen to the Infinite, that may be a matter of cycles. I presume *Builder* is capable of constructing hyperdrives?"

"If it is properly stocked, *Builder* carries enough components to build at least a dozen hyperdrives," Tidirok admitted. "Surely, this Infinite...once they have escaped, they will be willing to communicate? To negotiate? We can find a compromise, yes?"

"I would hope so, yes," Rin told them. "But this...this is a race that terrified the Alava Hegemony at the height of its power, that fought them to a standstill over hundreds of years. An enemy that brought a fleet this deep into Alavan space and may have defeated an Alavan sector fleet in open battle."

"We are not Those Who Came Before," Oxtashah murmured. "They were gods. We are children. I...I must review this information," she told them. "But I fear, my old enemy, that even our ancient conflicts may prove meaningless."

"I don't know enough about the Infinite to say," Rin admitted. "Everything I know for *certain* is on those data folios. All I can really warn you is that they are on the verge of escape...and having met them, that *terrifies* me."

JOIN THE MAILING LIST

Love Glynn Stewart's books? Join the mailing list at

GLYNNSTEWART.COM/MAILING-LIST/

to know as soon as new books are released, special announcements, and a chance to win free paperbacks.

ABOUT THE AUTHOR

Glynn Stewart is the author of *Starship's Mage,* a bestselling science fiction and fantasy series where faster-than-light travel is possible–but only because of magic. His other works include science fiction series *Duchy of Terra, Castle Federation* and *Exile,* as well as the urban fantasy series *ONSET* and *Changeling Blood.*

Writing managed to liberate Glynn from a bleak future as an accountant. With his personality and hope for a high-tech future intact, he lives in Kitchener, Ontario with his partner, their cats, and an unstoppable writing habit.

*VISIT GLYNNSTEWART.COM FOR NEW
RELEASE UPDATES*

 facebook.com/glynnstewartauthor

OTHER BOOKS
BY GLYNN STEWART

For release announcements join the
mailing list or visit **GlynnStewart.com**

STARSHIP'S MAGE
Starship's Mage
Hand of Mars
Voice of Mars
Alien Arcana
Judgment of Mars
UnArcana Stars
Sword of Mars
Mountain of Mars
The Service of Mars
A Darker Magic
Mage-Commander (upcoming)

Starship's Mage: Red Falcon
Interstellar Mage
Mage-Provocateur
Agents of Mars

Pulsar Race: A Starship's Mage Universe Novella

DUCHY OF TERRA
The Terran Privateer
Duchess of Terra
Terra and Imperium
Darkness Beyond
Shield of Terra
Imperium Defiant
Relics of Eternity
Shadows of the Fall
Eyes of Tomorrow

VIGILANTE
(WITH TERRY MIXON)
Heart of Vengeance
Oath of Vengeance

Bound By Stars: A Vigilante Series
(With Terry Mixon)
Bound By Law
Bound by Honor
Bound by Blood

TEER AND KARD
Wardtown
Blood Ward

CHANGELING BLOOD
Changeling's Fealty
Hunter's Oath
Noble's Honor
Fae, Flames & Fedoras: A Changeling Blood Novella

ONSET
ONSET: To Serve and Protect
ONSET: My Enemy's Enemy
ONSET: Blood of the Innocent
ONSET: Stay of Execution
Murder by Magic: An ONSET Novella

FANTASY STAND ALONE NOVELS
Children of Prophecy
City in the Sky

Made in United States
North Haven, CT
18 July 2023

39219083R00221